THE GUILD'S DESIGN

SISTER SEEKERS BOOK 7

BY
A.S. ETASKI

Published by Corpus Nexus Press
ISBN: 978-1-949552-13-3

www.etaski.com
www.miurag.Etaski.com
www.patreon.com/etaski
www.goodreads.com/etaski
www.bookbub.com/authors/a-s-etaski
www.facebook.com/asetaski

Cover Design by Eris Adderly
Book design by Guido Henkel

Dedicated to each of us who have made mistakes, have learned from them, and are open to learning from more.

CHAPTER 1

MY HEAD POUNDED, AND MY BODY WAS WEAK. I SAT IN A DARK
wood chair within a private office, certain I would fall if I stood up.
Soon, my gut would be writhing from that acute mix of appetite
and illness whenever I waited too long to eat.

Not an hour had passed since my last meal, but it felt *much*
longer.

I exhaled, having just peace-knotted Soul Drinker to my belt
at the Guild Mistress's request. The blood-red engravings seemed
duller on the black dagger's hilt and sheath, without a hint of crimson glow. Even when I touched it for the third or fourth time,
there was no pulse of magic as if something was trying to reach me.

I listened to the relic for anything familiar yet heard no insidi-
ous whisper in my mind. The Black Heart would never have waited this long to seize an opportunity to talk, especially after how our
fight ended.

The demon had been silenced.

I am the wielder of Soul Drinker.

Proving I could do more than carry it had been my only pathway forward, and I had no options now but to believe I had done
it. If I had lost the contest of wills in that dark throne room with

the Black Heart, then I'd have joined Innathi the Desert Queen in the Elsewhere.

I would be there with her and the others for all time.

I squeezed aching eyes closed as a shiver passed through me.

"Light-headed?"

"Hm?"

I looked to my right and across the table at Krithannia. The raven-haired Naulor was the Guild Mistress of Augran and the second pale-skinned Elf I'd met. Krithannia knew the first one as well: the blonde Druid, Tamuril. They referred to each other as sisters, though they didn't appear related by blood.

"Oh, no," I answered. "Just queasy."

"Here." She poured me a clean cup of water. "Sip this."

I accepted gladly, pursing my lips tight on the rim and gradually sucking on water while I surveyed the room.

Gavin was here, standing just behind me and sorting through objects on the table. I turned my head for a better look when the death mage set down a shallow metal bowl. He placed a bloodied cloth into it then used a candle flame to set the fabric ablaze.

What...? I stopped myself before I could ask aloud.

Oh, yes, I remember.

When I'd come out of my trance with the dagger, my sullen and studious ally had been pinching my nose with a cloth to catch the stream of blood. I'd asked him to burn it, insisting he couldn't keep it.

If you wish, he said.

Apparently, Gavin saw no point in waiting.

"Hm," grunted the other male in front of me, his scaly, black tail shushing along the floor.

Mourn.

He was the half-breed my Queen wanted me to bring home, and the only mercenary for hire who might keep me alive and unshackled long enough to discover anything about Jael at Manalar.

I was slow to look up at the heavily armed mercenary who never wore boots on his large, clawed feet. I could feel him study me closer even than the Pale Elf and waited for him to ask about burning the cloth.

Or whether I still heard voices in the dagger.

When he said nothing, I assumed either he knew more than I did or could see something in the auras which answered his own question. Either of these had often proven to be the case.

Meanwhile, my three guardian spiders roamed curiously around my body after I'd sheathed Soul Drinker and finally released them. Having been kept tied up in their bag while I struggled alone for what freewill I had left, they were much calmer, content to be out and moving.

While watching them, a memory came back to me and, with it, the realization of how close Krithannia must have been to my spiders at one point when they'd been wriggling to get out of their pouch.

They might have bitten her, as they had her sister, if I hadn't secured that knot as well as I did. If that happened, I wouldn't have been aware enough to give her the antivenom, although Krithannia probably already knew from Tamuril to look for it.

Hmm.

"A question, Naulor," I asked.

Krithannia blinked slowly, watching me expectantly before prompting, "Yes?"

"May I ask what you were doing with your ear pressed to my gut?" I coughed. "Or before that? You were chanting something when I became aware."

The Naulor was slow to answer; for an instant her gaze seemed far away. Simultaneously, Gavin focused on her, his eyes tracing her form. It wasn't with admiration but rather his familiar contemplation and study of one's aura.

My grip on my cup tightened a little. *What's happening?*

Then, she was back.

"The chant," she said, folding her hands in front of her, "was a spell to coax a shared strength between us, focused enough to include a third."

I squinted with suspicion. "Shared strength?"

The Guild Mistress tilted her head. "Are the Dark Ones unable to do this, even among their mages? I would be surprised. I had little trouble finding your song which responded as I'd expect."

My 'song'?

I lifted my cup to my lips and only had two more sips before I emptied it. Sarilis had spoken about the "song" of the Ley Tower, something I even sensed as it spanned such distance, but otherwise I wasn't sure what she meant. I could imagine our mages might "share strength" but wasn't confident enough to explain how they would do it.

Too often they're competing instead of sharing, anyway.

"Are you a touch healer?" I asked.

"No," she answered firmly, as if she knew how rare that was. "I also acknowledge it is possible that you didn't need my help. Nonetheless, my efforts would not harm you, and I would rather try to make a difference than do nothing. As for afterward..."

The dark-haired Elf smiled at me. "I listened for a heartbeat besides yours. I heard one, and it was set at the right pace. I am confident you are both well."

My cheeks warmed. The right pace? What pace was that, and how does she know? Did that mean unborn Naulor and Davrin grow at the same rate? If so, did that mean we could breed?

What would that look like?

I shook my head, asking instead, "You heard a tiny heart over my grumbling guts?"

I let the skepticism trickle into my tone as I held up my little finger to imply the baby organ's size.

"Meditating on your aura as I was," she nodded, "yes, for a short while. No longer, though. The spell is ended, and I cannot sense anything like that by standing near you nor by touching your shoulder."

Hmph. She could probably still read more than I could about her, though.

I looked at my empty cup and reached for the water pitcher when Mourn caught my eye and made a sign.

Huh? Oh.

"Uh," I grunted aloud, pouring my drink before speaking. "Thank you for explaining, Guild Mistress."

Krithannia smiled. "You're welcome, Red Sister. And I thank you for showing us your determination to help others. It is truly impressive."

Easier to do when you have no choice.

My mouth twisted with that silent remark as the Naulor Elf lightly rested her gloved palms on the table and turned to include Gavin. She seemed very tall when standing like that.

"I believe we can indeed work together to further each of our goals," she said. "But there is enough time to settle now after your long journey to have this meeting. We shall discuss this in greater detail after I've met with a few trusted contacts and gathered their confirmations."

She focused on me. "This will also give Morixxyleth time to consider his separate bargain with Sirana. I think it would be good to close the deals and set our expectations at the same time."

Her voice had a subtle, dancing lilt to it much like her Druid sister. It was easy to listen to.

"So be it," Gavin murmured.

I shrugged, nodding. "Sounds good. In the meantime?"

"For now, I invite you to take your rest back in your rooms. We are still determining more secure accommodations for your time in Yong-wen."

I smirked a little as my ally said, "More secure? So, we should expect to move?"

Krithannia nodded. "You should, yes. Although feel free to take the trays of food back with you. Mai and Ting can bring you anything else you need until then. There is a cord to pull on to summon them."

Gavin nodded as if he'd seen this cord while I blinked and made note to take a second look. It was obvious to me that Krithannia and Mourn would speak in private after we left, yet it was still easier taking this instruction from her than from any man I'd met on the Surface thus far.

"I expect you'll keep the relic and the soul shard safe," the Guild Mistress finished, her silvery-blue eyes moving from me to Gavin again. "In return, count on my discretion to limit those in Augran who know about these items or your presence."

Out of the corner of my eye, Mourn dipped his chin in agreement. He trusted Krithannia's word, plain enough.

And yet, she'd told me in my room that he'd been a "feral fugitive" when she'd found him on the Surface. I also hadn't forgotten that, on the boat, Mourn had admitted to one female contact in Augran who was a "past" playmate.

It was quite likely her.

Where did you two meet each other? Under what circumstances?

Mourn's sudden bass filled my ears, startling me for he hadn't spoken in a while.

"Rest up and spend your time as you like," he said. "But do not leave this building or draw attention to it. I will find you when something has changed."

Gavin nodded, gathering up his things without a word or grunt of complaint. He was probably eager to return and lock his door to begin writing all this down in his grimoire. I sighed and gathered my spiders and belongings as well.

If I might hear more about these two or how they'd attained their influence on the design of these Humans, I would have to be patient.

I CARRIED THE TRAY OF FOOD BUT LEFT THE WINE WITH THE Guild Mistress. I wanted nothing that might dull my senses while staying in this crush of Humans, even if the street scents floating in through the cracks had me consider it.

Curiously, the strongest Human scents no longer came from Gavin despite his standing next to me. I still hadn't detected much sweat from him despite his having been under vivid stress at least once during that storm on the lake. His pale skin could even be a little drier than back at Brom's inn.

My mind flew over the Deathwalker's description of the Nexus as given to Krithannia while we walked down the dark-paneled hallway back toward our rooms. Unsettling how he'd spoken of existing after his body's death and of waiting for the chance to reclaim it.

A ritual suspended but not destroyed by the Chief Warrant's silver dagger.

Somehow in the Nexus, Gavin had possessed some solid quality of essence mimicking flesh which could be cut off to "feed the crows" as he'd learned from them. A grotesque imagining, although that explained the shared dream on the ship when he'd appeared to me as a black skeleton.

I hadn't realized it was him until I'd heard his thoughts.

That Krithannia seemed to believe him suggested this hadn't come from either the Black Heart's tricks or my own splintering Reverie. These rituals seemed unlike anything our Priestesses could do, but we didn't have death mages I was aware of. Just sorceresses, wizards, healers, and seers.

"That is as it should be," Gavin had said.

Meanwhile, the Ma'ab would bring more of that Nexus death magic to Manalar. Jael was in their way, looking for some officer or clergyman to do… *Something.*

Goddess damn it.

I did not look forward to closing the door on my separate room to be alone with my thoughts. If I could obtain an obliging bedmate or maybe a quality tool besides my own fingers, I could entertain myself long enough for Mourn to knock without my head getting in my way.

Yet I was sure the Yungian girls in this safehouse would scream and faint again the moment they understood my proposal. Would a terrified youth manipulated into compliance be better than spending an unknown time alone and bored?

Bah. No.

I didn't have the patience to constantly guide an unwilling tongue or unfocused fingers. This was why I never pounced on buas like Micraen or Callitro without some genuine sign of their arousal, and why my attack on Auslan during my trials still felt unrecognizable to me.

The use of force or a hard struggle is only necessary with my Sisters, and we have the Feldeu to enhance things.

With the Red Sisters and my elders, I'd grown accustomed to sexual contests and learned to enjoy the exhilaration. Their methods forced me to earn my pleasure, and it was somehow different than what I'd experienced beneath the knees of my sister. I believed I'd had more choice over how I could respond to a Sister than I'd ever had with Jilrina.

I also knew now that Shyntre was the sole exception to my preferences with buas *because* of our mutual experience and "training" in the Cloister. Somehow, our fighting and his resistance made the release even *better*, because I knew he could handle anything I threw at him.

I admired him for it.

"Gavin?" I began as we reached his door.

The pale death mage looked at me and asked, "Is there anything you are willing to share about your contest of wills with the dagger?"

You want to talk? Really?

I blinked and then grinned. "Absolutely! I thought you might want to be alone after all the talking of private things with the Guild Mistress."

His icy pupils rested on me as one thinning eyebrow lifted. "Hm. On the contrary, I'd like your insights on her as well."

So would I.

"I can try."

"If you don't mind my taking notes—?"

"With your cypher?"

"Of course."

I waved one hand. "Lead the way, scholar of crows."

He grimaced at this but nonetheless allowed me into his room, closing the door after me and setting the bolt. Neither of us had any privacy spells like our hosts, but the bed and small utility table were in between the door and window, and we were accustomed to keeping our voices down.

Gavin set up his writing space, feet still bare and solid black toenails visible, while I set the tray of food down beside the bed and admired images painted on the pale tan walls.

"A lot of blue in both our rooms."

"What do you mean?" he asked, distracted.

"The Yungians like to paint water," I said. "And the paint seems diluted *with* water. The boundaries look like mist. There are streams, rivers, ponds... lakes."

Gavin grunted. "An apt deduction. For a foreign enclave which does all their business on a river flowing out of the Great Lake, I can see its importance and a strong theme in their crafts."

"What birds are these?" I asked, pointing to a pair with white and black coloring and wings outspread. "The long neck and legs, walking in water, of course."

They seemed to be dancing around each other in a marshland.

"They are cranes." He'd glanced up but looked back down at his work. "I recall seeing some when I crossed the Midway the first time, though there were none where I grew up. More common around the Great Lake and its neighboring lands."

"Aha." I paused. "Are they good to eat?"

"I wouldn't know, I never trapped one. Perhaps ask Mourn if he's ambushed them in a river."

I huffed a breathy laugh and dared to relax, removing my cloak, belt, and weapons to set them on the bed. "May I release my guardians?"

"If you wish. Are you ready?"

"For what?" I tugged open my pouch and set it down, letting the spiders come out in their own time.

"For anything you say happened after you drew the black dagger."

Hm. Plenty had happened, not all of which I was aware. Surely, he didn't need the more nauseating details, though.

"Well, first," I began, "I would tell you that the voice you heard speaking to you was the Black Heart, not the dagger itself."

"And what is 'the Black Heart?'" he asked, dipping his stylus to scratch his first marks in the leather-bound grimoire.

"It is a demon of the Abyss," I said with confidence. "I recognized its ways. They are much like home. It also knew the name of the Spider Queen but saw her only as a competitor."

Gavin nodded, his long-fingered hands recording in his cypher.

"The demon was the source of hunger, though the souls consumed by the dagger seem to pass through to be trapped somewhere else."

This seemed clear to me only in hindsight.

"Where are the souls trapped?" Gavin asked.

"The Black Heart described it as an 'Elsewhere.' It claimed to be the gatekeeper."

"Interesting," he remarked, motioning for me to continue. "What did the gatekeeper look like?"

I shrugged. "Whether it was true or not, it took an unimaginative shape. Shadow upon shadow. Floating. With red eyes."

"There was no form at all where you were? There was only void?"

"Oh, there was form," I recalled now. "I was inside a huge, barren throne room built within a cavern. There was a cracked throne on a platform, and some steep, rock stairs behind me without walls or railing which led to nowhere." I paused. "I saw red runes wrapped around the demon."

He grunted. "Did they match the runes on the dagger?"

"I didn't get that close of a look," I admitted, "but they were similar. Mourn said the relic has many kinds of magic layered over it and from the insight I gained confronting it, I know these were magical chains binding the Black Heart to the dagger. It couldn't leave that throne room."

Gavin paused to glance up at me. "Someone *else* put the demon there as gatekeeper?"

"Yes, exactly. The Black Heart wouldn't say who, but when it touched me, I linked with it and discovered it was… personal."

The Deathwalker frowned. "Punishment? Or vengeance?"

"Betrayal." I paused, looking toward the window. "Maybe by its own child. A trick, or perhaps the child became more powerful than it."

"Child? Another demon?"

I hesitated. I'd not forgotten the claim that the Black Heart had somehow given birth upon this world, and this was how it had escaped notice at first. *Whose* notice, I hadn't discovered.

"I can't say for certain," I said. "Only that the Black Heart saw itself as the parent of this entity which trapped it."

Gavin didn't reply at first, only completed his note. "So, what happened with the gatekeeper, then? How was it resolved that you came back?"

"I had to face it, mind-to-mind and will-to-will. We provoked each other until I learned how to match its strength in that place, wherever we were. I clasped it, held it near its throne, and encased it in crystal. Then it was quiet."

"Crystal?" he asked with interest. "How did you summon this?"

I shrugged again. "When my… talent first appeared back home, I thought I saw shimmering veins of crystal in the rock. I guess I used that as a focus."

"Hm." Gavin dusted something very fine on his most recent scratches, waiting a few flicks before gently blowing the excess off the page of the book. "And after it was encased, when you could not hear its voice?"

"I walked behind the throne into the Elsewhere."

"Can you try to describe it?"

I did the best I could, explaining how the colorful canyon and the waterfall at Koorul was a place that both Cris-ri-phon and In-nathi would recognize, made tangible by the souls consumed by the dagger over millennia.

"It was where they'd met," I said. "She'd been expecting her husband, not me, and seemed surprised I'd bested the Black Heart. But she was willing enough to talk."

"About what?"

"Some about the other wielders, how many were there with us, and how none had carried Soul Drinker for as long as she had."

"She was a bit prideful, then?"

I smiled. "She was a Queen in life. Though, they all fell to the relic in the end. That's why they were there."

I felt cold just saying it, and Gavin nodded like this was expected.

"Continue."

I did because if anyone might help me make sense of speaking with souls long "transitioned," it must be this Deathwalker.

"She described how she died, assassinated in childbirth by Davrin Elves wearing red. This was supposedly in revolt against their Queen for wedding and breeding with a Human, the Zauyrian Sorcerer-General Cris-ri-phon. Um, though we met him as Brom Troshin."

"The Deathless," Gavin stated, nodding. "And at some point, her own dagger was used on her to be present in the Elsewhere. Or perhaps the relic itself betrayed her?"

I blinked. "She didn't say."

"Hm. Perhaps she does not remember her final moments. Many spirits don't." He read over his last two pages. "So, we have a dagger created by an unknown hand to be a precision soul trap. Penetration with the blade draws in the Vis and Vitas of its victims and, if given enough time, keeps the Vis somewhere it cannot leave, preventing it from traveling in the beyond. An aptly named weapon, Soul Drinker."

Gavin tapped the table with his fingers while in a deep focus I did not disrupt, then pointed a thoughtful finger at me. "But you *did* benefit when you used it against the corrupted creatures of the warp rot forest, when the gatekeeper opted to share its strength with you."

I grimaced. "A false strength, as it turned out."

"Indeed. The Black Heart could do this by claiming the Vitas drawn by the dagger," he considered. "The sensation of strength and wellness was real enough but only temporary, as you discovered."

A low growl rose in my throat as I crossed my arms. I was a fool.

"However," he continued to contemplate, "for you to have seen and spoken to an ancient Elven Queen, the Vis of each soul *must* have escaped into this Elsewhere, passing by the demon, as you said."

I perked up, imagining puffs of mist split in half by the blade's magic, and part of it escaping the void waiting to consume it. *Hmm.*

"If the Black Heart's 'child' betrayed it," Gavin said, "perhaps bound it to this relic, then it was left to hunger. The dagger's true power is an unending torment, compelling the Black Heart's influence on the wielder to use it which, at the same time, denies full satiation of its appetite. Hm."

He paused, nodding as he gazed at his book. "That could explain some of what it said to me."

I listened with unblinking eyes, fascinated by his interpretation despite having been the one to experience all of this. He was an astute observer with space leftover in his mind to step back from it all and speak his thoughts. I realized I admired this about him.

Then, the Deathwalker frowned. "What connection am I missing, Sirana?"

"Uh. What do you mean?"

"The Deathless sought this relic for centuries, enlisting the Ma'ab's help, possibly in exchange for something he did for their leaders in the Nexus. He wanted it for the soul inside, to speak again with his former Queen, correct?"

I nodded, hesitantly.

"And this Queen was a Davrin Elf, not a Human woman. She bore many children with him and provoked an assassination attempt which seems to have been successful."

"Yes?" I agreed, unsure where he was headed with this.

"You were *sent* to find the Ley Tower by a Davrin Queen," Gavin said as if to remind me. "You told me your mission included killing Sarilis."

"True." My voice cracked.

"And now we've agreed to look for your sisters," he continued, skipping over Mourn's questions which had caused me such pain by the river. "But not before we stumbled into Troshin Bend and, by extraordinary fortune, uncovered this relic of significant relevance to both our present paths."

I stared at him. "I can't explain it."

"No? What about she who sent you? Did your queen foresee this, somehow?"

"Not...explicitly," I said, feeling that warning twinge of discomfort.

"Would she want this dagger?" he asked. "Can you see her speaking to the Desert Queen inside?"

My mind froze, and my arms tightened around me. My spiders crept closer in my periphery. "I don't imagine she would be eager to acknowledge another Davrin Queen exists."

"Indeed, perhaps not." Facing his table, the Deathwalker propped his elbows on either side of his book, steepling his fingers. His lank, black hair covered part of his profile. "Is there any link between these two rulers that you know of? Aside from their race?"

The nausea rose again.

My sister returned from exile and became a Seer for my Court. She was respected in V'Gedra as she'd never been with our Mother.

"Innathi had a sister," I murmured.

"Your queen?" Gavin prompted, twisting his head with a crack.

Panic.

"I'm not certain yet."

He nodded. "Best not to assume, then."

Argh...

But I wasn't assuming; I *was* certain! When Cris-ri-phon had attacked me in his bed, when I'd seen the Desert while awake for the first time, he'd recognized the same young face as I had!

Why couldn't I say it?

"Ishuna is still your Queen," Cris-ri-phon sneered. *"Good. I am grateful to know I am not too late."*

My heart pounded as I sat propped up on the bed. Gavin had been so close to figuring it out but stopped pushing me when I was right on the edge, deliberately blurring his answer when I'd been forthright with the Black Heart.

The Deathwalker *knew* about my shared dreams setting me at odds with Kurn and Cris-ri-phon back at the inn. When it kept happening to him, he'd even traded Kurn's sword to get the blue pendant back from Mourn, for fuck's sake!

I won't pursue this secretive web. It's too much to keep alone inside my head. I'll go mad!

The Deathless knew the truth about my Valsharess already. That meant my allies needed to know, too. Somehow.

"Innathi had a sister who was a Seer like my Queen," I blurted, waiting to meet Gavin's eyes. "I believe the Deathless recognized the same Seer when we mindlinked…" I swallowed painfully, finishing with a hand wave. *"He* was certain they knew each other long ago. That is relevant to what he does next, isn't it?"

Gavin stared at me, rightly baffled at the wobbling, indirect answer to his very direct question. Regardless, he put the frayed logic together and nodded acceptance. "Yes, quite relevant, if he acts as though the Desert Queen's sister and your underground ruler are one and the same. Perhaps some of this was glimpsed but not certain when your seer-queen sent you. It can be that way with my own patroness as well, when she chooses to speak with me."

My head ached again, and I bit my lip against remarking on the chaos such predictions had caused so far.

Had She foreseen this? If so, what was I to do about Soul Drinker? The only guidance She'd given concerned "machinations of the Hells fouling the crossroads," presumed to be the Ley Tower. Killing Sarilis was supposed to address that, but then the goddess-damned half-blood had to cross my path and make it even more complicated!

We might as well be back on the ship during that magical squall for how certain I was of where I'd find myself next.

"What do you plan to do with the dagger?" he asked.

As usual, my death mage scowled at me in his concentration.

"I don't know." I shrugged, feeling a burden lift despite my irritation. I reached for a salty, dried fruit on the tray. "Maybe take it back with me after all. Let the Queens talk and see what happens."

His brows lifted as if to imagine. It was an amusing expression. I smiled, popping in my first bite of cheese that truly brightened my mood.

Then he turned away and intensely started writing. I sighed, chewing my way through more cheese and several chunks of pale, crunchy roots until my head and my middle felt better.

Enough mashing my brain pulp about this.

"Are *you* ready to answer some questions, Gavin?"

His eerie eyes stayed on the page. "What do you wish to know?"

I sat up quickly on the bed. "What did you see when you looked at Krithannia? You said you'd never seen anything like her." I spread out my hands. "She appears like either an elder Yungian woman or an elegant pale-skinned Elf probably older than Mourn. What do you see?"

Carefully, Gavin set down his stylus and leaned back in his chair, putting his hands together in thought. He wasn't looking at me but at the door. "Do you recall her answer that she had always been the primary?"

I nodded. "What does that mean?"

"Well, like Cris-ri-phon, I sense an immense age in her life aura, well beyond her mortal appearance."

"What?!" I was aghast. "She's already centuries older than me!"

"Indeed. And yet *unlike* the Deathless, whose lifetimes must come from consuming Vis and Vitas in ways I recognize, the Guild

Mistress seems…" He paused. *"More* than whole, rather than shoring up against natural decay. She carries others but is still one."

I shook my head. "I am confused."

He tried again. "Her essence is complex and varied, aged beyond her body and woven together as if by the consent of all its sources. In addition, there is no apparent struggle to exist in such an…unlikely state. I cannot comprehend how it was done."

"Why not?"

The Deathwalker turned his midnight eyes on me when I didn't expect it, and I leaned back.

"Because the Vis and Vitas of the soul are susceptible to degradation or corruption," he said, "if not outright consumption, and no soul passes without struggle. It is in life's very essence to resist transition and attempt to retain its sovereignty. Existing in such a fluid yet *unchanging* state and, even further, acknowledging this is like nothing I have seen until now."

My ally reconsidered me as a seemingly renewed curiosity on his bed. "Now I wonder what the elder races are capable of when it comes to their existence and their deaths. How they differ from what limits I've known of Human souls for all my mortal life."

His words sent a chill down my spine, as I wondered now who the Guild Mistress really was. I should ask Krithannia how old her Naulor Queen was? Did either of them happen to remember waging a war in the Desert?

Mourn said she was too young to remember. Could he be wrong?

"How many 'essences' do you see?" I asked.

Gavin shrugged. "Not more than ten, I think. As I said, her aura is strangely fluid. I can't be sure."

Ten?

Krithannia had seemed delighted that Gavin had acknowledged them, that he could even *see* them.

Intrigued, she said. Hmph.

What was she? The Naulor equivalent of a Deathwalker? Shouldn't it be concerning to her that someone like him could so easily see her secret?

Bah. All that means is the Guild will try even harder to recruit and keep an eye on him. He just doesn't know it yet.

Still, it wasn't as if Gavin could move easily among Human circles spreading Elvish secrets without getting staked through the chest for his trouble. I bet she knew that already.

I checked behind me to make sure my spiders weren't in the way when I laid down, crossing my arm over my brow. I was overwhelmed again and unsure how much more I wanted to delve into these speculative subjects.

Our reasons for going to Manalar were set, and I'd confessed to him as much as I could about my Queen, the Deathless, and the dagger we'd stumbled onto.

Now this.

Gavin seemed content to let the discussion drop as he concentrated on his script, and I ate the rest of what was on the tray before settling back and closing my eyes. With a sigh, I relaxed.

Next, I was startled awake by someone tapping on the door.

What the—?

If that's Mourn, he's gone meek all of a sudden.

"S-Sho'shien?" spoke a tiny squeak of a voice.

I propped myself on my elbows. *A girl?*

Gavin either hadn't heard her or was ignoring the interruption. Outside the door, she took a breath and tried again.

"Sho'shien-si?"

I recognized the voice now. *Mai.*

Finally, he lifted his head. "What do you want?"

On the other side of the door, she must have jumped like a deer before setting something hard on the floor. I heard the patter of soft feet down the hall toward the kitchen.

Well, now. I felt accomplished communicating with Yungians by comparison.

"I'll get it," I said, the mattress making a lot of noise as I sat up.

My spiders skittered along the ceiling to accompany me to the door, and I waited for them to reach the jamb before taking to one knee and listening in silence for movement. Hearing none, I slid the bolt back and opened the door a crack.

There was no one there but something was left behind. I studied the dark wooden tray and its items. A glazed, blue pot with a spout, handle, and a lid; beside it, another in red but without the spout and sitting on a thick, brown cloth. Both gave off heat. Included were two decorated, glazed vessels in two sizes, white with delicately painted blue fish and red-crowned cranes. Lastly, a woven basket with a red cloth covered up whatever lay within it.

I sniffed. *Oh, my goddess...*

A dizzyingly floral fragrance floated up, blended with savory broth and herbed meat. It struck my nose hard enough to make me forget that I'd just eaten. My mouth watered as I tugged the tray inside along the floor before closing the door.

Mine.

"More food and drink?" Gavin muttered. "A bit decadent, aren't they?"

"If you don't want yours," I said as I lifted the tray with care not to spill, "I'll take it."

My scholar paused. "I may agree with Brom on one thing. I don't know where you fit it all in your size."

"I'm not *that* small. The Zauyrian women were smaller."

He tilted his head, pondering how I knew this. "I'll take your word for it."

Smirking, I looked around. There wasn't space on Gavin's desk or the bedside table, and I didn't trust that lumpy mattress with these pots and cups. That was when I noticed the dense, brown cushion turned on its end by the tiny storage space in the wall.

On the floor it is.

Gavin watched me set down the tray and carefully set out the cushion to sit down. His thin lips stretched with mild annoyance at the fussing, but I ignored him until I'd settled and removed my gloves.

"Do you want to try the soup or the...?" I lifted the lid and sniffed the floral liquid.

"Tea," he finished, granting a nod. "Yes. A little of each."

"And the...?" I unfolded the red cloth, discovering six, pale, sticky doughballs neatly arranged but not touching each other. In between each were individual bundles of dark greens. "Um..."

Gavin sighed and put down his stylus, replacing the stopper on his ink. I tilted the basket his way so he could see.

"Grain pods, perhaps," he said. "Although those are smoother and wetter than what the monastery made or what most taverns throw together."

"Grain pods," I repeated, plucking one up. The texture was tacky and strange, but it smelled wonderful. "Just bite it?"

Gavin shrugged. "Or warm them in your soup first. They may be gummy to chew like a berry."

Good idea.

I started pouring the tea and soup between four smooth vessels, more in mine than his before bringing them to him. "You want any pods?"

"You eat them."

Yes!

Once I returned to my seat, I held up the small handful of green tied with a bit of string. "What about these?"

"I have no idea," he admitted, lifting the tea first to sip from the cup without much concern for the heat. "This fare is wholly unfamiliar to me."

"Except cheese." I chuckled. "Everyone up here and below makes cheese."

"Huh. I suppose if they milk animals, cheese seems inevitable."

Smiling, I sniffed and nibbled the edge of one green bundle.

The taste was quite odd, the texture as if it had been pounded while wet and then dried. There was a bit of mineral and salt, but no taste of soil. It reminded me more of fish and was the farthest thing from coarse, bitter, but edible greens I'd found in the mountains.

Perhaps a water plant?

I'll warm this in the soup, too. Maybe my second bowl.

Gavin had struck just right about warming the grain pods in the hot liquid before eating them. There was a bit of mashed meat and vegetable inside, and the flavors melded so well together that I'd have to imagine I was a guest at one of the top Noble Houses back home to be eating this. Yet, this was far from the fanciest place in Yong-wen; I could tell from my walk down the streets.

Next, the crisp greens quickly turned floppy upon touching hot liquid, but they added flavor and texture to the broth once I'd let them soften. Unfamiliar on my tongue, yet every bite urged me to eat more of it, as if my body recognized the nutritious treasure within.

I sighed with supreme pleasure as I enjoyed the meal. How healthful were the growths which grew effortlessly beneath the Sun compared to what we could urge to grow in the dark, and what complex flavors waited to be joined in endless combinations.

The Humans have it well in their Surface abundance.

Gavin stopped writing during my meal, now staring vacantly into a corner with his hands in his lap. He'd gone so still, his eyes turning black, that I assumed he either slept upright or had fallen into a trance with his patroness. This didn't deter my appetite for I felt accustomed to his oddities, even if I didn't know why a ritually risen corpse bleeding black still needed to sip tea and nibble on cheese.

By the time I'd finished chewing and drinking from my bowl and cup, both pots were more than half empty, all five of the green bundles consumed, and the vanished grain pods had swelled enough to strain my stomach.

Uh-oh. That was meant for two Humans.

I grunted in discomfort trying to settle back against the wall, realizing too late that I wouldn't be sprinting anywhere without regret for a few hours.

I stayed awake to watch over Gavin and our belongings by playing leaping games with my spiders with my bare hands while keeping my ears open. I didn't want to move to grab my belt, the laxness a mark against me if Rausery knew, but—

Eh, she doesn't. I'll fling the tray at them and toss my babies before diving for the dagger…

I paused at this thought.

Tossing my "babies"? How else did I think of them?

My guardians. My little ones.

"You should know," Gavin had said by the river, *"that the Dragon-child is of the firm opinion that formal names are worthwhile for anything of value to you."*

Of course, he would.

Though if Innathi's tutors from millennia ago were correct about the Dragons creating the first language of magic, there was even a good reason for Mourn to be stubborn about it.

My spiders had value to me, yet they had no names. *No formal ones, anyway.*

I gathered them together, lifting them up to peer at their tiny, glinting eyes. One of them flexed her mandibles. *Heh.*

~*Listen?*~ I asked, waiting for that tiny chime of acknowledgement.

I heard it. A cluster of three.

~*Do you have names?*~ I asked.

They were still and quiet. Apparently, they didn't understand my command and were waiting for something that made more sense.

What to do now, pick names and try to teach them, this one means you? What good would it do if names wouldn't solve a problem I did not have?

Truly, we hadn't had issue with conflicting commands so far. They kept watch, attacked, or tended to themselves. Not much else. Even when one trilled in warning, it didn't seem to matter which one she was.

~*You are enchanted by a sorceress, touched with magic,*~ I thought. ~*At one point, you awakened. What did you hear? Names? Words?*~

They didn't answer. One settled down like she would wait for days for a meal to walk by. I sighed. What did I expect? That natural spiders counted time from birth like I did?

~*Hunt,*~ I commanded, releasing them onto the wall again. ~*Eat.*~

They understood that familiar command as they each climbed their own direction. Like the Red Sisters, they worked together but survived alone.

I smiled and turned my attention to Gavin sitting in his chair. If I listened carefully, I could make out a heartbeat besides mine, and it wasn't in my belly.

Gavin's heartbeat was slow with long pauses in between, and deep, like a drum. The organ had begun contracting almost from the moment I'd removed the Witch Hunter's dagger from my death scholar's chest. It had begun forcing a thick, dark fluid through the body of the gaunt, pale man.

Not entirely a corpse. No longer a living man.

Somehow, I was more comfortable chatting, eating, and resting in the same room with him than I was any other on the Surface. He was every bit as strange to others as I was, now a matured mage that did not need my protection yet still found value in traveling together. He wouldn't attack me in my sleep, either.

He has neither the cause nor the urge.

An easy alliance, almost as simple as my nameless spiders.

Now that the Black Heart wasn't raking my will raw all the time, I could enjoy a peace while lying down such as I'd only had in the Cloister before.

I grimaced as Gaelan and Reishel instantly came to mind. *Damn it.*

I stroked a tensing, overfull belly to soothe it, keeping my eyes closed. *Breathe. Relax. Listen to the street sounds.*

They were few and far in between, and it was still dark outside.

It must be very late.

After my stomach settled, I reached to adjust the waistline and tug at the crotch of my leathers. I felt a tingle and opened my eyes, noting three black spots in my periphery as I tested with another caress.

My slit warmed to the touch, responsive enough.

Hm. How long has it been?

…Oh, yes.

The ride from Mourn's hideaway to Port Fortnight when he kept interrupting me. I finally had to stop Nightmare and take care of my need deeper in the trees.

I glanced at Gavin. He remained as he'd been but if he suddenly became aware, he'd be displeased with his first sight. Maybe he'd offer nothing worse than an eyeroll before voluntarily leaving the room.

Maybe.

I hadn't performed any lurid act in front of him yet. The many rutting games and struggles between me and Mathias, Jacob, Kurn, and Brom at Troshin Bend I had dealt with when Gavin was either dead or elsewhere. I was glad that he hadn't watched any of it. Maybe I wouldn't feel so at ease now.

I *could* move into the room next to this one where I'd first been assigned, but I was comfortable, warm, and knew I could be quiet. I debated pulling my pants down at all; perhaps I could peak still clothed.

My ears tingled along the edges, barely detecting the broad, dry feet approaching in a long but light step out in the hall. I slumped in my cushion and called my spiders to me.

Mourn had arrived just in time to negate my dilemma.

CHAPTER 2

I FIGURED THE DRAGONCHILD KNEW GAVIN AND I WERE BOTH in here, given the meals for two left outside the door. He tapped with one knuckle enough to draw the attention of someone awake but not one deeply asleep.

Gavin didn't stir as I pulled on my gloves and rolled off my cushion to a barefooted crouch, giving my spiders time to jump onto my shoulders and slip beneath my braid. Meanwhile, the mercenary didn't call out or identify himself.

What would he do if he thought we were both asleep?

I could wait and see, or I could attempt to surprise him by opening the door when he expected no answer. I rejected the latter option as soon as I thought it. Surprising him might not be worth the bragging even if I managed it.

Mourn tapped again, and I glanced at Gavin.

Still in his trance.

Staying low, I moved to the door without making a sound, as much of a compliment to the floor's crafters as to my training. The floorboards were much smoother and fit more tightly together than at Brom's Inn.

I tapped back, echoing his pattern and turning my ear to listen. I was sure I heard his tongue flick out, and the next tapping came in low and to my left, with less force behind it. I smiled. *His tail.*

The Sisterhood had some basic tapping signals to communicate through walls, but it wasn't used unless we had no message pellets. My choices what to say were limited as I hadn't learned anything complex, but I doubted a fugitive from a city I'd never heard of— one who'd been on the Surface more than four centuries already— would be familiar with the rhythms.

Still. Plant the thought.

I slid the bolt back, tapped out *"enter"* with my knuckle, and took a step back. After a pause, Mourn sighed softly and took hold of the door handle, pushing but stopping at a crack to peek in.

Paranoid as I am. I guess the blood runs true.

When I saw his metallic eye glint, I signed, ★Quiet,★ before motioning to the death mage.

The mercenary slipped into the room with envious stealth for his size, pulling his long tail in behind him without apparent thought. He still wore his loose, dark pants and chest harness loaded with pouches and padded tools. Kurn's sword was still on his back as well, yet the only appreciable noise was in closing the door and setting the bolt again.

Mourn spotted the empty tray for two on the floor between bed and cushion but saved his bewilderment for when he peered at Gavin. Flexible lips drew back before Mourn sucked in air slowly through his teeth, his tongue pressed to the back.

I mimicked his bewilderment. *What's he doing?*

★Concerns?★ the mercenary signed.

When he did so, my eyes landed on the enchanted metal bracers which magically stored his weapons. They were a permanent addition to his body at an age younger than I was now, and likely to cripple him if removed improperly.

In his four and a half centuries on the Surface, he'd never found someone capable and willing to remove them. Given the humility required in admitting it and his apparent frustration at the time, I'd never doubted it. The mercenary had one advantage, at least.

He's always armed.

I shrugged. ★No great concern. I was eating. Gavin was writing but then slumped like this.★

★Has he done this before?★

I tilted my hand back and forward. ★He slept on the ship reclining with his eyes closed, but he 'left' with eyes open like this during the magic squall.★ My hands paused. ★You never saw it during the days I slept in your cave?★

Mourn considered that more seriously than I expected and shook his head. ★Not that I observed.★ He tilted an ear toward me. ★What happened during the storm? He 'returned' once it passed?★

I might have confirmed this for simplicity, but his tail and expectant look told me he'd caught the unspoken negative first. *Damn.*

★The death mage recommended your willpower,★ he prompted. ★Being his anchor during that time. What happened exactly?★

I pressed my lips together, shrugging again. ★I touched his hand.★

His eyes narrowed. ★Nothing else?★

I hesitated. ★I had my blue stone back. It may have aided me.★

Mourn considered, glancing at my chest like he could see it beneath my leathers. ★Try again?★

I grimaced. ★He recoils from touch. Is there need?★

He exhaled, looking toward the shuttered window. I listened but nothing seemed unusual.

★Would you leave him here alone?★ he asked.

Gavin was accustomed to waking up alone, yet I hesitated.

★Are you not bored?★ he added, probably as a small jab.

It worked. I felt the tangible pout between my legs as I made a face at him. *Well, I **had** been about to entertain myself when you arrived.*

I indicated the inn's room. ★This is private but not secure. The servants are frightened. They may speak of him to someone and draw trouble.★

When Mourn didn't deny this, I was sure of my answer. ★I will not leave him alone and unaware that I am gone. Not without need.★

The Dragonchild was dryly amused. ★Good. That's the reason I came. We have a secure place nearby which will serve him better the next week or two we are likely to be here.★

The next week or two...?

★Just him?★ I challenged.

★You may stay with him if desired, but if he's protected and content in his work, would you *want* to?★

You're teasing me, half-blood.

I squinted. ★What is your plot, mercenary?★

He shrugged broad shoulders. ★Did you not want to discuss a bodyguard contract?★

Anticipation and suspicion each lunged for control of my hands.

★Of course, I do.★

★And with such an agreement in place, would you not prefer to spend some of your waiting outside?★

You're definitely teasing.

I bit. ★Doing what?★

Mourn smiled closed-lipped. ★There is much to do in a city this size.★

Ostensibly, I knew that yet still swallowed. From listening to Mourn, I had estimated that ten cities of Sivaraus might fit inside all four of Augran's quadrants, and how well I knew that an outsider wandering aimlessly stood out and drew interest. Even hiding or blending in at tiny Troshin Bend had been difficult, and one could say I'd failed miserably.

The difference now was that I'd presumably have a bodyguard who felt drawn to cities. He claimed this was the largest one with which he is familiar.

★'There is much to do' as entertainment or task labor?★

He cocked a ridged brow. ★The former. What is entertaining to you?★

Sex!

Then my eyes slide to one side. *No, no…*

He'd think I was propositioning him when it hadn't even crossed my mind. He was too big, anyway.

Let's see, for fun. Stalking. Spying. Running, chasing. Wrestling…

I had to reach back farther to find entertainment that *didn't* involve getting my mouth on someone's genitals at some point.

★Sparring?★ I asked him.

Mourn seemed intrigued, nodding readily. ★This is an option.★

So easy. Huh.

★What else?★ I returned. ★What do *you* think is entertaining?★

He showed his fangs like he had been waiting to see if I'd ask.

Uh-oh.

★Food, wine, performance,★ he signed, his tail ticking them off with tip curls, ★music, games, competitions, metal crafting, fishing, exploring, trading, reading, history—★

★Wait, wait, stop,★ I jerked my hands, unable to visualize most of those where it pertained to Humans. I picked one. ★Performance?★

Mourn nodded. ★Some perform in the street, some in a paid hall upon a stage. Playing instruments, dancing, or singing.★

Oh, yes, those things the Matrons made their sons learn…

★Sometimes one or many are acting.★

I shook my head. ★What is that? 'Acting'?★

Skilled performers telling a story as if it is happening while you watch.

What?! Why?

My face scrunched in confusion, and I gestured impatiently, *Understood. This city is rife with plenty and leisure.*

Mourn was smirking. *Are you envious?*

I puffed air through my lips. *Why should I be?*

I was when I saw it.

Slippery cockweight.

I focused on Gavin, truly wishing he'd come out of his trance on his own and in a reasonable mood this moment. *No such luck.*

So, I try to wake him, I pointed at the death mage, *you move him to a 'secure location' where he can...work?*

Mourn nodded. *On something of interest to him, yes. Without interruption.*

He and Krithannia had nailed the Deathwalker's disposition, for certain. Now I wagered the half-blood was trying to figure out how to keep *me* waiting one or two weeks for news about Jael without causing too much trouble.

Once he's moved, I can look around outside?

For certain. I will be your guard and guide. We'll be disguised with a certain amount of freedom.

Freedom.

This was too generous. There must be something else he wasn't saying, I trusted my gut on it. But if we had a week or two to wait...

Eh, just ask.

Might there be willing consorts in Augran as well? I asked.

The Dragonchild blinked, and I smiled. The surprise was genuine.

⋆After what you told me of Troshin's inn,⋆ he signed slowly, ⋆I didn't assume that specific pleasure was at the fore of your thoughts.⋆

⋆It's not, it's down here,⋆ I framed my mound with open hands at crotch level and continued signing. ⋆A Red Sister's cunt isn't easily cooled by a few rough cocks. It tends to make us eager to straddle the next one, not avoid them like we're broken.⋆

Mourn kept a neutral face, although that long, black tail swerved slowly to one side, pausing before swaying the other way.

⋆I can look into it.⋆

The tone of his sign was noncommittal, but at least he thought it over. No doubt he was sure I would cause trouble this way. Without my knowing the rules or boundaries, he would be right.

I made my decision.

"Very well," I said aloud, keeping my voice soft as I stepped closer to Gavin, pulling off my left glove. "Let us see if we can summon him back. If not, we'll be waiting until dawn."

The Deathwalker's eyes were still void-black. His chest moved only a small breath every minute or so. I allowed my fingers to hover above the bluish-white hands in his lap, in case he could sense the impending interruption.

Nothing.

I rested the pads of my fingers on the back of his hand, the reverse of what he'd done back on the ship during the storm. His skin was dry and cool, though not frigid.

I felt nothing at first, but then brought my blue stone out from beneath my armor to hold it in my other hand as a focus. I tried to concentrate with Mourn watching me, to think a simple command as I did with my spiders, though I still didn't know if he could hear me.

~Gavin. We request your presence. The Guild Mistress has a proposal.~

A chill flowed up my arm as his bowed spine straightened. The pale blue of his irises returned. I held in place, shocked at the swift response, and Gavin pulled his hand away, the creases at his mouth tightening. I stepped back to give him space.

The Deathwalker coughed before he could speak, and the sound reminded me of when he had been just a man who had fallen into the dirt, unable to run from Witch Hunters anymore. The blood from another man's heart had spilled down his pale, pointed chin, staining his teeth red.

"Sirana?" Gavin acknowledged with a grimace. "What is it?"

I stared for a flick at the black teeth matching his fingernails and toenails then gestured to Mourn. "Perhaps you would like to explain, bodyguard?"

The mercenary did not contradict his role and spoke simply. "The Guild Mistress suggested we show you our library, and I agree."

"Library?" Gavin repeated, his interest and skepticism clashing as mine had.

"Yes. It is nearby. There are no windows, and the door to access it is hidden."

The scholar contemplated the ink bottle, page dust, and stylus on the table before him. He'd managed to slip the grimoire into the pack beside him before nodding off.

His head turned to me. "Did I speak? Or seem distressed?"

My brows lifted in surprise. "No. You were perfectly still and silent."

"Hm. Very well." The ever-frowning mage pulled out the wrap to tuck away his scripting tools. "I would be glad to move to a windowless library, if you are offering."

"We are," Mourn reaffirmed.

Belatedly, I began collecting my things as well and was ready to leave at almost the same time. Now I felt a little excited. Mourn had laid out enough bait and would not get outright refusal from either of us.

Though, I would wait for the other boot to drop.

WITH EACH OF US CLOAKED, GAVIN AND I CARRIED OUR BOOTS and stockings back to the kitchen while Mourn carried the saddlebags. My feet hadn't noticed much chill until we stepped down into the sunken, stone room.

Now that I'd eaten some of the Yungian fare, I admired the multitude of hanging plants and neat lines of colorful, marked jars with greater appreciation. I wondered what portions of that vast selection I'd consumed and whether I might sample more later. Depending how long we stayed in Yong-wen, I could ask to feast here again.

While Gavin and I were donning stockings and boots near the door, I heard a small gasp in the corner and found the servant who was *not* Mai clinging to the edge of a table, her hands and the protective apron dusted with white. A pale blob of something which may have formed the grain pods sat briefly abandoned.

We had been too quiet, and she must have been in deep thought. I thought it was very late for her to be working in the kitchen.

Or perhaps very early.

"Shi'sheh, Ting," Mourn said to her, somehow calming her with a hand motion despite that he waved his claws at her. *"Ni'he Mai pinquy lingken."*

I glanced up, stamping a foot into my first boot. *What about Mai?*

Mourn held his hand out with palm down. *"Za-ci'da dinhua."*

The girl bowed deeply at the waist; her powdery hands clasped above her speeding heart as she kept her eyes on the floor. *"Da'zhen ro, Wen-yung!"*

Gavin was turned away putting on his second boot, but I heard him sigh in that customary way which made me smile. I was close to the same point of rolling my eyes for how dramatically the girls bowed, fluttered, or shivered around us depending on which "spirit" looked at them. But I also had higher tolerance for formalities than he did.

Mourn seemed to enjoy them better than either of us and, in his knowing the language and culture, we could let him do the work.

It always did feel like work.

Ting remained in her supplicative pose until we climbed the exit steps. She waited through Mourn cracking the door and checking the alley with ears, nose, and tongue; she waited while he signaled us to follow and still hadn't moved when I glanced back before closing the door.

Whew. I've had my fill of that for now.

I still wasn't comfortable watching women act like the meekest bua servants. I was grateful for Krithannia as an example, even if she wasn't Human. She was the only female since Osgrid who seemed to have a spine.

Well, there was that former Manalari sailor hungry for a fight on the ship, but I'd beaten her too easily. So there was her and Brom's conniving daughter, Amelda. I had no impulse to punch the Naulor Guild leader or the Dwarven eve witch in the face, but the Human women were either floppy, bowing reeds cooking our food or bitter pains in my back if I took my eyes off them for two moments.

Surely, they aren't all like that.

Something in between would be welcome to see. Perhaps another idea to ask Mourn about this city.

"Before seeing this other place," Gavin murmured once we'd stepped away from the door, nodding across the alley, "I want to check on Nightmare."

Our guide nodded, peering across the alley at the stable's entrance and scenting the air. I could smell the nearness of the river we'd floated down from the Great Lake but less of the Lake itself. The large sister moon was half-size in the sky and clouds were wispy and dimly lit. The nearby streets were empty; even I was satisfied no one skulked to note our passage when Mourn signaled for us to cross.

Upon entering the stable, however, Gavin kicked a dirt clod hard enough to burst it, and one of the tending boys we'd met early in the evening stirred in the loft above our heads.

"Hu zeh nao?" asked this light sleeper, slim hands reaching for the edge of the loft.

Yungian eyes were open in the dark, but I was certain I saw him clearer than he could any of us with our hoods up. I was expecting further talk and social rituals to slow us down so jumped in surprise when Mourn moved fast, leaving the saddlebags on the floor. With two steps he sprang at the loft, pulling himself up as the stable boy inhaled to scream.

"Shhh, *aquan,*" Mourn hushed gently, his palm covering the boy's brow. *"V'dri."*

The youth's eyes rolled backward, and his body relaxed as quickly as it had tensed. Mourn caught him, tucking him back out of sight from the door, and replaced the boy's blanket.

I stared up at him. *What in the…?*

This half-blood couldn't so blithely do that to *me,* could he?

Gavin may have wanted to comment as well, but there was another boy smelling of manure and sleeping in the hay. We watched Mourn repeat the spell with him, easing both caretakers into deeper sleep before dropping back down to the dirt before the stalls. At the same time, the horses stirred, blowing through their noses and stamping their hooves on the wooden floor. Their tension was escalating.

My mouth twisted. *The beasts can smell a Dragon.*

Mourn signed to me as he picked up the saddlebags. ★I will wait outside. Bring him when he's ready.★

★Wait, where——?★

The mercenary left the stable, and I leaned to watch as he slithered back across the alley, approaching a slanted door framed in stone that I'd missed before. At first, I thought it was a water-catch of some sort behind the inn, then Mourn pulled up a metal bar attached to one end and used it to tug open one of two sky-facing wood doors. He disappeared underground, leaving the entrance wide open behind him.

Oh.

Comparing directly, I estimated the kitchen of this safehouse was built halfway beneath street-level while this nearby entry would lead to space fully underneath it.

He said there were no windows. Would they keep a 'library' down there?

I had my doubts since the door was apparent and accessible to anyone walking by. *Not very private.*

The live horses were calming down, and I caught myself frowning when I heard the stall door open at the far end. Shrugging, I decided to check on our mare as well, to see her with my own eyes.

Then I caught my thought. *Heh. 'Our' mare.*

I felt for the knucklebone which allowed me to command her. *Still in its pouch.*

When I peered inside the open stall, Gavin was diligently inspecting Nightmare by feel, moonlight, and whatever extraordinary senses he possessed. She was also chewing on a fresh rodent as though it was an apple, crunching bone and chewing wet meat, blood dripping from her dry lips like juice.

"Where did you find the rat?" I asked.

"Barn trap near a feed bag," he answered, motioning somewhere behind me. "Its life aura was fading."

"Hm. Fortunate find."

"They could use more cats." Gavin looked up at the rafters, his unworldly eyes trailing them. "It is an ideal environment."

"Oh? *Should* there be cats?"

He shrugged, checking a final hind leg and seeming satisfied. "I would have expected them. There seem to be owls instead."

"Hm."

The moment Gavin rolled up his sleeve to expose his arm, a chuckle slipped out of my mouth.

"Thirsty after her meal?" I teased, receiving that reflexive, bored look of his I'd fished for.

"If I might be studying in a windowless place," he said, preparing his scalpel for a fresh cut, "our connection must be refreshed so I can sense her at will during that time."

I nodded, observing the grotesque but familiar ritual. Nightmare lapped at the black wound on his pale arm, her teeth sharp as ever, her tongue a dark grey. She did not try to nip for a further fleshy treat as a living creature might have.

"Quite obedient," I commented as he pushed her head away.

Gavin kept his arm exposed, gauged the closing speed of his wound. "Nightmare being otherwise might be like me disobeying myself at this point."

I had just begun to ponder that when the death mage reached his hand out toward me.

"May I see your talisman? That should be reattuned as well."

I pulled out the knucklebone and dropped it in his palm, watching him do as I expected: dipping the carved bone into his wound, rubbing it with his thumbs, and whispering something intensely enough that his pupils disappeared. A few moments later, he wiped the excess ichor with his sleeve and handed it out to me, the pale blue returning to his gaze.

"Thank you," I said, looking it over. The bone seemed whiter while the runes were starkly black once again. Moments before, they had been rubbing off.

"Test it before we leave," he insisted when I moved to return it to my pouch.

Ugh. Again?

Mourn might be wondering what was taking so long.

Sighing, I clutched the bone. *~Nightmare, turn your head to me.~*

The long, dark neck lifted and craned my way. With her ears pricked forward like that, she could have passed for a curious horse waking up.

~*Step backward. Stop. Step forward. Stop.*~

Gavin stayed out of the way as his mount moved oddly within the stall, nodding with satisfaction. "Good." Finally, he noticed we were missing someone. "Where is Mourn?"

I jerked a thumb toward the outside. "Horses hate him, remember?"

"Ah."

We exited the stable with our hoods secure, and I indicated the passage leading down. Both doors were open now. Gavin looked skeptical.

"What do you call that?" I asked.

"A cellar," he muttered as though he was being tricked, "and a bad place for a library."

"He didn't say it was down there," I replied, truthful enough. "Just to bring you when you're ready."

Across the way, a large, clawed hand poked up and signed a simple, *Come quietly.*

He was aware we were dawdling.

The sign appeared enough like a beckoning that Gavin's long fingers tapped on a shoulder strap of his pack as he considered. Meanwhile, my time to refuse going farther with Mourn had passed the moment the half-blood had stepped out of the warp-rotting trees.

I tapped the scholar with my elbow, jerking my head before sneaking across the alley. I'd just made it to the top stair when someone in my periphery pitched themselves out of the kitchen door.

Jerking my head to the right, I reached for a weapon then recognized her and took my hand from my belt. I didn't have time to warn Gavin before Mai collided into his right side; she was lucky to have missed the spade strapped to his pack.

"Ai!" she cried, dropping her empty basket, and stumbling back. Dark eyes widened, her body stiffening with fear when the Deathwalker turned around to look at her.

I knew well the scowl she saw now. Would she pass out and collapse again as when I'd told her my name? Would Krithannia come out here to save her again?

Mourn popped his head up, quickly assessed the situation, and called softly for the girl's attention.

"Mai. *Yao sruncai?*"

"Ei?" she yelped, tearing her gaze from what must appear to be death given form.

"Yao sruncai?"

The Yungian girl managed one breath. *"S-sruncai'tem, Wen-yung."*

The Dragonchild beckoned to her; it was not a Davrin sign. *"La jie tem. Aquan."*

Wen-yung. Aquan.

Words I'd heard more than once; I made note.

Mai nodded again, cringing back from Gavin, and avoiding his face. Behind her, I glimpsed Ting peeking one eye out the kitchen door.

So much for sneaking down here unseen.

I wondered what Mourn might do about it, send us all to sleep?

Whatever Gavin thought of the situation, he picked up the empty basket and blocked the girl with his body when she tried to leave without it.

"Here," said the death mage, pressing it back into fumbling hands. He sounded more annoyed than anything else.

When her feet didn't move, Gavin gave Mai a firm push on her back toward the cellar. I was genuinely surprised that he touched her.

Finally, her legs broke free, and she hustled forward.

"*Aquan*, Mai," Mourn repeated, attempting to reassure her, though I caught his warning look which Gavin probably missed.

"What does she need?" I asked, quite curious by now.

"Vegetables for the coming day," he answered, returning underneath the inn to light a candle at the bottom.

I stepped back and let Mai skim by me. With Gavin at her back, the servant girl took the stairs two at a time to catch up to Mourn.

Quite a nimble mountain goat.

I turned my eyes and my grin to Gavin, waving to offer him a first look down there. "Vegetables. No library."

Feigning his patience poorly, Gavin stepped down but had to rebalance his load which Mai had thrown off before descending underground. I followed right after him. The stairs made a little noise beneath my step and a fair bit more for Gavin. All my senses confirmed I was in a place for food storage.

A cellar.

It was cooler down here than in the household above, and many types of dried, brined, and otherwise preserved foodstuffs lay down here. The walls on either side of me were lined with shelves storing numerous bottles and jars with deep standing vessels of clay tucked in between. Barrels had been stacked at the back and the front side near the street. Dried, hanging haunches, herbs, and bulb roots hung from well-spaced hooks in the wooden beams above our heads.

Most House manor kitchens had this space, too. Except for the precise, unfamiliar blend of preservation methods, this was probably the closest to home I'd felt in months.

With Mourn holding the light, Mai swiftly selected her ingredients to add to her basket, moving between shelves, baskets, and bundles while we stood around waiting. I remained upright without a problem, but it was amusing to see both Mourn and Gavin hunched over or leaning various ways when they stepped to make room for the girl while avoiding the swinging sustenance.

"Linmin woa," the servant kept repeating. *"Linmin woa! Wen-yung, sho'shien, lantiu'janshi! Linmin woa!"*

"Yuatin mi, Mai," Mourn answered. *"Yuantin mi."*

I doubted the girl could be consoled at this point, but I listened to the repetition while Gavin inspected bundles of fibrous, hanging plants.

Wen-yung. Sho'shien. Lantiu… Janshi?

I knew that last one. *Clear sky warrior.*

Krithannia had suggested this instead of offering my real name to the spirit-wary people of Yong-wen. I extrapolated the other two from the servant girls' actions thus far.

Wen-yung was Mourn, for certain.

'Sho'shien' must be Gavin.

With many bows, mumblings, and clear permission from the Dragonchild, Mai quick-stepped up and into the open air, heading back to the kitchen but leaving the door open. Belatedly, I realized she'd been wearing the heavy, outdoor shoes which I'd seen in the kitchen.

Mourn followed her, reaching to close the double doors of the cellar, and muttering something as well. The next moment, I heard the metal bar being set back in place. I doubted it had been frazzled Mai who'd done it.

Another spell.

He certainly possessed an envious array of casual magic. I could believe Innathi's thoughts on how Humans tended to worship Dragons.

It is always a struggle for a Queendom when a To'vah becomes known… for they shall be fervently worshipped by the ignorant and superstitious. Their strength is alluring to many, and they are too eager to accept gifts of metal and magic.

Indeed, and one of their half-bloods would also accept rubies, strange blue stones, and jewelry from little, old women.

With a massive, slow exhale, Mourn turned around and rejoined us, handing the candlelight to Gavin.

"That was fun," he said, his tone loaded with irony.

"She ran into me," Gavin protested, his voice brusque. "She wasn't looking where she was going."

"He's right, she wasn't," I seconded. "Came bounding out of the house like a *Sathoet* was chasing her."

Mourn darted me a glance, his tail coiling, but held up a finger to Gavin. "May I request one favor, Deathwalker?"

"Depends on what it is," he replied.

"A simple request. Do not reach for anyone in Yong-wen unless they are attacking you. Of course, there is nothing to be done if they run into you, but do keep your hands from them."

"I did not touch her," the dead monk denied.

"Um," I began, and his eerie eyes looked at me. "You pushed her when she didn't move fast enough."

Gavin wrinkled his nose. "A nudge only. She needed the help."

Mourn pointed his claw. "That. You are not mortal anymore, Deathwalker. Please do not do that again."

The gaunt man lifted his chin. "I'm unlikely to if you still mean to show me this library."

"I still mean to. But, unlikely or not, will you agree to this favor?"

Gavin sighed. "Yes. I know it is better that way."

"Good. Thank you."

"Wait, why?" I asked, glimpsing the mercenary's expression as he turned toward the rear. "What was so wrong about it?"

"You spotted Ting, didn't you?" he asked, turning right at the final row of shelves.

"I did." I motioned to Gavin, and we followed the hybrid to discover what he was doing.

"A death spirit of a very old legend just reached out with his pale, inhuman hand and touched her," Mourn said, sounding irritated as we leaned around the shelves to see him prodding at a dirty spot on the wall. "Whether Mai could keep this to herself or not, that is not her choice now. I do not know what effect this will have on her and her family but, generally, families touched by death are shunned to prevent it spreading."

Oh.

"Superstitious as Manalar, then," I commented, folding my arms. "Are you worshipped here like Musanlo is there?"

Mourn found the trigger he sought; something clicked, and he pushed to move a section of the stone wall back before sliding it to the left—this time, the feat seemed entirely physical, unassisted by magic but requiring significant strength.

"Come," he said. "The library is this way."

Quietly, I scoffed. *No answer is an answer, you know.*

Just a less precise one.

The stone hall beyond was barely wide enough for the half-blood and he had to duck his head. It was a tight and awkward fit for me and Gavin to get past him so he could close the door behind us. He didn't make us reverse the walking order.

"Walk forward until you reach an alcove on the left."

Gavin led with the candle before him, and I was trying to keep an irrational and inconvenient paranoia under control with barriers on all sides of me and Mourn walking a bit too close behind. Once we reached the tiny recess which seemed to have no purpose, the light was too close to my eyes, and my vision blurred with tears.

I heard Mourn say, "I must blind you both."

Fuck, it's a trap!

"Another secret room?" Gavin guessed.

"Correct."

I gritted my teeth behind my lips, promising I'd be less on edge once I saw a few of those promised scrolls and books and didn't have a candle in my face.

"Is a blindfold sufficient? Sirana carries one."

"Yes, and you may just blow out the candle when you're ready."

The males paused to look to me, and I carefully bound my eyes in the small space, my elbows brushing either the wall or Gavin's ear. I waited tensely, debating whether I only had cause to relax once the bargain was set.

Whichever way. I'm worth more alive than dead no matter who I meet up here.

With my acceptance of my fate, Gavin blew out his candle, and I didn't remember what happened next.

My stomach lunged, and then I was about to topple off my feet. Gavin staggered first, quite loud, and heavy as he fell. The handle of his spade clacked and dragged against a stone wall. Simultaneously, I dropped to a knee rather than fall, planting my hands on a surprisingly soft floor until I felt steadier.

A thick scent struck my nose, like a cross between the Wizards' Tower and a blacksmith's forge without the heat. This had felt similar to sharing the jump circles with Shyntre.

"You may remove your blindfold," Mourn said to me.

I pulled it off in an instant, blinking until I could make out the fingers of one hand pressed into an ornate rug. I could see the intricate designs but not any colors until Mourn rumbled in Draconic, which called a warm glow to several lanterns. Though I winced at the light, I also saw the rug woven with threads of brilliant red, yellow, purple, and blue which implied flowers, fruit, fire, and water.

It was beautiful. And would take a decade to make.

"The library," Mourn welcomed us simply.

With Gavin I regained my feet and looked around the large room. If we were below the safehouse still, not transported somewhere else entirely, the space could fit within the footprint of the architecture with room to spare. I smelled the aged parchment of scrolls and books which filled the alcove shelves lining two of the walls. There were two heavy, wooden desks, four matching chairs, and one red, oversized chaise.

Large enough to fit a To'vah-krav.

There was also a spread of curiously blank wall. It was just well-dressed stone, yet my fingers twitched as I wanted to touch that spot, to study how it was made and perhaps by whom. Was it Dwarven work? My gut thought it was. It looked much like the build at the Ley Tower.

Dwarves in Yong-wen?

Though I felt a hint of excitement, I had not seen a one of them in my brief walk of the streets. According to Rithal and Osgrid, however, they existed in Augran at large.

The half-breed seemed curious why I stared at a blank wall when Gavin was already drifting toward the nearest shelf. Mourn turned his head toward a dark corner of the room, however, and made a strange noise. Something between a growl and a whistle.

Suddenly, as if in answer, two small, reddish eyes peered out at us from the shadow between two bookshelves. I heard the creature gurgle a rush of air, as if displeased and trying to growl.

"What is that?" I murmured.

"Graul."

"Graul?"

Mourn wasn't talking to me.

"Avayorn, Graul," he continued in a calm and smooth tone.

The beady eyes shifted from me to Mourn, who motioned his hand forward. *"Qeif esp, fevekic."*

That's not Yungian.

Was Draconic good for speech as well as spells?

The creature, after sufficient evaluation and consideration, emerged from the shadow and slinked toward him on four legs, dragging its belly along the carpet. Its scales were a similar color to Mourn's, deep black with purplish undertones. The scales did not seem as glossy as the To'vah-krav but, unlike the hybrid, the little beast possessed a full hide of them.

Black, leathery wings folded very close to its body, each foot had five digits with claws, and the tail was long and whip-like. The neck seemed a bit short for its tail but still had enough bend; the beast could look behind it without having to turn its body around. It did just that, as if eyeing the warm spot it had left.

"You created a small, Draconic guard dog?" Gavin asked as Mourn crouched down to lift the creature up.

I heard a rasping purr as the big mercenary cradled it in his arms then a hiss aimed at Gavin, as if it had understood his comment. It struck me that the reptile had moved stiffly across the floor and had not stretched its wings out at all.

Looking at the eyes, red like most of the Davrin, I could also see a haze reminding me of the few riding lizards that reached an age too old to be a mount. I also spotted a tiny bit of growth: coarse hair sprouting on its chin and the tips of its swiveling ears. The hairs were white and silver.

"I don't think Mourn created this," I mused, sure now of what I saw. "This is a drake, yes? An old one."

Gavin frowned. "A what? Drake?"

Are there no drakes up here?

"Just what you see," I said, motioning with my hand. "Small, winged lizards I've heard live in the tunnels underground."

"Only heard? Not seen?"

I shrugged. "Not in my city or in the close tunnels around it, but others have."

"Oh?" Mourn asked, obviously interested. "Why no drakes in Sivaraus?"

"Are they in Vuthra'tern?" I countered.

"Sometimes."

"As pets?"

He frowned as I glanced at Graul. "No."

"Then you know they are elusive and hard to catch or keep. I always heard they're more trouble than they were worth soon after some noble bragged about her exotic pet."

I paused as the drake released another hiss which was almost a chuckle. The long tail coiled around Mourn's forearm like a snake —or like Mourn's own tail had coiled about that wild pig—and the tiny beast turned its head to hiss at me next. Finally, the wings moved a little bit, more clearly stiff with age.

"How old is he?"

"For a drake, Graul is ancient," the half-blood acknowledged, rubbing the pad of his forefinger between the little reptile's eyes. "He is perhaps a century younger than me."

Graul enjoyed this attention. The purring sound came from a vibrating flap of skin along his throat.

"Perhaps a century?" I remarked. "That's uncharacteristically imprecise of you."

Mourn smirked. "He couldn't count when we found each other."

"He can now?" Gavin asked, disbelieving even as Mourn nodded.

"I taught him."

Ah. So, unlike the Matrons, the Dragonblood managed to keep a drake for a pet and teach him tricks? I supposed that wasn't too surprising.

"What's he doing in a library?" I asked.

"Guarding our hoard."

The surreal look of pride on the little beast's muzzle almost had me doubling over in laughter. I might have if my pack wouldn't have pitched me head over heels.

"Really?" I asked, failing to hold a hearty chuckle as I peered around. "I see no jewels."

"Just don't poke your nose into his nest."

Simultaneously, Gavin and I looked to the shadowy spot between the bookshelves. Graul rumbled with clear hostility, and we looked away.

"I can accept a library as a 'hoard' worthy of protection," said the Deathwalker, direct but not aiming to placate. "However, you never stated that you might be taking us to *your* library."

Mourn grunted. "Not mine alone. Krithannia adds to it more than I do."

"Adding to it for how long?" I asked, and Gavin seemed to appreciate the question.

"Hm. Almost four hundred years, now."

Gavin's eyes widened slightly.

"Graul used to travel with me on our tasks," Mourn continued, possibly missing my scholar's thirsty expression. "Now it hurts his bones and I ask him to watch over this place. The Yungian family who owns Luni Ti—"

He saw my expression and clarified, "The family who owns this inn are more than pleased to have their own 'good luck Dragon' protecting the foundation of their business."

"Ah, so we *are* still beneath the safehouse?" I asked.

He nodded, rubbing the ancient drake gently around the shoulders. "We are. Sometimes Graul finds his way out of here, and they feed him or give him a pillow to sit on and watch them work. I hear the stories when I return. No breath attacks yet." Mourn looked at me with a wry smile. "He likes being worshipped, I believe."

And likes to mimic.

I blinked. "Wait. Breath attacks?"

Graul coughed, making the air in front of him pop when Mourn answered. "Yes. Breaths of air."

Gavin and I glanced at each other; we weren't sure what this meant, but we maintained our distance.

"Uhm, well, he is... cute," I said, unsure if that was the right word.

Gavin shook his head but gazed once again about him as he stood on the plush carpet. "If the drake lives here, are you implying that both of you are prepared to leave me to sift through your 'hoard?'"

"If you like," Mourn answered with surprising aplomb. "There will be time to do so. Krithannia must gather further information for your mission and any word of Sirana's sister. You may stay in the room up above, or you could browse the scrolls down here. I don't have many options on short notice."

Both of us knew Gavin's answer to this, but he had some good questions to ask first.

"Can I leave without you being present if necessary?" Gavin asked, eyeballing the texts with growing curiosity now that the drake was calm in Mourn's arms.

"You can, through that wall," Mourn indicated the plain stone I'd been admiring. "It will take you outside to the alley, but you would not be able to get back into this library unless I escorted you again. You must be certain it is time to leave."

"What of food, water, and life's other annoying interruptions?"

I smiled at that. Sleep and voiding waste, no doubt.

"Do you still need those?" Mourn asked seriously.

"Inevitably, but no longer daily." Gavin indicated the drake. "I am also asking about him."

Mourn nodded. "Ah. Life's necessities."

He walked over to a panel with a handle and a shelf in front, barely disturbing Graul as he slid it effortlessly with one hand to reveal a small recess and platform. One side held a few clean cups, plates, and bowls, and the other a rune-marked circle.

My gaze traced backward from this to a narrow ramp of carpeted stone leading to the floor. *Hm.*

"If you require sustenance," Mourn instructed, "place a cup, a bowl, and a plate on the runes and wait. They will send something back to you."

"Will they?" Gavin said with a bit of a sneer, no doubt thinking of Mai's petrification when looking at him.

Mourn smiled. "They won't know it is you. Fang Ro Gi is accustomed to answering the runes, especially when he and his wife know I am back in Yong-wen. They will assume it is me or Graul and be discreet."

"Wait," I interjected. "Graul uses this, too?"

"He does. He is a very clever drake."

I was looking at the ramp again, so Gavin asked first, "Will they send a meal like before, or should I expect chunks of raw meat?"

"There will be meat, and they may send both." Mourn shrugged. "I prefer it cooked, but Graul less often."

Gavin accepted this, settling down with the idea of remaining here for a time. "And the other half of life's needs?"

"Similar closet, over there." Mourn indicated a panel door at a well-lit corner with a handle and hinges. "It transports waste to the manure pile behind the stables."

There was also a square cut out near the bottom, fixed with a swinging door with the hinges at the top.

"And Graul uses that, too," I added, easily able to imagine the beast slithering into and out that passage.

"Yes, he does."

"Clever," Gavin said dryly while I openly snickered at the idea of using a jump circle to aim dung on top of the road apples outside. The Deathwalker looked at the snoozing Graul. "What recommendations do you have for sharing space with this drake?"

Mourn looked down at the scaly bundle in the crook of his arm, who was now peeking suspiciously through an eyelid. "Just don't try to lift him up or needlessly wake him from a nap."

"Done. But what more of 'breath of air' attack you mentioned before?" Gavin indicated the room. "I'd wager you and the Guild Mistress are wary of feeding fire with all this parchment around."

"You are correct. Even the lanterns are heatless. They will remain lit. Feel free to move them around."

"Very good. And Graul's breath?"

"Just gusts of air capable of shoving a large man off his feet or pushing him into a wall."

"'Just' air," I mused.

"Well," Mourn added, "if you are too close to him, he may try to suck the breath out of your chest. Taking part of it forces you to pass out. Taking all of it can collapse the lungs and suffocate a man, though Graul has not killed many this way."

That was a bit scary, although Mourn did not mention that such an act would be costly to the little beast in his advanced age. It would have to be necessary, I thought, with Graul under imminent threat.

"A good thing I do not always need to breathe," Gavin remarked, "though I don't see a point of crowding him to test it."

"And that is good enough for us, Deathwalker."

We waited patiently, giving the death mage time to think and decide for himself what we already knew. Except for sharing space with the crabby little drake, he was being offered a private library with servants sending food and drink without having to interact, without being interrupted at all.

This was exactly what Gavin would have wanted for any lengthy time spent in this safehouse, and it was truly generous. I must think that Krithannia was indeed "courting" Gavin for something beyond breaking the Bishops' magic at Manalar.

But an elder Elf like her has time to be patient.

There were too many books and scrolls here for Gavin to read even if he spent a solid week in here, but I wondered what my death mage might find down here as he poked about?

Inevitably, he nodded. "This is impressive. I will be glad to stay here while we await further news."

Mourn smiled, looking pleased though not in the way that sent my senses alert and wary, searching for something overlooked. He stepped to set Graul down onto the comfortable chaise, receiving a minor protest from the drake who curled up again soon enough, blinking curiously at us.

The mercenary also removed Kurn's sword from his back and stepped to one of the few other wall spaces available; this one had a couple of empty hooks. He placed the Ma'ab weapon one-handed atop two of the hooks, displaying it at a flattering angle.

"Only one trophy on your wall?" I asked, bemused by his action.

He admired it for a flick before turning away. "I would rather leave a new piece here by itself until I have a chance to study it. It will be added to the others soon enough."

The others?

"Just weapons?" I asked. "Or do you do the same with things like enchanted rubies or blue saphgar?"

Mourn looked at me with brow arched. "It depends on the piece, though moot in this case, as neither of those will join my hoard."

So, he had another collection aside from this library and probably nearby. One of metal and gems and other crafts, and a clear habit far more like his sire than his mother. Unlike the books he collected with Krithannia, I doubted Mourn would so readily accept her recommendation to show us his treasure pile next.

And she probably knows not to suggest it.

While my mind wandered on that wealth yet unseen, Mourn had pulled a heavy box from beneath one of the desks, setting it on top before working the lock.

"I will give you this before we go," Mourn said, keeping his voice easy on the ears in this underground lair. He lifted a pouch from out of the box before closing it, then stepped to hand the laden leather out to Gavin.

"Before you go?" my ally asked without reaching for it, glancing at me. "And where will Sirana be spending the next week or so?"

So, he finally thought to ask.

I shrugged. "I want to see Augran, and I must work out my bargain with Mourn. I plan to come back here and check in with you, of course."

Mourn didn't counter any of this, and Gavin frowned at me, then him.

"You will be a proper bodyguard?" the death mage said in subtle challenge. "She has had a strong hand in my journey and is not disposable to it."

I blinked at what might have been the most generous thought he'd volunteered about me.

A corner of Mourn's mouth rose high with genuine amusement and he bowed his head, still offering the pouch. "Sirana will be safe with me. I will bring her back here whenever she should request it."

"Very well." Gavin accepted the pouch. "What is this?"

Mourn glanced to where Graul dozed on the chaise. He leaned closer to the death mage, and I leaned closer to them. I needed to for how quiet his voice became.

"Snacks. If he is agitated or aggressive while you access the books near his nest, offer him one. Use sparingly."

Gavin blinked his death's eyes in a richly amusing way, and I chortled. He grunted, weighing the treats in his palm. "Hm. An animal usually has a warning before it uses its ultimate defense. What is his?"

Our host nodded. "He makes a sound like a sheep's bladder if one fills it with air and makes it tremble so fast that it hums."

"I've never heard that."

"It is unique. You will hear the warning. The flap of skin at his throat will also puff out and stretch to a bright lavender color. His tail can still lash hard enough to cause a welt or bleeding cut should it strike bare skin."

Gavin's mouth twisted a bit; it wasn't a smile. "Do I toss it to him?"

"No, place it down and step away. Don't throw it at him." Mourn finally showed his teeth in a smile. "Unless you want to play rough for the rest of the bag."

Gavin felt for the snacks inside with dexterous fingers, contemplating as Mourn touched a brief farewell to his companion from the Deepearth. Then he signed for me to walk through the wall with him.

Outside.

My death mage required nothing more from me than a wave as I left with the mercenary. I did not envy the scholar being shut up in a room with only books to read, but I *did* envy that he'd received exactly what he wanted most. With an amusing companion, as well.

May I be as fortunate to find exactly what I wanted in this city.

CHAPTER 3

Reprising the unsettling sensations of leaving the Wizard's Tower, I walked through the magic wall with Mourn. As he'd claimed, we stood in the back alley. On his recommendation, I'd left my full traveler's kit and its weight behind with Gavin and Graul.

"You'll not need them," the mercenary had assured me, smiling a little. "And you need not confuse the gossip of how many newly arrived spirits there are in Yong-wen."

Heh.

That was the most persuasive part. I'd already done the "new arrival" walk wearing my true face, hauling around excess rations, waterskins, wilderness tools, bedding, and miscellany, and accepting many gifts of food in exchange for people touching my cloak for "luck." It was exhausting.

This time I would walk this city as I once had around the Palace and Sanctuary back home: just leathers, cloak, belt, with the tools used for defense and maintaining order—although *whose* sense of order wasn't worth debating.

The familiar mindset and light weight helped my posture, as did knowing any needs for shelter, rest, and sustenance would be met as my new bodyguard deemed most practical.

Well. Almost new.

The moons had slipped behind the high, curved rooftops, and dawn would arrive within the hour. Half the street lanterns were lit still, and while the cobbles were not as crowded as last evening when we'd arrived, I could hear that Mai and Ting weren't the only early risers in Yong-wen.

Assuming the two ever slept with us in the house.

★To begin,★ I signed, ★can we *not* walk blatantly down the streets this morning as we did last eve?★

Mourn still smiled when he looked down at me. ★Are you sure? This is the only place where you may walk as you are. The rest will be us running the rooftops or as on the boat, wearing a Human disguise with comments on your accent each time you speak to someone new.★

To the Abyss with my 'accent.'

I squinted with suspicion. ★Running roofs? I can't jump these streets, I haven't the equipment.★

★I do. But I enjoy walking Yong-wen more.★

I exhaled. ★If we are to reach a bargain, Dragon son, you should be direct. What is it you want from me in this?★

He gave it some thought. ★Perhaps to observe your new poise, Red Sister? The relic is no longer distracting or speaking to you, I can tell, and you have your blue stone back. I am still learning who you are.★

★As I am you.★

But at a slower pace.

★Wait,★ I realized, ★you took the ruby from the table, right? For your bounty?★

He nodded, confirming, ★I did.★

★When will you turn that in to the Ma'ab?★

★I won't be. I'll turn it in with my handler. He returns it to the Ma'ab and collects the bounty on my behalf.★

Smart for slowing targets on his back but oddly trusting for a treasure-collector.

And when will you do that? Where?

After sunrise. Here in Yong-wen.

Oh? Do I get to be present or must I hide?

He smiled as if this were the first activity that I'd shown interest in. *Present, if you wish. He would probably have some questions for you about Kurn and Castis.*

Who is 'he'?

You'll see. If you don't change your mind about being 'blatant' in Yong-wen.

I sighed. *Until then?*

He glanced at the main road, motioned for me to follow as he began walking toward it. After a moment my knees finally bent, and I caught up to him.

"Side trip, nothing harmful," he answered before I repeated myself. "You are safe. Enjoy what you can."

Sighing again, I walked next to the tall hybrid, observing the earliest workers quietly disappearing into doorways while peeking out at us. We took a streetsweeper off guard, coming upon him with his back turned. I chuckled at his enormous, open-mouthed expression and exaggerated scuttle away, bowing repeatedly before falling backward over a small rise.

"One might mistake you for the Valsharess here," I muttered in Davrin.

"Are you envious?" he asked me again. "Or incensed?"

"Fuck you, no. I'm confused. Skeptical. Like I'm missing something."

I caught myself admiring how softly Mourn placed his wide, bare feet on the curiously clean stone. Admittedly, the streets were well designed, constructed, and maintained. Even with my shorter legs, it was easy to avoid the few mud clods, dung, and puddles in my path without bobbing or leaping.

"After the sampling of Humans I've met," I continued, "I'd think you must be lying to say that walking in the open like this has *never* caused you trouble." I made a face up at him. "Unless it's simply your size which makes them cower."

"Hm. The claws and tail help."

I blinked. "Is that a jest?"

He smiled. "Not really, but in truth, it is their stories and how I choose to help shape them that levels the trouble."

"Legends, yes. You take advantage of their ignorance."

"If you and I lived the same lifespan as Humans, that might be worth debating."

"Oh, so it's not?"

"New 'ignorance' is born every day in Augran, you can never teach everyone or see their knowledge last. The shaping never ceases. Should I stop helping to shape this city, then the time has come to move my hoard."

He glanced down at me. "Not strange, is it? If the Davrin cease shaping the short-lived races who do so much work for them below, either they are giving up the slaves or giving up the Great Cavern, yes?"

I shook my head; I never saw either happening. "Alright, noted. So, you see Humans as your unwitting slaves?"

"No," he said with a chuckle. "But a healthy and stable city is good for cultivating ideas and crafters of wonders. There is far less skill and wealth to trade if they are starving or overwhelmed with disease."

His saying this reminded me of his interest in my sharing Shyntre's pellets with his apothecary. *Hm.*

"When you live so much longer than any Human you've met," he continued, "why *wouldn't* you want to see what ideas could be cultivated with only a nudge where needed?"

"Interesting," I commented, sounding like Gavin.

Now I wondered who he'd been speaking to in coming up with these ideas and approaches. Certainly not any Davrin. His sire? I knew nothing at all about the Black Dragon of the Deep, but Queen Innathi had been clear about the To'vah being known for sculpting whole regions to their design.

She implied this manipulation harmed the Desert Queendom, theorizing that her sister Ishuna, had met a Dragon at some point.

It was clear the half-blood beside me embraced this side of his heritage much more than his Mother's. He'd been direct why that was.

"It is less gratifying that you grasp the nuance of a slave name and not my true one, Baenar. It is a dead name, let it stay so."

I could believe there was once a Matron with hubris enough to assume she could control a To'vah-krav to the same level as a Sathoet. I didn't know what happened to her, though, or how the "slave" got out.

Now isn't the time to ask.

For a while I had been using my mental map from yesterday, recognizing landmarks in the dark which did not rely on color. I expanded that memory as we entered a new section off the main streets. It had no merchant fronts, but more dwellings surrounded by taller trees, shrubs, and crafted paths and bridges around constructed ponds.

Gardens. Hm. Nice.

Despite Mourn's claim about walking in the open, I soon noticed that he was favoring the shadows and keeping obstacles between us and the dwellings. We crossed one constructed border, a fence made of plants set in a straight line, and finally moved in toward a house. The landscape must be tended constantly to keep these straight lines. I bet Tamuril would hate it, but maybe Krithannia encouraged it.

We paused near a small garden patch, hiding behind a standing stone which would protect the soil from excessive wind or driving rain from the North. It even seemed to have a drainage system, and the thick scents of herbs and unusual blossoms floated up from rich soil.

Growing food, too.

I tapped Mourn's shoulder so he would look at me signing. ★Where are we now? You're avoiding being seen.★

He signed back, ★Losing followers before we knock.★

★Knock?★

Mourn turned then to approach the back door of the nearest dwelling, motioning me somewhat behind him and to his right. This was a better position than a bua got back home, and I had no cause or desire to stand in front anyway. He lifted a hand and tapped with the four tips of his claws.

One, two, pause… One, two, three, pause… One, two, three, four.

He paused and continued patiently, adding another tap to the cluster each time. I truly did not know what he intended. The sound was not threatening, I didn't think; more like the breeze pushing a nearby decoration to swing into the red painted door. The sky had lightened to blue-grey and, by my count, the Dragon-child had reached a successive total of nine taps before I finally heard soft feet drawing near on the other side.

"Shuzi ai'nali?" asked a female Human.

"Yunqi," Mourn answered in an odd tone with a lot of bass.

She hesitated and I waited to see what she would do.

Ultimately, she opened the door only wide enough for her face, looking out first, then up. Her body reacted like the stable boy who had peeked into my hood rather than the streetsweeper. After that she opened her door as wide as it would go and managed a fine bow at her waist.

I blinked with surprise when she straightened, recognizing the very first elder woman who had approached us the previous day.

The silver haired Yungian had offered the "Dragon spirit" a necklace, and Mourn had traded it for a vial which she had palmed and sped away as the crowd closed in on us. She wore not the yellow and pink cinched gown of before, but a plain tan, loose garment covering her from neck to ankles, lightly smudged with dirt.

"Wen-yung, duo'shan tsoa woia," she said solemnly, her feigned calm implying she thought we could not hear her heart or sense the flush of heat from her body.

Mourn seemed to pretend he couldn't sense her fear and asked her a question. She began to shake but nodded many times, gesturing for us to come forward past the threshold.

Following Mourn in, I noted the mat to the side and sighed in silence, beginning to remove my boots without being asked.

"Hm," Mourn hummed pleasantly, smiling at me as he gently wiped off his feet.

I looked to the side rather than roll my eyes. This custom was *not* conducive to coming and going quickly, so we'd better be as safe as Mourn assumed or I'd be running around barefoot before the first week was done.

The Yungian woman stared at us with open mouth before breaking into motion to retrieve a previously drawn bucket of water and cloth with impressive speed. At first, she moved as if to wash his feet herself, but the hybrid thankfully spared her that embarrassing display. He took the cloth with thanks, dipped it, and scrubbed his own feet.

The elder matron looked at me curiously, and I obliged her by taking down my hood. She immediately put her palms together and pressed them close to her breasts, lowering her eyes.

"Janshi-tsao," she said.

Warrior something. Hm.

I hoped that she did not require a response because Mourn did not translate that for me. Instead, he said something lengthy which ended in a question. I was dismayed to see even an elder woman of this city emoted as much as Mai and Ting. She did nothing to hide her thoughts in her grand gestures and expressive face while listening and responding to him; the creases and wrinkles even enhanced the emotion.

Perhaps that's where the caits learned it.

Soon she guided us, still talking, through clean and flower-scented work rooms to a much smaller one lit with a portable lantern. I smelled illness and stopped myself at the door after Mourn squeezed himself through. Peeking in, I saw the room contained nothing but a pallet on the floor, layered with blankets nesting a small Human child.

Mourn and the matron talked a bit more, their voices quiet, as he crouched down next to the pallet. His tail shushed along the floor beneath his cloak as he briefly inspected the small Human, who was young and thin enough that I could not tell the sex.

Straight, dark hair topped the youth's head, some of it plastered with sweat. Even though the brown skin offered an impression of health when compared to Gavin's gaunt pallor and sunken eyes, this lasted only until I studied the small lips and around the eyelids. They were oddly pallid with darker, bluish-purple flesh and tiny veins visible beneath the closed eyes and around the lips. The exhaustion and shallow breath seemed to imply a rare, quiet moment for one very ill.

I watched Mourn's palm cover the whole of the child's chest above the blankets, then he whispered something that made my ears tingle.

Draconic, again? Didn't the vial help?

Almost instantly, deep brown eyes fluttered open, and the tiny heart began to race as the youth drew in a much deeper breath and began to cough, turning away to the wall. The sound of it was raw, deep, and hoarse, and I could see the pain etched on the babe's face as it tried to stop the fit without success.

"*Suni,*" said the woman mournfully.

Mourn removed another vial from his belt and gestured the matron forward to assist in getting the youth to drink it. This took a few moments, and it was almost spit back up, but he spoke another phrase in his sire's language, more than once, sounding as a much different song from the Yungian speech.

"*Weloh ir yinigeld.*"

His words seemed to augment the swift change in this tiny space. The cough quieted; I heard a clean breath which did not rattle. The matron grew excited, flapping her hands as she kept her eyes fastened on one I presumed was her offspring, even if she seemed a bit frail for bearing children.

When the two finally rolled the babe back, it stared at Mourn with wide eyes and no voice. I did not think it was petrified into speechlessness but watched intently, noting many details up close and in wonder.

The Dragonblood obliged the child further by pulling back his hood, revealing straight, black hair like the Yungians while adding his pointed, Elven ears, and his short, ivory horns to his bestial visage. I heard two soft gasps from the Humans.

"*Ankang'lu,*" Mourn said as he stood up with the child still staring.

"*Shi'sheh, Wen-yung!*" the matron cried as moisture trailed down her cheeks. She looked from Mourn to her child. "*Xijuan, shuohua!*"

"*Shi'sheh, Wen-yung,*" the child repeated obediently, blinking dark eyes at last.

"*Wodei, Xijuan,*" Mourn answered, his face peaceful and his teeth hidden as he nodded to the child.

I could admit relief that we did not linger in leaving. Near the backdoor, Mourn bowed his head to the matron—I tried to mimic while I put on my boots—and the elder mother moved to open the door for us. She thankfully refrained from gushing words of gratitude, but her eyes were still moist, glittering in the dawn light.

I was glad to get away from so much heavy emotion even as my own eyes watered from the rising Sun. Once we cut through the shaded side into a neighbor's garden, I signed, ★Guessing you healed the infant the rest of the way?★

★Yes. The illness held too strong to cure her with only the vial I gave before. She needed a magical boost.★

★The child is a cait?★

★Female, yes.★

★How many years aged?★

★Not more than six.★

I pondered. ★You knew them from before?★

He shook his head. ★Yesterday was the first I met the grand-mother.★

★Grandmother. That was her daughter's daughter?★

★Her son's. But yes.★

★You came straight here. You must have located them before coming to get me.★

★Krithannia helped.★

★Why?★

★She's good at finding families.★

★No! I mean, why do what you just did? Won't you be drowned by everyone asking you to heal their children every cut or ailing?★

He smirked. ★That's why we were subtle. I also asked her to wait five days to make certain the child is well before telling any-one.★

I growled, and his ear perked up. Mourn looked at me and slowed to a stop so we could face each other. We were far enough from any dwelling that he chose to speak aloud.

"What troubles you?" he asked in my native tongue.

"Beyond performing magic to amaze and awe," I replied, "how does sneaking in gardens and healing sick daughters 'shape' your city?"

Mourn folded his arms, frowning with disapproval. "The woman was brave to be the first to approach me. She has listened to the stories enough to offer me a small treasure with her request. I wager she had to have sprinted to retrieve it by the time she heard we were here."

I listened but caught myself tapping my foot.

"I accepted her gift with the promise that Xijuan would 'gain Dragon luck' and reclaim good health," he stated. "I assured this promise would be fulfilled quicker than I might have because *you* are here, Baenar, and you are my priority."

I blinked. *Trying to distract me again.*

"Alright, you've explained the 'side-trip,' mercenary," I said, "but not my question. Why do it at all?"

He sighed, the tip of his tail flicking. "The girl was with her widow grandmother, slowly dying of illness because her father did not want Xijuan near the older brother, their only son. Remember what I said, those touched by death are shunned?"

Hesitantly, I nodded.

"Add to this, Yungian daughters do not matter in passing on land and wealth to children, the same as sons do not matter among Davrin."

I frowned. That was interesting. *And insulting.*

"The grandmother was desperate, she had tried everything," he continued, "but no one would help once she'd consumed 'too many' resources for one girl. Now, Xijuan will live and, in a mere fifty years, that same girl may be telling her own grandchildren of the night the Dragon Spirit came and saved her life."

"And you assume to still be here?" I asked.

Mourn smiled tightly. "This is as their ancestors have done for three centuries now. Those children and their children's children still look to the shadows for protection, and never whisper a word of the Dragon's passing to those outside of Yong-wen. Loyalty like that can never be bought with coin, Baenar, and I've promised yours and Gavin's safety with this as well."

I felt another flush through my chest but had no reply, at first. I knew how small actions bred consequences, but I had yet to contemplate "shaping" a series of them for three centuries. That was my Elders' claim to secrets and power, D'Shea and Rausery, and even *they* were used to thinking of individual competition and motives, not healing sick buas.

I'd never imagined that a whole community might follow the same goal through more than one generation, especially based on a story of a legend with periodic appearances. I thought Humans turned over their populations too quickly to be reliable in how they would react to races like ours.

That's what Rausery claims.

Mourn was telling me otherwise, that it was something different he had determined about Humans from long term exposure.

He seems to have made a haven by using it wisely.

★Very well,★ I signed. ★Impressive. I understand you must give something back to maintain their cooperation.★

His shoulders relaxed. ★Good enough.★

I smirked. ★How did you figure this out? Just stumble into it or did your sire guide you? Or the Pale Elf?★

He tensed again, and my eyelids fluttered as his tail lashed once.

Oh, he doesn't want to answer that.

"Speaking of giving something back," he rumbled so low only I could hear him. "Are you still willing to bargain with the wellness pellets as well as the ruby?"

My eyebrows raised, and I crossed my arms. "Oh. You want to negotiate now?"

And change the subject.

He showed me teeth. "You'll be hungry soon, a good bun place should be open, and we may talk in a nearby people's garden with plenty of cover."

"Ah-huh, and after this?"

Something fun maybe—

"We'll meet my handler and hand over the Ma'ab ruby."

Damn it.

I sighed. "Tasks first, then play?"

Mourn offered an odd smirk. His eyes shone metallic in the early light. "We'll see."

Leaving me dangling, huh?

"Wait too long," I threatened idly, "and I'll go hunting alone."

"Hunting? For what?"

I grinned, inviting him to guess.

"Ah," he said like he remembered, but I reminded him anyway.

"You said you'd look into consorts for me."

He placed a hand on his brow and rubbed a patch of scales there. "One task at a time."

"Fresh buns, hiding amongst trees, our bargain, your handler," I ticked off.

"Correct."

"I'm ready. Lead the way, mercenary."

FOR THE SAKE OF EXPEDIENCE AND ASSURING THAT A MERCHANT who sold hot food at this hour took his payment, Mourn left me in an alley peeking around the corner, while he mundanely bought a basket of meals as a disguised Yungian. The bowing between them was slight and casual, and they smiled and chattered to one another while the exchange took place.

Hm.

Upon reflection, I hadn't been in the merchant center of Sivaraus often enough to observe how those exchanges usually went. Even the times I was there, I wasn't their peer. Those merchant matrons would have acted differently around either Noble or Red Sister, as I could expect of this merchant if Mourn *wasn't* disguising himself.

Does it matter that they're all male?

That I couldn't say. Mourn's statement that "girls" weren't important for passing wealth in Yong-wen had me feeling less irritated by Elana, Mai, Ting, the grandmother, and her Xijuan granddaughter if I considered them like bua servants at a House manor or the Palace. The ones expected to handle the Pytes, to keep things clean, wash the clothing, obtain and serve the food…

That fits perfectly.

Why did it take me this long to see it? Or had I begun to with Elana but forgot until confronted with a city full of humble female servants? Brom's servant had two children to teach as she worked, though. None of the buas ever would.

Mai and Ting didn't have children yet, but perhaps that could change at any time. Elana had mentioned the sires "leaving," and it wasn't good for her. Even her son, Lain, had seemed shamed. At the time, I'd assumed she'd chosen the men to catch "kids" when she'd decided it was time.

Maybe she hadn't? Or had expected but had no power or enticement to make the fathers stay? If so, that meant no men protected her except Brom.

And she called him kind for it.

To me, he was no different from a Matron granting shelter and expecting the buas to work and obey in order to stay. After what happened at the inn, what would happen to her and those two kids now?

Although this chain of thought led me to a place to be less irked by Human females in general, it also opened several unsettling possibilities which could be right under my nose.

Then I saw Mourn returning with the food and sighed in relief.

"Ready?" he asked me.

I sniffed the tempting scent of the food basket. "Been ready."

We walked deeper into the alley before crossing two streets toward a small copse of trees called a "people's park." He chuckled as I kept sniffing the air, his full height returning as the illusion faded.

"So, we're going to sit in the grass and eat?" I asked.

"On an old stone bench, but yes."

The greenery thickened enough to obscure an easy view of the nearest street and its shops, but anyone looking into the park would still be able to see something moving along the path.

"Is the bench on this main walk?" I asked, looking down at the surprisingly level flats of stone with grasses growing between them.

"No. We'll have some privacy from casual eyes."

I was more willing to believe him when we stepped onto the soft ground and climbed up and then down a modest hill, and then up another. Blossoms were thick in some places; trees or bushes with white, pink, and red were just beginning to open for the day.

The "old bench" was overgrown with vines. Mourn didn't care where he sat on it as he cracked a couple of the woody ones. I waited to be sure the pitted, lichen-touched structure held his weight.

Fine.

I sat as well, having to work to settle into a place where there wasn't a hard knob of wood prodding my bones or backside too much. I waited expectantly as Mourn peeled back the cloth on the basket to show me six pale steamed pies like the one I'd been given on the street last night.

"Three each?" I asked.

"Anyone looking at us would suggest one for you and five for me," he said, amused too easily by this.

"Well, that's not balanced, is it?"

"It's not. Choose and enjoy."

"Are they all the same?"

"No. Be surprised."

Very little thus far suggested I would regret that, so I dug into the basket for one at random and took a large bite. My stomach awoke, encouraging this course of action. The pie was sweeter than the one last night, but retained a well-cooked mixture of vegetables, sauce, and a little meat within its stretchy wrapping.

It's also…

"What's that?" I asked, licking my lips after clearing my mouth in a swallow.

"What's what?"

"I feel…" I stammered as the sensation became a real, living thing inside my mouth. "It's hot!"

"Ah. You can detect the spice," he said, having eaten half his pie in one bite.

"You knew?" I snarled. "A trick to further amuse yourself?"

"Apologies, no," he said with a grimace. "I cannot detect certain fruits the Yungians use which have this 'heat.' Some spices, I can taste. The rest, others must tell me, and I can only believe them."

"But you didn't warn me, either."

"I forgot to ask the merchant," he said seriously. "I haven't shared these with another in a long time, but I will not forget again. I promise."

The grumbling continued in my head while I blew out then in, trying to cool my tongue, but it didn't last. The strange heat soon seemed to peak but sat like a coal in my mouth. I knew better than to take another bite.

I handed him the pie. "You eat this one, then. Are they all like this?"

He took and bit into it, confirmed to be unaffected as he chewed and swallowed. "I do not believe so, but you will have to try them. I can't taste this for you."

This was not the type of excitement I'd been thinking about, but despite the heat I was still hungry. I grabbed another pie, sampling it with more wariness. This one, thank Goddess, was like the savory one from last night. I worked on it diligently and Mourn seemed to relax as if he was forgiven.

Be surprised. Pfeh. Good way to make myself sick in the wilderness, trying random pickings from someone else's basket.

I encountered another of those spicy pies and handed that one over to my bodyguard as well. I confirmed two more were edible before starting the conversation which had been going on in my head.

"Question."

"Hm?"

I noticed his tail curved around the back of the bench and back through the middle between us. I could see the end waving languidly in the grass. *What the fuck?*

"Yes, Sirana?"

I blinked and looked up. "Oh! Right. Does it make sense to liken the young females here as having the same roles as common-born buas back home?"

Mourn's face was neutral, bordering on skeptical. "It's a place to start, I suppose."

"And Noble-born? Those exist?"

He nodded. "They've stumbled on the same concept for governing themselves, yes."

My brows lifted higher. "Ah. Familiar enough to be relatable when you arrived on the Surface? You said Yungian was the first 'young' language you learned."

He shrugged. "Neither my experience nor my younger decisions were that direct, but I will not deny having seen both the best and the worst of various systems through their generations."

"Oh? Do short lives repeat such that it might inform on the future of where you and I came from?"

"Again, no comparison is that direct."

"I believe you, but I just got here. A learner has to start somewhere, and I want to learn."

Mourn sighed. "Very well. Do not set rigid expectations of Yong-wen, but you may see similarities between how they spread the work and hoard the wealth to be in some ways like a Matron's manor."

That was the starting point I sought.

"So, could this mean your hesitation to point me toward an available consort stems from most 'consorts' being caits, not buas?"

The Dragonchild gave me a look like I'd been leading him by the nose. I could admit I had been.

I shrugged. "If she knows how to use her mouth and it makes your search easier, I'll take a cait instead of a bua. I can bend."

Mourn groaned, briefly covering his eyes with his palm so I couldn't see them. I chuckled and ate my pie.

"Come, they *must* rut in this city for how many babies they have," I pointed out. "And if they figured out Nobles, they figured out leisure. That includes sexual leisure. In fact, I'd be willing to consider doing what *you* usually do when the urge hits."

He darted a sideways look, one gold eye shining. I grinned, unrepentant.

"Come on, merc," I coaxed. "You said you had playmates. I am certain Krithannia has been one, even could be right now, but surely she's not the only companion you've had up here."

"I will not discuss that with you," he said. "Do not suggest it again."

The resentment was clear and echoed Shyntre's frustrations with my presumption. Prodding him further was a mistake.

I sighed and worked on my third pie, slowing down as my stomach was nearly full. The silence was awkward.

"I am accustomed to multiple playmates," I said slowly. "Frequently at once, and of any age in the Sisterhood. It is relief of stress for me, Mourn, and sometimes a chance to hone my grappling skills."

He arched a brow at that last one.

"Either way, good for me." I looked at my half-eaten third, unsure if I wanted the rest. "I lost my last grappling fucks with Brom and Kurn, and I feared I would die or become a slave *because* I failed. My Elders would say to take the lesson and run, but I can and still want to enjoy sex for leisure again. Something less threatening or violent. I am asking you for the best way to accomplish this, since you know so many things about this city."

The Dragonchild let out a slow breath. He'd finished his pies but didn't so much as glance at mine. "I've never visited the prostitutes here and am not sure I want to set that precedent."

"Prostitute?"

"A female consort, but she is paid in coin per encounter."

"Wait, like a merchant?"

"Correct. Groups of women sometimes live together in a house and act as merchants of that sexual leisure you want."

"Really?" I said, excited. "That's an interesting idea!"

Reluctantly, one corner of his mouth lifted. "I suppose it has both admirable and disappointing qualities, usually depending on how few or how many men behind them are involved."

I blinked, confused. "What do you mean?"

"Imagine a group of buas able to live together and conduct their own business for sex," Mourn said. "They are independent from a House in Sivaraus and get to choose their clients and keep what they earn. Perhaps pay an amount of that to help maintain the city around them."

Fascinating, but…

"There could be no such place in Sivaraus," I said, beginning to see where he was going with this. "A Matron would step in to govern them, by force if necessary. The buas could not keep or manage the wealth. The bua house would be a threat if they could refuse just *any* female. The chance of insult is staggering."

The mercenary pointed at me, the glimmer in his eyes intensifying. "Precisely. It is the same as the men think here, though I've seen some madams push back against it. It depends on her contacts and how willing the 'government' is to leave her and her workers alone. The answers are few, not often, and not for long."

I frowned. "So, you do not visit the prostitutes or want to set the precedent because your gold goes to the 'men behind,' not to the consort who serves you?"

"Correct. And many are too young for my comfort anyway."

I nibbled on my pie. "Then what do you do when the urge becomes so strong that your hand isn't enough?"

He shrugged, not denying my assumption he had these urges. "I have no 'casual' source for that release, Sirana, I must negotiate with care. Whomever I visit would benefit and suffer from an imbalanced response to the 'honor' of being mounted by a Dragon Spirit. Independent concubines are rare and usually well-hidden to be so selective, and I do not know any alive and active right now."

Wow.

"Sssooo, because you are worshipped here," I said, "you do not have sex here because it too easily destabilizes the Humans' lives."

Oddly, this made him smile. "Correct. Better to seek one who does *not* worship me and has claimed their own independence in ways which have nothing to do with me. Even then, if there are too many witnesses, it destroys their lives, either immediately or a bit over a longer a time."

I planted my chin in my palm, grimacing. "A bleak outlook for you living for centuries around so many Humans and one Elf."

Unless he might have coupled with Tamuril as well?

He looked mildly insulted. "I do not require much sex."

That's a negative.

Was it true that he simply did not need sex? Was he more like Gavin in his preferences, or was the scarcity entirely from learned consequence?

I narrowed my eyes a little but kept my skepticism to myself. "So Krithannia would be your best choice right now."

His tail, still tucked beneath the bench, slapped the earth. "We're not talking about her, Baenar."

A pity.

"Fine," I said. "But this means you *don't* have an easy way to direct me to a willing consort as I appear naturally. What if I wore a disguise? You need not participate or be present, just set me up and I can do the rest."

Mourn exhaled, clawed fingers loosely entwined. His tail was still flicking at the grass. "Disguised as Yungian when you do not know the language or customs? They would see you for a spirit immediately. Disguised as a Manalari for your speech, and to take you to a brothel outside of Yong-wen…?"

I leaned closer for these new insights.

He shook his head after seemingly dismissing several possibilities. "Similar issues with most 'consorts' being women with men behind them, who may or may not know *how* to use her mouth on you."

"What?" This truly surprised me. "How could she not?"

Mourn smirked but he wasn't truly amused. "Because she can passively lie on her back to please a male client. It takes more effort to learn a practice on another woman which more Humans find distasteful anyway."

"Distasteful?!"

"And fewer women have the money or need to pay for sex. It's not profitable for the workers to push the service."

"Back up," I insisted. "Distasteful? How dare they think that?"

Mourn shrugged. "It's because of the woman's moon cycle."

I was getting a headache. I rubbed my temple. "And what is that?"

"Related to how Humans populate areas so quickly. You should know about it if you'd truly take a woman as easily as a man."

I watched him, quietly paying attention.

"A Human womb prepares the most fertile 'cradle' to catch a child about every Mother Moon cycle."

My eyes widened and my mouth opened. *"Every* moon cycle?!"

"Yes, though not synchronous. I agree, it is stunningly quick. And if she doesn't catch, it sheds this cradle as blood outside her body instead of reusing it. So, part of every month, she is seeping red between her legs."

He looked at my horror and shrugged. "It does not harm or weaken them, and the blood is clean. Perhaps this is another way they give back to the soil throughout their short lives? But it's not well understood even by them, and more work to stay clean and dry. Another reason there are more male sailors and travelers than female."

By the web pit…

"Ohhh," I breathed. "You're warning me I could easily encounter a female whose slit is bleeding. Anytime?"

He looked at the trees. "Yes. And this part of their function has created some of the most disparaging legends the Humans tell. The moon cycle is a large part of why girls are not valued, because they are taught to feel shame of this… hm. Challenge to stay clean. This fear and disgust are the same both in Yong-wen and Manalar, whether hidden and unspoken or blatantly hostile. Their thinking has led some men to evil acts against their own mothers, sisters, and daughters."

I felt a chill as I remembered Jacob's insults to me in the shed. He had been quite fixated on what "filth" might be coming out of my slit. I'd been confused.

Huh. Not anymore.

"That's why I would never be the same status as you," I said, "even as a spirit. They would assume I moon-bleed, too?"

"Most likely, though they may not think of it consciously." Another shrug. "And to complete my thoughts on visiting a brothel outside of Yong-wen, I am sorry. I couldn't assure your health or safety, either, since I have no recent contact with someone trustworthy. There are issues with disease in some places."

I slumped. "Oh."

He nodded. "That is one reason I am interested in these anti-fester pellets of yours. If the Humans could learn to make them, they could have lasting benefits to these women especially."

Ah. I sighed, admitting to myself I wasn't as likely to "go hunting" by myself as I'd teased. *This is complicated. I don't know enough to keep me and my baby safe.*

That was not to say that Cris-ri-phon hadn't been equally complicated and dangerous in about every way even with his ancient knowledge of Davrin. Or because of it.

And Kurn just simply wouldn't back off and let me be.

"Would…?" I hesitated. "Um."

Mourn looked at me. "Hm?"

You wouldn't serve that purpose, would you, 'body' guard?

I bit my tongue, thinking of his Matron-Aunt with the name he'd give me, and how the other "named" half-bloods were expected to serve the Priestesses. Before Kerse had rebelled, he'd been trained by his mother for almost as long as Mourn had been alive. The two males were nearly the same age, I realized, but the Dragonblood had escaped much younger.

Might this be why Mourn was so wary whenever I brought up sex, he expected me to ask him to serve my urges?

Nah. He's still too big. I'd be stupid to push him when he's only warned me about prying with Krithannia.

"Never mind," I said. "I admit I have no solution that would not cause more trouble."

"Indeed, aside from stopping on the edge of the road when the urge strikes."

I jerked my head up in surprise.

Is he…? I squinted. *Is that a smile?*

"Are you *teasing* me about that?" I accused.

He looked like he wished he'd bitten his own tongue. "Well, no. It was a good sign of your recovery. I didn't mind."

I prodded his forearm with a finger. "But you did interrupt me on purpose. Until I had to stop Nightmare and go into the trees."

Mourn considered this and nodded, his lavender tongue flicking out quickly. "Apologies. Your arousal was becoming…strong. As you moved against the saddle."

He could smell it?

I blinked. "Oh."

I had made certain he hadn't been walking too close to me but recalled the wind had changed often enough to make it moot. I flushed hot, unable to read his face despite that I knew exactly how Gavin would look saying something like that.

"I will grant you were being subtle," he added as if to ease my tension. "The Deathwalker wasn't paying attention while sitting on the same horse."

"Uh-huh."

Did I wash well before that? I can't remember.

I asked, "Was it, um …a foul smell?"

His response was slow and cautious. "No. Just distracting."

Distracting.

So, not disgusted but not tempting enough to drop his watch. Did that mean he enjoyed it, even a little? Did he watch me stroke off in the trees?

Argh! Stop it. He doesn't want to flirt.

My eyes had begun to ache despite the cover of my hood, and I measured the moving shadow of the plants with the increasing intensity of the Sun. "Should we negotiate our bargain for Manalar, or is it time to meet your handler?"

The mercenary seemed to consider that, and when I didn't push for either one, he opted to avoid the first option. Again.

"Let us close my current contract first," he said, standing up off the bench and waiting for me to do the same. "It may grant us added insight on the current situation."

"Very well."

Goddess knew I could use all the insights I could get.

84

CHAPTER 4

Our hoods stayed up to help against the Sun's glare, and if not for the To'vah-krav's head and shoulders rising above any man we passed, I might have drawn less attention for how busy everyone seemed.

He was correct in that, while we *were* noticed, we were not surrounded with beggars wanting healing and luck. They glanced, whispered, and pointed, but only children took to trailing us while hanging far back. No adults approached with treasure for any favor by the time we reached our destination.

The self-restraint of the populace was impressive. I wondered about the core source of their collective reasoning. They did not truly seem afraid of *him* but perhaps they feared related things I couldn't know. Perhaps his presence was all the "luck" they needed, or that asking for frivolous favors for yourself was seen as greedy or shameful.

Hm.

As we moved North, the change between merchant fronts and multi-level dwellings wasn't as distinct in this area as in the grandmother's. I'd noted plenty of script on wooden signs and lining doorways in curious ways. I could not read any of it so had to rely on what I could see in guessing their specialties and services. In addition, we passed fenced yards which were clearly not for leisure, but the messier crafts, agriculture, or livestock best tended outside.

The breeze picked up before we rounded what would be the final corner. I smelled fine dusted stone and heard the unmistakable sound of a hammer striking a chisel. Another set tapped in a different location, quick and precise, so I expected to see hands sculpting large statues out of massive boulders.

What I didn't expect to see was a blend of agile Yungians and stocky Dwarves moving about in the same open-air yard and working on the same six pillars of dark and light grey stone. It also surprised me that most of these working Dwarves had similar brown skin to the Yungians, even though they also possessed red-blond and red-brown hair and beards like the ruddy-skinned Rithal.

One elder stood out among them, bearing an enormous, iron-grey beard kept neat and plaited with like-colored metal clasps. He was also quite pale from what I could see of his face. Despite obvious age, he was as broad-shouldered as the others, wearing similar dark clothing and boots made of tough material lightly dusted with chalk.

This Dwarf wasn't one of the five others working on four statues but rather was the one moving between them, consulting and critiquing. He even seemed to praise from the way he clapped a younger Dwarf on the shoulder, almost knocking him forward. I saw a wide spread of teeth appear in both beards a moment later.

Like Graul, the greybeard seemed a bit stiff when he rotated one arm as if to stretch the shoulder, but the four Yungians present and crafting their pieces betrayed no contempt for this I could see. They either sculpted intently or acknowledged the grandfather Dwarf with the ever-present bow or nod of their head.

Mourn and I approached the segmented fence which separated the yard from the street, but it appeared able to swing open at nearly any place like a gate. The workers had no walls other than those of the dwellings surrounding them, but they still had a high roof above them which would shed the rain into large barrels at the corners, with further channels built to scoot any overflow some-where I couldn't see.

I saw no females here, either, and was uncertain how different this might be from Sarilis's Tower or Brom's Inn. I pushed back my cloak to show my armor and weapons and waited either for Mourn to speak or someone to notice us.

It didn't take long, but it was eerie.

The younger Humans hushed each other's tools, setting them down before rising and folding their hands in front of them, un-smiling but nonhostile. The Dwarves, in stark contrast, all smiled and climbed to their feet, some with a grunt or two. They looked to the greybeard, who finally turned around.

The twist to his smile was visible even through his thick hair.

"Ahh, *Wen-yung*, welcome back," he rumbled in an accent complex enough I could never read his lips even if he trimmed the beard back. "Ya come with wisdom tah share?"

The elder Dwarf paused with significance, turning pale green eyes on me. I found the color and slight lack of focus unsettling. I couldn't say why, but I did wonder how well he could see me at this distance, for he did not step closer to the street.

"I do, Elder Baradum," Mourn answered with a slight bow at the waist. "Where is Qin Tran?"

"Onna short business trip. He'll be back within th' week. I'm overseein' the current project while he's away."

"I see. I have news of some urgency, concerning the Ma'ab."

"*Bakgwei*," whispered one of the Human sculptors, spitting on the ground as the other jaws tightened.

So, either they understood the Trade tongue, or they simply recognized Ma'ab. I wagered on the former to be safe, and because it did not make sense to me that the *entire* enclave would keep themselves ignorant of the common trade language just outside their walls.

Especially working with Dwarves enough for one elder to trust another while he's away on 'business.'

"Aye, can do," said the greybeard. "I'll receive it. Come inside."

I glanced up at Mourn with a frown. ★Your handler is not here. Can this one close your contract?★

The half-blood only made two signs, suggesting I refrain from hand sign for now and to come along.

No sign? What's going on?

I tolerated being stared at while Elder Baradum opened one of the gates and Mourn and I entered the yard.

"Keep honin', kids," the greybeard ordered next, pushing his palm against the red door on the right side.

"Aye, Groda!"

We followed the Dwarf inside to their acknowledgements, and the relief to my eyes once he closed the door was immediate. It was cool and dim, the walls just bare, dressed stone rather than dark panels of wood.

The halls were certainly designed for Yungians. The elder Dwarf was prone to brushing the walls or clipping the corners with his shoulders as he led us back and past a front room filled with tools, a kitchen partly below street level, an eating area, and several closed doors before bringing us to an office.

Belatedly, I realized I still had my boots on, as did the Dwarf. I could see dried mud from outside tracked inside from previous trips in addition to this one. There were also two brooms leaning together against the wall which the elder needed to twist his torso to avoid knocking over.

Mourn noticed my confusion.

"Boots!" I said in Davrin.

"We'll sweep it up when we leave," he whispered back.

"We will?" I protested. *"Why? Isn't he disrespectful of the home he keeps with your handler away? Can you trust a Dwarf who does that?"*

Mourn's mouth twisted dryly. *"I admire your observation and deduction, and my thanks for the concern. This will work out. Keep your boots on."*

I huffed. *More complicated than the Palace, this enclave.*

I ceased arguing as we were led into a recognizable office lit from above. There weren't any windows near the ground but several high up, and a few more even built into the roof to catch the Sun's light. On the dark walls hung more black script on long scrolls, framed in red and yellow as if the writing was meant to be an image. There were a couple true images painted in watercolors as well. More of the lake, the cranes, and…

A purple serpent swimming around an island? Hm.

Meanwhile, the elder Baradum took the man-sized seat behind a desk which was somehow too high *and* too narrow to fit him. Behind me, Mourn had to use his strength to roll a glossy slab of dark marble on a rail, thus "closing the door."

"What…?" I gaped.

"Would ya think one ov the best masons in Yong-wen," said the greybeard in amused Trade, "might refrain from showin' off what he can build when folk come tah visit, *lasschen?*"

"But that 'best mason' isn't you, you're sitting at his desk." I arched one brow. "And what did you call me?"

"Wheuf," he puffed through his lips, disturbing his whiskers, and looked at Mourn. "Report wasn't kiddin' about her accent. May be useful, may be a pain in the *naiken.*"

Report? I narrowed my eyes at my escort then said to our host, "I can't understand half the words you slur, Dwarf."

Mourn cleared his throat loudly. "Let us start with introductions, please?"

The greybeard smiled, his teeth certainly aged and a bit yellowed. He settled his elbows on the desk, interlacing thick, gnarled fingers, waiting like he was quite familiar with my bodyguard.

"Sit," he invited, motioning to the slim but sturdy chairs nearby.

I folded my arms and waited, reminded to reassure my spiders when I felt them shifting beneath my hair. *~Still, still. No danger.~*

Just a creature who survived to an age to be arrogant about it.

Mourn looked between us and sighed deeply as neither of us sat down. "Sirana, this is Talov Baradum, of Clan Baradum in Taiding. And he *is* my handler, I assure you. The exchange outside was for listening ears. We're merely borrowing this place to meet."

I studied the Dwarf behind the desk. "Ah, so you *can* close the contract with the Ma'ab?"

"I can," Talov replied with a slow nod, "an' free him up for the next one." A mischievous look crossed his face as his eyes flicked to the Dragonchild. "Have a couple contracts lined up, if ya'd take a look."

I did *not* need the wave of nausea that hit me to imagine what might happen if Talov somehow tempted Mourn to take a different job.

Talov lifted a bushy eyebrow. "Ya alright, *lasschen*? Ya look sick."

We should have negotiated in the park.

Mourn's tail thwapped the floor as if to regain our attention before he continued. "Talov, this is Sirana *d' Vloszia Dalnanin*, my new client after we've wrapped up. I shall pass on the other leads, thank you."

"I see."

I could breathe again, and the elder studied me for a few moments as the sickness gradually left me.

He said, "Sirana di Vloshee-ah Dalnah-neen. A pleasure tah meet ya."

I blinked. The pronunciation was still foreign, but the Dwarf's first attempt was quite good.

I unstuck my tongue as I nodded. "Red Sister Sirana, Talov Baradum. And you were forewarned what race you would meet?"

"Ya. Yer a Davrin Elf, like in the old tales." His massive shoulders lifted. "Also knew, long as I've known the kid here, that yer kind were still 'round somewhere. Could see clear as day the black Elves on his mutter's side."

The kid?

I started at Mourn's feet and trailed my eyes the long way up. The half-blood didn't protest but he was smirking. Talov chuckled quietly.

I asked, "And how long have you known 'the kid?'"

"A couple centuries," he replied with a sudden yawn coming upon him. He covered his mouth with a hand, as if to keep something from flying in.

Oh, we can do better than that.

"How long have you known Talov Baradum, Mourn?" I asked.

The Dwarf quickly interjected, "Ye don't have tah answer her because she's got tits, kid."

Why, you—!

"*Ish'ket, Driekeinsau!*" I spat.

The greybeard puffed up. "What did you call me?"

My mind blanked. *I have no idea.*

Then I rallied. "What did you call *me* earlier?"

"What? When?"

"*Lasschen,*" Mourn slipped in calmly, trying to mediate. "It means 'young female' in Dwarvish. It's not an insult."

But it was in Tragar, I was sure. *Lochek.* It was close, but the sound held something meaner inside it when Kain said it.

"*Ish'ket Driekeinsau,*" Talov repeated, putting his fingertips together and leaning forward a bit. "Sounds like I *should* know whatcha said, Sirana, but I don't."

"I apologize, Talov," Mourn mediated. "I didn't realize she knew Tragar insults."

My face heated. *He knows what I said?*

"Tragar?" Talov repeated, squinting with thought. "Oh, yahhh... Those deep Dwarves, all white eyes an' beards. Ya said they were mean as shit."

"They are. They don't normally come far out of their strong-holds." Mourn looked down at me. "I am truly surprised you speak the language, Sirana."

"I don't!" I protested. "As you said, I've had enough contact to know insults."

Talov rumbled in his throat, still smiling. "Always the first thing we learn, eh? Don't like them much?"

"I've fought Tragar," I answered, staring at a spot on the floor. "Twice. They are dangerous."

"But I wager not *the* most dangerous thing down there," said the elder Dwarf, who couldn't resist prodding me. "That's reserved either fer the Davrin themselves, or those others. That native race. The squid things."

"Ornilleth," Mourn answered. "We also call them mind flayers."

"Sounds apt. Stuff ov nightmares."

I held my gaze on one of the scrolls on the wall, resisting the urge to hug myself. *Yeahhh, let's not talk about them.*

The room was silent for several beats when Mourn answered, "Four hundred and ten."

I snapped my head up. "Hm? What?"

Mourn smiled. "I have known Talov for four hundred and ten years."

Four of his five and a half centuries…?

That meant they were roughly the same age. I swallowed, struck with the twin thoughts of knowing Tragar lived far less than that, and that this was another in whom Mourn's trust would be unshakeable.

The Dragonchild was absolutely testing my poise.

Surface Dwarves can live five hundred years? No wonder he looks so old.

"Do ya want tah sit?" the Dwarf invited again.

This time we accepted, and I asked the first question which came to me. "Did Talov used to travel with you as well? Until it... hurt his bones? Now he's your 'handler' while you go out alone?"

Mourn chuckled. "Yes, Talov was quite a traveler in his prime decades. But now he must hold back, so he calls me 'kid,' still."

"I see."

Talov's face had softened a little bit as he watched us talk in our seats. He grunted approvingly. "Interestin', he told ya because he wanted to."

I shrugged. "As Krithannia said, his bargain with me is his own."

"Ahhh, lovely Krithy." The Dwarf's eyes twinkled. "An' what do ya think ov her, Davrin?"

"A clear elder and leader," I replied. "The Guild is lucky to have such a mistress behind them."

His cheeks bunched up in a wide grin. "Ya? The pale skin don't bother ya?"

I made a face at him. "Why should it? She convinced me she is smart and determined and has far more experience than me."

"That all it takes fer a Red Sister? That's interestin.'"

"Why is that?" I challenged.

"To hear her talk, her people have somethin' big stuck in their throat about the 'dark ones.'"

I shrugged that off. "Well, I don't know what that is."

"Ya don't?"

Well, besides what we did to Tamuril.

"Believe it or not," I said, "meeting her was a relief after meeting several Human women, who are worthless to help when their men attack or try to trap me."

Talov started chortling and didn't stop until he had to cough. He granted me some deep, thoughtful nods. "Aye. Hm. Not all of 'em, but, aye. Lot ov fear, still."

"Unlike the one Dwarven witch I met," I added, steering the conversation like a hand cart rattling over potholes. "She helped me when she did not need to. I believe she made the difference for me."

The greybeard blinked, immediately back with me rather than whatever he'd been thinking about. "Aye? A Dwarven witch?"

"Osgrid," Mourn supplied. "She has left Troshin Bend, finally."

"Ah, good fer her."

"She had to," I said. "Anyone who smelled of 'witch' after the *Dyos Guerrimos* arrived had to leave."

"Oo, good pronunciation!" the old Dwarf complimented.

"I have a good tutor," I replied with a smirk.

"Oh, aye, we'll get tah *him*. Heh! Gerrit's Balls, I wanna hear this whole tale over a drink an' near a fireplace." Talov looked mournfully around the room which was missing these comforts and sighed. "But maybe business first. Let's confirm th' bounty proper. Ye have what the Ma'ab paid well for in advance, kid?"

Mourn nodded and reached for a pouch on his webbing, removing two small bundles. Each was carefully wrapped in a water-resistant skin and tied securely. He placed those plus the ruby on the table.

"*Hervogand*," Talov murmured, looking intensely pleased as he picked up the gem pendant first and handled it as any of his mining kin might do, whispering something to himself.

"That was the most difficult piece to retrieve," Mourn said, directing his gaze at me.

I smiled back. I was not the least regretful about his delay, considering the circumstances.

The Dwarf nodded. "Once the big *ocks* started using it poorly in th' open? Heh! No doubt. Let's see what else."

Indeed, other than the *Ridhian* I'd recently handed over, I did not know what these other pieces were. Talov made as if he was unwrapping gifts with careful measure, his beard bristling around his mouth as he pursed his lips in concentration.

He unwrapped one which contained a ring that I remembered to be on Castis's hand, plus an ear ripped off from straight force.

"Excellent," Talov said as if he recognized the ring, too. "That's one."

"Why the ear?" I asked. "What does that prove? It could be from anyone."

"Ma'ab have their own type o' sorcerers. They can tell. All they need is a bit of flesh."

Hm. Could Gavin do the same?

Inside the other bundle was one of Kurn's large, male fingers, and I couldn't hold back a sneer.

At least it isn't his prick.

For once Talov didn't remark on my expression. "That's two. Good work, kid. This'll help. An' I take it he suffered?"

Mourn nodded, finally going into his report. "Over time, yes. Drugged, interrogated, sleep-deprived, nerve-flayed, taunted with glimpses of his father, his backside penetrated with an object. His stallion poisoned by warp rot in his presence before going mad himself. Then, finally, stabbed in the heart."

With his Vis and Vitas sucked out, I thought, pondering the quiet relic on my belt.

Presumably Kurn was still there but maybe helping to create that Desert I saw, lacking the strength to become self-aware like Innathi was.

While the greybeard pondered, his callused fingers touched one of the clasps keeping a beard plait tidy. "Sounds about right, but not typical fer ya to violate like that. Special case?"

Mourn smirked, indicated me. "That was her, not me. Most of his suffering was Sirana, including the kill."

Talov looked shocked then struck his palm against the table. "Ha! She stole th' bastard from ya?"

The mercenary looked at me, calmly refusing to take the competitive banter. "It happens rarely, but I waited too long. The murderer was Hellbent on targeting *her* next. He suffered as the contract stated he must, but Sirana paid a cost. It's balanced that she also took the kill."

Talov followed the half-blood's lead and considered me with less overt glee. "Hm. Anything especially punishing ya want me tah pass on? The Ma'ab like details."

I lifted a finger. "First explain how Kurn's father can be a century-old warrior still fighting and breeding blunt-heads like him."

Talov's iron-grey beard shifted with the twisting of his lips; he might have been suppressing a laugh. "Kreshel Divigna?"

"Yes. Kurn bragged about his being sired by the 'Eternal Hellhound.'"

The old Dwarf nodded. "Eh. Something th' Ma'ab Ascended did tah him. Unnatural, that's obvious. They love sending him out tah terrorize but keepin' a lid on how he's still around. Why no one seems able tah kill 'im."

"They have kept this even from the Guild?" I asked.

"Yup, from everyone. Trust me, we'd want tah know how, if they can make more like him, and how often. What they need tah do it." Talov shrugged. "So far, he seems the only one, an' that's good."

The series of questions without answers gave me a terrible feeling as I again thought about our missing Priestess and her Sathoet. Kurn had only seen the demonblood. As far as I'd been able to prod, he hadn't even heard of another who looked like me until Brom gave him ideas.

At least the 'yellow-eyed demon' Jacob had seen coming back to town had probably been Mourn, not the Sathoet.

As much as I wanted to ask what his multi-century Dwarf might have heard about a vanishing black demon with a white mane, I hesitated to engage in two clashing aspects of my geas by trying to follow the trails of two half-bloods at once for my Valsharess.

I have one sitting beside me, and he's not likely to leave now.

Mourn had said he wasn't helping to train the Hellhounds, and he didn't know why I asked. I could infer that meant the Guild hadn't heard of the capture and Kurn's insider glimpse was what it took to know.

I can't take this strain every day…

Just stay quiet. Do not bring it up.

"Details on Kurn's suffering," I murmured, as if that explained my inexplicable silence. "Well, after he used the ruby on me, I turned it around and used my sapphire on him."

I pulled it out of my armor, and the Dwarf appeared equally interested in this stone, leaning forward with his fingers sliding slightly forward on the desk.

"Saphgar, not sapphire," Mourn corrected immediately.

Of course, he would.

"Yes," I granted, "but does Talov know what that is?"

The half-blood paused, and the Dwarf chuckled and spoke for himself.

"I do not," he said eagerly. "A new stone?"

"It only exists deep down," Mourn said.

"The Tragar are the only ones to mine it," I added. "They seem to be the only ones able to see it for what it is."

"Ya?" Talov lifted a finger toward Shyntre's pendant. "That's a beauty I doubt any might miss."

"It doesn't look like this until a mage has worked on it," I said. "It appears as the most ordinary rock in its raw form."

"Oh? Mm! May I see it?"

"What? No!"

"Ach, ya know how tah tease a Dwarf, Blue Eyes."

Mourn shook his head, leaning on one elbow with his tail waving. "That's partly my fault, Talov, but it's complicated. Let her finish her thoughts on Kurn."

"Awright, I'm listenin'."

Oh, yes. I smirked. "Well, first, this stone *isn't* imbued with magic like the ruby but *reacts* to magic. My wizard said it responds to my will when I wear it, but in ways not well-studied yet. And in a face-to-face conflict with Kurn's ruby, his theory was proven correct."

Talov made a small cooing sound, motioning me to continue.

"While we were traveling from the Ley Tower to Troshin Bend, Kurn attacked me while I was bathing and chased me into a canyon."

The Dwarf made a disgusted face like he wasn't surprised but nodded.

"I had my saphgar, he had his ruby, we both got tangled in my magical webbing. He tried to do to me what I presume he did to the Ma'ab owner of the *Ridhian,* for which he was being hunted?"

"Yup."

"Except I blocked him, drugged him," I glanced at Mourn. "I would have killed him that night except *someone* stopped me."

Talov's eyes twinkled as he glanced at the hybrid. "Ya, that woulda been too quick."

"Hmph." I rolled my eyes. "Not for me, but anyway. The next time we rested, I dreamed of, well, sex."

Talov perked up.

"Relieving my frustrations and stress with someone *willing,*" I clarified.

"Oh, aye?"

"Yes. And Gavin observed my dreams and strength of will influencing the Ma'ab fugitives in *their* sleep."

"Both of 'em?"

I grinned. "Yes. Such that the brute rutted atop the mage in their bedrolls. They both enjoyed it, I promise, but were confused in the morning because one had a sore, sticky pucker hole and the other's prick stank. I understood later it was their first time."

Mourn showed his surprise, either at my crude description or because the information itself was new. Talov's brows sprouted up in such a way as to keep the smile on my face, then the Dwarf guffawed, leaning back in his seat.

With a pinch of concern, I clarified, "The Ma'ab don't need to know how I did this."

"Oh, agreed! Got 'em drunk will be enough." He chortled, pinching the bridge of his nose, and wheezing a little. "Well. Given what I was told about our lump head targets, I think I see the seed of what led to ya shoving something up his ass."

Mourn tensed and murmured, "You don't have to describe that part, Sirana."

Talov tilted his head but didn't suggest either way.

I exhaled. *We'll see when I get there.*

"Kurn blamed me for everything going wrong," I continued, "and wanted to finish what he'd started in the canyon. Brom Troshin proved the more powerful man, however, and blocked them. The two Ma'ab couldn't trap me without the sorcerer's help and alliance."

"Mm, aye," said the Dwarf with a level nod, keeping his eyes on me. "But even the sorcerer failed, hm?"

I glanced down at Soul Drinker, and Talov followed my gaze. "You must know the essence from your 'report.'"

"Only that ya stabbed the town governor with that thing," he admitted. "And that it didn't kill him."

My stomach clenched. "You know for certain?"

Talov nodded, eyes glancing at Mourn and back. "I'm happy that yer the kid's client now, tah be honest. Figure Brom Troshin isn't gonna let it lie. We'll see 'im again."

I felt the bite of resentment bleed into my shame. "So, you're saying I should have made certain and finished him before I ran."

"No, *lasschen*, not sayin' that." His elder's voice was low and soft, his eyes calm. "Knowin' what I do 'bout that sorcerer *and* that blade,

I'm not sure ya coulda survived the attempt. Either he or the dagger woulda overwhelmed ya then. Better ya ran when ya could."

I leaned forward. "What *do* you know about them?"

"Long story, an' comes with a price."

Damn it!

"And Krithannia shared a little already," Mourn interjected. "Sirana also bested the Abyssal influence after she regained her strength. The blade is hers in truth, now."

Talov looked pleased, but I was frowning when I said, "So, it *was* a better use of time to lodge the hilt of Kurn's dagger up his netherhole. He deserved to suffer."

"That all it was?" the Dwarf asked perceptively. "Payback? Punishment? It was 'fun?'"

I glared at Mourn. "No. I wanted to force him to tell me who was *following* us. The 'blood-bound demon' Kurn saw at the canyon who stopped me from killing him!"

"And the one who stopped him from attacking you after the Witch Hunters shot you," Mourn replied. "Remember, after Gavin was killed, I thought you would leave that night."

I sighed, rubbing my face, and Talov hummed with amused sympathy.

"I can see this tale will keep us guessin' and addin' for weeks, yet," he remarked. "But backin' up. Ya compelled Kurn tah fuck his accomplice instead ov you. Drugged him—"

"Twice," I said. "Shoved dissolving pellets up his nostrils. And poisoned him with a fever paste which turned his pole floppy, so he couldn't force another female as he did the Ma'ab noble."

Talov patted his palms together like a playful conspirator. "Good, good. And? Anything else ya want me tah tell our contact."

"Before the warp rot got him and his precious stallion through his own arrogance and stupidity?" I shrugged, my scowl still in place. "I presume Mourn was responsible for the sleep deprivation and 'nerve-flaying,' as the 'lump head' was manic that morning, running like something was chasing us."

The To'vah-krav nodded confirmation. Gradually, I waited as more memories of that mad forest returned.

"I stabbed him in the heart with Soul Drinker, so his Vis is trapped, and unable to 'travel.'"

Talov studied me. "Ya know that word? Vis?"

"Gavin explained it."

"Ah. Well enough. Mmm, I'll leave that last part out of my report, but good tah know. The Ma'ab wouldn't like that ya still *have* their fugitive, in a sense."

I hesitated, then added, "I also experienced Kurn's 'confession' of the murder, as he died and passed into the blade."

Talov straightened, more serious. "Ya mean ya saw it?"

"Saw it, heard it, felt how *he* felt... his memories of killing the noble woman with Castis there, helping. Kurn blamed her for removing him from Hellhound training, even though Kreshel Divigna was the one to inform her that he failed."

"Really? Go on."

I grimaced, wishing I knew if this was a quality of the relic or if it was me. Would it happen every time I used it to kill?

If I ever kill with it again.

"Kurn imagined controlling a spiked chain with his own will. Those are the weapons of the Hellhounds?" I looked at Mourn. "Like I heard in the woods. Your illusion."

The Dragonchild nodded.

"He also dreamed about his skin being imbued with 'markings' which would prevent him from dying by an enemy sword."

"The tattoos?" Talov blinked, then he exchanged a look with Mourn. "Tha's *very* interestin', Sirana."

"Why?" I asked.

"We've been speculatin' but nothin' confirmed till now. A couple recent attacks up North, Hellhounds sent in first. That's not unusual. But, before, it was just the 'Eternal' that couldn't be killed, whose skin turned a blade's edge. But now other Hellhounds are resisting th' same edges. We didn't know why, but Kurn failed training an' knew it was the tattoos?"

I nodded. "Yes."

"Hervogand," he said again; it was an appreciative sound filled with wonder. "D'ya remember anything else from his 'confession?'"

Reluctantly, I went through the attack on the woman again, partly prepared because of Kain's coarse language unexpectedly spilling out of my mouth. I still remembered what I'd done to Lana, after all; it wasn't much different from Kurn. Toward the end, I heard what the big man had said to Castis, the entire reason he was at the Ley Tower with Sarilis in the first place.

We shall meet the army at Manalar with anything we can find to break down the walls. We'll be champions greater than the Hellhound infiltrators. I will be rewarded...

"The vials from Sarilis were intended to help break the temple walls, which was what they sought. To be pardoned and go home after exile."

Talov nodded encouragingly.

"Kurn mentioned their work being greater than the Hellhound 'infiltrators'. But...nothing else useful." I shrugged. "I thought it was an odd word. Could a Ma'ab *infiltrate* the temple when they look so different?"

"They're gonna try," the Dwarf said with confidence.

"Manalar has enough crypts and ancient underhalls which the Bishops have probably forgotten about," Mourn said, "that it's possible with enough intelligence."

"Oh," I said, understanding without asking how these two already had that intelligence. "Well, then. I'm sorry he was not more specific."

"Always good to hear recent talk ov solid tactics, Red Sister," said the greybeard. "Gives us directions tah watch more closely."

"Us," I repeated. "You mean the Guild?"

Talov's eyes crinkled at the corners. "Aye. If Krithy is mostly here in Augran, I'm mostly up in Taiding. Th' Ma'ab are in my back-lands. My Clan's been watchin' 'em since they first spilled outta th' North like an avalanche."

"How long ago was this?"

"Oh, fifty or sixty years before I was born. Some chillin' stories of those first years. Heard the Ma'ab didn't appear as Human as they do now, an' they were grabbin' mostly Noiri and Darge women, but also as many slaves as they could get."

Talov drummed his fingers. "They entrenched themselves quick, an' no one's equipped tah dig 'em outta Ennikar, so we just wait fer the Ascended tah get bored. They stir the shit in the ice every so often as we learn more about 'em."

"Why are they said to be headed for Manalar?" I asked. "Aren't they passing by Taiding and Augran doing that?"

Talov smiled, although not nearly as warm as I'd seen so far. "The Clans ov Taiding have made the Ma'ab regret attackin' us. We have a couple millennia on them fer entrenchment, but they know by now we won't follow 'em back home, or wherever they march.

"Augran was too big by the time the pale pricks made it past us. This city's got th' ships, controls the waters, and can defend well enough, but the men here aren't conquerors, mostly traders. And, really, end ov the day? It's what Manalar *has* that we don't that th' Ma'ab want."

"The sacred pool?" I guessed.

The Dwarf was impressed. "Yup. If the Ascended claim that, figure how tah make it work for 'em, they can flank Augran an' Taiding later. It seems we've got a cluster ov death mages that are past death, so the Ascended got time."

This made sense, but I still narrowed my eyes at him. "Then why are you taking contracts from them? Helping them if they are a threat?"

"To learn more about 'em. Even better if they want us tah kill some ov their own. Serves a dual purpose."

"Then the Guild is not neutral in this conflict," I stated.

"Nope," Talov agreed, "but better tah obscure motives where we can. Not like we really want either side tah *thrive* in their current form. Allow me tah say we're *really* glad that the kid found your Deathwalker when he did, with the monk plannin' what he is against both sides ov his blood. He can't do it without our help."

Gavin was probably equally glad, yet I dared not overlook she who could be lost in the middle of it all.

"Have you heard of one who could be a Davrin and seen around Manalar recently?" I asked, unable to pass up the opportunity.

"Ah," Talov grunted. "Yer sister. Hm." He shook his head. "Not yet. But I know Krithy's working on it."

My stomach felt tense. "What about Tamuril? I thought she was heading out this way. Has she been in contact with *her* sister?"

The Dwarf was surprised with this one. "I wouldn't know, and that's more Krithannia's privilege tah share, anyway."

Blocked again. At least the elder Dwarf respected the elder Naulor's business.

As I sat back, Mourn said, "We'll discuss this more after we've worked out our bargain."

"Now?" I asked. "Have we closed your contract 'properly?'"

"Generously," he replied, "with your many additional insights."

"Indeed," Talov seconded, "appreciate it, Elf."

Oh, no. What the fuck was wrong with me? I should have saved those insights for *my* bargain, not his!

"So," I repeated with a trace of that irritation. "Do we bargain?"

"I think we could use a break outside of this office first."

Fuck!

Mourn read my expression and clarified, "I *will* bargain to be your bodyguard while searching for your sister at Manalar."

"But you keep putting me off," I growled.

"I am still considering what is fair payment. This doesn't happen frequently, but with your objective, there is nothing obvious I would ask for which is also balanced."

"True," Talov added, a slow smile spreading through his beard. "The kid doesn't take a contract where he's not satisfied with the terms. It's as much benefit tah you as him that he's stubborn like this."

"How so?" I asked, my tone heavy with skepticism.

The greybeard's grin bloomed in full. "Heh. Ya've never bargained with a devil, have ya?"

I stared at him, incredulous.

"Not th' wide brush stroke the Witch Hunners call 'devils,'" he clarified. "I mean th' kind that don' much care for the demons gobbling up unfortunate souls before they can nab that coin themselves."

Any disbelief I felt as he began, I swallowed it back down.

I knew there were demons. Mathias may have doubted their existence, but that had never been a luxury for me. I could have doubted the Black Dragon's existence, too, but here was his son sitting next to me.

I could suggest the Grey Maiden and the Nexus was a vague concept or a vision, but then Gavin's corpse had sat up again, bleeding black, and a deathless sorcerer hadn't died of the red-runed dagger when Kurn so easily had.

If there are demons, Deathwalkers, and Dragon sons, then of course there are devils.

I just had yet to meet one.

So, I took the bait. "Have *you* bargained with a devil?"

Talov shook his head. "Thankfully, no. But I've known those who have, usually in a moment ov weakness. Ya never win what ya think ya have, and they don' look for balance in their payment. The more foolish an' ignorant ya are, the better fer them."

The elder winked at his long-time contact while still speaking to me. "The kid won't do ya dirty like a devil, Sirana. Just be patient with him. He's stubborn anyway but has a history ov caution bargaining wit' a pretty *lasschen* like you."

"Talov," Mourn warned, his tail seconding him as it scraped along the floor to the other side of his chair.

"What? I should remind ya what yer Da said?"

"There is no need to remind me. Enough."

The last word sounded like a growl.

"Awright, awright. Smooth yer scales."

The Dwarf backed off but didn't look at all remorseful for bringing this up. My experience with the half-blood thus far taught me to be cautious about assuming what "this" even was.

Wishing to change the subject, I exhaled audibly through my nose. "Well. If your Ma'ab contract is well and truly done here, Mourn, I am willing to take that break. No more tasks for a while. Something to take my worries from my sister, perhaps, if I must wait on the Naulor."

"I recommend the noodle house on *Roi-kung* fer midday," Talov suggested. "Try th' tea, anything's good. An' the *dorji-ka* is around the corner if ya wanna study some new moves."

I arched my brow. "New moves?"

"Fighting moves."

"Oh?"

"Oh, ya!"

Mourn stood up with a sense of finality. "Thank you, Talov."

The greybeard smiled up at him. "No cost, no stress."

Smiling despite my suspicion, I stood up as well. Only then did the ancient Dwarf push himself out of his seat, offering me a small bow.

"The Guild thanks ya both fer your contributions. Take that break an' enjoy. Ya've earned it."

CHAPTER 5

WE LEFT THE MASONS' YARD WITH OUR HOODS UP AGAINST THE Sun and the sculptors' eyes following us. I caught even more scents rising with the warmth of the day and saw so many colors in full force beneath the light. It all threatened to overwhelm me after meeting in the dim mason's office, though I adapted much like stepping out of a cave after a long rest.

It was only that the crush of signs for a city were vastly different from the wilderness.

All the Yungian residents noticed Mourn and me on the street, the word traveling ahead with anticipation. Some were reverent in their expressions or gestures, others kept their eyes on the ground, and a few drifted behind us for longer to obtain that good look at their Dragon Spirit passing by. They didn't crowd or obstruct us, but I could not help keeping my eyes and ears on our environment more, I thought, than my protective escort.

Although, that didn't stop my thoughts.

What did Talov think needed reminding? What did your sire say about 'pretty lasschen,' and what will it take to confirm your bargain with me?

I wanted to ask even though Mourn's irritation had been clear. I didn't agree with Talov's assessment of the dynamic between me and the Dragonchild. The idea that Mourn could be flustered by the thought I might be "pretty" was ridiculous, although I appreciated this valuable insight on "the kid" in making this assumption. It made it easier for me to imagine similar caution with a "pretty bua" like Auslan.

Say my Consort also had my skills, and he roamed around a foreign land, seeking extra protection I could provide. Hmm.

What would I ask for if Auslan had little wealth to offer me? It was a good question but not a difficult one. I quickly settled on his pleasure skills, sensual services if he didn't have anything material to trade. I knew he'd be open to this, and so would I.

If Mourn had suggested this himself weeks ago, when he could smell my renewed health and arousal in the saddle, for example, then I might have been wary about the strength imbalance but doubted I would have been insulted. Sex could have different value to different Elves, and even the Humans put a price on it, but regardless, the experienced ones knew how to work for it.

This was my big obstacle. Mourn wasn't open to this method of payment. He'd said so on the boat, very close to my face, when I'd asked about playmates and business partners overlapping.

"I have never... **never** bargained for information using sex. Neither offering nor accepting. I also do not offer my skills in exchange for a mounting. I am not that easy or hard up."

So indignant.

But at least I understood where that response arose better now, as I contrasted the idea of a "feral fugitive" escaping a Queenless city with observably *different* behavior on the Surface more than four centuries later.

Reassuring frightened servant girls, visiting old matrons to heal their sick granddaughters for a single necklace, and insisting Gavin and I consider the long-term implications of what we did around them.

It was obvious that Mourn took his actions more seriously than any male I'd ever met, and he had been clear about this since we landed in Yong-wen. He'd even introduced me to two non-Human elders that he trusted to get their opinion. This meant the half-blood was not routinely led with arrogance or hubris, either.

Fortunately for me, neither Talov nor Krithannia had loathed me on sight, despite my Dwarvish insults or what another of my race had done to the Guild Mistress's druidic sister. They had weighed me as an individual, as Sirana, considering what I knew and what value I could prove from my conflicts and my adversaries so far.

I'd grasped their expectation that I do the same in return.

So, if Mourn did not consider sex as a viable payment, and if no treasure I possessed could be traded to balance the task ahead, then what else *could* be "fair" in his golden eyes?

What *had* his sire said? Was it a deterrent or encouragement?

"Hai," I said quietly as we turned a corner onto a quieter street.

"Hm?"

I spoke our native tongue with no hand sign. "If you have never exchanged your skills for sex, and if I can't trade the dagger or pendant and only have the wellness pellets, yet you suggest I don't loot for more, what about gaining information such as I learned from Kurn? If you have a target meant to die anyway, especially down South, I could serve in this way."

Mourn frowned. "That seems a grim service to ask of you. The Deathwalker is better suited and may even have better control of gleaning that information from the dying."

I growled at such quick dismissal. "Merc, I am running out of ideas, unless you want me to start encouraging suppressed Witch Hunters to fuck each other next."

The sound which escaped surprised us both. He had *laughed.*

He also clipped it off quickly. *"Ahem.* Hm. That *would* be justice. May I ask how you did this? And how much control you really have?"

My eyes bugged out. "You would consider? I was jesting! Plus, I strongly doubt *you* would approve of such punishments."

He scanned some rooftops. "You haven't met Reprisal."

"Who's that?"

"Not in Yong-wen."

"Not what I asked."

"Let me think about that. You might like them."

"You'll *think* about our bargain until after Manalar falls!" I grumbled.

He was still smirking. "No reason for that level of defeatism, Baenar. I merely suggested we needed a break."

"Oh, I beg your lenience, *Wen-yung*, if I remain distressed about Jael while we 'negotiate.'"

He cocked a ridged brow at me. "You can do nothing more than you have, Sirana, which is quite a lot. Don't discount how many eyes and ears you've convinced us to use in search of her."

Irritable now, I shrugged. "I can neither discount nor take solace when I haven't the haziest idea what resources are at your disposal."

"Very well. How about you tell me about her?"

I opened my mouth and closed it again. *Huh?*

"Why?"

Mourn shrugged. "Tell me about Jael. How did you meet?"

I swallowed when it all came back so clearly.

Hm. Why not?

"I met her during a battle with mind flayer thralls. Three Ornilleth came to capture slaves, but we blocked and destroyed them. Afterward, Jael was among the wounded army, not yet a Red Sister like I was. My task at the time was to make certain the healers did not poison their competitors in other Houses."

The Dragonchild listened as he led us around his favorite city. By now, we'd walked far from the gardens and merchants that I noticed more wafts of dung and working sweat on the wind.

"She was the fieriest cait around me, in the fight and after," I said, smiling. "Even bleeding and seeing my uniform, she met my eyes and refused a Fifth House healer, calling her out as having a grudge. So I ordered her 'better' away. It felt good being able to do that to someone so far up, even if it caused her trouble later."

Mourn hummed in mild amusement, and I paused, exhaling as her face remained comfortingly clear in my memory.

"Her eyes are like polished copper, really bright in any light source. My Elders were already thinking of recruiting her, but I recommended it anyway."

"Is that all it takes?" he asked. "A feisty, public challenge to someone of greater status to receive a Red Sister's recommendation?"

I exhaled. "No, we… the Red Sisters look for caits who aren't content with the games of the Court or in their roles at home. They are misfits likely to be sacrificed for some other's ambition, so, why not ours? If she passes trials and can be trained, she need not be contentious or aggressive all the time, but… sometimes it helps us take notice."

"And you noticed Jael," he said.

I nodded. "She was the youngest Daughter of the lowest House, Twenty-Fourth, and the Priestesses were already watching her. After she insulted the Fifth Daughter on the battlefield, someone quickly sent Sathoet to harass her."

"Harass her?" Mourn sounded displeased.

Briefly, I pursed my mouth. "In that way powerful females enjoy using their males against weaker females. Jael wasn't going to last unless the Sisterhood claimed her."

"Hm."

I paused at his grunt, trying to read the Dragonchild's face after my oblique description.

Were you used this way to punish caits lower than your Priestess-Matron?

His tail betrayed anger, but that could be from many sources. I couldn't tell, but he reengaged with my story.

"You said that the Priestesses were watching and thus were easily convinced to torture the youngest Daughter for an insult. Do you know how long or why they were watching?"

I shook my head. "No. I heard the Sanctuary likes to torment the lowest House because they can. Occasionally, an Aurenthin goes missing. I never rose high enough in the Sisterhood to find out where they go or what becomes of them if they aren't recruited by the Red Sisters."

"Hm. I see." He mulled this over but eventually set it aside to move on to the eventual outcome. "So, Jael was retrieved from the Sathoet and passed your trials?"

I hesitated. "Some would have said she did not."

His brows raised. "How so?"

"Well, I... interfered in those trials. She was dropped naked out in the wilderness and supposed to return to Sivaraus on her own resourcefulness. I knew from *my* trials that the Tragar were in that area when they hadn't been before. She didn't stand a chance alone, so I convinced my Elders to let me go look for... well, um."

"For her?" he prompted.

"No, they forbade that. Otherwise, our top leader would kill her outright the moment I brought her in."

He looked disgusted. "What?"

Shrugging helplessly, I touched my chest, where Shyntre's pendant lay beneath my armor. "My Elder gave me and another Sister permission to look for this stone, the saphgar in the same area, because I knew that's what the deep Dwarves wanted and why they were so close to our borders. If Jael could be kept away from them at the same time, well, that was fortunate."

"Ah, workarounds. I understand," he said, and it sounded genuine. "What happened when you 'searched without searching' for your sister?"

I smiled despite myself. "Mm. Well, the Tragar had already found her. Or I think we accidentally pushed her into them. We could only jump into the fight. Six against three, and two were psionic, throwing rocks at us with their mind." I straightened up. "We won again."

"Not an insignificant accomplishment," he granted. "And these were the two times you fought Tragar? Your trials and aiding Jael in an imbalanced fight?"

"Yes."

"Then what?"

"Well, she was bleeding badly, so I gave her my healing potion." I skimmed past the taboo of that as well. "Jael ran and made it back by herself, and I got the stone I needed for my Elders to justify my being there. A lot of Sisters didn't want to accept her at first, but... she survived and proved herself like I did."

"And she will always know that she wouldn't have had the chance without you."

I swallowed at the way he said it. "It was the same for *me*, in other ways. If I hadn't been given a chance to prove myself by Sisters older than me, if none had *ever* come to help me, I'd be gone now. We need to pass it along without seeming weak in doing so."

"Hm. Sounds like a brutal gauntlet to pass through, but I can well imagine the loyalty this breeds in a closed group like the Red Sisters."

We'd been walking West when I noticed the roads began bending to the South. I realized that we'd walked the width of the Northern enclave, but there were still many streets, yards, and dwellings on either side of us. I hadn't walked the *perimeter* of whatever border separated Yong-wen from the rest of Augran.

Nonetheless, this far West from the "fish road" docks on the riverside, farther still from the merchants and crafters and dense city dwellers, I noticed manors spaced farther apart, plant and tree-lined roads leading up into gentle hills, and larger fields and pastures. The roads were dustier and less tightly cobbled. Fortunately there were rows of tall trees providing us with shade as the Sun climbed higher.

Even farther out, I finally spotted horses as well as field workers. I recognized plantations when I saw them.

Mourn spoke after a lengthy pause. "Sirana?"

"Yeah?"

"May I ask if you've closely encountered Ornilleth as well as Tragar? Perhaps in the thrall battle? Did one get close enough to touch?"

A rock dropped into my stomach.

Shhhiiit...

"No," I said. "Not in that battle."

"When?"

My head felt light, and for a moment my vision swam. I slowed as I grew unsure of my balance. Mourn shortened his gait, watching carefully without touching me.

What the fuck? This *wasn't* the geas, I could tell the difference!

And yet... I... couldn't *speak!*

"Keep walking," he said, lightly touching my shoulder, which seemed to ground me.

I obeyed but did so slowly, remaining jealously close to the trees for their shade and pulling my hood forward over my eyes. Yungian gazes were still upon us but, at this distance, I'd be surprised if they made out more than two dark blobs of starkly different heights.

When Mourn next spoke, his voice was quiet and without questions.

"I was once part of the only squad that could face mind flayers in Vuthra'tern. I had something like a 'sisterhood' with whom I fought in skirmishes or planned culls. We were mixed, caits and buas, by necessity."

"Necessity?" I repeated, confused.

"Vuthra'tern is much smaller than Sivaraus. If you have twenty-four Houses, there were only eight as I grew up, and not enough new births to create more."

Oh.

"I admired my leader," he continued. "An elder female, for many decades. She was a capable commander. Her only intent was keeping us alive."

His words were deliberately chosen yet, at first, I wasn't sure why he laid each thought out the way he did.

"She was a mage," he continued, "who used stones imbued with magic to mimic those we fought against. When we wore them, we could hear each other's thoughts, anticipate each other's moves, and share in the morale and the threat. It made us stronger, fighting as one but, unlike the Ornilleth, we could separate at the end of it and be stronger, still."

There it was. The other boot finally dropped.

I blinked, shocked to realize liquid drained down my cheeks. *Tears?*

"I've never done anything like that," I said. "And I'm not a mage."

"Hm. But you can use a stone most valued by Tragar as a focus to influence suppressed desires of sleeping men. You can anchor a Deathwalker during a magic storm and be unaffected by it. And you bested the Black Heart of Soul Drinker through sheer force of your will."

A sound caught sideways in my throat, and I swallowed it down. "Just say what you're thinking, To'vah-krav."

He exhaled through his nostrils. "You possess a mind talent which appears psionic to me. But, as a Baenar, you weren't born this way. Something happened to change you."

I licked my lips, my mouth drying as I barely noticed the scenery around us. "Do you want to bargain? That knowledge for my sister."

He chuckled soberly. "It's not urgent, and I've seen ample evidence that crucial fragments of this are not yours to share. Too much strain on your mind and body risks your pregnancy, and you have carried for quite some time despite belonging to a Sisterhood which likely doesn't encourage catching children."

"Yes, foolishly so," I said before I could stop myself.

"On the contrary," he said, gradually leading us forward on the road. "I'd like to know something about the sire. Tell me."

I frowned, blinking away the last of my abrupt tears, although my throat still hurt. "Tell you what?"

"Anything. Your choice."

A warm breeze passed us at our backs which somehow still smelled like the Great Lake, even this far away. I sniffed the air, cleared my nose, thought about Auslan for a score of paces in which Mourn didn't speak, verbal or otherwise.

I remembered my most recent dream of him, of the strange prison and him reaching out into the Desert through molded stone. I remembered our embrace before I'd woken up about to enter the warp rot forest.

His voice, his warmth.

His hope that I'd come back alive.

It felt so real.

"I keep dreaming of him in the Red Desert," I said. "While I've been up here. But I've never *been* to the Desert."

Slowly, Mourn turned his head. I could read the incredulous confusion even from my periphery. I didn't blame him.

Of all the things I *could* have said about the sire of my baby, this flew in from nowhere. I could have said he was the most beautiful Consort there was, and that he'd help make a beautiful baby. I could have left it at that.

Hmph. Why not share the rest of this foreboding confusion?

I smirked as I looked up at the half-blood. "Sometimes, when I'm asleep, my beautiful bua has gold eyes. Like metal, much like yours. Not like the sickly yellow of the Sathoet. When I'm awake, his eyes are a natural scarlet."

"Uhhh…" Mourn paused, uncertain. "Are these dreams from after we met?"

I shook my head firmly. "No, these dreams are from *before* you stepped out of the bushes, Dragon son. Before I reached Sarilis's Tower, where you noticed me. But... I will tell you that, as a novice, I once saw a portrait of a different bua with shining gold eyes in the Sanctuary. For some reason, my dreams mesh my baby's sire with that portrait, though they do not look alike."

I hadn't forgotten that my Valsharess thought Shyntre was the sire, and for that reason alone hadn't killed me. I was still confused why She made such an assumption.

"A portrait," the Dragonchild repeated, intrigued. He wanted me to continue.

It was a relief, somehow, to go freely in this direction no matter how mad and random it sounded.

I shrugged. "It was unnamed, but Cris-ri-phon dreamed of the same bua when I arrived at Troshin Bend. If what I saw truly happened, then he once found the bua in a Desert prison, but I don't know how long ago..."

My voice audibly trembled as the pitch and volume felt squeezed off, and my left hand trembled. Mourn seemed to notice. I found that I couldn't say who Innathi thought the prisoner was, though I wanted to.

"My younger sister gave birth to a son in hiding. He was kept well-hidden for centuries, fully grown when my General stumbled on the prison... The bua possessed most unusual eyes.

"Something his Mother did to him..."

"Mourn?" I asked. "Is there a Desert Dragon?"

He sounded taken aback. "What?"

I chuckled, my throat wringing it out until it was dry. "You heard me. Is there a Desert Dragon? I assume there is a Dragon around the Great Lake. He's purple, right?"

"Ah... I believe you are correct on both accounts." He paused. "But I haven't met any of them except my Sire. I don't know how many there are or where they dwell."

I wasn't sure how far I should believe that. His tail was not as calm as he might claim.

"So, only your sire talks to you?" I asked.

"Correct."

"How often? Since you've left the Deepearth?"

He weighed answering me at all. "Not frequently, but yes. We speak."

"How? Does he leave the Deepearth to find you?"

"No." He paused. "My Sire visits my dreams. We talk in a lucid state."

Well, well.

A nice trade for blurting out my tangled nightmares.

I took it all together. Mourn's Mother dead from his birth, him spending his youth fighting psionic enemies with mimicking magic before running from his Aunt-Matron with a shadow drake clinging to his back. This last admission of being tutored directly by the Black Dragon while he slept cinched why this hybrid son of my race acted in almost no way like a Davrin.

Finally, Mourn chose a road East which would take us back to the city center. The flowers on the lines of bushes were fragrant and larger than anything I'd seen in the wild thus far. They were beautiful.

"Do you dream frequently of the Desert?" Mourn asked.

I nodded. "For several years now."

"When did it start?"

My jaw clenched, and I stopped, leaning over as my stomach heaved. Hesitantly, I tapped the saphgar stone at my chest, and Mourn took my shoulder to steady me.

"So, these dreams have become more frequent on the Surface, especially after meeting the Deathless?"

Ow.

"*Fuck*, yes!" I gasped.

The Dragonchild chuckled, taking both my shoulders to help me straighten up, massaging and pressing the muscle in ways that seemed to help the nausea to pass. My spiders didn't so much as twitch in my hair at him being so close, and eventually I breathed out with relief.

"Thank you," I said as we started walking again.

"Welcome. Anything else you can share about the dreams on the Surface?"

"Well, the first was when I met Tamuril," I said, "and again at the Ley Tower. But they were brief. They grew longer and more intense the night Cris-ri-phon revealed himself to me. It began when we were both asleep, like Kurn and Castis, and grew stronger with each day I was there. Gavin theorized I was…drawing the ancient memories out. And I had to leave before it got worse."

"Ah. Hm." Mourn crossed the road to stay in the best shade, and I followed him. "Did I observe one of those dreams while you recovered in my cave as well?"

His question brought it back like a hammer.

The Davrin merchant, Toushek, holding a golden shield. He argued with a female skeleton in the prison with Cris-ri-phon and his Deathwalker staring behind empty iron bars. They were too late to retrieve the golden-eyed bua, but something else was there.

It was big. Furious at the desecration, calling a windstorm and shaking the earth. Filling the chasm with sand.

Metallic gold eyes floated in the dark. *★Thieves.★*

A bloom of panic spread through me as I blinked out of the dream back into the daylight.

"Sirana?"

I blurted out, "Did I draw memories from *you* in the cave?"

"No, no. At ease," Mourn assured me. "I learned how to kill Ornilleth up close with my blade. I can shield my mind against psionics almost without thinking. Whatever you saw, it wasn't from me."

Was that why he was so hard to read? My relief was palatable that he wouldn't be easily influenced.

I sagged a little. "Can you teach me to shield like that?"

His dry lips stretched in a thin smile. "I can't teach you to shield your mind from your own mind, Sirana."

I rolled my eyes upward, which was a mistake as the Sun blinded me. I rubbed them, protected them behind black gloves as I continued.

"I mean, how did your squad become separate minds again? Did they ever need to practice pulling away?"

"Hm, yes," he said, "now you mention it."

Yes.

"So, do you know methods that might help with unintended dream-links?" Finally, I took my hands away and blinked rapidly, refocusing on him. "I am doing better while awake, but sleep is when my guard is down."

He nodded. "As I would expect."

"So. If we're here for a few weeks anyway, I know Gavin would appreciate it. He's said I must practice staying out of his dreams."

Mourn covered his surprise with a smirk. "That must have been pleasant."

I rubbed my temple. "Oh, he's pure Deathwalker while unconscious as well. It's surreal. All mist and blood, swaddled maidens, and black-boned skeletons."

"Any crows?"

Unexpectedly, I laughed. "Swarms of them!"

"Hm." The Dragonchild considered this seriously, and I tried not to hold my breath. "If I can develop practices for you, physical and mental, which might help your sleep, would you share your dreams in what detail you recall when you wake?"

"Sure," I agreed immediately. "Why not? If you'll listen to my confusion."

"Very well. I will stay in the same room and observe you, or perhaps we will sleep at the same time as well." He paused. "Perhaps you can learn to dream lucidly. Even if you don't feel rested, you aren't utterly lacking in direction or control of what you see in this state."

"I don't know," I replied skeptically. "Gavin's dreams are vividly lucid, yet he seems to have no control of what he sees."

"He's given his oath to a higher power," Mourn countered. "You have not. Lucid dreaming may still help you, as it helps me."

This sounded both intriguing and terrifying.

"Very well. Thank you." My mouth twisted with bland humor. "Wait. Did we just negotiate yet another trade *except* for the one I need finalized?"

Mourn chuckled. "We did. Intelligence is the simplest of trades, and you have more to offer than I've seen in decades. It is the dangerous jailbreak from a fortress which is known to be the center target of an imminent war which requires much more negotiation for compensation."

I exhaled, feeling better despite that unfortunate truth.

Better, and hungry.

"It's midday," I pointed out, shielding my eyes as we passed out of the trees and approached the dense dwellings and streets. "Can we go to that noodle house Talov mentioned?"

Mourn showed his teeth. "Sure. And, afterward, the *dorji-ka* is a good place to start for seeking physical and mental balance."

"Yeah? Hm. Alright, deal."

If he meant I might learn some new fighting moves, I was definitely interested.

I HAD BEGUN TO BELIEVE NO BLAND OR POORLY PREPARED food existed in Yong-wen, even as I resisted such simple-mindedness in the delirium of my enjoyment. Clearly, it was the company I kept that had me eating like a Top Tier Matron.

The noodle house was doubly-sound in this reasoning. Mourn was offered only the best when they knew whom they served, and Talov wouldn't recommend incompetent merchants who might make their pregnant diners ill.

Assuming he knew. I couldn't see how he would *not* know, but he'd never mentioned it.

"*Mmm,*" I hummed, sipping the savory broth from the bowl's wooden rim, inhaling its steam to taste it twice. I washed down my well-chewed mouthful of slick, seasoned noodles and chunks of tender vegetables. I'd already eaten the egg which had been the final ingredient added on top.

How do they discover what flavors mingle so well?

Mourn's tail weaved with bright enjoyment as he watched me eat, forgetting his own bowl in his palm until I was a quarter done with mine. Then he demonstrated how to use the eating sticks.

I narrowed my eyes in study with my mouth full. I'd already grown impatient and was digging the big pieces out of the broth with my fingers, the same way as the grain pods last night.

"I still don't see the point," I commented after he'd deftly slipped a dripping prawn between his teeth without it slipping and falling back into the soup.

"The sticks slow you down," he answered, sharp teeth shredding the crustacean tucked in one cheek. "You must concentrate on your meal, and you are fully present. Good for knowing when you are full."

I pulled out a pale cube with a dark green rind and ate that, sucking on my fingers before pointing at him. "Down below, most have their meal stolen if they take too long to eat it."

"I remember," Mourn replied, using the sticks despite having perfectly serviceable claws to pinch anything he wanted from the bowl. "Another reason I like Yong-wen."

I sighed then realized I *did* need to slow down, or I'd feel as drowsy and uncomfortable as I had after cleaning the tray in Gavin's room.

We stood alone in an open-air shelter decorated with red and yellow paper tassels; it was located out of sight of the noodle house and across the way from the *dorji-ka*.

We had already upset the Human routine at the food stand by requesting their goods without a disguise. The high-pitched chatter and fluttering and bowing were incessant, and Mourn had stood there and smiled, keeping his teeth hidden when he wasn't talking. I wagered Mourn couldn't have sent them coin by messenger falcon and have them accept it.

How does he stand it unless this attention is what he craves?

"So, indulging in sex gets your chosen Human in trouble," I began after clearing my mouth with another gulp of broth. "But…"

He sighed, setting his sticks across his half-empty bowl, and arching a brow at me. "But?"

"But," I chuckled, "taking their food for no payment is harmless?"

"Better than harmless," he replied. "The Mina Hin might have to turn away customers for the next month if they run out of food to serve before the end of each day. Two bowls of *shuram* gifted to us will bring the cook business and good word far beyond what they were worth in coin."

"Aha." I found a prawn as well and dipped my fingers for it. "And does proving the Dragon Spirit needs to eat ever disappoint anyone?"

Mourn smiled. "No. The Dragon Spirit enjoys mortal food when visiting, and it is an honor if he chooses your shop. The tradition is a long one and keeps them guessing while maintaining good practices. The result is better food for the people year-round, and the best in Augran, I think."

"Wait, does that mean you deliberately did *not* give the same boost to the morning pie merchant?"

"He was boosted last time I was here," Mourn answered. "Being favored twice in two sightings isn't a balanced approach. It may cause destructive envy."

I acquiesced with a nod, taking another slurp of broth.

"I will add that your presence adds even more," he said, slowly grinning. "They see you eating with your hands, licking your fingers, unable to resist their offering, and yet you must be from somewhere unrefined. They are trying to discern why you are with me."

"Unrefined?" I took mild insult to this as I also became aware of a well-dressed youth spying on us.

This one sketched in a book. *Sigh.*

"Think it over, Mourn," I said, "is a *spoon* that difficult of a concession for soup? Must they find the hardest way to eat soup to feel superior in Augran?"

Mourn chuckled, continuing to use his sticks. "That's not how it came about, though do imagine trying to scoop up the shaved noodles with a spoon."

"Stab it with a fork, then."

"I've tried. This is still easier." He plucked up a wide noodle and laid it across his tongue, pulling it in. "I will grant you that not *all* Yungians use these, but they are common in Yung-An, seen from the Great Lake to the Lonely Ones."

"The what?"

"Steep, craggy mountains to the West. Part of the same chain as where you crawled out, but Yung-An is farther North."

I squinted at him, opting to finish my last bites and drink the broth before deciding whether I wished to pursue further talk of faraway landmarks.

No. No, he mentioned something else much more interesting.

"What would you wish to be the story of why I am with you?" I asked. "Will you give them an answer by the time we leave?"

Mourn seemed surprised. "Perceptive. Yes, they'll have at least two answers by the time we vanish: the story they collectively decide upon, and the story I tell the right persons to spread by gossip. Everything we do until then balances the credibility of each."

"Mm-hm. And what's the story you'll tell the 'right persons?'"

He looked cheeky. "I'm still thinking."

"Oh? Well, then I have an idea."

"Uh-oh."

His tail stilled as he looked up from beneath beetled brows, and I snickered, blinking with mock bewilderment.

"What? Tell them I'm a 'life spirit' balancing the arrival of Death," I suggested, deliberately obtuse on the topic of sex he expected to revisit yet again. "That we walk together as the South prepares for war. Maybe if they believe it, that could balance some damage done for Mai."

"That's not…" he began then stopped. His tail lifted then settled back behind him as he reconsidered. "Well. Hm."

Wait. *What's this, now?*

After a few beats, listening to the wind chimes down the street, I prompted, "Yes?"

Gold eyes skimmed over me. "You don't *look* like a life spirit they'd recognize."

"I wager that also depends on how you present me," I replied, peeking over the rim of his bowl to see if he'd finished. He drew it back slightly, and I grinned. "What do I look like to them? Anything I can do or change to make this idea easier to swallow?"

Mourn watched me. "Do you mean this, Baenar? Changing something in your behavior to help one girl and her family?"

I shrugged. "We have the time. *You* did it just this morning. Why not? What do I need to do?"

"Hm." He frowned in concentration. "With your weapons and poise, you look like a hunter or warrior spirit, perhaps an assassin. I don't think there's anything we can do to change that, but your eyes may allow us to bend that boundary a bit."

He hesitated again; his uncertainty was amusing. This time I decided to wait him out.

"Do I understand correctly," he asked, "that you feel no taboo if strangers see your breasts?"

A laugh of surprise escaped me. "That's correct. Assuming *they* don't lose their sanity and attack me. But, just as important, under what circumstances might these strangers see them?"

Mourn tossed his chin to the *dorji-ka* across the street, from which I'd already seen several men with smooth heads come and go. "Martial practice."

"Oo!" I looked that way with renewed interest. "You mean naked wrestling? My sisters and I do that."

"No," he corrected quickly, "model sparring at most, and top-less is enough for me to work with. Full contact isn't safe, and full nudity isn't necessary. Displaying discipline over impulse would be better for the story and, thus, for Mai."

My glance up suggested he was trying harder to stay focused.

"Hm. Heard and understood, To'vah-krav."

He looked at me, considering. "I still intend to show you cen-tering techniques to help your sleep as well, and this will help."

"Ah." I smiled. "Fun *and* advantageous. Although I must warn you, my breasts have felt like rocks have tumbled over them for months. A strike there could take me down like a bua hit in his egg sack." I winked. "But a Red Sister always gets up. When do we start?"

Mourn huffed a laugh, contemplated his bowl with the eating sticks crossed over the top. With one thumb, he swept them to the side and lifted the bowl to quickly finish his meal. I stared as his throat moved, gulping down those larger chunks without chewing them. He finished and reached out for my bowl. I gave it to him.

The Dragonchild nested one inside the other and said, "First, let us return these to Mina Hin. Then we introduce ourselves to the Shi family *dorji-ka.*"

CHAPTER 6

Mourn's shoulders blocked the narrow entryway to such an extent that I had the opportunity to release my spiders on the nearest wall.

~*Follow me,*~ I instructed them. ~*Stay hidden. Come only if I call.*~

They scurried up to the ceiling as I reflected on the weight and firmness of Shyntre's pendant. My inner voice seemed clearer to me; the effort itself, lighter. Odd, but welcome.

I brought my attention back as the initial din of the first greeting rose while Mourn wiped his feet and I removed my boots and stockings. I didn't know what *Wen-yung* planned exactly, but I'd agreed to follow his lead. We began with a bow to the "Master" Shi of the sparring house, and I stayed alert to further signals.

"*Lantiu'janshi,*" Mourn bowed to me, describing something in Yungian. I hadn't the first idea what it might be.

"*Ai!* Honor, great honor!" the elder man said to me in Trade. "Yes, you summon and push *ging* with us, a great gift!"

The crinkles at the corners of his eyes deepened as he saw my surprise in understanding his words, if not his meaning. His dark eyes met mine for two beats before looking down. As far as I knew, he never met Mourn's eyes.

"What is '*ging*,' Master Shi?" I asked.

The man with a touch of silver at his temples blinked with surprise and looked at the hollow of Mourn's throat in question.

"Aura," the half-blood answered. "She knows *ging* as 'aura.'"

I did?

"*Ai!* Understood! Here, we push aura together." Master Shi cupped both his hands and drew them in. "Come in, come in!"

"*I don't know how to summon or push auras,*" I remarked in Davrin as we stepped forward.

"*You will and certainly can,*" he answered, his tone warm. "*You'll understand.*"

Let's hope so.

Mourn stepped first into a large, open room layered with sleeping pallets touching each other. There was a bare, narrow walking path around the perimeter. On my right and facing the street, a line of narrow, glass windows near the rafters allowed natural daylight inside. The popular dark paneling on the wall on my left had no windows but was adorned with a neat row of script-scrolls like what I'd seen in the mason's office.

I sensed my spiders nearby, turning my head enough to see their careful entry to reach the molding of the doorway.

~*That's good there, babies.*~

I heard their understanding of my endearment, yet still no names came to mind.

I gazed back at every man inside the *dorji-ka*, counting eleven who had shaved their heads bald. Mourn had explained in advance that these would be the youngest and newest learners demonstrating their commitment and devotion to what was expected to be a life-long chosen practice.

The rest of them, fourteen of twenty-five, were the older practitioners and experienced teachers. Each had dark hair of varied lengths, all bound up similarly to the Dragonchild's: segmented with bands and looped up at their napes. None were in that high, tightly coiled bun as I'd seen on older women.

Mourn removed his cloak and hung it on an open hook near the door before working on his harness. I realized then that he had the longest hair here.

Heh. Another multi-lifetime tradition.

He'd truly been up here a long time, and he was granting me access to observe some of his territory which was clearly personal. Why? Did he believe I couldn't destroy any of it, by accident or with intent, in what I might tell others later?

My Queen *had* predicted I would return to Her. *Perhaps that will happen whether I bring the half-blood with me or not.*

Mourn shrugged out of the complex webbing of his harness to hang it over his cloak. Any man by this point who was not yet naked to the waist with his feet bare and on the mats took this opportunity to catch up. The sight would have brought out a laugh of delight if it wasn't my turn.

Being watched by all these Human eyes trying to be subtle in their glimpses and sweeps, I followed Mourn's example as well, hanging my cloak on a hook next to his. Then I removed my gloves and bracers, placing them with my boots and stockings. I hung my belt off the floor, at the last moment swapping places with the cloak, using it to cover my tools and weapons from view.

"They won't touch a spirit's belongings," he whispered, standing near and observant like a bodyguard would.

I nodded while working on the leather armor covering my torso. *"Better they not study Soul Drinker close up, agreed?"*

"Agreed." He paused. *"Where are your guardians?"*

"High wall, inside," I said without lifting my chin or eyes.

"Ah. What triggers them to jump or bite?"

"I call them. Um, psionically."

"Indeed? And if you should spar with anyone? Throw a punch?"

"They can't see that well. They listen for my distress, even if someone is choking me and I can't speak."

Something like Kurn's hands or thorn-covered vines.

"Hm. Very well."

Mourn reached to help remove the last of my armor, and I let him take it with a pinch of curiosity what happened next. He set it with care against the wall next to my boots while I tugged down and straightened my wrinkled, black shirt, flapping it briefly to cool my skin. The looseness and air felt good, though I noticed Mourn subtly suck in a breath through his teeth with his light purple tongue pressed up against them.

He said he 'tasted' the air that way, didn't he?

"What else?" I murmured, lifting the hem of my shirt slightly. *"This?"*

"If you are willing," he said, careful not to move his head or give nonverbal cues in either direction.

"And my pendant?"

"I'd prefer you leave it on while you train, along with your bottoms."

My lips formed a tiny smirk. *"Very well."*

I pulled my shirt over my head, shook it out, and managed to make it stay hanging over my cloak. Now I was bare-chested and barefoot like everyone else here, although I was the only one wearing a necklace and my leather "bottoms" fit tight to my form and were quite unlike the woven, loose fabric worn by all the males.

My pants were as flexible as they needed to be for a fight while also negating risks of being grabbed or snagging them on something sharp. I wasn't sure how I would keep the saphgar from swinging to knock me in the teeth or to prevent someone using it to choke me in a grapple.

Full contact isn't safe, he said.

"Eng zhuvyi!" called Master Shi at the other end of the room, and I jumped.

"Calling their focus," Mourn translated. *"Not ours."*

I watched anyway as all but the eldest turned their backs to me and spread out evenly. They stood not in rows but as if each stood in the center of a circle equidistant from the other men around him. It was impressive; it took practice and cooperation to take up that formation so quickly.

And self-discipline.

For I had *felt* the thought-wave of general interest in my breasts.

"One more thing," Mourn whispered.

"Yes?"

"If you are willing, loosen your hair and leave it down. That will aid the story for Mai, as well."

I was already reaching to unbraid my hair when I frowned. I hadn't seen any women in Yong-wen with their hair down yet. I was about to ask him what that meant when he stepped away.

"Join me at the front when you've finished."

I sped up a bit, combing my hair with my fingers and shaking it out before moving out to trace the wall around the room.

Here we go.

It was true that I lacked the shame or "taboo" to walk shirtless and be seen, but my experience with Humans kept me wary and my step light at first. I watched for glimpses of expression like Kurn's or Brom's in the Yungian faces, since most of the bald ones failed to keep their eyes on the mat.

I was also trying to understand my own gut-warming response to a room of half-naked males. Mourn *hadn't* asked whether there was a taboo in the reverse, of males stripping down like this in front of me.

I quickly realized there *was* one, and it struck me quick and hard.

None of them had known I was coming. If they had, they certainly did not know that I'd walk to the front with my tits out. This meant their own half-nudity was how they usually congregated.

This was *typical* for these men.

Was the nudity total at some point in their practice which their women never witnessed? Buas back home never observed how the Sisterhood lived and worked together.

That was an interesting possibility.

Whew. Well, shit.

Males showing this much skin around each other voluntarily *and* without a female present to direct them wasn't done outside of an orgy or ritual in Sivaraus. Not unless they wanted to invite accusations of "jutting."

The short, contemptuous word encapsulated the prohibition of buas crossing cocks while leaving their caits and matrons out of the play, unable even to watch. This could be punishable by altar sacrifice, depending how flagrant they were and how furious the injured female was.

That's… that's not what all these Yungians are here for, is it?

The mental image which followed caused my breath to hitch.

It wasn't in anger.

No, no, no! My mouth tightened. *Don't be like Kurn and assume they're willfully flaunting in front of you!*

*This **can't** be as lurid as it seems.*

Mourn had said we were here for martial practice and to somehow help Mai. I simply hadn't prepared myself for the full impact of what that *looked* like until I'd finally stopped watching my back.

"Are you frightened?" the half-blood murmured after he'd exchanged a ritual greeting with Master Shi and turned back to me.

Mourn heard my heart racing. I noticed how, without his cloak and harness, he was a bigger version of the nakedness laid out before me, adding to the flavor. He wore the magical bracers, of course, and I briefly wondered why the Humans weren't mimicking him in *this* look, too.

Unexpectedly, the image of the Dragonchild by the river without his pants on either returned as well.

Hoo-bua…

My face felt warm, and I smiled with as much confidence as I could muster. *"No, I am not afraid. I think I'll enjoy this more than I thought. Show me what we must do to help the cait and her family."*

His serpentine pupils shifted downward, expanding a little as his gaze landed briefly on my chest. He noticed how much the nipples stiffened with the exposure; mine were the largest nubs here.

"Do you have a warm-up routine?" he asked in Davrin. *"The mentor is curious."*

"Of course, I do."

I frowned a bit that the man hadn't asked me directly since he *could* speak Trade, but let it go as another cultural habit. This was Yong-wen, after all: Mourn's cultivated garden.

"Am I to perform it alone while you critique it?"

"No," he said, *"I will perform with you. Something similar but not the same, working from what you choose. The others will observe, and they are welcome to join. Then, we will walk through their ritual."*

"Alright."

The mercenary and I had already walked the roads a lot this day, so my basic stretching wouldn't feel as though I'd just woken up. Not that I *tended* to wake up in a languid state in the Sisterhood, anyway. I'd either be hustling into my gear to leave as quickly as possible, or I'd unfold myself from heavy limbs, wake up others to stretch, wipe down, and *then* hustle into our gear.

My "routine" was boring and practical, I knew, and Mourn *had* said "ritual," which implied the Yungians placed a greater importance on this part than I did. I wished I had been allowed to watch them first for hints, but it made sense that the group wanted to see the sole visiting foreigner's workout first.

I shouldn't dampen their expectations; that would make Mourn look bad. *I must make this interesting.*

Master Shi suggested then that all men take to their knees, which they did together. They were perched upright, shoulders balanced with backs straight, hands resting on their gently spread thighs. Their posture was excellent.

Nice.

I mentally removed the last article of clothing covering each man's legs and loins, and grinned.

Yes, I can do this.

First, I slowed down my routine, giving me the time to elaborate on my stretches while carefully nudging my range of movement a little farther than usual. With the first, barely audible hum of approval from somewhere, I added more flair in ways some Court buas would dance at a party with their hair down. This assumed I could reasonably turn it into a slow stretch or a holding position which developed strength.

If I was a bua, I knew caits would enjoy watching this, too.

My motions involved plenty of bending, arching backward with arms or legs curved and akimbo, sometimes playing my whole body parallel with the ground.

Then I took to standing on my hands. My toes pointed toward the ceiling, and the blue pendant swung close to the ground while my hair actually touched it. My sore breasts reversed their usual resting positions on my chest, and I'd made sure the men could see that part.

Appreciation.

With my palms flat on the mat and strong arms holding me steady, I felt the mood in the room shift even more when I split my legs and bent my knees to keep my balance longer. I paused, holding the pose for as long as I could, certain by now that the merc knew this wasn't my "routine."

But he wasn't signaling me to stop.

Mourn had been moving along with me for most of the time, choosing complimentary displays that I could see my Lead Jaunda doing to show off her strength rather than moving like a sensual bua wearing an eye-catching bit of jewelry.

The Dragonchild had turned, showing his flank to the others while still able to see me; he kept his legs closer together in adapting my strength-building positions. Although his own hair was tied up, he was also using his tail for extra balance in some entertaining and entrancing ways.

Sometimes it was hard for me to concentrate, and a smile creeped up on my face more than once.

By now, I'd picked up that this could be about displaying a *suggestion* of the act which creates life. I felt certain without Mourn saying it; something about this demonstration of health and strength was meant to start a story about a "life spirit" being with the Spirit of Death.

Perhaps being topless opened the possibility to consider me as a fertility spirit, a role beyond her weapons.

If so, a pity my pregnancy isn't more obvious.

On the other hand, maybe all of Yong-wen would assume the Dragon son was having *another* son or something. That gossip would spread like fire, no doubt. Better that my belly was flat enough to conceal what nestled there, assuming none of them can see the aura like Gavin and Krithannia.

If they could, there was nothing to be done at this point.

The men enjoyed my demonstration. The large room had warmed with significant Human scent while they'd enjoyed several opportunities to imagine what my ass and slit might look like beneath my formfitting leathers. None of them reacted with affront or hostility as Jacob had.

When Master Shi and Mourn signaled their thanks for the demonstration, I was sweating and breathing deeply. We bowed to each other, the silver of my pendant briefly sticking to the skin between my breasts. Although not one Yungian had joined in with the exercises, I was certain this had to do with what erections might be visible if they stood up.

A significant gain, not a lack.

Hopefully, this was indeed something Mourn could work with.

"At ease, great spirits," the eldest mentor said now, motioning to the mats with that same crinkled smile. "Now, we draw in the air, transform it. Regain the center of our *ging*."

Heh. I could try.

Taking the same position as the men, I caught Mourn's sign to face *him* rather than the room. I followed his lead, certain that we gave the young men time to calm their pricks. I suppressed a smirk.

Although the rhythm of synchronous breath filled the entire room, and although I'd been told "inner quiet" was the goal, my eyes wandered *a lot* while my heart slowed. I could not resist looking them over when all eyes were either closed or unfocused somewhere on the ground before them. They were no longer looking at me, so it was my turn.

I settled on a young one with modest fuzz regrowing on his head who had dark markings on the skin of his left arm. They were deliberate and possibly permanent. The image looked like a white flower from Tamuril's garden next to a human skull.

Tattoos, Talov said.

Right after him, I spotted an older man with long, looped hair who had the image of a small crane drawn not far above his right nipple, which was a darker brown than many.

Hm. How many others have tapestries on their skin? Are they magical like Hellhounds—?

Mourn signaled at my periphery, his hand out of sight of the rest of the room. I looked up at him then down at his hand while barely moving my head.

★Hold my eyes?★ he asked. ★I can help this first time.★

I frowned slightly, signing next to my thigh. ★A spell? Or word?★

★No. A hum. Practiced with my squad for calm and clarity.★

Ah. The methods for my mind he'd promised.

Suddenly, I felt nervous. How quickly the time had come that I had to trust he wouldn't put me to sleep or into an instant trance like he had the stable boy.

137

Yet how much could he have *already* done to control me if he'd so chosen? Compared to all he'd been sharing with me, *showing* me about his preferred methods to influence.

For this entire day so far.

Just meet his eyes, Sirana.

Aligning my breath with the rest of the room, I settled my gaze on that dream-like color, watching the minute changes in his vertical pupils. An important difference between this Dragonchild and that portrait I once saw; the ancient bua's pupils were round, like mine.

Like a pure Davrin. Not a Dragon.

Mourn began to hum. It was a pitch so low that I wasn't sure the Humans heard it like I could.

They might feel it, though.

Gradually, I relaxed. My breath slowed alongside his as the hum and metallic gold filled enough of my attention to lessen what I had given to the skin, scents, and breath of the others. The effect wasn't a dulling or muddying of my senses; they remained sharp. If someone walked in or if our situation changed, I could come awake instantly.

I knew we would.

Before I realized it, I'd reached a state where the quiet constancy was oddly comforting. Restful. I'd never been here before, but I could stay a little longer.

I am not in danger.

By the time we stirred and used our eyes to see each other again, the afternoon light streaming through the windows had changed its angle enough for me to be mildly concerned. It hadn't seemed much time had passed, yet my legs begged to differ.

Ohh, ouch.

"*Stretch slowly,*" Mourn whispered, demonstrating a good way to unfold and stand up without pulling a muscle or stumbling on slightly numbed feet.

He probably didn't need it, but I sure as fuck did. I'd have to learn what I did wrong.

The room came awake at once as the Yungians returned to their feet, smiling and rested. Not a one of them had a pole tenting their loose trousers. I smiled a little. *Pity.*

Still, this was extraordinarily *pleasant*, somehow. I tried to put it in words, pondering. My mind was clear, and a moment later believed I knew.

I am still the strange outsider here, but their suspicions aren't boiling over. I acted with intent to entice them, using my body to encourage arousal and sensual thoughts, and not a one of them couldn't bring himself back under control.

Unlike the Ma'ab and the Witch Hunters, even Brom and his daughter Amelda, the men in this room did not blame me for the thoughts no doubt entertained while I demonstrated my "routine." They could handle those thoughts on their own, and they didn't need anything from me to do it.

It was possible among men, and I was impressed.

"How do you feel?" Mourn asked.

I smiled. *"Surprised. But heartened."*

His tail said he was pleased before he did. "Good sign. Are you ready for their demonstration?"

Should be fun.

"Of course. I'm eager."

INSTEAD OF BEING ASKED TO MIMIC THE OTHERS, I WAS INVITED to watch the practice forms of two "brothers" who were called to the center of the room while the rest moved to the perimeter. Master Shi, Mourn, and I kept our place at the front while five or six learners moved to each remaining walls.

"Renshu and Hulin," said the master of the *dorji-ka*.

The young men bowed deeply at the introduction.

"The brothers from Shi Mu Kuo."

"Brothers," I murmured. *"Is this a fighting group like my sisters?"*

"They can, but these two are blood brothers of the same mother and father." Mourn nodded subtly toward Master Shi. *"The master's nephews. Their sire is his brother."*

I nodded once. *"Got it."*

When they began, I observed exercises meant to limber up their bodies. Both had warm, tanned skin and enough dark hair to plait into a queue like Mourn's. Unlike his, which was twisted and bound over several times, the end of their shorter plaits had been brought up and secured at their nape to form a single loop.

Their hair was so easy to grab in a fight that I wondered if it was deliberate, an additional challenge to impress the Dragon Spirit? If I sparred with anyone today, I'd be moving my necklace and hair out of easy reach.

Once I looked beyond this, I started to notice deliberate postures and smooth, choreographed moves which wouldn't turn into a spar anytime soon. Instead, the brothers used their hands, pushing them out with loud breaths and sudden barks of sound that I truly did not understand; some made me jump.

At my slightly annoyed look, Mourn signed an explanation. ★One method to control and focus their aura.★

What?

★Are they mages?★

★No. Life aura.★

I thought Gavin's talent was rare.

★They can see it?★ I asked.

★No. They feel it, as you do.★

I did?

★Why focus life aura? For what?★

★Keep watching.★

I did but saw nothing obvious, scanning lines of defined muscle and strength in their forms, for certain. When they tensed up, abdominal muscles appeared, capable of absorbing a blow to soft organs. Still, this seemed like posturing, suggesting a fight without starting one.

Finally, after two more circles, I watched their feet, realizing they stayed either along an imaginary straight line or a surprisingly clear curve. This pattern held no matter what their shirtless upper bodies did with their hands and arms, which now seemed like these upper moves were meant to distract the eye.

Hmm.

I saw a body and situational awareness I'd missed at first, but this was the familiar starting point for me. Among the Sisterhood, the Palace Guard, or even the army, the feet were often the first and best glimpse of competence in handling their weapons. I barely thought about my feet anymore; they knew what to do.

Soon, the two brothers shifted into complicated moves, their feet secure across the mats and their steps controlled. As a bua dance, it was entertaining, but I wasn't sure what it told me of how they fought to win. Perhaps I just didn't know how to interpret it.

Could all this careful footwork translate into blinding action under the right pressure? *I'd like to see that.*

Although I was a good observer, we didn't reach this point before Renshu and Hulin stopped, bowing to soft grunts of approval and adding to the exchange of bows as they received their praise and critique from Master Shi. Then they moved toward the wall.

Three men with longer queues entered the center next, older than the two brothers and with more refined forms and poise. This performance was satisfyingly complex for the added man and held my attention, but they still didn't fight before yielding the mats to the next four men.

Whew. Tease.

Again, they presented their forms, each of these an elder above the previous three with more loops to their queues. To my pleasure, they attempted to strike each other and worked as hard to avoid it.

Nice.

Clearly, the Master planned to keep the smooth and fuzzy headed learners off their makeshift stage today and thus easy to anticipate the final group of five, which included Master Shi.

Hm. Mourn had tapped on the grandmother's door with the same counting method, adding one more for every separate cluster of contact. Curious coincidence or another cultural ritual?

Regardless, a stronger musk filled the *dorji-ka* with the intense practice of the eldest men at once. They feinted strikes more often, never landing, but sensing the breeze against one's sweaty skin apparently counted as a hit. I hadn't been wrong about their feet, either; watching these eldest Yungians gave me pebbled skin more than once. The experienced mentors were stunningly fast, and I wagered all their motion began with their feet. The rest seemed to flow like water.

So many Davrin in the army never absorbed this lesson or fell early into bad habits and shortcuts, and they'd had decades more to practice than these Humans. I was far from the best but, under Jaunda's training, I got the foot lesson after the first time I lost.

I smirked at the memory. *My Lead has a way of driving her point home.*

When the final bows arrived, Mourn could hear my heart beating.

"Enjoyable?" His tone was unassuming.

"I think so." I exhaled, still wondering if I'd missed something. *"Have you ever sparred with those older men?"*

"I have not."

"Who do you train with?"

He just smiled. I rolled my eyes.

Master Shi drew the Dragons Spirit's attention, and I waited patiently through another complex social exchange by perusing the room of half-naked men. Several of them seemed torn about which spirit to gaze upon more.

I was fiddling with my pendant when I sensed my spiders and quickly located them. They'd moved much closer: still high on the wall above Master Shi.

~Good choice, babies.~

When Mourn finally turned around, he seemed to be cautiously considering something.

"*Yes?*" I prompted.

His smile and tone held a calm irony. "*Good work. They are open to accepting you as a fertility spirit as well as a warrior. That is the first step we need.*"

I could hear the unspoken in the void. "*But…?*"

"*They would be honored to watch us spar, you and me.*"

I quirked one brow, calm despite my twin trickles of excitement and trepidation. "*Real contact or whiffing the air?*"

"*I've explained you have a foreign style which doesn't practice pulling punches, but that you can give us a demonstration by attempting to land a blow on me. I will only dodge and block.*"

His eyes flicked to my abdomen to make his point, and I wrestled with whether this was exactly what I wanted or an insult.

"*Attempting,*" I echoed. "*And what will be their opinion if I cannot land a blow?*"

"*You are not expected to.*"

"*You mean you don't expect me to.*"

He didn't deny that. "*It will give them a sample of what you can do.*"

"*And you, as well?*"

"*No need. I recall the canyon, the god warriors, and the warp rot.*" He showed his teeth in a way that looked a little feral. "*You're plenty lethal, and I know you will make a genuine effort.*"

Well, that relaxed one knot in my mind.

"*What about your tail?*"

"*Avoid it.*"

"No, I mean does landing a blow on your tail count?"

"It does. But probably at the cost of becoming immobilized."

"If you pounce that fast, your body might crush my gut."

Mourn showed his teeth a little more. I squinted with suspicion. Clearly, I'd missed something. I caught up an instant later.

"The pig at the river," I said.

"Precisely. The pig."

He had pounced not to crush that prey but to drag it off its trotters; his tail had helped immensely.

I glanced to one side. Some of the men had begun to smile as if they could read the banter without a translation. Meanwhile, a swath of tiny bumps spread over my back and shoulders yet again, reaching the front a moment later where everyone could see.

"Sounds fun," I said brightly. *"Let's do it, Dragonchild."*

I TIED BACK MY HAIR IN THE CENTER OF THE ROOM USING THE cord of Shyntre's pendant. Not only did I need my hair out of the way while fighting but also needed the saphgar within my aura without swinging to hit me in the face. Instead of my spiders tucked beneath my hair at my nape, it was the blue stone.

This works.

I admired the dark mats beneath my feet. They felt firm, evenly stuffed, and liquid resistant. I could believe they would absorb enough impact that, assuming I landed well in the first place, I could avoid injuries and even some bruises.

Mourn and I stood facing each other, barefoot and in our starkly different black pants. All watched with anticipation, and he didn't make us wait. I caught the signal to bow to him as he bowed to me. Neither of us lowered our eyes, and Mourn's tail seemed to have a life of its own as it swished quietly across the floor.

Ah, yes, that tasty pig.

We didn't use the same step-the-line form as the groups before us. Beginning with a game of patience was pointless here, as I would not be able to goad him into acting first as I often could my Sisters. At the same time, he anticipated a direct attack and was ready to block, so that hardly seemed entertaining.

I was trained to use all my tools in a lethal fight, and there were many more options for surprises with a belt. But what tools I'd brought were mostly gone and what was left hung beneath my cloak on the wall. I must think of the stripped-down essence of those moves now.

I began with a feint, darting in for a low sweep before springing up and kicking out at his chest. He slipped back out of reach, his arms ready to block any follow through. He could have grabbed my ankle had he been on the offensive and determined to hit me.

My response would have been to grab his wrist and find pressure points while watching for that tail, but then we would be on the ground within moments of the conflict.

Which was how all lethal fights ended anyhow.

The Red Sisters did not bluff, and with the Prime's blade always at our backs we'd be foolish to think that would work. The longer our fights dragged out, the more tired we got, and the clumsier and more sluggish we became. Posture too much and die.

The nature of this performance must be as visible to the Yungians as it was to me. Mourn defended against moves designed to finish a fight, quick and painful. Only real attempts to injure or maim him could show any of my "style."

If a succession of strikes appeared anything like the smooth patterns of the Shi brothers, it was because one action led to another and might have worked in a split instant I couldn't predict.

I did not look at the audience; I focused wholly on Mourn. The Dragonchild and I made no sound but for the soft slap of our feet, knees, elbows, or hands striking the ground. No one around us made any noise. He was faster than anyone I'd fought before, and I did not have the height or strength to throw him. I likely couldn't trip him, and without tools or weapons, he was tough to distract and tricky to get close to.

One uninhibited strike following three wayward feints finally got me near enough that he shored up his guard and did something unexpected. I saw it coming because I recognized the way his thighs bunched, and his aura seemed to compress with his stance before releasing like a bowstring.

The same signs preceded his leaping to the hayloft to quiet the stable boys.

Ignoring the Human exhalations at this astonishing vertical feat, I rushed forward when his talons left the ground. Somersaulting to get under him, I spun to use his landing against him, kicking low to force his feet to move before he was ready.

He just jumped again, lashing at me with his tail.

Fucking f—

The merc landed with two quick skips backward, his tail acting as a fine counterbalance. If I'd had any kind of blade, pellet, or powder, I'd have pitched it at him. But I didn't; I was tired with a trickle of sweat on my brow.

Enough.

With a deep draw of air, I dashed into a new sequence of feints which ended low near his flank. Mourn readied to block, his balance unshakeable, his long arm prepared to urge my body past him with a sweep. He towered above me.

But his stance was wide enough.

I dropped and turned with my momentum to get underneath him. Counting on his hesitation to use those heel spurs, I smacked the thick of his tail with the heel of my hand, landing that coveted strike.

The Dragon Spirit collapsed like the Abyssal Web around me. His tail whipped around my torso and squeezed.

I couldn't breathe.

His limbs tucked in tight, boxing me in. Sharp teeth bared a finger's width from my face. I heard a rumble as thinning, black pupils vanished inside irises of molten gold, and his body swamped me with a sudden wave of heat unreal for a living thing.

At least I would've injected the poison before I died.

I couldn't speak, so I slapped his shoulder and signed where I hoped he could read it. ★You win!★

A moment later, the pupils of his eyes relaxed along with the coils of his tail, but he took a deep breath at the same time as me. He won the claim for space, crushing my chest, and I winced, wheezing, *"My tits…!"*

My bodyguard looked down, saw that he squashed them flat, and leaped off me as quickly as he'd fallen. I sucked in a huge breath of relief, so dizzy I was slow to recognize the hand he offered. When murmurs and excited chuckles reminded me that we weren't alone, I grabbed his hand, and the Dragonchild lifted me to my feet.

"Did I hurt you?" he asked.

He was dead serious.

"I'm fine!" I gasped, an adrenalin-laced laugh escaping from my throat. *"Oh, Goddess. Reminds me of home."*

My skin felt scalded from where he'd pressed against me. Blood raced in my ears, and my arms and legs quivered. My sex awakened without conscious thought, and I was reluctant to move away from him at first.

As if an important part of the fight lay unfinished.

My eyes slipped shut. For an instant, I was back in the Cloister, my pants about to be yanked down. I wouldn't resist; the victor always took the first turn on top.

Whichever fresh hole she wanted.

"Sirana?" Mourn whispered.

Fuck.

Now I stood inside the *dorji-ka*, hazarding a guess that I should bow first to end the match. Turning with a languid smile, I realized belatedly that Mourn, Master Shi, and two elders were still unsettled.

What?

I'd been challenged to hit him, hadn't I?

Smoothing out my smile as I bowed, I took solace in the younger Humans around me buzzing with amazement.

"Great fight," I said in Trade. "Much fun."

The mercenary gauged that my smile was genuine and finally relaxed his shoulders, offering me a formal bow as well, ending the contest to Master Shi's satisfaction.

"Are you alright, Sirana?" Mourn asked in Davrin as he stepped closer. *"Is there any pain in your abdomen? Even a bruise?"*

I chuckled, patting my middle after tensing up. *"No pain, no bruise but to my pride."*

"Very well. I will ask again later when the rush wears off."

"If you must. Oh, I'll be hungry soon, but I'm thirsty now. May I have a drink?"

I wasn't the only one. Only a couple words passed between Mourn and Master Shi before three learners left to retrieve clean water for everyone. Soon, Mourn and I returned to the front to sip from small wooden cups. I ached to gulp it down and ask for more but knew better; I didn't need the belly cramps.

"What concerned the elders?" I asked. *"They don't know I'm pregnant, do they?"*

Mourn studied me then smirked. *"I think you scared them."*

I scoffed. *"And you didn't?"*

"No, not me. Your face while you fought was... Hmm."

"Hostile?" I guessed.

"Savage."

I wrinkled my nose. *"What?"*

He suppressed a smile. *"Certainly a dangerous spirit."*

"Isn't that the point?" I shrugged, sipping. *"I was just concentrating on hitting you."*

"So you were, and you did. Well done." Mourn glanced at the murmuring Humans. *"I understand it was at once impressive and frightening to our observers. Now they know you can focus your life aura as they do, as a warrior, but the elders in particular felt a lethal menace."*

I grimaced. *"Oh. Does that hurt what you're trying to do with Mai?"*

He shrugged, scanning the *dorji-ka*. *"Perhaps not. I knew you wouldn't go half-measure, Sirana. I will just tell them the truth."*

I narrowed my eyes. *"The truth?"*

"Yes." He smiled at my suspicion. *"That you are deadly where you come from. That you have been trained for a hundred years to protect your elders with your body and skills against silent adversaries they cannot imagine."*

I puffed on the surface of my water before sipping again. *"That's a slight exaggeration."*

"Not really. They cannot imagine Tragar, Sathoet, and Ornilleth, and your training extends past the youth of their grandfathers. This is all they need to accept what they feel bearing witness. You are with me, and I vouch for you."

I nodded, feeling odd with the explanation. *"Well... Thank you."*

Mourn grunted, finally noticing my spiders above his head. *"Hm. Would you like to check on Gavin when we leave here?"*

"When will that be?"

"Soon. We've taken all their afternoon. They must return to their families in the evening."

"Ah. Then, yes," I agreed, smiling. *"I'll be hungry by then."* I paused. *"And I think I need Reverie."*

Mourn nodded, appearing calm and centered, his earlier distress from our conflict either lifted or hidden.

"We'll meditate again before you sleep, and I will observe you. Now that I know what to look for, we'll see if there are ways you can better protect yourself in your dreams."

I smirked, my voice laden with irony. "Sounds fun. Let's do it, Dragonchild."

CHAPTER 7

THE DAYLIGHT THROUGH THE HIGH WINDOWS WANED ENOUGH for lanterns to be lit while Mourn and I dressed and armed ourselves near the exit.

I had trouble getting Shyntre's pendant out of my hair, and the merc took it upon himself to assist me, acting like such grooming was familiar between us. He could *see* the tangle, so I played along as the tips of his claws grazed my scalp. We didn't have to cut the cord or a snarl to get it loose, and soon I could return the necklace around my neck.

Human eyes distracted by our display and the new flickering shadows from open flames helped my spiders slip out into the hall to wait for me, and I collected them before the elders caught up to us. After the quiet but earnest flood of thanks from Master Shi and others for our presence and participation, the Dragonchild opted to lead us out the backdoor into the alley rather than the main street.

Outside, we paused to check our surroundings before slipping across the next street, and I was relieved when he led us the way with the least people. We had to be more careful about stepping in dung, but we could utilize the shadows and narrow passages for cover and privacy even in early twilight.

Perhaps even a self-made legend grew fatigued bearing the constant awareness and praise of others, or perhaps he acted on my fatigue as a bodyguard would.

I pursed my lips. Every time I thought of Mourn as my guard, I thought of Jael and how long it seemed I must wait for news on her.

It's only been one day.

The unnamed payment I still owed the Dragonblood also lingered, without which we could only go so far together.

No. Not an option.

I couldn't fail to convince him to protect me at Manalar, but I didn't know how close I might be to desperation in cinching the deal. Mourn simultaneously assured me he *would* bargain with me but would not bargain with me *yet*.

What is he waiting for?

This pressure had vanished inside the *dorji-ka;* the exercise and exotic sights had been wonderful. I was glad for the break but, unfortunately, the uncertainty of our obscured path forward returned as a lump of nausea following me all the way to the safehouse.

As soon as we approached the rear of the stable, I remembered Nightmare. The memory tumbled directly into images of Gavin reading scrolls and somehow dealing with a sore, elderly drake that might need snacks in exchange for access to shelves close to his dark cubby. I smiled to myself, but then noticed the stable's busy noise.

Much greater compared to yesterday and this morning.

How would we enter the cellar unseen to return to the library? Was Gavin's mare still there and unmolested? Should we check?

The death mage had said his undead mount was freshly attuned to him, that he'd know if something changed. But maybe he was eyeballs deep in books and would ignore such interruptions.

Mourn signed, *The mare is still there.*

I blinked, wondering if he'd read my mind or my face. *How do you know?*

★I can smell her, and I sense the death magic at the rear where it should be.★

★Very well. Why is it busier? Should we be concerned that there are more guests at the inn above the cellar?★

★This is partly supply replenishment, but you are correct that guests have returned to Luni Ti. Krithannia only cleared the place for our arrival.★ Mourn smiled. ★The owners still need their livelihood.★

I frowned. ★Is Mai in danger from guests if the death-touch gossip started already?★

★It might not have but, either way, she isn't here tonight.★

★How do you know?★

★She isn't a regular worker here. Krithannia brought her and Ting when we were expected to give the regulars the night free.★

I squinted. ★Wait. If the pale one had a choice, why select inexperienced youths who were afraid of us?★

★You would have to ask her.★

That wouldn't be an option for a while, so I let it go in favor of watching for the opportunity to slip into the cellar. The wait was shorter than my typical stakeout at House Itlaun when I sought to speak to Auslan.

The density and variety of scents were better in most ways, too; my Consort as the reward at the end was all I lacked. Instead, after sneaking in, binding my eyes, and trusting Mourn with the jump circle, we ended the trip with a deeply inhaled mix of parchment, leather, and metal with very little dust.

Gavin was here as well; I heard him shuffling objects atop a desk, followed by a rattling exhale that *wasn't* him.

I lifted my blindfold, glimpsing Mourn's arms pull back from my sides. He'd been prepared for me to fall, but I'd kept my feet this time knowing what to expect. The place was well-lit by heatless lanterns the color of natural flame.

"Graul," Mourn said warmly, receiving a bizarre purr from the winged reptile as the drake lifted his head.

Mourn's old companion from the Deepearth had curled up on the far corner of Gavin's desk, Kurn's sword still hung on the wall, and the library was almost as neat as the first time. The only signs of ruffling the stashes had come from the death scholar himself.

The beast is not belligerently territorial, then.

A short stack of leatherbound books and codices sat on the desk without obvious signs whether they'd been studied yet. The former monk currently had three scrolls open, one on either side with the third directly beneath his unnatural gaze. His grimoire and ink bottle were placed on his right between two open scrolls. His stylus lay still in his long-fingered hand.

Gavin and I met eyes when he looked up. I wiggled my fingers in greeting before his icy eyes moved to follow Mourn, who drew close enough to greet Graul with a touch to his muzzle. I released my spiders onto the wall to explore where they would.

"You've returned already," Gavin remarked.

"The Sun is setting," I replied. "We've been gone all day."

"Hm. I hadn't noticed."

"Without windows, how would you?" I grinned. "Find anything interesting?"

"It would be difficult not to."

"Disagree. Just leave everything on the shelves."

The Deathwalker could still snort through his nose, and it only sounded a little dry.

Meanwhile, the Dragonchild massaged where Graul's folded, purple-black wings attached to his shoulders before slowly moving partway up the neck. The drake's groan was unsettling in its likeness to my Sisters after a hard cycle working before Reverie, like pressing the sore muscles hurt at first but he knew it would ease the stiffness.

Curious, I joined the three at the desk, peering over the surface. As expected, I couldn't read any of the script even if it happened to be in Trade. "What language is this?"

"More than one," Gavin replied.

"What?"

"Trade, Dwarvish, and a Northern script hinting at sounds which could be Ma'ab."

Mourn sounded impressed. "You found them already."

My scholar looked up at him. "Them?"

The mercenary motioned to the desk. "The Guild uses these books and scrolls for tutoring Dwarvish and Noiri, together. They cover the basics, and you are correct, they would lead to understanding some Darge and Ma'ab as well."

"Ah, Noiri. Interesting."

Mourn smiled. "The Ma'ab haven't been here long enough to have their own written language when they brought none with them. Although their speech sounds much different from their neighbors, they ripped the operational text from the Noiri and Darge, as those are less complex than Dwarvish."

"Logical. Hm." Gavin considered. "I imagine the Ascended and the highest caste have a special script."

"Correct, again."

"You've seen it?"

"I have. It resembles little that is known and is likely an elite cypher rather than a spoken language."

Gavin nodded. "Do you have any examples?"

"Very few."

"But they exist?"

With a nod, Mourn stepped over to a specific shelf as if he remembered where each item rested. He tugged out a thin leather bifold and placed it on the table where Gavin could reach it. I watched my ally turn it open where it lay and lean closer to the contents.

"Scraps of original text, kept together," he said. "Not a copy."

"You are welcome to copy them into your book if you wish," Mourn invited. "If you can read them with any certainty, Death-walker, we'd pay well to know what they say."

"We?"

"The Guild."

"Ah." Gavin pursed his thin, greyish lips as he turned two of the scraps around in a couple orientations, contemplating each for several moments. "I will meditate on these. Perhaps my mistress can guide me."

The death mage returned to the trilingual passage he was working on when we arrived. "Will you translate the Dwarvish here into Trade for me?"

Graul champed his muzzle with something like a snicker as Mourn stepped around the desk to look over the dead man's shoulder.

"Go slowly so I can transcribe it," Gavin added, dipping the tip of his stylus in ink.

The Dragonchild followed this request so closely that the words made little sense to me at first. Once I'd grasped that it was a mundane passage about borrowing clan currency in Taiding, I had mostly stopped listening when they continued to discuss a few odd "rules" in Talov Baradum's language.

The familiar hollow in my middle was growing, and I glanced at the runed platform built to send food and drink from the kitchen above. It looked like neither Gavin nor Graul had used it yet, but I stood up to get a closer look.

What did Mourn say before… place a cup, a bowl, and a plate on the runes and wait?

I did so, folding my arms to keep from interfering with the magic. After a longer delay than I expected, a small but familiar *suck-pop* signaled the vanishing of empty dishes.

"Ah, apologies, Sirana," Mourn said from the desk.

"For what?" I turned around. "You explained how to use it. Simple enough for a drake should be simple enough for me, right?"

The half-blood seemed surprised but amused by the self-jest; he nodded. I also noticed Graul staring, the end of his tail flicking as his hazy gaze fixed on the rune circle like he thought the food had already arrived.

"Want to share?" I suggested.

"They may only send a normal amount for me and Graul," Mourn replied, as if I should be careful being so generous.

"I've eaten plenty and well today, my thanks for that. After the exercise, I only want a half-belly before Reverie, anyway."

"Hm. Very well." Mourn glanced at Graul and back. "We accept."

My scholar looked up from his grimoire, turning his head my way. "You are resting here?"

"I have my pendant." I patted my chest. "I'll be quiet. Like on the boat."

Gavin narrowed his eyes and looked at Mourn. "You are staying as well?"

"I may not sleep, but yes. Likewise, I can be quiet."

"Why here, if you are both under constraint?" the Deathwalker asked with a touch of irritation.

I watched the tips of Mourn's white horns swivel around as he scanned the library with deliberation.

"This den has other, unseen protections in place which we need tonight," he said.

"Oh?"

"Yes. Not only can Sirana have her first secure rest without Soul Drinker draining her," he looked at me, "but she may also take her peace knowing she won't influence other sleeping citizens of Yong-wen by accident."

I frowned. "You didn't mention that. Do these 'protections' dampen mind magic, somehow? How will I practice dreaming anything lucid?"

Mourn shook his head. "I didn't mean to suggest your mind would be suppressed. You are protected from magical *intrusions*, and you are out of reasonable range even if someone is sleeping on the kitchen floor. There is only Gavin and me, but we know what to watch for."

"And Graul," I added.

"Graul is immune to psionics."

"Wha—? He *is?!*"

"Dreaming lucid?" Gavin interrupted, tucking a knuckle under his chin with a loose hold on his stylus.

Now he was interested in our loitering in the library.

"Yes," I said, "Mourn knows methods I could practice. They might help stop me from joining the dreams of others."

"Curious. Does he dream like this himself?"

"I do," the merc answered, removing his cloak and harness as he'd done in the *dorji-ka*. "It's a quality of my Sire's blood."

"Interesting," Gavin said.

More than that, I think.

Mourn turned around to face the Deathwalker. He was bare-chested again. "You sound to have your own impressions of what this means."

"I doubt dreaming while lucid is any one experience," Gavin said. "But I am present in my dreams in a way one could say I am lucid while having them, and the memories hold similar to memories made while awake. My death transition also seemed like a dream in which I was awake as well, and this state still... continues."

"You mean the trances?" I guessed. "When your eyes are open but fully black?"

The Deathwalker watched me a moment but nodded with reluctant agreement. Perhaps he'd been unaware of that detail until now.

"Would you call them visions?" Mourn asked.

Gavin shook his head firmly. "No, I would *not*."

"Why not?" Mourn asked, also sounding interested.

"Describing what I see and learn as 'visions' would suggest I am an oracle with misplaced confidence interpreting actions or events which have not yet happened or never will."

Gavin lowered his stylus from beneath his chin, shaking his head again with palms on the desk. "What I see is nothing like that. It has never been. I see the long-dead and those in transition. The past and present. I see no future which matters to the events of the living. Even in those ways pertaining to the service of my Lady, I only know what I must know *when* the time arrives, not before."

"So you have said." Mourn nodded in thought. "An articulate and convincing assessment that you are not a seer. I am impressed with your perception that there are many paths which lead to a lucid state when the body is at rest, whether a Dragonblood, death mage, or psion."

"I wanted to ask about that," Gavin said, nodding to Graul, who was still lying on the desk watching the food delivery hatch.

It was still empty, and I frowned. *Seems to be taking them a while.*

Mourn folded his arms and leaned against the second desk while I sat on the long chaise, testing the softness for my eventual sleep. I should have been more engaged in this talk as part of it was about me, but I yawned while Gavin asked his questions.

"You said Graul is immune to 'psionics,'" asked my scholar, glancing at me. "What is this word, psionics? And why is this the case for the drake?"

The mercenary had been expecting that. "This is a word from the Deepearth. We have denizens so strong with this talent that we need a name for them. A *psion*, or someone displaying a talent like Sirana's, is a sentient not using magic but is nonetheless summoning similar effects, albeit in a more limited range."

"Magical effects without magic?" Gavin repeated skeptically.

"Yes. Magic and psionics are the will made manifest. There are a myriad of ways this may happen."

Gavin began taking swift sets of notes when Graul suddenly puffed and snarled excitedly as our food arrived.

I smirked and got up to inspect the three separate bowls of steaming, orange-glazed noodles, sticky vegetables, and *a lot* of braised, seasoned red meat. It smelled as delicious as everything had so far. No doubt these mixed well together, despite each component presented separately.

Kind of like a magic spell. Heh.

The tray contained a tall pot filled with a cool drink plus a short one with something hot to the touch. There were two small cups for the drink, but they'd sent only the damned eating sticks for the food. With a sigh, I placed two empty bowls in front of me and attempted to pour roughly equal portions of each between them, listening as Gavin and Mourn continued their talk.

"What are these 'denizens' called?" Gavin asked. "And how many?"

"*Ornilleth* and *Tragar*," the Dragon son shared readily, repeating them so Gavin could write it down. "Tragar look like Dwarves with skin and hair like Sirana, but greyer, and without pupils. The Ornilleth…" Mourn paused. "I am not sure if you've seen anything that resembles them before."

Gavin started basic. "Bipedal?"

A nod. "Hairless. Tall, gaunt, purple-grey skin most of the time. It's their heads which are distinctive. Have you ever seen or heard of squids?"

"What?"

"The eight-armed, soft-bodied swimmers in the Great Lake. Large eyes, a hidden beak within the arms which can crush crab shells. They have slick skins which can be many colors."

Gavin shook his head. "No, I have not."

Mourn smiled. "They are intelligent for their size. An Ornilleth looks like someone attached this strange water creature as the head for a body with a skeleton like yours, Deathwalker, but with far less muscle. The head has four tentacles instead of eight."

I paused in blowing on my hot drink, which I'd discovered was a floral plant brew like Tamuril made. "A flayer on Gavin's skeleton?" I blinked toward my scholar and back. "My gratitude for the future nightmares, To'vah-krav."

Mourn chuckled, and Gavin looked at me. "Is it accurate?"

"Well… yes," I admitted.

The scholar wasn't insulted; he just dipped his dry stylus to keep writing. "Why did you call it a 'flayer,' Sirana?"

"Ornilleth means 'mind flayer,'" Mourn translated for me.

"Ah. Do they 'flay' minds, then?"

"In a few ways, yes. A single Ornilleth can attack the mind of another, triggering a headache so intense that you pass out."

"Mm-hm," Gavin said as if to encourage him.

"However, their greatest strengths lie in linking minds and communicating their thoughts and memories without speech as one mind, a hivemind somewhat like bees."

"Do they have a queen?" Gavin asked instantly.

He might not know squids, but he knew bees.

"They do, though neither female nor male," Mourn answered with confidence. "Called an 'elder mind.' The mind flayers work together to bend the wills of individual minds of other races to obey the elder mind. They remove the ability to choose and disrupt memories, either by obscuring them, twisting existing ones, or inserting new ones. Lesser abilities have physical signs. Moving objects or forming barriers from force of will alone, without using hand, tool, or voice. They are primarily a slaver race since they can and do compel others to perform the hard labor for them."

"That's unsettling," Gavin commented.

"It is. I am glad they have never migrated up here." Mourn's mouth tightened to a dry smile. "Bear in mind, Deathwalker, I have also seen the most powerful mages take identical actions to the mind flayers, using magic as their power of choice rather than psionics. The Ascended and Brom Troshin are strong examples, wouldn't you agree?"

The half-blood's eyes flicked my way as well. Gavin and I nodded without hesitation, though I wagered I was more troubled than the scholar. I turned around to tuck the eating sticks into one bowl, thinking of my Valsharess and Her Priestesses of Braqth. And my sister.

They bend wills. Compel to obey, remove choice. Enslave to perform labor for them. That all fits.

I hadn't realized how alike we were to the Ornilleth, but the difference was only the tool and who could use it. With a sigh, I crossed the library and handed half of the meal to Mourn while it was still warm.

"Thank you," he said, accepting it.

I nodded before retrieving my own food, the shadow drake watching my every move. Graul had turned his head multiple times between Mourn and me by the time I returned to the chaise. Perhaps the creature assumed my proximity meant I was the one meant to feed him.

I avoided eye contact after my first bite because I wasn't going to share.

Mourn chuckled and resolved this confusion by retrieving the drake from Gavin's desk with one arm, placing the beast on the empty desk next to him so they could sit together.

The Deathwalker and I watched Graul nip morsels of meat from between Mourn's claws once he'd pinched them out of the bowl. The little beast snapped his jaw happily on the meat a few times before swallowing.

Their antics made me feel better eating with my bare fingers again. I licked and sucked the tangy, orange sauce off after every noodle. It tasted as good as it smelled.

"You were comparing powerful mages with Ornilleth," Gavin prompted.

Mourn nodded while he fed his drake. "Powerful mages can enslave as many minds and cause as much disruption up here as an elder mind does below. This occurs from the sheer number of individual mages born added to their likelihood of finding a tutor."

Gavin pondered this and seemed to agree. "Are psionics unique to the underground?"

"No. Some Humans are born psions like some are mageborn, but there aren't nearly enough of them on the Surface to be apparent. The majority of common Humans suffer less for encountering a psion of any kind than they do from entire cities structured to support self-serving mages."

Like Manalar and Ennikar.

He didn't need to say it aloud.

"I see," Gavin nodded. He'd never stopped writing. "So, why are there more psions in the Deepearth? Are there fewer mages?"

Mourn nodded. "Far fewer mages below, yes. The Davrin Elves weren't always in the Deepearth, but they are now the greatest source of magic."

"Ah," Gavin said. "This is why the Dwarves have stories about them."

"Correct. The psions claimed the deep caverns first and became strong teaching each other to become one. Magic *could* compete with psionics, as it turned out, but understand that the deep psions view this as encroachment. Magic is a foreign threat to be destroyed."

"Fascinating," repeated the scribbling scholar.

I had never heard it put that way before but was ready to believe it. If Dark Elves hadn't always been in the Deepearth, if the Ornilleth had come first, then we must have arrived from somewhere else. My Valsharess, the dreams of buas with golden eyes, mindlinked memories with an ancient Sorcerer-General, and talking with Soul Drinker itself had all but proven that origin to be the Red Desert.

But why did we leave? Only to end up deep underground and competing with mind flayers and hostile, grey Dwarves?

Gavin reread his notes thus far. "And Graul is immune to psionics because…?"

Mourn showed teeth. "Ah, you didn't forget. Shadow drakes have lived alongside Ornilleth and Tragar for I don't know how long. They developed a defense which has proven nearly impossible to overcome."

"And what is that?"

"Shadow jumping."

Gavin and I frowned with suspicion when the drake suddenly pranced, turning in a circle while emitting an excited hiss. For once, Graul focused on us rather than Mourn's bowl of food.

"He looks proud," I said.

"He is," Mourn admitted, offering another morsel, which he nicked before I could blink. "Graul understands we're talking about him."

"I guessed as much," Gavin said, eying the creature. "He seems extraordinarily self-aware, although I am uncertain to what extent or with what nuance he grasps our speech and ideas."

"Not all drakes are this self-aware, but he's lived around languages for centuries," Mourn explained, gently rubbing the throat pouch with the back of one finger after Graul had swallowed. "He understands enough to follow directions or a simple plan."

"Impressive. But what is shadow jumping?"

Gavin glanced at me at the question. I shook my head, nearly finished with my messy bowl of noodles.

"Shadow jumping," Mourn said, "is like the jump circle through which we enter and leave this library, or which sends us food and sends our waste out, except it needs no runes or imbuement. It is a natural talent of the black drakes."

"Black?" Gavin asked. "Implying there are other colors of drakes?"

"There are, yes." The Dragonchild rubbed his companion's muzzle while he continued, his tone admiring. "The black drakes can pass through barriers by 'jumping' a short distance if there are shadows on the other end. The darker it is, the farther the leap may be. While Graul's jumps are limited up here in the day, shadows fill the entire Deepearth for his kin. Jumping this way both breaks a psionic link and prevents one from forming."

Graul chuffed through his nostrils and hummed with the additional scratching.

"So," I said, "never mind what I heard about Matrons who tried to keep drakes as pets. Not even the Ornilleth can hold them for long."

"Correct, Sirana." Mourn looked proud. "They use this ability instinctively. The moment they do, a mindlink or compulsion breaks."

Huh. I wish I could do that.

Graul turned in excited circles before Mourn fed him his next treat, obviously enjoying the conversation centered on him. I should have been annoyed but couldn't muster the pettiness once I realized I was smiling despite my envy.

"So," Gavin picked up at another place in his notes. "Psions aren't populous enough on the surface to expect that a mundane man in a city would run into a will-bender every year, correct?"

"Correct. For most, probably not in a lifetime." Mourn was finally eating the noodles and vegetables with his sticks, speaking out of one side of his mouth. "The potential is inborn but given how short Humans live and how likely they will be alone in their society, learning even a modest level of control is not guaranteed. Most psions are exiled from their society or killed before they learn control."

"They are found out," Gavin said with a too familiar grunt.

"As they decline, yes."

"Decline?"

I swallowed, stared at him eating as the Dragonchild continued. For once, I did not want his food.

"Without a tutor in another psion, such individuals are likely to grasp at other minds randomly, seeking connection in the chaos the way Ornilleth do. If they do this so much that they do not recognize their birth-self, they fall to insanity as their mind splinters into separate names and clusters of memories in one body. I've witnessed some Humans being killed by their own family for seeming to be possessed by multiple demons."

I clutched my stomach as it jumped.

"What?!"

Mourn and Gavin looked at me, and my voice grew soft.

"I-Is that what's happening to me?"

My tone drew Mourn out of his frank discussion to grasp the impact of what he'd just said. He exhaled and didn't try to back out of the new sinkhole he'd created for me.

"It seems like it to me," he admitted, "that your mind may have reached out this way with the Ma'ab, Brom, and Gavin."

Not just them. To Lana. To Reishel and D'Shea. Wilsira, K-Kerse, and the flayer inside the prison…

What about Jaunda, Gaelan, and Jael? Auslan and Shyntre? I had dreams about *all* of them but didn't know if I'd hurt them.

How many more minds would I "grasp" for?

How could I *stop* it?

Mourn's voice cut through my panic. "I want to stress, Sirana, these are the *early* signs. You know perfectly well who you are when you are awake. You also have more time and resources than the unfortunate Humans I've witnessed. From what the Guild could piece together, these psions were all born alone and had no one who understood what they were, much less guide them as children. You have another advantage in being grown already and having this understanding."

You weren't born this way, Baenar. Something happened to change you.

I forced my mouth to work. "But you said I need another psion as a tutor, or I *will* go insane?"

Again, the half-blood paused. "It may be a good idea to seek one in time, but we have several tasks to take care of first, I'm sure you recall."

Of course, I do.

"You've proven you are far from mental collapse, Sirana," Gavin added.

Such cause to shout for joy. I blinked several times. I would *not* cry. "Do you know where to find one up here? A psion who's *not* going insane?"

Mourn pursed his mouth in a way that confused me. With his particular shape—not quite reptilian muzzle but no full Elven jaw and lips—I didn't realize it was an indication of grim humor until he spoke.

"I do. But he's a little busy preparing for a Ma'ab siege."

What?

Gavin set down his stylus and folded his pale hands together like he'd just finished a puzzle. "Do you say Captain Isboern is a psion?"

The Dragonchild looked to him. "Yes, but it would be better if the layman doesn't hear that. They'll misunderstand the same as they would a Davrin or a Deathwalker. And in truth, I haven't witnessed one like him before."

"Like what?"

"Captain Isboern appears to have full control of his talents, equal to a single Ornilleth, though he is only twenty-five years old. I don't see how this could happen unless he had the best-case scenario for the recognition and training of his talents."

"Which would be?"

"If his entire community is familiar with and accepting of psions yet somehow aren't a hivemind. More like the Tragar than the Ornilleth, on account that not every Deep Dwarf is born psionic."

Gavin tilted his head. "Interesting. Which community is the Captain from?"

Mourn shook his head. "We know Isboern came from some-where out West, in the Lonely Ones. While not a Manalar native, he arrived with a purpose five years ago and is already a beloved leader. A psion using his talent with the same subtlety as the Bishops could do this. At the same time, he'd be resistant to their methods."

"Hm. Do you think he's simply 'disrupted' the Bishops' memories? Or inserted new ones in the populace to be so 'beloved?'"

"I don't think so, no. I wondered the same thing when I became aware of him. I've since been close enough to determine he is not as powerful as an elder mind, nor is he always *using* his talent like they are. He is a singular identity who can simply act on a good read on people, and those actions speak for him the same as any man."

"Hm."

Gavin finished his notes in quiet while I weighed continuing with my own questions, even though the hot food and soft chaise seemed to be dragging down my eyelids.

I wondered if Krithannia had spoken with Tamuril about this Manalari Captain, especially after the Druid left me at the Ley Tower. I could still see Tamuril's expression when I'd made the mere suggestion that Jael had been sent to assassinate Captain Isboern.

The Naulor had gasped with such horror.

I'd been certain then Tamuril knew him, and she had tried to get me to come with her.

"Sirana?" The Druid reached out and plucked at my dark cloak. "Come. Come with me. Let us talk as we travel away from here. I have others you may speak with. They know more than me."

If the blonde Naulor knew something about psions, had she somehow recognized the way I was strange? Did she realize what was happening to me? Was she at Manalar now, looking for Jael or trying to warn the Captain about us?

"You look tired, Sirana." Mourn had finished up his bowl without my noticing; Graul was licking at the sauce inside. "Shall we practice the meditation again before lying down?"

Being honest with myself, I feared what I might dream when I did. Blindly, my fingers sought Shyntre's pendant beneath my armor.

You have more time and resources than a Human...

"One last question, Mourn?"

"Yes?" he invited.

"Are Surface Dwarves sometimes born psionic like Humans? The way Tragar are born about one in four?"

The way Mourn grimaced, I knew at once that must be another long story, and he answered with caution. "Not anymore. But... perhaps another time?"

I sighed, glimpsing Gavin making that note in my periphery. "Agreed."

Graul and I each used the waste closet, then I stripped down to just my shirt and pants before joining Mourn on the plush carpet facing him.

Although the Deathwalker attempted to return to his translations and transcriptions, I sensed how frequently he paused to watch Mourn and me. We breathed together, and I gazed at the half-blood's face until it went out of focus. As my trepidation lessened, Mourn quietly began to hum.

So low. Barely detectable.

I relaxed, searching for that still space to settle in, where I seemed to float but was neither blind nor unaware. My mind drifted pleasantly as tension left my body.

When the humming stopped, I remained as I was, not wishing to leave. My bodyguard stood and gently took my arms, encouraging me up. I accepted and allowed myself to be guided to the long chaise where I could lie down. I noticed Gavin sitting back in his chair as well, his hands relaxed off the arms of the chair. His eyes were black and empty.

When I settled on the cushion, Graul was already there, curled on the footrest with his eyes closed. A folded blanket appeared from somewhere, and Mourn laid it over me, saying nothing.

Within moments, my consciousness dropped into Reverie like a pebble into a pond.

DARK SAND LAY BENEATH MY HANDS. FINGERTIPS DETECTED A lingering heat from the previous day. If I dug down just a little farther, it was warmer still beneath the surface.

Silence surrounded me. Not a sound nor a breeze passed my ears; no hissing of grains in the distance. The sky above me was dark as well. Moonless, with only starlight.

I waited as those tiny threads of silver light proved enough to see that the sand was red.

Oh, Goddess. Who am I this time?

And when? What era, if not the Elsewhere trapped in stasis? I dreaded looking but lifted my hands from the sand, inspecting palms and arms which offered the first hint.

Davrin. Female. Alright.

If not the Sorcerer-General, was I Captain Xala again? Was Ishuna nearby, looking in a mirror and unwilling to tell me where her son was?

Where is he?

I got to my feet, turning in place, in awe of the vast hush. Frightened of it. Was this another trap? Could I leave this weighty calm when I wanted?

When I must.

My ears detected the faintest whimper, and my feet turned toward it, taking that first step without hesitation. I breathed deeper, felt better while hearing my breath and my heart with my legs at work, creating the shush of warm and cool sand beneath naked feet.

Who am I this time?

I stood on the dune, listening for another heart besides mine. My stance was balanced, and it felt safe to look out at the horizon.

I peered outward.

Two shadows.

Perhaps they were a mirage, but two figures waiting on either side of me, far from each other. I couldn't tell yet if they drew nearer.

A moan, another whimper. Much closer.

That way.

I continued, aware when my breasts began to ache. Glancing down again, I recognized my naked body and the blue and silver pendant. My hair was loose down my back. My hand covered my gut, and I found it.

The hard, warm spot low in my gut.

I am pregnant.

My eyes narrowed, glancing again at the two figures far away.

I am... Sirana.

No mask or illusion this time. No uniform, either. Just naked and carrying.

I crested the next dune, finding the other source of sound in this impossibly quiet place. He lay in a low trough, buried in the sand up to the waist as if the Desert had tried to swallow him but he got stuck in its throat.

His back was to me. The Davrin bua was slumped over as if exhausted, as if he'd been fighting the inevitable. He wore nothing that I could see, and I admired what I could of his figure.

Then I saw the blond streak in his hair.

I gasped, "Ta'suil!"

His head lifted. He'd heard me, knew his name. My baby's sire twisted his spine trying to see me, and the healer sank a little deeper. He whimpered with despair.

"No, stay still," I said. "I'm coming."

On naked feet I circled around him, careful to kick the least amount of sand into the depression. Both his beautiful hands pressed to the shifting sand as if he could hold it in place, and he looked up when I crept into his view.

I remembered his smile.

"Sirana," he breathed.

Then he frowned; he was worried.

"Do not come down here," he said. "You will be trapped, too."

"I can't leave you here," I said practically, again glancing to the dark figures on either side of me. "And I don't trust them enough to ask for help."

They didn't seem to be getting any closer.

"Ask who for help?" he asked.

"I can't see them. They're too far away." I pointed a hand in each direction, my arms straight out. "They're just standing there."

My Consort nodded with nothing to suggest. He licked his lips, his tongue seeming dry. I was afraid to ask how long he'd been here without water.

"Here," I crouched, taking a crab-step down into the steep trough. My arm reached out. "Can you take my hand?"

"I can, but the sand is…pressing in," he said. "A single hand cannot pull me out, and two cannot dig enough sand away before it will fall back in. I am sorry. I wish you could fix this alone, but you can't."

I didn't understand his tone any more than I did how he came to be here. Why wasn't he panicking? Why was he not pleading for me to get additional help to get him out if two hands weren't enough?

Is he just that tired?

I paused so that the sand would stop sliding down with me; I needed to think. Not a single hand could pull, nor two to dig. What else? I was naked; I had no tools or rope.

My Consort smiled again. "Shyntre told me he made that for you."

I blinked. Looked down. *Oh, the saphgar.*

"He did?" I asked. "When?"

"After you left."

I smirked. "He didn't tell you why, did he?"

"To protect you, of course."

Of course. Stubborn wizard.

Then I blinked, a rush of concern flooding back such that I choked on my next breath. "Are you still in solitary, Ta'suil? In the Cloister?"

He hesitated to answer, considering it with wavering lips, as if he wasn't sure whether to laugh or weep. I got the sense I shouldn't have asked.

Maybe I don't want to know.

"It is... better than it was," he answered.

But I couldn't get him out of that place any faster than I could this sand trap.

"Where are we?" I asked.

"My dreams," he answered softly.

He looked up again, focusing on my abdomen the same way Gavin did.

"You can see it," I stated.

Finally, he smiled again. "I can. I am honored you still carry. I did not expect it would last even this long."

A fierce pain stabbed my chest. "Well... I think it makes strong mages hesitate to kill me. I'm still alive because I carry."

He grimaced, nodding. "I am sorry. That is as I saw it would be."

"You did? When? Did you do it on purpose?"

He looked away and whispered, *"I was trying to save you."*

No mattered what else happened, I knew that he had.

Ta'suil waited at the bottom while I waited to one side, indecision and a lack of solutions keeping us in place. If this was a lucid dream, would we sit here until we woke up? This empty place was the most like being awake I could remember. Time seemed to pass the same.

Was there anyone to ask for help? Was the Dragonblood watching somehow? Perhaps he was asleep.

No, he wouldn't sleep the first time.

Maybe one of those shadows was him. If I called, would he hear me?

"I'll be right back," I promised, waiting until Ta'suil signed his understanding before I climbed up to the edge of the pit.

I looked out around me again, struck by a chill.

Shit.

Not only were the first two figures still there, but there was another one straight ahead of me. This third one gave me gooseflesh.

It had eight limbs.

Shit, shit.

None had drawn any closer, yet I sensed that they *waited* to do so. They wanted to. What prevented it?

Finally, I looked behind me. *Wow, that's new.*

"Ta'suil?" I asked.

He hummed to signal he listened.

"There is a... very tall, spear-shaped rock to *this* side now. It wasn't here before, but it's in between the two figures."

And across from the third one.

My Consort was so quiet that I thought he hadn't heard me.

"Ta'suil?"

"Yes, uhm," he sounded to be gasping for more breath. "Does the 'spear' look like a tower with a thin tip? Made of red rock?"

I nodded. "Yes, exactly. If that's a tower, it's huge."

"Oh." He swallowed. "Another of my dreams, Sirana. The spire is often in my visions, always in the distance. I can never get closer as I walk, but no danger comes from it, either."

I wasn't certain about that. One of the Sister Moons rose behind it, her silvery light just touching the base of the spire. Because of that light, I could make out the haze at the base which looked either like mist or...

Dust.

If it was, it was a big cloud.

The incredible silence was about to break, the quiet pushed out of this space and past me by what hurtled toward us.

"Sandstorm!" I called, slipping down just off the edge to duck the fast-rising breeze.

That was a bad move. This trough would fill with sand. We were about to get buried, and we were both fucking naked!

"Ta'suil!"

I looked at him, and he looked back, eyes wide and fully aware of the danger. Spotting flecks of gold in his eyes, I almost choked when I inhaled a grain of sand. The golden streak of hair was gone.

He reached up with his hand. "Sirana! Get down here!"

"Shyntre?!" I screeched as I slid down, kicking sand which buried him a little more. "Where's Ta'suil?"

"I don't know! Give me your hand!"

"Why?"

"I'll shield us!"

Good idea. I seized his hand as the first gust of air flowed down and smashed into us. His skin was hot, his grip hard.

Too fucking real.

"If the sand buries us," I shouted, "your shield won't hold. We'll suffocate either way!"

"I know!" He struggled against the sinking sand. "Help me!"

"How?"

"Dig! Then pull me out as the wind takes more sand! I'll make sure it doesn't fall back in. Then we fucking run!"

Better idea.

Pulled my hand back, I dug around his waist as the wind began to howl. I could barely see from particles in the air. Shyntre kept his magic shield to one side, letting the sand build up on this as multiple, whirling spouts of dust and grains sucked the sand from the bottom as I flung it desperately aside. This was working so well that I almost thought the windstorm was *helping*.

When enough sand moved, Shyntre grabbed my shoulder and tried to tug himself out. His hips shifted but he failed to free his legs. I used my arms faster, like the ground rodents burrowing, loosening and tossing the sand so it could be instantly whipped away in the gusts.

Most of the fine sediment didn't leave the trough but landed on the invisible, magical barrier above our heads. Maintaining it was a clear and growing strain on my wizard. He was sweating, turning the red grit to mud sticking to his skin, and I knew we didn't have much more time.

I got up, wrapped both arms under his damp pits, and braced my legs. With all my might, I pulled him upward.

His body shifted, slipping partway out.

"Yes!" he gasped, suppressing a cry of pain while he quivered from fatigue. "Try again!"

Once more.

Using my legs, heels sinking into the side of the hill, I lifted again. *"Hoomph!"*

I could feel him wriggling his way out while I held continuous pull against the sucking sand. Moments later, my bruised and scraped wizard was free; I held him in my arms.

"Sh-shit," he cried. *"S-sira—!"*

The shield containing all that sand finally gave way, about to cover us in an avalanche.

My eyes fixed on our fate when something popped in my skull.

~*NO!*~

The enormous mass of sand exploded as if struck by a giant's fist. Half of it scattered to either side of the pit while the other half shot straight up into the air like a geyser's spout carried away on the wind to rain down elsewhere. The trough sand was already rising up past my ankles. I held Shyntre tight in my arms.

"Last chance," I shouted, jerked my feet free. *"Run!"*

His magic spent, Shyntre obeyed, scrambling up the slippery incline with me. The sand stuck head to foot to his sweaty skin; for one instant, his legs wouldn't hold him. I gripped his arm and climbed, pulling him, pushing us both until I thought I could no longer breathe.

Finally, we reached the top. The wind rushed past, and I saw no shelter. Pulling my weakened wizard's arm over my shoulder, gripping him around his waist, I hauled him farther from the sand trap.

We stumbled on a small cliff of exposed rock to hide from the wind, and we collapsed beside it, wrapping arms tightly around one another for further protection. I moved closer, wrapping a leg around his hip to defend even another handspan of his dry, scraped skin from the scourging storm.

I didn't feel the grains abrading bare skin like he did, and I didn't understand why. They *should* be taking bits of my skin as they whipped past just as they did his. Shyntre buried his face in my neck, and I heard a whimper like Ta'suil's.

Then he grew quiet. Soon, he stopped trembling.

We waited for the windstorm to pass.

Before long, it grew quiet like before, and my determined mage hadn't vanished with the storm. Shyntre clung as if he didn't trust the silence at first but eventually took a deep breath and leaned back. He looked as confused as I felt.

I studied his face, met his eyes.

Goddess, that is gold in his eyes.

My wizard looked exactly as he should, as he always had from the moment I found him in Phaelous's Tower.

Yet it felt like my first time seeing him.

"What..." he began, licking his lips, then spit out sand. *"Peh!"*

I tried not to chuckle before he finished his question.

"What changed, Sirana?"

"What do you mean?"

"You. Here." Shyntre twisted his neck with care, looking at the calm night sky. "Why is the sky so clear? I-I'm not really here, I know it."

I bit my lip. "Do you know anything about a spire?"

Shyntre shook his head. "No."

"Oh. Alright."

"Wait. Why do you ask?"

"Well, that's where the windstorm came from." I pointed up and over the rock which sheltered us. "It's that way."

Shyntre frowned skeptically then sat up slowly to get to his feet. I helped him, and we stepped around to climb atop the rock for a better look.

The spire was gone.

"Well, fuck," I muttered.

My wizard didn't fling any dung at me for this. One side of his mouth curved up as he shrugged his shoulders as if to let it go. He looked around for himself before stopping in place.

"What?" I whispered, following his gaze.

The eight-limbed shadow was still there.

"Oh," I said. "You can see that one? What about the other two?"

"Other two?" he whispered back, looking where I showed him.

He swallowed, the fear confirming he saw one of the two for certain.

"You don't see the third?" I whispered.

Shyntre shook his head, afraid but still confused. "Why isn't she getting any closer?"

"She?"

He gave me a look like I should know better than to ask him for a name. He asked me again, his tone serious. "What changed, Sirana?"

Well...

It was my turn to swallow. "I found a..."

My voice stopped. Whether it was the geas or gut instinct, I didn't know this time, but Shyntre noticed and lifted his hand to take back his question.

"Never mind," he murmured, glancing toward the two shadows on the horizon he *could* see. "Don't tell me. It's better that way. Just keep doing what you're doing."

"I will." I offered a tentative smile. "Seems like it's helping."

My wizard agreed with whatever "it" was, but his eyes dropped so I couldn't see the glimmer of gold. His gaze had fallen on my stomach the moment before his fingers reached out to touch what he could see there.

He stopped. Hesitated.

"Go ahead," I said, "if you want."

Shyntre's shoulders slumped, and part of the fight seemed to go out of him. "I shouldn't. She'll only use it against me later."

I dared not ask what he meant by that, but I tried to think of something else to offer some hope.

"She told me I would come back," I said. "That She saw it happening."

Shyntre nodded, his eyes straying off to one side again. "I believe it, unfortunately."

Ouch.

"Why?"

"I wish you could stay up here." He met my eyes then looked down again. "Both of you. I just want you both to be free."

My chest flushed with emotion, but my mind blanked on how that could even work. What would I do, alone, with just an infant to raise?

"Uhm…"

Shyntre looked up, watched my face for another moment. Then, as if in defiance of his own caution, he leaned in and pressed his lips to the corner of my mouth.

A kiss.

Did the naked wizard just *kiss* me?

"Maybe next time," he murmured, "we won't dream of getting sand in every crease."

"Oh?" My brows shot up, and a grin soon followed. "Ohh. Next time? Like… maybe in a library?"

The wizard smiled with the first touch of humor I could remember in recent memory. "Maybe." He looked down. "Thanks for helping us. Ta'suil needed this."

"But you're the one I ended up helping."

He nodded. "Me instead of him. How it needs to be."

Belatedly, I saw the sky turning purple around us; the stars were dimming quickly. I felt close to waking and knew it somehow.

"How do I know if you need help again?" I asked.

My wizard shook his head grimly. "You don't. But… If it happens, just come wherever it is." He looked around, his gaze shying away from the faraway Drider. "Such a quiet place. This has never happened before."

I smiled without showing my teeth. "I'm glad it helped."

"Yeah. But… I have to go back now." His eyes fixed on mine. "And you should let me go."

Well, damn.

I OPENED MY EYES IN THE LIBRARY, FOR ONCE NEITHER JOLTED nor startled upright. I sensed my spider guardians at once; they rested on the ceiling above me. My chest filled with the deepest breath I could draw. The pendant radiated warmth between my shirt and the blanket. The room was as quiet as most of my dream.

Well, almost.

I heard air whistling through small nostrils and looked down to see the old drake still nestled on the footrest. Thank Goddess I hadn't kicked him in my sleep.

To my left, Gavin's desk seemed still enough to be empty but when I turned my head, the Deathwalker sat in his trance still. His pale hands were at rest, flopped off the arms of his chair; his grimoire and writing supplies lay undisturbed.

I did it. I stayed out of his dreams.

I suppressed the burgeoning cry of accomplishment and looked for Mourn. At first, I didn't see him and wondered if he'd left despite his promise to guard.

Then I spotted him on the carpet in the farthest corner. He seemed to be meditating again. Kurn's Ma'ab sword laid naked across his open, callused palms, the sheath placed on the floor beside him.

As soon as I sat up, the Dragonblood opened his eyes. We stared at each other a moment before he released the blade to sign with one hand.

★Your stone was glowing. Lucid dream?★

★Vividly,★ I replied.

★Do you feel rested, or not?★

I paused. ★I don't know.★

★Lie back down. It lasted barely two hours. You might sleep true this time if you allow it.★

Only two hours?

I studied how still Gavin was, how comfortable the drake looked. I didn't have anywhere to be, I had nothing to do, and I wasn't hungry yet.

Gradually, I accepted this odd languidness, turning over to settle down again. I tugged up the blanket with a quiet sigh.

Webs bind me if the Dragonchild wasn't right again. My mind rested in truth, and I wouldn't wake for hours.

CHAPTER 8

ONCE THE FOUR OF US WERE AWAKE AND MOVING AROUND THE library, we each took our turn using the waste closet with me going first. Afterward, I waited for Mourn to ask me to describe my dream to him.

That was our bargain, after all. He'd proven his knowledge about psions which he'd hinted at during our walk. He'd provided my first mental exercise, the *dorji-ka* breathing, before I fell asleep. Lastly, he'd given me a safe place in which to try.

It must be my turn to trade.

The red dunes had been uncanny in their quiet and clarity. I faced no confusion or haze, no shifting faces or eras. I knew my name, who I was, and I recognized those with me.

"What changed, Sirana? Why isn't she getting any closer?"

That protection Mourn claimed must have worked beyond my boldest imaginings if it had kept the Abyss out of Davrin dreams.

What I didn't understand yet was Mourn's claim about my being out of "reasonable range" of influencing anyone in my sleep. He wasn't wrong about that pattern; those most deeply affected by an unconscious mindlink thus far had been lying near me and asleep as well. But there was one clear exception, or maybe two.

The Deepearth seemed like it should be out of range.

Just a little.

"Hungry?" Mourn asked me instead.

The practical comes before the mystical, I suppose.

"Yes, please."

Graul stretched out his wings with care before gingerly hopping down from the long chaise he'd shared with me. He seemed to be feeling better, moving with greater flexibility as he waddled along the carpet and returned to his dark cubby between two standing shelves. His hiding place was deeper than it appeared; his tail disappeared without his turning around. After some scuffling, I heard the brief clink of metal striking metal.

"Checking on his hoard," Mourn answered before we could ask.

"There must be a larger burrow beyond the bookshelves," the Deathwalker observed.

"Indeed, there is."

"And he collects what, coins?" I asked.

Mourn smiled. "And other shiny things."

"What does he do with them?"

"Practices counting. Sleeps on the pile."

I chuckled at the mental picture. "Is that somehow more comfortable at his age than a soft, stuffed cushion? Is he just mimicking you, or do all shadow drakes collect a hoard?"

The half-blood's smile didn't fade, but he seemed deeply reflective. "In this, he is mimicking me. You are correct other shadow drakes don't collect pieces of civilization and commerce, though they may have other stashes within their nest." Mourn shrugged. "I doubt any of them count, though."

"So, it is his ritual?" Gavin asked. "One that satisfies and maintains a bond with something larger than himself?"

Mourn blinked Draconic eyes at the Deathwalker. "Insightful, and I suppose the answer is yes. His collection has gathered a modest bit of magic over the centuries as well." He nodded to me. "To answer your question, because of that magic, sleeping on the pile is more comforting to his body than the chaise. Another reason he would attack if you sought to disturb it."

"Ah." I waved my hand. "No worry there, Dragon son, I neither need his 'shiny things' nor would I tease him in such a way. Especially knowing it is his medicine."

Mourn took me at my word as our breakfast arrived within the runes of the kitchen delivery chute. I couldn't yet see what it was but waited for the scent to hit me.

"Does he, um, fly anymore?" I asked on impulse.

"Not really." Mourn divided the food using the sticks instead of tilting the bowl. "He can glide short distances but tends to jump shadows, for the landing is less likely to injure him. I can help some with healing but it's not as easy as it used to be."

So, the beast is truly nearing death.

I glanced at Gavin but refrained from asking him if he could sense it when Mourn handed me a wide, shallow bowl out to me. There wasn't a strong scent for once, though I knew it was fresh food.

I saw tidy, separate portions of yellow, segmented fruit, sticky balls of puffy grains squeezed together, two bread-like buns both drier and fluffier than the slick grain pods, and a dense, red paste not unlike the bean paste Gavin had made at the Ley Tower. Nothing was warm, and some were cooler than the air in the room.

"Is this a typical daybreak meal in Yong-wen?" I asked.

"It may be what is on hand," Mourn answered, preparing to eat after offering some to Gavin, who shook his head. "It is still dark out. Many fires aren't stirred up yet, so the hot meals come later."

"I see, and I'm not complaining." I smiled, wondering how he could tell the Sun hadn't risen yet. "Um. Could I try using the sticks again?"

The Dragonblood showed his surprise but retrieved another pair from the hatch for me before taking one of the sturdy chairs. I watched him thread his tail through the gap at the back with obvious practice until it rested like a snake on the carpet. Then I studied how he used the sticks again as he resumed eating.

The one on the bottom doesn't seem to move much. Hm.

I tried a few different hand holds until one was comfortable to maintain then managed to fish out a sticky grain ball followed by a fruit piece, snagging them with my teeth before they could slip. At least the pieces were bigger and not slick as noodles, and the paste was easy to scoop and suck off the ends. However, I simply picked up the bun to bite into it and satisfied my curiosity as well. Whatever the complex, finely minced filling was, I knew it lacked one thing.

"Hm. They didn't send you any meat this time."

Mourn smirked as he ate a bun with his fingers as well. "I don't always require it."

"And the successive owners of this inn know that?" I chewed faster to get to my next bite.

He arched a brow at me. "For three hundred years. Enough time for the Yungians to have noticed I eat whatever they eat. It's easy to tell when they make special things for me which they think are more suitable for a spirit than their normal fare."

He dug a glob of the paste then plucked up a fruit bite and ate them together. I tried that as well, shocked at the wholly taste on my tongue when they mixed. It was like a sauce which would go well with the bun.

"How is it easy to tell?" I asked as I attempted the fruit, paste, and bun in one bite.

He chuckled watching me, swallowing before he spoke. "They don't have the practice. It took a while to convince them my favorite foods are what they make and eat themselves, largely by only eating half of the special stuff. But that's why I'm their *Wen-yung.* Many believe their food is a big source of their luck, and the reason I keep coming back."

I laughed. "Isn't it?"

He kept that smile. "I admit I look forward to eating here each time I come in from the wilderness."

"What about Graul?" I asked before both our bowls were empty. "Does he need any breakfast?"

Amused, Mourn shook his head. "With how much he ate last night, he may not eat again for a day or more. He doesn't like the fruit and *byi* balls much, anyway, though he will lick at the *triu* paste."

That was enough to surmise the shadow drake would be sleeping on his "hoard" for the day, slowly digesting his feast.

Meanwhile, Gavin was on his feet and perusing the shelves for something new after putting the Noiri-Dwarven scrolls away. The three books from yesterday remained on the desk. My eyes landed on his grimoire, and I recalled how much he'd been writing in that last night as the To'vah-krav lectured on his centuries-long observations of psionics.

"What are you going to do when you run out of pages, Gavin?" I asked, looking to Mourn. "Could we get him a second grimoire, perhaps?"

"We could," he agreed. "Yong-wen has book makers."

This irritated my scholar at once. "I prefer to add my own pages and rebind the book. I have the tools. I only need the supplies."

Mourn and I stared at him before the mercenary asked, "Have you done this before?"

"Twice." The gaunt death mage touched a few spines with one finger. "But the paper was too costly to add more than five sheets each, folded to add ten new pages."

"Hm." Mourn's tail moved languidly on the floor as he held his empty bowl with both hands. "We can bring pages for your grimoire by the end of today."

I perked up. *Where to this time?*

"And at least three arm-lengths of book thread," Gavin said by way of acceptance. "Tougher is better. I don't care if it is not supple."

"Also available."

Mourn stood up to take my bowl; baffled, I let him. He returned the used dishes and sticks to the chute, where they soon disappeared. I glimpsed half of a bun still in his bowl just before it vanished.

"Hey, I could have eaten that if you were full," I said.

The Dragonblood chuckled, shaking his head. "I can't believe you spotted that way over there."

"How do I explain? My baby's hungrier than I am most times."

His tail moved with continued humor as he turned around. "A good sign. But to address your concern, that is how I let them know I am satisfied, and they need not send more. If the dishes are sent back empty, they take it as a sign I am not yet filled and send a second helping."

I pondered that sensible solution for a solitary place. "Still a pity about the waste."

"It's not wasted. Someone eats it."

I snorted. "Do the servants fight over your scraps, do you think?"

"Probably," he admitted, "though I don't care to know. Do you need to use the closet before we go?"

That was a good idea.

I stood up to reenter that tight but practical space, experiencing the chilly, smooth-wood seat and awareness of depth beneath my ass. The circle of runes was surprisingly far down, and any smells didn't linger or become strong. I assumed the vanishing act was like the dishes and triggered on contact but, unlike them, this happened without any delay.

"Is it fair to assume," I said, coming out of the closet, "that if anyone drops something down there, we'd have to dig through a massive pile of manure to find it?"

Mourn chortled, nodding. "Correct."

I smiled. "Has that ever happened?"

"I have nothing to say on that."

A sensation of pure glee filled my chest when I saw his face, surging out as a guffaw of comprehension.

"Got it," I said. "I'm glad me and my Sisters didn't have access to something this convenient. The pitching of objects down the hole would be endless."

I heard a brief, low laugh as he nodded. I stepped out of the way to let him visit the closet while I put on my boots and bracers. My spiders had come out of their hiding places, crawling along the ceiling to wait above my head by the time Mourn exited and closed the door behind him.

"I wanted to ask something," he began.

"Hm?" I reached for my belt.

"Would you leave your weapons belt here?"

I blinked at him then at his densely decorated harness still hanging in its place. "You aren't wearing your harness?"

He shook his head. "I won't need it."

"Are you sure?"

Mourn gave me a dry smile and lifted both his wrists, reminding me of the bracers and his permanent cache of weapons.

"Oh, right. Um. What about the relic?" I asked.

"Do you truly see yourself using it after looking around yesterday?"

"Well…"

"It can remain here," Gavin said from across the room. "I won't touch it."

I looked to him sitting at his desk with his new selections; his posture suggested he was waiting for us to make up our minds to leave.

"And it will stay exactly as you leave it," he added.

"Alright," I said slowly. "I still want my cloak against the Sun. And a blindfold as back-up."

Mourn nodded. "Of course. Myself as well. I hadn't planned on walking shirtless in the streets."

That put a smile on my face. "Pity."

He narrowed his eyes, but a quirk at one corner of his mouth suggested he accepted the jest for what it was. Yet, as he let the silence stretch, my face turned warm. I cleared my throat, pointing straight up.

"They must come with me," I said as my smaller guardians started down the wall. "They have never left me willingly, and they were weakened from stress when Brom captured them and kept them in a chest."

Mourn considered this and nodded. "At your nape, out of sight?"

I nodded. "As usual."

"That'll work."

He turned to don his cloak, and I did the same before extending my arm to collect my babies.

Besides collecting paper and thread for Gavin's grimoire, I didn't know what we'd be doing today but looked forward to moving in the fresh, cool air.

OUTSIDE LUNI TI AND AGAIN IN THE INN'S BACK ALLEY, IT WAS predawn with clouds covering the stars and moons. I smelled that a light rain had passed, and another could come at any time. This hadn't deterred the same number of early workers from the previous dawn. They moved carts, cleaned the streets, and relit the lamps which had been snuffed in the rain.

"Whew," I began, speaking our native tongue. "The sky looks nothing like it did in my dream."

Mourn peered down at me. "Subtle."

I shrugged. "Weren't you going to ask as soon as we were alone?"

"Maybe." He motioned me to walk with him. "Or it might wait."

We began in the opposite direction from before, and I growled softly, rubbing my forehead with my fingers. "You mean to say, you'll do as you've bargained but accept the payment when you're ready?"

Mourn nodded. "I only want to know one thing now."

"What?"

"Was your queen there?"

Augh, please, don't let me lose my breakfast…

I slowed down, breathed deep with a steadying hand on my belly. I took another and answered, "No, she wasn't."

Not this time.

He hummed with a nod. "Very good. And good to know."

We started walking.

"And you said my stone was glowing?"

"It was, but this seems to happen when you are communing with a mage or imbued object, like the Deathwalker or Soul Drinker." He frowned. "I'm still trying to figure that out."

I shrugged. "I thought it just glowed in the presence of magic."

He shook his head. "That's not what I've observed."

"Hm. Maybe just strong magic. That's what it used to do."

"Used to?" he prompted. "What changed?"

My mouth twisted. "Three Red Sisters were sent up here."

"Ah."

He didn't follow up; he knew already this triggered the geas.

"It took a lot of magical focus the first time to turn it blue," I volunteered. "Saphgar is just grey in its raw form."

"But it can't be imbued with magic."

"That's what our wizards found out, yes."

"Why was it given to you?"

"My Elder knew I'd changed, and she was trying to help me survive." I shrugged. "It used to shield my mind from thought-reading and will-bending spells. We tested it, me and her, and I know it worked against two Priestesses trying to manipulate me."

Wilsira just kept trying, though.

Mourn looked around as I watched his feet and mine for dung, then he turned us toward someone's back garden, asking, "Is the benefit once provided not so apparent anymore?"

"It was…more difficult to defend against Kurn and the *Ridhian* ruby," I admitted. "And that was the first time I tried to shield my mind from another since reaching the Surface. It certainly *didn't* shield me from Brom's dreams but made them stronger."

The half-blood frowned like that didn't make sense. "You were wearing the saphgar the first time you and he both slept? For certain?"

I nearly tripped and stopped, frozen in place as I recalled the night Gavin died vividly. The dream beneath the waterfall in Koorul, and Brom waking up intensely aroused, desperate to couple after once again meeting his future wife and queen.

Ishuna's sister.

"Sirana?" Mourn asked.

"No, I wasn't wearing it," I whispered with dismay. "I… I'd taken it off. I was trying to hide it from him."

"Aha." The half-blood took a slow step, urging me to continue in more ways than one. "What about when you held Soul Drinker for the first time?"

"I was wearing it, then, for certain," I said. "That was when they… all attacked me in the kitchen. I could feel what they were trying to do. I resisted every moment."

"I believe you, and I would say your pendant clearly still provides you critical protection, even if the boundaries are shifting." Mourn was quiet for a few steps. "Gavin was right. When you traded it to me, you lost that buffer, and the demon in the dagger tried to break you." He shook his head. "Had I known, I wouldn't have made the trade."

I laughed with a touch of bitterness. "I wouldn't have, either."

"The Deathwalker is a strong ally of yours, I hope you realize. To see all this, trade for the stone, and return it to you for nothing."

"Oh, I realize!" I laughed again. "Though the trade wasn't for *nothing*. He didn't want me mindlinking with him when he sleeps. He asked me to stop."

"I don't blame him. Hm. A related question."

"Yes?"

"The night you influenced Kurn and Castis. Were you wearing the stone then?"

"I was, yes," I said, "but I didn't see their dreams, nor did they see mine."

"How are you certain of this?"

I smirked. "Well, first, I only remember *my* dream. I parsed out what they'd done with each other from physical evidence. Second, in all Kurn's accusations, I'm certain that if he'd seen *my* dream, he would have cursed me for sending him a nightmare about being a 'black witch' with tits wearing a removable cock between her legs, using it to fuck her sister up her netherhole until she came so hard, he spurted into his companion's ass at the same moment."

Mourn was silent for several more steps. I savored being able to say that out loud in my own tongue, to sound like a Red Sister again. It was also a pleasant recollection.

I *still* missed Jaunda grabbing me when I least suspected it, missed the way she pulled me into the sluicer or her quarters, or just pushed me against the nearest wall. If we weren't wrestling, she always kissed me first, leaving me breathless before the leathers came down.

"Wow," the To'vah-krav said.

I chuckled. "So understated, Mourn."

"Do I understand correctly," he asked with obvious care, "that the Red Sisters have sex with each other more often than with others outside your group?"

"You could say that. For most, anyway. It's encouraged." I shrugged. "There was strict ranking, though. A novice is dominated to sate her elder Sisters' appetites until she learns to dominate as well."

"Ah."

I stopped talking when I realized my slit was warm and more than a bit damp; I could feel my netherlips rubbing against my leathers, and it was starting to feel really good.

Ah, Goddess, where can I go to rub this one out?

"Is that…" Mourn cleared his throat, and I felt more warmth from him as his cloak drifted around him. "Is that why you seemed aroused after I pinned you in the *dorji-ka?*"

My gut caught fire for an instant. *Oh, yeah, that.*

He could have pulled down my leathers and spread me out. I would have welcomed a quick and hard rut on the mat afterward.

I swallowed *that* response, instead showing my teeth in a smile. "Yes, Mourn, precisely. I can't convey how *truly* dismayed I am that you have no regular place you go for that release. One good sparring like that, and I yearned for the roughness of the Cloister more than any moment since I left."

A light grey sky brightened the East as we followed the road out among the open pastures again, where dwellings and muddy work yards grew sparse. Mourn was frowning deeply inside his hood; he looked to be concentrating on a problem.

I wanted to think he was reconsidering mine.

"So," he began, "you were… properly prepared for attacks like Brom and the Ma'ab before they happened. In some ways, being forced is similar to how you and your sisters play?"

My brows lifted with surprise, though I saw his point and shrugged. "Yes. We're not often sent up here, as you know, so it was circumstantial that I might have been 'properly prepared' for an attack like that.

"However, we're trained to be resilient under pain, pressure, and humiliation. It's not unusual for Red Sisters to learn pleasure from it as well. I did." I pursed my lips in thought. "Because we learn like this, the rest of Sivaraus, especially the Nobles, fear us for what we might do to them."

"As was done to you," Mourn said, "so you do to others."

I nodded, noticing the curve of distaste on his lips. "As we are ordered by our Prime, but that's not all we are, Mourn, nor do all of us think so simply. Our play is real, and it is what it is apart from the city. While we have our eldest, everyone goes through this. No exceptions. I survived and found Sisters I *wanted* to play with, and we watched out for each other. I am not exaggerating when I say our other options were to die or break alone in a cell somewhere."

Mourn grunted as he studied some trimmed rows of bushes. "I understand, I think. I've been around long enough to know why some leaders think this is necessary." He looked at me again, his eyes touched with regret. "I will take from this that you speak the truth."

Had I been lying?

"Truth about what?" I asked.

He looked out at the green fields. "That after a…"

"A fight?"

"A fight," he granted, "like at Troshin Bend, I will accept as truth that part of your recovery is seeking penetration for pleasure, on your own terms, instead of avoiding it."

I smiled, and it was genuine. "Yes. Exactly. I'm not keeping my legs closed because of *them*. Jael would be bitterly disappointed."

His face was quite amusing; he almost looked shy.

"What?" I asked. "Did you not believe me before?"

"I believed you, but I didn't understand," he replied calmly. "There's a difference."

"Hm. Fair."

"Thank you for explaining more," he added. "I will try harder to find a way you can claim that release in Augran."

You will?

Goddess, now I was hot as I'd been on the sparring mat, just without the breathlessness and fighter's surge. No doubt I didn't need to lick my fingers before sliding them in deep.

Argh!

I exhaled loudly to get his attention. "Mourn. I've waited more patiently than I knew I ever could, but I need some release now. Is there any place I could go to... do the same as I did on our way to Port Fortnight? Just quickly."

He swallowed, looking above the bushes and out at workers heading into the open fields. I grimaced.

Bad timing again, damn it all.

"There," he said, motioning toward one of the few copses of trees nestled between the road and the fields. "Still darker on the west side. I think we can disguise our shape long enough for you to finish."

We?

I tried not to sound teasing. "You aren't sending me alone while you wait by the road?"

"I wouldn't be a good bodyguard if I did that." He motioned. "Come on, before the Sun climbs higher."

The quick jog over the rough dirt and patches of weeds to reach new cover was just what I needed to get my blood pumping. I laughed softly as we came to a halt, felt a quiver of anticipation as I chose the widest tree trunk in the cluster to brace my back against.

"Here?" he asked.

"Yeah, here is good," I panted, already tugging loose the leather thongs at each hip. It was a pleasant change that my belt and weapons weren't in the way when I pushed my pants down to my thighs.

With a touch, I confirmed I was already slick between sensitive netherlips, plenty of wetness to spread around before dipping my fingers in. Even if Mourn wouldn't join me, even if he would only stand guard, he was still close by. He would probably smell me again, like when I'd been rocking in the saddle.

Not a bad smell. Just distracting.

Plenty of mental spice to get started.

Lubricating my fingers, I slid them along my slit and went in firm. I tested my stretch while rubbing the heel of my palm in a circle against my keen little nub. I closed my eyes to concentrate. Tilted my head back.

Oh, yes…

A shadow fell over me, and two hands braced against the trunk above my head. My eyes popped open, my private moment getting warmer as Mourn's cloak shifted on either side to shield me from easy view.

I stared up at him, my hood in place as I felt my spiders shift then settle down again. "What are you doing?" I whispered.

"Obscuring our forms while you finish."

I couldn't believe my eyes. "You're going to *watch?*"

"I shall keep watch, yes."

He didn't bat an eye. I was certain he had understood, yet I couldn't read his intent beyond what he'd said.

"That's not what I—"

My sex pulsed impatiently at the interruption, and truly, what was the worst he'd do: stick his cock somewhere warm and ready?

I could enjoy that.

"Oh, fuck it," I growled, returning attention to my drooling slit where it belonged.

So be it. Watch me, then, Dragon son. Listen, breathe me in, and try to stand guard at the same time, you obtuse, teasing… oh!

This blatant, soggy indulgence wasn't just me imagining. The large hybrid granting me such generous cover could act as calm of voice as he pleased, but his tail wrapped twice around his left ankle, the constriction practically strangling it.

A hint even harder to miss was the pole trying to turn those loose, coarse bottoms into a tent.

Enjoying the scent, aren't you?

I rubbed harder, gasping harder, well aware of the squishing noises from my crotch as I stared at his hard, bare abdomen and hidden erection. My eyes drifted over his odd patches of scale blending with smooth, dark skin. I wanted to trace the irregular lines where the two transitioned but kept my hands busy with myself.

My thighs had begun to quiver when he murmured, "What are you thinking about doing to me, Red Sister? Right now."

I heard a subtle warning.

Are you serious…?

"*Ungh*," I grunted, grimacing as I lost momentum trying to think of something that wouldn't insult him yet wasn't an obvious lie.

Ahhh, shit. I had nothing.

"Touching your scales," I confessed hoarsely. My hands didn't stop even if they slowed down.

"Do not," he replied like it was a helpful suggestion.

I snickered. "I won't. My hands are full."

He grunted. "Tell me what you are staring at."

That one was easy.

"The pole right in front. Rising to attention."

"Ah."

His voice paused, his hips shifting slightly so that the ridge traveled across his gusset. I hummed with appreciation.

So, he can be playful.

"Would a clear look at that 'pole' help your concentration?"

My eyes popped but didn't leave his crotch.

Ohhh, you are fucking teasing, now.

"I'm getting close," I said.

"Not an answer, Red Sister."

My fingers plunged deeper, then faster, like I was getting fucked by a Feldeu. I heard him breathe in through his teeth. His tail unwrapped from one ankle, and for a moment, I thought it would dart toward me. Instead, it weaved and coiled up on itself.

"Fine," I huffed. "I want to see it."

"You've already seen it," he reminded me. "By the river."

My breath escaped as a hot hiss. "You weren't aroused."

He did not deny this. I heard his tongue flick out above my head, then one hand left the tree trunk.

A thumb hooked the top of his pants, and I almost choked.

What in the web does he want?

"Would it *add* to your peak?" he asked. "Or are you just curious?"

Ffff…

"Seeing it would add," I admitted.

"Agree not to grab me."

"Huh?"

"Agree not to grab me," he repeated, tugging the black cloth. "And I'll show you."

My ears brimmed with the sound of my galloping heart. I could neither blink nor take my eyes from where his thumb dipped into his waistline. It took several moments to absorb what this was.

Another small bargain before we settled on the big one.

Another test.

I found my voice at last. "A-agreed. I won't grab you."

"Not your hand or mouth, or any part of you," he added. "Only look."

I'd never wanted a male to spin me around and plunge inside me more than right then. I couldn't seem to catch my breath.

"Agreed!" I panted. "No touching. Only look."

My hand squeezed and massaged my cunt, trembling as I held my climax back, waiting for him to decide if this verbal agreement was enough.

He hesitated, as if considering a regrettable lapse in wisdom. I made a sound between a chuckle and a growl of frustration; he certainly had *me* trapped between reason and babbling stupidity!

"Show me your cock, Mourn." I breathed in once and released it like at the *dorji-ka*.

It helped.

"Keep your word, Dragonborn, I'll keep mine."

His hand moved slowly, stretching his waistline down far enough for me to see hints of black hair at the base of his shaft. It wasn't as thick as the white fur might be on a bua, but he wasn't hairless around his groin.

I missed that by the river.

The hybrid reached with his large hand to lift his genitals out, gently tucking his pants beneath a recognizable Elven scrotum enlarged for his size. My own hand sped up again, throttling my cunt as he wrapped his hand around his prick and gave it a long pull. Clear liquid dripped from the tip, forming a long string to the soil between my boots.

"Oh, my goddess!" I whispered, sharpening my pace.

Any curiosity I'd had about what else he'd inherited from his sire was thoroughly satisfied.

"What?" he asked, a bit short of breath.

"Stroke it again. Please…"

His hand wrapped around it with plenty left to feed into one's mouth. Although his glans had been covered by a typical foreskin while flaccid and seemed Elvish, it had now engorged to reveal a startling shape and incredible breadth such that not even a blind Davrin could mistake it for the cock of a pureblood.

The head looked like a deep-piercing arrowhead and reached a size that would stretch my lips open more than D'Shea's largest Feldeu. It wasn't difficult to imagine how the pointed, purple-red tip would trace the back of my throat as I tried to suck.

The black skin of his shaft pulled taut over random, hard nubs like there could be scales underneath as well. I saw a ridge like a dorsal stripe along the top which gave him a slight curve upward, as well as a spot on the underside which dipped down to form the thickest part of his length in the middle.

He also had a modest bulge near the base, smaller than Kerse. I wondered if it could swell more, such that Mourn might "lock bodies" like the Sathoet while joined with a female. Though unsure how I felt about it in this moment, I could still believe this cock had been born of a Dragon, not a demon.

"Oh, wow," I whispered as heat flashed through my gut. "What a remarkable ride."

Mourn's hand paused for an instant but then stroked faster along his shaft, smearing his own gloss over that turgid trident.

"Oh, yes. Keep going."

My cunt clasped at my fingers, and I moaned high in my throat without looking away. My fingers pressed hard to the hot spot inside my slit, my other hand manipulating my sopping netherlips with intense focus. Sideways and around, my determined fingertips danced until my clit was at last content with their lavish attention.

"*Ffiuuck, yesss*," I growled as… *At last!*

I reached my peak and fell with profound relief over that edge.

My eyes squeezed shut against the strong grey light as my body relaxed into that first wave; I felt it crash into me as my release soared through my core. My throat exchanged gasps of air for chirps of cascading pleasure as my broken tension drained deliciously away.

Above my slumping head, I heard Mourn's breath, ragged in a very familiar way. Then it hitched once.

Stopped.

Is he...?

The Dragonblood crouched slightly, his hood covering his face but for feral teeth. His grip aimed his cock at the roots of the tree as his toe talons dug deep into the soil; claws scraped and cracked the bark next to my ear. His tail lashed as if trying to snatch something out of the air before the distal third of it started vibrating in place.

A long stream of cum landed between my boots.

I pressed my back to the trunk, eyes fixed, legs shaking and desperate to stay upright. My sticky hands grabbed my bare thighs, and I braced to hear him groan, as the tip of his cock gushed clear fluid in five strong pumps, all of which splattered the tree roots beneath me.

Oh, fuck!

His cock's issue had stopped, yet he couldn't relax as he grunted in place. *He's still coming.*

His tail and his toes seemed to be the best indicators of when he was truly finished. The former flopped lax to the ground, and the claws finally pulled back out of the dirt.

Wow.

My head swam.

...what just happened?

I'd begun to catch my breath when he pulled his spine upright, his chest swelling with air, and his tongue flicking out, missing my face by a finger's width. He let his equipment hang over the waist of his pants as it slowly deflated.

"Don't... touch anything," he reminded me, as if I needed it.

Judging how he flinched from a breeze, no doubt he was extremely sensitive.

Just as well. I was still trying to clear my head.

"I'm certain you weren't keeping watch," I said.

"Most of it," he protested. "Regardless... I set a ward and our lines were obscured before you started."

If I was honest, that was what me and my Sisters would have done during a fuck-break outside of the Cloister.

Mourn drew in a deep breath, let it out, and lifted his head until I could finally see his face. He appeared as usual—calm and hard to read—as he pulled his relatively clean genitals back inside his pants.

I sighed, realizing far too late that I hadn't brought my belt, so I didn't have any cloth. I used my blindfold to wipe down my hands and crotch; it wasn't enough, and I could have sworn Mourn almost laughed.

His tail did, regardless.

"What?" I asked, squinting up at him as the morning brightened behind thinning clouds.

"Apologies," he said. "I hadn't thought about this possibility when I asked you to leave your belt behind."

Heh, I should have.

I smirked, shrugged, and swept up my juices the best I could. If the scent lingered in my pants, so be it.

As I got my leathers settled back into place, tying the second set snug at my hip, I said, "You seemed pent up."

"Mm."

The half-blood was scanning the roads again. A horse drew a cart fairly far away on someone's plantation; they weren't coming this way.

I asked, "Were you planning to join when I insisted on a break?"

He thought about his answer for several seconds.

"No," he admitted, looking at me again. "But it has been a long time."

I smiled a little. "Dare I ask how long?"

Mourn huffed like he'd expected the question. "Before I started tracking you."

"Oh, shit," I said, blinking in genuine surprise. "So... now you're good for another three months?"

"Possibly," he said seriously, surveying the fields around us. "Thank you for keeping your word."

Keeping my...? Oh.

I crossed my arms, waiting with a grin on my face until he finally looked at me. "I found out yesterday what happens when you are touched in a time or place you aren't expecting it. Wiser to keep that word, yes?"

The mercenary held my eyes like it was a challenge but softened to let out a chuckle. "Well. I am glad you aren't insulted in how I joined."

I pursed my lips in confusion. "Hm. Why would I be?"

He shrugged and turned halfway, signing politely to start walking. I refrained from rolling my eyes.

Sure. Why not? I still had no idea what we were doing today besides finding Gavin some paper and thread.

We left the copse of trees to regain the dirt road. The damp air from the rain grew warmer. The Surface noises never stopped through my afterglow. I listened to our feet walking, to Mourn's tail occasionally scuffing the ground, to flying and chirping birds above us and breezes through leaves and grasses. Among vague and distant calls lived that subtle hum of life plus activity from Yong-wen's center.

Yet just silence in the half-blood walking next to me, and unsettling enough that I quelled a string of separate urges tempting me to break it. I would eventually, but I discarded question after question as either inane, assuming, or invasive.

I returned more than once to the last question I'd asked.

When I cleared my throat, his tail pulled into a tight snake's curve.

He turned his head. "I apologize for my tone in speaking to you, Sirana."

I closed my mouth. *Huh? Tone?*

"Especially as you hadn't invited me," he finished, "and I didn't ask."

My words dissolved in a new haze of confusion, and I had to start over.

Damn it.

I sighed. "Could I convince you of something simple, Mourn?"

He seemed tense but ready to talk. "Convince me of what?"

"I *enjoyed* your tone, how you spoke to me. It was a surprise but not an insult. Your cock alone, intriguing as it is, could not have aroused me so high as when you presented it with your voice. Lust talk can make it better."

I grinned in the face of his skepticism. He needed a little more convincing. *Very well.*

"Mourn, you could not have been clearer what you wouldn't tolerate from me," I continued, "while telling me you wanted to play. Your 'tone' coaxed me to speak my thoughts, so you knew what interested me. Your actions were *informed* by my answers, yes?"

With apparent caution, he nodded.

"An even trade," I noted. "Meanwhile, you held yourself to the same restriction, though that was not in our spontaneous bargain. You even kept your tail from touching me, which seemed incredibly difficult."

The Dragonblood narrowed his eyes. "Is that how you see my actions?"

I shrugged lightly. "If you would invite yourself into a Red Sister's play with no experience and very little foreknowledge, I think you found a persuasive way to do it."

I paused to judge how far he might be convinced. Regardless, this was true for me, and my sex finally felt satiated.

"You're complimenting me," he said, like this had just occurred to him.

I pulled my hood over my eyes before tilting my head back to laugh.

"I wouldn't be complimenting you if our places had been reversed," he growled.

"So what?" I replied. "We're different minds. Vastly different ages, skills, experience. I insist that you hear me, though. You never coerced me, and you didn't insult me. Whatever way you see this, that was *much* more fun than slapping my slit alone. Thank you for the play, and I would be open to it again."

Mourn pondered that in silence for another score of steps, his tail active as his thoughts and almost as complicated.

"Heard and acknowledged," he said. "If not understood, yet."

I huffed a laugh. "That is acceptable."

Far easier was it to accept some quiet between us. The many questions I'd had seemed unimportant now that I had countered his assumption of insult.

Especially as you hadn't invited me, and I didn't ask.

He had not planned on playing, and he admitted that. Was it an impulse, or a temptation too strong to resist?

I don't require much sex.

I was beginning to doubt that.

Mourn was the opposite of impulsive, claiming a lack of options which didn't trouble him over Human lifetimes. Then along came me, the first Davrin cait he'd met in centuries, and she wants to rub herself to climax out in the open against a tree while he watched.

Hells, I'd have joined in, too.

Don't grab me, and I'll show you.

Not your mouth, or any part of your body.

Only look.

I glanced up at him briefly but stifled yet more questions. Two lingered in my mind for longer than the others.

Was your Matron's House as bad for you as Thalluen was for me?

And how did you escape?

CHAPTER 9

LIGHT RAIN RETURNED TO YONG-WEN FROM THE GREAT LAKE at the same time Mourn and I exited the small countryside to tread the cobbled streets. We strolled in silence for all that time, as I'd resolved to let him speak first when he had something to say.

Early signs suggested it would be a long wait. For once, the To'vah-krav had more going on in his head than I did in mine. I wagered his unplanned play had stirred up a memory, probably a wound from the Deepearth which he hadn't thought upon for a significant amount of time.

Possibly longer than I've been alive.

A sobering thought.

This followed weeks of an experienced mercenary contemplating where I'd come from while he patiently aided me to sort out my churning head where wounds new *and* old conflated.

The pressures of the Ma'ab, the warp rot forest, and a sorcerer with a relic from a previous Matriarchy. All warring with my geas protecting the current one. Not to mention bartering for Jael, going to Manalar with Gavin, and now knowing Captain Isboern is a psion in control of his own mind...

A part of me feared Mourn might try to back out of our bargain because of this moment he had chosen to engage. My only defense was to heap his many actions and words onto my own fear to smother it.

If he runs from this on account of watching each other toss our pleasures in a field, then he's far less balanced than he claims.

I could not avoid trouble with my geas if Mourn tried to force us out of an agreement, but his doing so would signal a lack of self-awareness I did not believe was the case.

At the same time, if the Dragonchild would lay at my feet a similar blame in sex as Kurn, Brom, or even Jacob, then I must see it for myself. Soon was better, and this was the best chance I'd get.

The challenge was to be as patient as he had been with me thus far. I imagined it like my first stakeout at House Itlaun and my Elder's forceful words of advice.

*Until you learn to appreciate pure observation of the moment rather than **expecting** anything to happen, your missions will feel agonizingly long, with ample opportunities to ruin your chance of witnessing those actions which come naturally. If you ruin too many opportunities from youthful impatience or willful ignorance, you'll never learn to see your chances as they come. You'll simply run out of options or be forever blind to them.*

I'd once thought Elder D'Shea had had too much wine to speak so grand yet vague about my future or how much control I had over it. Yet, her words seemed relevant here.

She was older than Mourn, with a defiant son who'd been stolen from her and also resented her for the many "chances" she didn't take on account that she *couldn't,* because of Wilsira and the Valsharess.

My Elder lived with a geas of her own for centuries…

Shyntre's existence and his shackles to the Palace and Sanctuary suggested a great many more cuts from the Abyss's Web upon my Elder's mind than the Dragonchild had ever faced in Vuthra'tern. D'Shea would know about running out of options even when one wasn't ignorant or young.

She would have no patience for a novice stuck in one, the other, or both, but she'd always said I could bend, and I could learn.

I can do this, Elder. I see this opportunity, but I know there's no way to rush what comes naturally.

Mourn and I roamed about without apparent direction while avoiding the thickest crowds. While he only paused to note the changes since he'd last been here, I mapped this new city to a level of detail I'd never expected to enjoy firsthand.

The architecture was truly distinctive, with scents, work yards, and the rare glass front window offering me hints of the many crafts and services we passed. I missed much more for not being able to read the scripts. Nonetheless, I saw enough art and sculpture of similar creatures to know what sort they venerated.

Dragons and cranes, of course. Horses make sense. Fish, crickets, and... chickens? Male chickens. And massive, horned bulls with low hanging testicles.

I smirked at the last one, though the next animal to give me pause was the red and orange firebird. Mourn noticed.

"Bird of wonder," he offered, his first words in several hours. "Or in Yungian, *quijizi.*"

I didn't catch how many syllables that had. "What does it mean to Yong-wen?"

"Rebirth," he said. "As when a forest burns. In the stories, the spark is dropped by a flaming bird, whose flight and further spreading of the flames will allow new growth to rise from the ashes."

I blinked. "Forests burn?"

The half-blood smiled a little. "Every year. Caused by lightning striking tall trees, or a careless fire tender. It helps clear out dead wood, quickens seeds, and refreshes its soil. The cycle lasts much longer than a Human life, however, so it is also a catastrophe which may force many to move elsewhere to avoid starvation."

I frowned. "There aren't forests to burn in the Desert, right?"

"Correct." He looked confused. "Why do you ask?"

"Cris-ri-phon wore a ring with that same bird, I am certain. Is it a Desert symbol as well?"

"It might be," he said, sounding like he didn't know. "It would mean something different in their stories."

But it was clear he didn't know those legends. He certainly didn't help cultivate them.

My stomach growling audibly before Mourn thought of food, but he hesitated on where to go.

"I'd like more of those steam pies," I suggested, "if they're not sold through."

He nodded, his shoulders lowering a tiny bit. "Very well."

I smiled as he retrieved them in disguise like last time. If his mind wasn't fully present in showing me the wonders of his haven, I didn't need him to stumble through a presentation of something new, making his escort today more awkward.

We reentered the green stretch of land along the North, stopping in some dense trees to eat standing up because the bench was taken. There were two pies left over to take with us when we continued; Mourn didn't have a large appetite.

I noticed we went deeper into the park than we had last time. "What lies this way?"

"Niss."

"Sorry, what?"

"Niss, the Northwest quadrant of Augran."

"Oh, right. And the other two, remind me?"

"Alran is across from Niss," he said. "The Northeast is the oldest part of the city leading toward Taiding."

"Ah, that makes sense. You said Alran is heavily Dwarven as well."

"Correct."

"And what is Southeast?"

"Bor. A mix of older Paxian and Noiri traditions with some Dwarven as well."

His tone brought back our discussion on the boat, and I grinned. "Sometimes horse-riding Kurgan come to Bor from off the steppes, right?"

Mourn blinked like he was surprised I remembered. "Correct."

"Alran, Bor, Yong-wen," I recited, tapping my chin. "Niss. That was the quadrant you said was changing rapidly right now. Heavily Paxian with a lot of refugees or exiles from Manalar."

"Hm." He was more than surprised; he sounded pleased. "Indeed, yes. Good memory."

"Any particular reason we are headed this way?"

Mourn frowned. "Not really. We aren't going to Niss if that was what you wondered. It wouldn't be as safe for you."

"Very well." Knowing this much, I could relax more into the stroll. I *had* begun to wonder.

Over the next hour, I estimated the park was about a quarter the size of Yong-wen's commerce center, not counting the docks. The animals seemed of light and small variety, those that benefited more from being near the settlement than out in the wild with greater competition, with their habits not too disruptive to how Humans did things.

Hm. Like down around Low Gate, with more fur and feathers.

We exited out the other side of the park nearer to the mason yard where we'd met Talov Baradum. At no point in the last three hours was there not at least one Yungian watching from a respectful distance or to whom we came close enough that they bowed their heads and vanished.

"This is truly astonishing, you know," I said.

"Hm?"

Still distracted.

I smiled. "Parading around as if to convince every Yungian alive that you are real and without threat or crowding you. Now you have spirits of life and death keeping you company. I wager the youngest have had as good a look at me as the eldest have ever had of you. If you didn't want it this way, we wouldn't have covered about every street and trail in Yong-wen the last two days, yes?"

He drew in a breath and released it. "Correct, Baenar."

A step back in familiarity.

"I don't mind the exercise after all those days in a ship's hold," I said. "I need my endurance. But as I'm participating willingly, could you offer me insight as to how walking in broad daylight with you helps your plans and stories?"

He grunted. "Fair question."

Yet he still needed to think over how to answer.

"Short term plans," he began. "This gives ample opportunity for different eyes to understand what we search for at Manalar. Also convincing beyond any statement I could give that a Davrin Elf is of great interest to the Dragon Spirit."

I was truly taken aback. "We're doing this for Jael?"

"Yes. It will also refresh any old descriptions so we will know more quickly if any other Davrin are sighted on the Surface."

"I thought word about your interest and doings didn't leave Yong-wen."

"Not as quickly, but it would be impossible to prevent all talk about me." He shrugged. "May as well keep it accurate in one place."

I squinted. "Doesn't that place a target on your back elsewhere? Surely your skin is valuable to some mistaken mage ruler."

Mourn chuckled. "I'm not easily seen elsewhere. They're still describing shadows and demons outside Yong-wen."

"What of one tracking you who could be your equal?"

Suddenly, he looked interested. "Like who?"

I hesitated, thinking it obvious now that the hybrid had the only Davrin-Dragon cock on the Surface.

"Another Dragonchild?" I answered. "One sired by the purple one in the Lake, perhaps?"

Mourn stopped on the street to stare at me.

"What?"

"Huh," he began. "Is that pure thought experiment?"

I scratched an itch beneath my hood. "Yes?"

"Impressive." He nodded as we started up again. "There *was* another Dragonchild in Augran when I first got here, and the stories of him *did* place a target on my back when I moved into the area. We discovered each other soon enough, competing for the territory to collect for our hoard here." He paused. "One of the few times I had no option but to fight."

"Clearly, you won," I said with a smirk.

"I did." He smiled. "With Graul's help."

I chortled. "You're not jesting?"

"Absolutely not. Never underestimate the advantage a shadow jumper can give you in a close contest."

"Heh. I shan't. So, does this mean you..." I waved my hand. "You would rather know sooner than later if another Dragonchild or Elf comes near? So, you maintain some accuracy in the Humans' short-life stories."

"Correct. If one who could be my equal knows I'm here, it's better to draw them out than spend even greater effort to obscure my own presence. When I do that, Human and Dwarven eyes miss more signs of another power moving in."

The thought struck that this had worked extremely well in drawing *me* out. Even Sarilis way out at the Ley Tower had heard the stories, and he pointed me in this direction. It hadn't mattered that I'd never considered a Dragonborn. I still came this way.

"Hm. And this is what you learned from your predecessor?"

"Correct."

"What if 'another power' moving in is female?"

Mourn smirked down at me. "I am either allied with her or I become aware of her long before she will become aware of me. Usually, I have options other than killing."

The latter part was piercingly accurate, and I was not long parsing out the former. "You consider Krithannia your equal?"

"Easily. She may be more."

No pinched pride there.

"And you became aware of me and Jael long before we knew you were there—"

"Correct."

"—but we're too young to be your equal," I finished my thought.

"You have that potential, and I would be foolish to ignore it. The same with the psion captain, the Deathwalker, and the 'death-less' Sorcerer-General. Such figures appearing among the younger races can only be allies or competitors, given enough time."

"True," I agreed. "Are any those you call enemies? Not just competitors."

I felt his reluctance before he said it.

"Enemies..." Mourn looked upward. "That is a word which takes a great deal of personal harm to earn, Sirana. It is not so easy as it once was."

Sirana. Back to the more familiar.

"I do not use this brand lightly anymore," he continued. "I've witnessed how this is a mistake, and a weakness in my long-term thinking around the young races. A competitor who lives as long as I do isn't always an enemy, and it is better not to limit myself by getting my pride involved. An enemy who cannot truly destroy me and will die within fifty years may not be worth the consequences of tormenting or killing them for an insult."

"That's...very interesting, Mourn," I replied, turning this over. "I've never heard the like."

"I know."

Hmph. Where did he learn to think like this? Not among my own, the Tragar, or the Humans I'd met thus far.

They would all consider this a weakness. Letting an insult go only gave permission to invite another.

At the same time, he wasn't wrong about simply outliving them. If a Human happened to insult him but would die soon enough and was powerless to harm what mattered most, why bother granting them such attention and wasting one's energy and focus? This was exactly what those I considered enemies wanted. So far, I'd had no options but to give it.

"Is this why you take contracts instead?" I asked, imagining his way of living. "Not for pure greed, but the 'young races' can deem each other peers while you cannot. Thus, they determine their own enemies, and sometimes that's to your benefit to help cull some of them for gold you plan to obtain anyway."

Mourn smiled wryly. "That's accurate enough. I've said I prefer a healthy and creative city. Some figures are too unbalanced and detrimental to that long-term goal. Even being short-lived, they cause destruction that outlasts them by decades.

"If their system will allow it and the consequences of a kill can be understood in *their* own history, not mine, then for certain I can 'cull' a few harmful actors for gold I would obtain regardless. This also helps me learn who the actors truly are."

"Hm! I think I understand." I was smiling now. "I didn't before."

He smiled back. "No reason you should. These urges and some of these 'long view' lessons come from my Sire."

"When he speaks to you from down below," I recalled. "In lucid sleep."

Mourn only nodded though his tail seemed hypnotically calm as the visible part attracted as much attention on its own as the two of us did together. I noticed we would soon approach the *dorji-ka* just past the next crossroad.

The half-blood was talkative again, and for that, I was glad. He still sought to share information and understanding with me. It seemed, in his "long view," that he wanted me as an ally, not a competitor.

In this moment, sadly, I was both.

I can take a small risk, perhaps...

I tapped his elbow and motioned ahead. "Any chance I could learn a few of those 'forms' I saw the younger ones do before we bargain for Gavin's paper? No sparring, I can keep my top on, and we don't have to stay all afternoon."

I wagered Mourn's surprise was a pleasant one though held a newer caution.

"And if you become aroused in a room of half-naked buas, Red Sister?" he asked with dry humor.

Quiet delight bubbled out between my lips.

"I will look," I said. "I won't touch."

Those were the correct words to convince him to agree.

"YOU MAY HAVE TO COMMUNICATE MORE IN TRADE," HE BEGAN, accepting one of the two leftover pies while I chomped into the other. "So I need to tell you a few legends before we get there."

Now I understood why we hadn't taken the main street directly to the *dorji-ka* and weren't in a hurry. We meandered a long way around into the alleys, giving Mourn and me time, privacy, and a chance to eat, while he spoke quietly in Davrin.

"If any suggest or ask if you come from the South with your accent," he instructed, "do *not* claim it. You are a sky warrior of the Great Lake who became a body of flesh in the mists of the Archipelago. You are searching for your sister spirit who has not returned from a dangerous mission. In those mists, you encountered the Yungian spirit of Death, *Sho'shien*, who was also looking for a physical form."

"Sho'shien," I confirmed. "I heard Mai say that."

Mourn nodded, his first bite of his pie consuming a third of it. I waited for him to chew and swallow before he continued.

"This is the story for the Deathwalker in their midst as well. *Sho'shien* is being carried within a monk of Hia-Yo, long exiled from Manalar."

"Wait, who? Are there Yungians at Manalar?"

The half-blood shook his head. "Hia-Yo is the Sun God."

"You mean, Hia-Yo is Musanlo?"

"Different perceptions and stories, but yes, the essence is the same."

"Alright. So, I got a body in the magic mist, and met an exiled monk of Musanlo carrying the spirit of Death. What happened next?"

"Gavin had been returning to Niss by boat and accepted the spirit of *Sho'shien* into him, and *Sho'shien* taught a new spirit to speak to Humans using Gavin's tongue. Because of this, your speech sounds like his. You stayed with him as you sought your sister's path and, soon after, I found you both near the borders of Yong-wen."

"Got it." I pondered. "Why was *Sho'shien* looking for a physical form on a boat?"

"The war coming to the South," he answered, smirking a little. "*Sho'shien* in Yungian legend is drawn to Ma'ab battles, to help assure the souls of the dead make it to the heavens and are not eaten by the Ascended. Gavin's arrival in Yong-wen helps the story that *Sho'shien* is still protecting the free souls of warriors who fall in battle. This also tells the people here that the conflict at Manalar is inevitable and imminent."

I was astonished how close this story was to the truth, with wise explanations for what could be noted by any witness without giving away too much. The story covered only where I'd been recently, prevented a need to fake or lie about what lay South of here, while at the same time explaining Gavin's appearance, knowledge, and vowed direction.

It also supported why Mourn and I had been walking around to give them a good look of the new "sky warrior" spirit.

To make it known their Wen-yung seeks another who looks like me.

We finished our pies before I asked, "Have you told anyone this story, yet?"

He nodded. "Master Shi, yesterday. Which means his brother, Shi Mu Kuo, will know it already, as will his sons, Renshu and Hulin, who were there yesterday practicing their forms for you."

"Understood. Which means it is safe to assume a great many others now know the story as well?"

"Correct."

"In that case, what *is* a sky warrior of the Great Lake?" I asked. "And how does showing my chest yesterday help Mai after *Sho'shien* touched her?"

Mourn's mouth stretched with amusement. "A sky warrior watches over the Great Lake. Your dark color of flesh signifies the storms when the celestial beings are fighting devils in battle. Your eyes and sacred pendant signify both the calm sailor's sky and the water's tumultuous depths."

Okay…

"These together with your beauty and proven femininity, showing your breasts," he nodded to them, "offers that balance of protecting the life of the Great Lake while sometimes being called to spill blood into it."

Hm.

"Wait, ahm," I glanced down at my chest. "Beauty?"

Mourn looked surprised. "Yes, beauty. Trust me, though you look foreign and frightening when you fight, you have ethereal beauty in their eyes as well. You are as they expect sky beings of eternal youth to appear to them."

I shrugged. "Well, we're not eternal…"

He arched a brow. "You may as well be if it takes a thousand years for your hair to turn fully blonde, which only makes you look younger than you began."

Fair point.

"As *Janshi-lantiu* traveling with *Sho'shien* himself," Mourn finished, "this gives you a connection to their homeland, Yung-An, to the North and West. The Lake waters touch both Augran on the South shore and their largest city, Yong-ch'hai, on the North shore, settled near the other end of the Archipelago."

I tried to fix that to my growing mental map. A pity Gavin couldn't be here taking notes. "Alright, last question. Why did *Wen-yung* find *Sho'shien* and *Janshi-lantiu* and bring them here?"

"Very good." He approved of my pronunciations. *"Wen-yung* is their mystical guardian of their city gates. All the Dragon statues you have seen represent me challenging powerful spirits near their borders and discovering their intentions before either allowing them in or turning them away.

"I sensed you two in Niss, and that's why I return to Yong-wen now. With the war and missing Lake spirit, you were both deemed part of the balance and allowed to enter Yong-wen."

"With escort," I added.

"With escort," he agreed.

"Good to finally understand. So, the next part of the story which helps Mai slough off the touch of Death is…?"

"We're still working that out."

"We?" I grinned. "Should I remove my shirt again?"

"We will read the room, first." He glanced at me pointedly. "As a spirit should always do."

"Of course," I chuckled.

That wasn't a negative.

"SPIRITS, WELCOME! *WEN-YUNG*, YOU HONOR US A SECOND SUN, greatly!"

Through this greeting, Master Shi's expression contained intriguing nuance: the pride, the pleasure, and the awe I'd seen all over Yong-wen, but also a subtle concern and fear. Perhaps he was thinking back to yesterday for potential insult or some other punitive reason *Wen-yung* would return so soon.

He doesn't visit the same place twice very often.

The master of the *dorji-ka* stepped back and bowed, during which I secretly released my spiders. By the time he straightened up, Master Shi had his expression back under control, yet he waited with eyes up, hoping for a hint of an explanation. I anticipated Mourn was of the mind to be generous.

"*Janshi-lantiu*," he began, motioning with respect to me, "is curious about your forms which cultivate *ging*. Your house is the first with these disciplines she has seen in her travels in the mortal realm. She asked to return today."

"Ah!" Master Shi's concerns melted from his whole demeanor; he turned to bow formally to me. "Sky-watcher and protectress of life, these are but daily cultivation of our own small spirits, like a farmer tending his field."

"Indeed, such workers are small and easy to overlook from far above," Mourn added. "But when watched up close, even spirits see they possess ancient knowledge of the good life, practice and knowledge passed for millennia. *Janshi-lantiu* has recognized this and wishes to study closer."

As Master Shi bowed his thanks to Mourn and then to me, my eyebrows crept up my brow. Would we speak *entirely* in Trade to include me? Was I expected to speak in these same songful, poetic tones?

I hope not.

I didn't know what to say at first, although I did bow. This master had seen me as "savage" and "inhuman" when sparring with Mourn, who insisted I also represented "ethereal beauty." Better that I do not fake too much either way. My Yungian titles still shifted anyway, becoming mixed.

Warrior from the clear sky. Sky-watcher. Protectress of life.

At least these names suited me while the Dragon Spirit nudged the Humans on behalf of one unimportant servant girl.

"I do not want to watch," I spoke at last. "I want to practice the young learner forms."

Master Shi's shock seemed genuine at first then became exaggerated. "I... I have seen for certain, sky-watcher, you are no beginner in ways of an ancient *ging* warrior!"

It took me a moment to see this as a knowing compliment rather than him missing the obvious.

Sigh. So be it.

I called forth an equally exaggerated smile and a smaller bow of thanks, grasping for a similar farmer metaphor. "Thank you, Master Shi, but I lack hubris to demand stomping into your field during the middle of your growing season. I must present my, ah, ancient *ging* at the beginning. Like everyone, yes?"

"Ah, you are most wise, protectress, most wise. Even old men like me start anew with each student and continue to learn from there. I look forward to what you teach me."

Master Shi bowed *again*, and I bit the inside of my cheek, glancing at Mourn, whose eyes seemed to be laughing. Nonetheless, after I responded to his request to remove and carry my boots, his hand had a subtle sign for me.

Well done.

I exhaled as Master Shi spoke his thanks and waved us in; at last, we were led down the hall to the practice room. Once we stepped in, "reading the room" was not hard but strikingly different from the first time.

The younger ones could barely contain their collective thrill, and there were *more* of them. New ones had heard of what they missed yesterday and arrived today with the hope that we might walk through the door again.

Lucky them that Mourn changed his usual methods.

The Dragonblood slowed as he appraised the room, as if to reconsider the wisdom of being here, but even I knew it was too late. We couldn't turn around without landing a critical blow to the pride of those with whom he'd cultivated a mutual, multigenerational respect.

"No worry," I murmured in Davrin. *"We're not here all afternoon, and I'll keep my shirt on. I just want to learn those basic moves. It may help my mind exercises before I sleep."*

My reaffirmation aided Mourn's mind, as both he and Master Shi conferred long enough for the eldest man to introduce this idea and present the plan to the room. Although, without any suggestion of psionics or sleep.

This time master spoke twice, first, in Trade so that I understood him for sure; he used the farmer likeness again about cultivating their life aura with discipline and "good form." Then, presumably, he repeated this for those Yungians whose knowledge of Trade was shaky.

"Is it unusual for some to live in Augran yet never learn the Trade tongue?" I whispered.

"Not really," he replied. *"I'll explain later."*

While Mourn and I removed our cloaks, the eldest nine of the experienced fighters—those with the longest hair looped at their nape and the man with the crane tattoo on his breast—separated from the younger students. They spread out evenly around the room, their manner suggesting a tutor's presence on behalf of the master.

I counted from yesterday the same bald eleven and five others with fuzz or hair not long enough to gather at the nape. These included the master's nephews and the young man with the white flower and skull tattooed on his left arm. In addition, there were seven I hadn't seen before, but their hair conveyed they were also young learners.

Nineteen young men. All of them shirtless.

And now, Mourn was, too.

I had begun smiling at some point; I wasn't sure when but even knowing this, it was hard to stop. The climax I'd enjoyed in the field felt like a warm-up; I still had plenty of energy.

Master Shi bowed to Mourn, summoned five specific youths to the center, and invited me to join. Eagerly, I stepped barefoot onto the mats, though a couple expressions betrayed disappointment that I hadn't removed my shirt.

I wouldn't mind, buas, but my deal with your Dragon Spirit is more important.

"Feet like this," Master Shi began, generously demonstrating three ways I could settle into the position based on my favored leg or stance.

I focused on him and his feet, changing my posture to see which I liked best. The five youths with me also practiced but the three bald ones were distracted and swiftly called out by the master; the two with fuzz at least chose one stance and stuck with it.

The same way the demonstrations yesterday had added another man to the complexity of advanced exercises, Master Shi continually added another step or motion until I was reasonably competent—for a first lesson—at following through on eight of them from memory.

"Good!" he said, releasing us from our silence with a clap of his hands and a bow which was returned. He looked at me. "Practice until body flows like water, *Janshi-lantiu*. You learn like a blessed sailor's wind."

I grinned, comprehending that three more groups needed to practice before we could move on to the next level. I returned to Mourn, who motioned that he would practice what I'd just learned with me. He took the same, basic stance.

"Oh." I glanced about the room and saw all the men in loose groups of four or five practicing at their level. "Um, alright."

Mourn smiled but said nothing as we cycled through the form several times. When it became repetitious and a little boring, his body language challenged me to move faster, and I answered without speaking.

"Every learner has a limit where 'faster' is too fast," he murmured in Davrin, *"after which you become sloppy. We are looking for that limit today, no more. Speed comes with practice between sleeps. Every waking body has a limit beyond which they cannot step until they sleep."*

I squinted. A lot of words to say I couldn't match the advanced men in one day. I heard the soothing rhythm, though, and nodded. *"Got it."*

Meanwhile, the Yungians weren't the only ones trying to keep their minds off pleasing body shapes. Such fun to watch Mourn's tail dance with his feet once my movements took less focus to "flow like water."

"Sloppy," he whispered.

But only up to a point.

I heard another clap of hands.

"Good! Second form. Genbao, Bohai, Deshi, Kuluo, Reqi, Janshi, please come to center."

"That's you," Mourn nudged me, seeming relaxed.

I grinned and returned to the center to learn my second form of the day, eager to try something new since the first one was becoming a rut. Partly on alert to the demeanors of those surrounding me, I learned where to put my feet and how to move my core and arms for this new balance.

This one would take more time to fully adopt.

I also figured out who was who as Master Shi gradually filled in the blanks for me. The fuzzy-headed young man with the flower and skull on his arm was named Deshi. He had an unusual feeling about him which stood out to me, although I wasn't sure why beyond his tattoo.

Likewise, something about the demeanor of one called Bohai called out having a higher status than the others. His hair was a little longer than Deshi, yet he seemed less practiced. I caught him watching me once, but he looked away instantly and I did not catch him again.

As for the last three, Genbao, Kuluo, and Reqi reminded me of my "middling" Sisters who formed the core and maintained operations of the Cloister. Not only did nothing seem distinct about them, but they possibly preferred *not* to single themselves out by way of a markings or attitude.

This didn't mean they were less capable, only that their skills didn't lie in distraction or breaking a pattern. Between my birth and eye color, "blending in" like this had always been beyond my reach.

I took in this new form while looking them over, continuing a moment after I realized Master Shi had called an end to the demonstration. I caught up on the bows.

"Good!" The master clapped his hands. "Now, practice, honored warrior."

I returned to Mourn with a hop in my step that made him chuckle as he took this next stance. His tutor's expertise showed as he lifted his hands toward me.

"I think they've forgotten that you haven't removed your top," he said as he moved. *"Speaks as well for you as them."*

My cheeks were hurting a bit; I made myself stop smiling long enough to stretch out my jaw. *"May I ask a question?"*

"Yes."

"Why does the one named Deshi feel unlike the others?"

He blinked. *"Ah. You noticed?"*

I shrugged, breaking my pattern. *"I can't explain it, but it's there."*

"He's a mage," Mourn told me. *"You're sensing him relaxing two auras, his ging and his affinity."*

"Oo!" I cooed. *"Can you see which one?"*

The Dragonchild smirked at me. *"He wears a hint on his arm."*

"The white flower and the skull?"

"It's a winter rose," he told me. *"And yes, a human skull."*

My brows quirked high. *"Is he a death mage?"*

"Very good. Untrained, but I am guessing he is aware and may be searching for a tutor. The dorji-ka helps him stay aware of how his magic changes as he grows."

"So he doesn't do or say something strange," I said, *"and be shunned or draw Witch Hunters like Gavin?"*

"Precisely. Deshi was born in a better place than Gavin for his magic. He has more time and will follow a different path."

I chuckled. *"A pity Gavin couldn't be his tutor."*

"Heh. Even if your ally were open, it would take an ambitious Yungian to approach the Spirit of Death for an apprenticeship."

The room grew warm and pleasantly scented from the bodies exercising; the controlled breath and brief barks from the men added to our conversation. The newer fragrance also helped me detect the old layers of those same scents, suggesting the long and regular use of this space for this purpose. I still enjoyed the scenery.

"What about the one called Bohai?"

Mourn seemed to identify him without trouble. *"What do you sense about him?"*

"Status," I said with certainty. *"He's someone's son. A noble?"*

Mourn nodded. *"Close. He is the youngest son of Master Shi's brother."*

"Ah. Youngest brother of Renshu and Hulin?"

"Correct. He wasn't here yesterday but is today, like the rest who heard of our surprise appearance."

Mourn waited until we'd completed the set as fast as I could manage before the rhythm slipped. Then we switched back to the first form I'd learned without exchanging a word, working toward my limits once again before Mourn spoke.

"What made Bohai stand out to you?"

"Experience," I said, panting now. *"Mannerisms I recognize, supported by Deshi having shorter hair but is better practiced. This suggests to me that Bohai feels secure in his standing. Longer hair with less work."*

"Hm." Mourn smiled ruefully. *"Very good. I might wish otherwise, but Humans learned a similar balance to the Davrin here."*

"I knew plenty like him at Court," I huffed, striking out my arm and loose fist just short of Mourn's mirrored pose. *"I learned with the Palace Guard before the Red Sisters came for me."*

"Point taken, but I suggest granting leniency in your thoughts over equating him with a noble Daughter of a Matron House."

"Oh?" My tone was challenging. *"Why?"*

"His father and grandfather remember they were once common merchants from Yong-ch'hai, now with a noble's wealth in Yong-wen. They are shrewd traders but not nobles of divine writ. The Shi family is more generous with their wealth than many in Augran, beyond any Matron I knew."

"Hm." I frowned in concentration as we moved faster. I was running out of breath. *"Example?"*

Mourn showed his teeth in a pleasant way. *"Shi pays the learners chosen for this dorji-ka. The students have food, clothing, shelter, and a worker's pay while they practice. Many become part of Shi's guard or for the greater Yong-wen. This stability saved Deshi, who may be poorer than Bohai from luck of birth but is motivated and allowed to grow his ging. Especially beneficial for one with mage potential."*

"Good example," I granted, glancing Deshi's way. *"He is almost grown yet is untrained?"*

"Humans age quickly, and death mages are rare outside the Ma'ab capital," Mourn said. *"There are no schools which would be tolerated, and they don't tend to seek each other out. Deshi could live his life never finding a teacher, but what he learns here will help him keep his balance without one."*

"Even if he wastes the potential?"

"If he doesn't find a way to use it, he may pass it on to his children."

"Hm."

By now I'd been given ample practice for two beginner's forms, but I wasn't sure how much of their afternoon we had taken up. Nonetheless, Master Shi opted to demonstrate a third one which included the elder Shi brothers, Renshu and Hulin. I smirked, guessing they might have protested that the thirdborn son had practiced with the "sky warrior" while they stood on the side.

Perhaps their uncle tries to make peace between siblings.

I didn't mind this at first. The two brothers were older, their form more advanced, and built upon the two I had already learned. This new one took true focus and effort on my part to keep up.

While I learned these moves, the Shi brothers proved practiced enough to attempt catching my gaze without messing up, thus evading Master Shi's reprimand. I was caught by surprise, meeting their distinctive, Yungian eyes as each brother showed me his tongue in a brief, suggestive lick of his lips at the same time.

I frowned. *What?*

The brothers looked away when Master Shi acknowledged my mistake and demonstrated for me again. Then they tried to catch my attention again when their uncle focused on another student.

Furtive little fuckers.

Renshu and Hulin were highly aware of each other's success when I looked directly at one while he avoided getting caught by Master Shi. I knew this familiar nature between siblings, especially Noble Daughters.

I surmised these buas were less likely to hold back an ill-considered impulse if one thought the other might gain at his expense. While not an insult on its own, I considered it a known weakness if a sibling could never resist.

It was also unexpected behavior from how most Yungians acted with Mourn in the room. Hadn't he even suggested I "grant leniency" and not equate the Shi brothers with Noble Daughters?

What the fuck.

Master Shi noticed my own distraction, catching me peering at his nephews. I wasn't trying to hide it.

"Recenter," he instructed, taking a standing position on one leg, bringing his hands together, and closing his eyes. "Now, initiates."

He sounded a little mortified.

The older students all stopped and followed suit. I mimicked them but didn't close my eyes all the way. The breathing exercise helped us to start over without the brothers' searching eyes and darting tongues, but my read of the room had shifted.

It took twice as long for me to gain the precision I needed for the master to clap his hands.

"Good." Master Shi bowed a little deeper this time, as if in apology. "Practice until it flows, sky warrior."

Mourn set his face to neutral when I returned to practice with him. We didn't speak as much this time as my memories stirred and it was harder for me to focus.

"What did they do?" he asked softly.

I doubted he'd missed it, but he gave me the space to describe it. Smirking, I had to start over midway through the third form as I thought it over.

I kept it simple. *"They look at me the same as higher Daughters at Court once looked at a bua after he gave his attention to me instead of them."*

"Aha." Patiently, he completed the motions with me twice more. *"That's why I feel your aggression."*

"Eh."

I finished two more sets before I could put my thought into words.

"Have these elder sons forgotten they are not nobility?" I suggested. *"Do they want to deny being merchants?"*

"Possibly, but they are also not matured."

"How 'not mature' are we saying?" I resisted glancing their way.

Mourn's tail was under fine control right now.

"They should grow beyond this within five years, unless their sire and uncle encourage it, which I know they do not."

That wasn't too bad. I'd known Nobles who wouldn't "grow beyond" that rivalry impulse for fifty years or more. If ever.

Because their mothers and aunts encouraged it.

"You're not wrong that some forget their humble beginnings," Mourn added. *"This happens often by a third or fourth generation. The children have not known the same hardship if their grandfathers' legacy flourishes. They hear the success stories but inevitably have unfamiliar challenges to carry it forward and may see their fortunes decline."*

I nodded that I'd heard him but looked at his taloned feet on the mat. He avoided poking holes in them with every careful step.

"Are you insulted?" he asked.

My mouth curled as my practice slowed down instead of sped up. *"No. Disappointed, perhaps, but then, I thought their discipline was oddly perfect yesterday. I should know better by now."*

The half-blood accepted this. We didn't speak through the complexities of the form, until at last I felt the surety in my feet. By that time, most of the room had stopped for a water break.

I breathed in deeply and let it out, accepting my first drink as *Wen-yung* persuaded them to give him two cups of water. I chuckled when he handed a second to me but didn't refuse it. Mourn watched while I finished the first cup. He wanted to say something.

"What?" I invited.

"May I ask for your first thought when you realized their desire for your attention interfered in your learning?"

I thought back on it; it had been brief and ignored in the presence of Master Shi.

I sipped on the second cup. *"I thought I would like to challenge them to hold that confidence while learning my fighting style instead. I'm sure the spoils of the victor would humiliate them."*

The Dragonchild nodded as though this was the answer he expected, but he contemplated so long I thought he must be plotting. I kept my lips pressed to my cup, slurping slowly.

"A question," he began.

"Hm?"

"Is there any young man here with whom you would enjoy one-time play like with a consort?"

My eyebrows sprang up, and I took a bigger gulp of water before lowering my cup. *"Mm. You don't mean here and now?"*

"No. Elsewhere. I'm curious. Given the opportunity and security, would you choose a man present?"

Easy.

I started to smile. *"I'd choose Bohai, if only to remind his brothers they aren't entitled to everything due to birth order."*

Mourn chuckled, his tail forming a mischievous curve a bit like Graul's. *"Judging from his first look at you, I think Bohai would be willing."*

I cocked one brow at him. I'd noticed as well but thought Mourn must be teasing me again. *"You don't play like this, Dragon son. It's too small of mind to entertain you, at once bad for the Human's life and for your long-view."*

"Correct, I don't play like this," he agreed. *"I've seen it destroy women who did not deserve it, and I do not care to repeat the experience."*

"But?"

His gold eyes checked on Master Shi and his elders, who were talking quietly as we were, then returned to mine.

"But the women I harmed with my attention had far less power and fewer choices than their male family members. Sometimes the men grow complacent in their privilege, especially when it's granted and defended by their fathers.

"Once such traditions are entrenched, few women can jostle them, but female spirits are still whispered of humbling mortal men in their hubris. I am certain you could, Red Sister, and it would only add to their legends."

I couldn't believe what I heard. *"Would it not harm your reputation?"*

"Humbling is not harmful, unless you mean you would draw blood or break bones for you pleasure?"

I wrinkled my nose. *"Definitely not."*

Mourn nodded, satisfied. *"I can help make this the opportunity to find that willing bua you asked for. This could also help us in aiding Mai."*

I puzzled on this even as I became aware of a separate pinch of disappointment. The stark realization landed in my stomach, dissolving through me like a ball of salt.

But I'm more interested in you.

Fuck.

Bohai was cute and possibly an easy lay, but yesterday, Mourn had sparred and pinned me like a Red Sister in practice. Today in a field, he had pulled out an exceptional staff, showing me what he had to offer. He'd even climaxed and let me watch.

Make the opportunity, hm?

The mercenary did not include himself among the willing buas in this room, and he was not one to be coaxed or pressured. I couldn't visualize seducing him by backing him up against a wall and demanding a kiss.

Good way to threaten my bargain.

I'd also offered to do what I could do to shift the inevitable gossip which might destroy a frightened, powerless girl whom I'd made faint by telling her my name. Somehow, choosing Bohai would help make up for that mistake in Mourn's eyes.

Damn the web.

I sighed, my hands resting on my hips. Finally, I shrugged. *"What do we do first, Wen-yung?"*

He grunted, sounding pleased. *"Could you pin a few beginners on the mat as you would one of your Sisters?"*

Exciting thought.

"Bohai's older brothers?"

"Them, too, if you wish."

I started to grin. *"For certain, I can pin as many as you like."*

He answered with a smile of his own, small but genuine.

"I will talk with Master Shi."

CHAPTER 10

I WAITED ALONGSIDE MANY QUIZZICAL BUAS WHILE THE DRAG-ON Spirit conversed quietly with Master Shi and his elders. I thought the eldest Renshu and his brother Hulin looked a little concerned and tried not to smirk.

I had time to reflect that it wasn't wholly them or their impulses which had sparked this bit of intrigue; they were just the excuse. Even a benevolent legend could use small transgressions to further larger goals.

Master Shi and his two elders approached me with Mourn beside them. The first thing I noticed was the eldest's greater calm than I expected. He was smiling, though it was subtle.

"Janshi-taso," he greeted me with a bow.

Before he could continue, I bowed and spoke. "Master Shi, thank you for the gift of the three forms. It is exactly what I wished for."

He was momentarily flustered and changed his speech on a whim. "Ah! My honor and pleasure, great spirit. Your sharp eyes see much which is unspoken and difficult to explain. We teach for ten days or more what you learn today! You set your roots quickly."

His compliment ignited an unexpectedly pleasant feeling.

"Wen-yung informs me," the elder continued, his cheeks flushing a little darker, "that you offer to gift our youngest with experience of you in battle, though protected from death." He held up his pointing finger. "Not teach or practice! *Experience*, as our guardian spirit did."

I was glad for the clarification. "I offer experience, Master Shi."

"Good, good."

He and his listening elders chuckled in what seemed a suspicious way to me. What had Mourn told them, exactly?

"The young talk too bold and should be tempered with proper respect for spirits who come to us in the flesh," the master said, answering my unspoken question. "Forgive them, sky warrior, they are children and can still learn. My *dorji-ka* and all the brothers Shi would be honored to witness your true form."

My face heated as I bowed acceptance.

"We have a gift for you," the master said, turning to take something soft which another elder had been holding between his hands. "To honor your form, protectress."

Hm?

I watched as he unwrapped a dull, thick cloth to reveal a folded length of startling crimson weave. I gasped with genuine surprise, encouraging visible smiles. The texture resembled the Yungians' dark, loose bottoms but with more shine. It seemed too small to be a set of pants, however.

"May I?" Mourn asked.

The master ducked his head. "Please, *Wen-yung!*"

The Dragonblood plucked up the red cloth, letting it unfold and raising his arm high enough that the end fell just short of the ground.

"A sash?" I asked in Davrin.

"Let me show you. Remove your shirt and lift your arms."

I grinned, staring at his metallic eyes as I crossed my arms at the hem. Our contact broke only when I pulled the dark shirt over my head and tossed it aside. By then, the half-blood had stepped behind me and began by wrapping the soft, red fabric across my sore breasts and the blue pendant, pulling it snug around my ribs before crossing the length in the back and feeding the ends over each shoulder.

His fingers and claws trailed my skin in a few places as he wound the cloth around me, and a swath of tiny bumps rose on my skin in response. My nipples pressed hard against the novel texture, fully visible when Mourn stepped around to the front to cross the sash over each individual breast this time, twining the ends and pulling them snug once again.

He moved back around to start over, enough length remaining to create a form-fitting top protecting my skin from nape and collarbones down to just beneath my breasts. The carefully folded sash would also keep the saphgar in place and hide the cord from grasping fingers.

"I wear this color red when I protect my home!" I said, admiring the subtle sheen to the fabric.

I sensed their shock, and Master Shi bowed the lowest I'd seen yet.

"Yes! Color of blood, of life!" he said with obvious delight. "Without blood, there is no life, no past, no ancestors, no fortune! Red is our most lucky color, *Janshi!*"

I spotted the tiny smirk on Mourn's lips as he leaned to smooth a twist beneath my pit. He'd known this already, and he certainly made the sash as attractive on a female form as he could. I was impressed.

"All the room is staring," I whispered as he finished securing the back.

"As they should," he said.

A compliment from him, too? This was quite a day.

"Better for you if they are distracted, Sirana. Pin as many as you want."

I bounced on the balls of my feet, testing how far my breasts moved. It wasn't much. *"May I use pain points? They cause no injury if they're brief."*

His tail shushed over the floor. *"Their teacher asked you to show your true form, Red Sister."*

I hummed. *"Understood."*

This was going to be fun.

Next, I moved out onto the mat with Mourn and the elders, listening as Master Shi explained our next "lesson" in two languages. The light from the high windows was beginning to dim while their master called the youngest forward. The older students set about lighting their glass lanterns fixed higher on the walls.

Renshu and Hulin stood close to Bohai, laughing at him with a bump and a tease not unique among the nineteen males presented.

Hm. So many to spar with.

And I'd boasted as many as the Dragon Spirit liked.

Okay, then.

"Your task, my students, is blind defense from lightning bolt," Master Shi continued while an elder drew a white circle around us with a white powder. *"Janshi-lantiu* has only one goal, to take you from your feet. You must *stay* on your feet *and* inside this circle with her for only one minute quartered, beginning when she first strikes."

Fifteen seconds each. That, I can do.

"We shall measure your form, speed, focus, and fluidity. Any who last the full time shall be deemed *dei-ju* next week."

From the looks on their faces, this was a good incentive.

The elders and Mourn stepped out of the circle. I glanced his way, but the half-blood offered no last moment advice. Belatedly, I realized he also hadn't mentioned anything about a strike to my middle being dangerous to my unborn. It seemed odd but suggested two things.

He doesn't want gossip of a pregnant spirit to begin at all, and he must have supreme confidence in my pinning nineteen beginners...

"I call a first volunteer," Master Shi finished, looking among the nineteen young men.

Deshi stepped forward just a bit faster than another student, and they grinned at each other. It was almost a baring of teeth.

"Deshi," their master confirmed, bowing to me, and stepping out of the circle.

Ambitious, I thought.

We faced off with a bow, of course, and Master Shi used a single hand clap to signal I could begin at any time.

My excitement dissolved any trepidation as my mind removed the civil bindings from my body. I imagined being home in the Cloister with Gaelan and Jael.

You need to land a Sister before you can fuck her, Jaunda once said. *Anyway that works.*

I admired the fit, male form in front of me. Deshi was not a Red Sister but not a Courtly bua, either. Somewhere in between, not too tall or too wide.

"I like your tattoo," I whispered, my smile growing as we stepped around each other once.

Deshi blinked in surprise.

What's wrong, bua?

No one had said I *couldn't* speak.

"A winter rose, yes?"

He exhaled as if he might answer, and I sprang at him.

The youths could not restrain their voices as the first among them tried to evade me. Deshi was faster than I expected but nowhere near Mourn's speed. I kept the pressure on him, never backing off until I finally got him looking up as I hooked his ankle with mine.

We fell, landing with me on top, yet the move he'd begun to make but then dismissed made me suspicious. It might've worked.

Did he just throw his own test?

Master Shi clapped. "Good! Twelve seconds."

I stared down at Deshi's cat-like eyes, relishing the heat of his skin and his wide, innocent expression as his heart pounded against mine.

"Keeping secrets, death mage?" I whispered in his ear.

His prick stiffened against me.

"Opponents, up and bow, please."

I sprang up, pleased with this first spar. I grasped his hand to lift him up with me. Thanks to those loose pants, Deshi managed to hide his erection while bowing, then stepped out of the circle and behind the others. I chuckled as the student who'd tried to be first stepped in second.

"Jijuin," his master confirmed.

We bowed and began to circle. Even without having a tattoo for me to remark upon, the bua soon looked me in the eyes, offering the perfect chance to discover how he responded to my best predator's face.

Like he was a mouse.

I snarled as I lunged at him, the most noise he'd ever heard from me, and Jujuin cried something like a bleating curse.

He lasted about five seconds before I pinned him.

"Opponents, up and bow, please."

"Move your feet, sweet meat," I remarked in Trade, grinding harder to further quicken another stiff one pressed against my belly.

Jijuin quivered as I pulled him up, and we bowed.

"Janshi," he acknowledged before he left the circle.

Yeah, you'd let me do what I want.

None of them were ready for a Feldeu, though.

Five bald Yungians followed next, and I didn't have to use any pain points on them as I found for each of them a unique expression or a few choice words that drew involuntary reactions before I attacked.

I had broken a sweat, each student collapsing well within that quarter minute, close enough to smell my skin as I reveled in my contact with their naked arms and torso. Most sported erections they couldn't control by the end, which I always "marked" through my leathers just before pulling him to his feet.

I overheard one of them say I'd "pierced his *ging*" as he left the circle. I'd been admiring his ass at the time, and a vivid image struck in my mind.

Better me than my Lead, tight pucker.

By now, Master Shi understood it wasn't that my "form" was especially disciplined as much as dirty and effective. Fortunately, he was pleased to allow the lessons to continue for his young males.

Further aroused with each inevitable "victory", I bore in mind they were novices using block and evade tactics. None had attempted to strike at my stomach, which had kept it fun, and some had done well. They were trying their best and were hard to catch. Deshi held the record.

Twelve more to go.

The Shi brothers were standing back, observing, perhaps anticipating while I bowed to the next bua with fuzz on his head.

"Tun-rei," Master Shi acknowledged, clapping his hands to signal.

This one aimed to be tough against his fear, having watched long enough to believe he knew what to expect from me. Tun-rei thought I couldn't unnerve him so easily as the first ones.

We'll see.

For the first time, my predatory grins and lusty taunts vanished into a distant, expressionless stare as I fell into Deepearth silence. My body held still as if for an ambush in a tunnel, though I stood in plain view. I focused on the bua alone, thinking as I did when I commanded my spiders.

~Don't look.~

His heart murmured in response as the *dorji-ka* fell quiet. We stared at each other for the longest match yet.

~Not yet.~

Tun-rei looked not at my eyes but somewhere on my face while I peered at the depth of his pupils. My mind relaxed as I dismissed the chance of a rear attack, a risk I was sure I could take.

A test for my bodyguard as well.

~Look. Now.~

His eyes focused on me.

~Behind you!~

I struck when Tun-rei jerked his eyes to one side.

And floored him immediately.

"One second."

The youth barked a curse, and the others hooted and laughed.

"Never look away as you spot the cougar, Kuobu," Masher Shi said. "Opponents, stand and bow."

The bua was glaring but he kept his anger on the mat, not me; he managed a bow without sneering at himself. While he walked away, I saw him dig a finger into his ear as if trying to clear it out.

He heard something.

I exhaled, deciding not to use that tactic again.

The least predictable.

The next two buas chose a similar behavior and approach to Tun-rei, but I discovered what "pierced" them soon enough without using void silence. I gave them a few extra seconds of evasion, if only to put them in a sweeter mood when they landed belly down. I ground against their asses like they could feel my Feldeu before I pushed up and off them.

They were red in the face joining the other learners.

"Two mistakes, same result," an elder remarked as I caught my breath.

My sweat had turned gritty and my heart pounded beneath the red sash. *Nine more.*

"Water," Mourn said once I was alone in the circle.

Huh?

I looked, and he motioned me to him. "Your body of flesh still needs water, *Janshi*."

He was right; I was parched. I also felt the familiar hollow growing in my belly, no doubt to growl aloud by the end. Murmuring surrounded us during my break as the young men compared notes and the elders shared thoughts with each other.

"Any pains down low?" Mourn asked.

I shook my head, breathing deep against the sensual restraint of the red sash holding everything in place. *"No, I'm fine. I'm enjoying this."*

"I can tell. You do well using their fear against them."

I shrugged. *"Eh, they've never been in a real fight where they could die."*

"True for most. Watch the one with the broken nose. He's the exception."

I nodded in thanks as I drank the rest then handed back the cup. *"Understood."*

Before we got to that one, however, young Bohai with his full head of hair volunteered to be next, seizing the moment where I was better rested. I sized him up, taking my time, my eyes lingering on his slim waist, on the naked, brown chest and darker nipples.

He was the first opponent to speak first as he bowed.

"Deadly beauty."

His thick accent betrayed a tremor of excitement.

Oh, my.

It showed that this was Bohai's first day seeing me compared to his brothers' second; he still retained his awe without question. I answered his bow but grinned impishly, tucking my thumb into my pants and pulling them down to show off the top of my white fur as I straightened up.

"*Psst*, Bohai."

The Shi son looked, his eyes widening.

"Ready, pretty *bua?*" I asked.

His face deepened in color, and my grin held only on him as I covered back up. The thirdborn son laughed, the first of its kind and quite musical, then breathed out to recenter himself to take his stance with a nod.

"Am ready, *Janshi*."

His demeanor was the closest I'd seen in any Human male to my favorites like Micraen and Callitro. He was leaner than others around him and a little shorter, though clearly stronger than the buas of the Palace or Wizard's Tower.

Hm. Yum.

If this mood survived the next fifteen seconds without turning into a pout, I could choose him for reasons apart from annoying his older brothers.

Master Shi clapped his hands.

The thirdborn Shi son did well with his feet, walking his line even though my winks and lewd glances over his form distracted him as much as my other tricks had unsettled those before him.

When I lunged in, he was fast enough to draw me into two different directions before reversing his own feint when I didn't expect it, causing our shoulders to collide and knock us off balance.

Shouts rose briefly around us as I spun behind him and leaped onto his back, tugging his hair and biting his neck like I would a bedmate. Bohai cried out but not in pain.

I anticipated that he would try to throw me forward; the only other option was to drop to the ground and end the match off his feet. Once his move was committed, my ankles dragged along his flanks as I hooked one arm and hauled him over to one side with me.

The Shi son fell to the mat, and I scrambled to press him flat and flop onto him like I was settling down for the night. He didn't resist at all, and he was rock hard under my swiveling pelvis.

"Good! Nine seconds."

I laughed while pushing myself up, grasping his hand like the others and helping him to his feet. Bohai hunched over to hide the tent pole, but everyone already knew it was there. He was eight confirmed arousals out of eleven.

"Pfft, *dinfu*," muttered one youth who hadn't yet volunteered, but the one next to him had.

Reqi elbowed the contemptuous youth, whispering something short but earnest in Yungian as they both glanced over at Mourn.

Wen-yung watched the ring impassively. It wasn't clear whether he'd heard them or not, but if I had, I was willing to bet so had he. In everything but the water, however, he wasn't getting involved.

He probably wanted to see how I handled it.

Next, I faced off with Genbao, a bua from my first form lesson. He wasn't playing games; he simply wanted to test himself, and I could not sense much reason to taunt him. He lasted eight seconds with no erection, but he did get the wind knocked out of him when I flipped him.

"J-Janshi…" he finally wheezed, bowing before backing out of the ring.

After him, the bua who had scoffed and muttered entered the ring. I waited for him to be introduced to me then waved my hand in a blithe greeting without bowing.

"Hello, Sumao," I said. "Before we begin, what is *dinfu*?"

Dead silence. Then a couple students quietly groaned.

"Ah…?" The youth glanced at Master Shi, whose face was like stone.

"The honored sky warrior has asked you a question," the elder said. "She should be answered before she conducts your task."

Sumao looked like he wished the ground would open beneath him. "I meant Bohai, Master. Not our honored spirit."

Renshu and Hulin laughed louder than others at this, slapping their little brother's bare back and making him grimace.

Master Shi grunted, motioning for the brothers to quiet down. "That does not answer her question, Sumao."

I waited, still smiling.

"Dinfu is…" Sumao rubbed his hands together. "A flirt."

I heard several snorts from witnesses.

"Bohai," I asked with light curiosity. "Are you a flirt?"

The thirdborn glanced at his sniggering brothers and sighed, his brow stuck in a frown. "It is said, *Janshi,* but *dinfu* is woman or spirit who wears masks to trick men to give their blood and leave sons behind. *Not* me. I have no sons."

Some laughed in the back with that last remark.

"Thank you." I turned back and adopted a stance, my tone the same as if I'd just heard a good recipe for soup. "Ready, Sumao?"

The laughter got louder though Master Shi and Mourn simply watched. The bua didn't have much chance, he was already terrified. My opponent lasted four seconds, but I stared into his eyes and pressed my knee against his nuts rather than grind on top of him.

"Lucky," I hissed, "that I promised no blood to your master."

Sumao did not grow an erection before I got up, and I did not offer him a hand.

Six more.

And soon, the elder Shi brothers must volunteer. I held this in mind and breathed to sooth the spike of indignant anger. It wouldn't help.

It was also hard to tell if I succeeded. The next youth let his intimidation overwhelm him the same instant when he met my eyes. He was another one-second pin, but the next two volunteers were overly aggressive, determined to prove themselves challenging mortals after the last two boys.

At the same time, the *Janshi* approached exhaustion.

Fuck.

I had refrained from causing much pain so far, but the third to the last one, the fighter with the broken nose, went on the offensive, attacking me first. I had no option but to draw him back to look for an opening.

Then he went for my gut, his fist glancing off my hip as he kept bulling forward. I didn't even think before hissing the command word of Callitro's ring on my finger, striking him in the face so hard he staggered.

Taking my chance, I swept his legs and soon had a knee in his spine, his arm bent back with my fingers digging into three nerve clusters I'd found on Kurn. The fighter's bloody mouth was open as if screaming but made no sound.

"Eight seconds," Master Shi said, his voice louder. "Opponents, stand and bow!"

I released him without a word, we bowed, and he left the ring with his back straight, simmering with controlled defeat. Surreptitiously, I glanced at the hand that hit him. His teeth should have split my knuckles, but there wasn't so much as a bruise.

Huh. The ring or psionics?

Or both?

While blood was cleaned off the mat, I noticed it was dark outside and sighed quietly. I hadn't the extra energy for either humor or posturing when Hulin finally entered the ring.

So the eldest son plans to go last. Lovely.

My stomach growled audibly then, reminding everyone that this spirit was still getting used to feeding her new body.

Not far from the truth.

Hulin grinned. "You hunger, *Janshi?*"

My eyes flicked toward Bohai. "Quite."

The younger bua blushed again as his brothers laughed boastfully, as if the flirt included them. Master Shi's voice filled the room.

"Opponents, bow."

We obeyed, ready for the clap of hands. Almost immediately, something drew my eyes down.

Hulin's feet were poised as if he was about to lean toward Renshu.

Hm.

If we were Nobles at Court, I would assume Renshu planned something with Hulin which would slow me down for the last fight of the night, thus, the elder brother could be the only one to stay on his feet for the full time.

The task was to chase Hulin, and my chances were low that he would evade me and stay far from his brother. His eyes were bright, eager, and most importantly, patient. He was fresh while I was near drained.

I dismissed several tactics I'd already tried, and those I hadn't were uncertain to work.

Damnit.

Then I heard tapping behind me, roughly where Mourn stood and just beneath the mutters and shuffling feet as more than a few began to feel the lateness. I held still so as not to start Hulin's task too soon.

I heard it again.

His tail.

As when the mercenary had been tapping on Gavin's door.

Something was definitely amiss. Pity that I couldn't read his signals.

In my periphery, Renshu jumped in surprise, looking away from the ring behind him.

At Deshi.

I attacked Hulin just as Renshu arrogantly pushed the other man away, and voices exploded around us as Hulin dove to his brother's side of the ring. When we passed his older brother's and nothing unusual happened, Hulin's set face tightened further.

Two more seconds in, the second-born looked scared. Distracted.

Renshu had missed their opportunity.

You little shits. What were you planning?

I discarded attempts to take the middle Shi brother down quickly, instead letting him stay on his feet for the first ten seconds. The bua hadn't expected to defend against constant punches and wasn't as good at defense as some of the others.

He'd have plenty of bruises in the morning.

Finally, I crouched low and darted in, striking Hulin's stomach with enough force he doubled over and lost his breath. I shoved him facedown on the mat and kneeled upright on his back long enough for Master Shi to clap once.

"Thirteen seconds! Good! Opponents, rise and bow."

Hulin needed extra time to obey, shaking a little to regain a full chest of air. I took the opportunity to offer a bow to the master as well and read his face.

I saw tiny crinkles at the corners of the elder man's eyes though his mouth was set in concern. Master Shi exchanged a glance with Mourn before signaling the final spar for the evening.

A precious second wind had returned in the wake of my penultimate victory. When Renshu entered the ring, I'd regained my breath and my good humor. I smiled widely to see the corners of his mouth tighten when he glanced in Deshi's general direction.

No sense blaming him for having already lost.

"Ah, firstborn Shi!" I called, bowing to my opponent. "Welcome to the last challenge. Come, show me what your body can do so I may have my evening meal with the Dragon Spirit. I'm hungry."

The wealthy man's son swallowed and bowed. *"Janshi-lantiu."*

Although he pretended otherwise, I'd already pierced his *ging*, and Renshu had no other tricks up his sleeve without his brother to distract. My last spar of the night was clean and unremarkable.

Almost boring.

"Eleven seconds! Good!"

I was on my feet and bowing before the eldest brother could witness me doing it. Instead, he caught up to me as I tilted my head back, lifting my arms to the ceiling, and let out a yell like at the end of a battle.

"Yaaaaaaa!"

I did it! I sparred and pinned them all!

Voices rose to fill the room, some with calls, some with chatter, none of which I understood. Mourn approached and gently took my arm, guiding me to the side.

"Very well done, but we've kept them again," he murmured with quiet humor. *"They're late for evening meals."*

I laughed, *"So are we!"*

"We shall leave soon. Get your cloak, shirt, and boots. Leave the sash as it is, we can remove it later."

Mourn handled the parting rituals as I struggled to keep my mind out of its exhaustive haze, donning my shirt and cloak first. I summoned my spiders to be waiting at the door when I stepped out into the hall to put on my boots. The tiny protectors slipped beneath my cloak unnoticed.

"Sky warrior, thank you," Master Shi said with sincerity and respect. "You are true-made for the battles within the storms. You took our breath, changing direction every instant! None here could stand against so many, one after another, with none getting past the wall you guarded."

A snicker almost slipped out. *Well. They **are** novices.*

I exhaled, placing an easy smile back on my face, and bowing to him. "Thank you, Master Shi. I needed the practice in this new form."

"An honor, *Janshi-lantiu*. May it lead you to win your quest, and to find whom you seek in our realm."

My expression softened. I hoped so.

I liked that well-wish.

OUTSIDE IN THE DARK, MOURN PICKED ME UP FOLLOWING THE third time I tripped on something. After two instances, I didn't fight him, knowing he could carry me quite far on foot.

"Shiiit," I groused, covering my belly as it cramped intensely.

"Stomach sick?"

"Not yet. Aching and empty, though."

"We'll get you food and talk in the morning."

"Talk about what?"

"Obtaining Bohai for you, among other things while we're waiting for Krithannia. You've given me some ideas."

I couldn't think at first, but then a few ideas of my own shifted in my overheated head. "Hey, why did Renshu push Deshi there at the end?"

"I think he brushed too close behind him. Why?"

"Hm," I grunted. "I heard you tapping your tail behind me about the same time I realized Hulin meant to dart toward Renshu first."

"Oh?"

"Yes. Then Deshi conveniently annoyed him, and Renshu missed a cue."

"Hm. Strange."

I tilted my eyes at him. "No, it's not."

The hybrid kept his eyes forward on our path but invited, "How so?"

"First, Deshi is not a novice, so what's he doing there?"

Mourn smirked. "We'll talk about that later as well. Water. Food. Rest. In that order."

I exhaled coarsely. "What about a cloth bath? I'm covered in sweat, mine and a chamber full of buas."

"Wait until you've eaten."

I shifted for more comfort. "Mm. This is better when you aren't wearing a harness."

"As I'd expect."

My body's rush was wearing off, and I'd been staring blankly in the time it took to reach the next street over. My hunger pangs brought me alert.

"Ugh," I groaned. "So, who had the best time?"

Mourn chuckled, shaking his head. "Hulin at thirteen seconds, but only because you opted to use him as a practice dummy for ten of them."

I grinned. "You noticed."

"It was hard to miss."

"He deserved it."

"Agreed. He'll be sore tomorrow."

I checked over his shoulder, checking his tail. It danced lightly from side to side.

"Of the rest," he said, "Deshi ranked at twelve."

"Uh-uh," I protested. "He doesn't count, either. He threw his fight. I hold that Deshi is *not* a novice."

"Very well. Then Renshu came in at eleven."

"That's better."

He looked at me, his golden eyes visible in the dark. "You are satisfied with this."

"Useful, isn't it?" I replied, yawning. "This important son doesn't have his pride completely thrashed, so you may still ask about Bohai. But the firstborn is humbled and denied a prize for which he would have cheated with his brother."

"Ah." Mourn paused, shaking his head. "You'll have to tell me more of Sivaraus Court sometime."

"Heh. I doubt anything I say would surprise you."

"Hm. Perhaps I could be, now that I know how Red Sisters spar."

I snickered. "Not quite."

"Oh? What's missing?"

"I don't have the magic cock with me." I made a motion like I stroked a pole of my own. "But even without that, normally we're naked, so all those buas should have been marked with my slit smears to be accurate. I might have even sat on a few faces and demanded their tongues."

He wasn't sure how to respond, and in my exhaustion, my lips had become too loose about the Sisterhood.

"So," I said. "Will this help Mai? Somehow?"

Mourn nodded, still looking ahead. "I think so."

The hybrid adjusted his hold on me, securing it, and I sighed, relaxing against him and closing my lips for a while.

Later, we reached the barn behind the safehouse where Mourn sniffed for Nightmare. ★All is well,★ he signed.

The breeze had shifted, and I could smell the food already. I almost bit my fist to keep from whimpering.

"Soon," he promised.

The Dragonblood had my complete cooperation to reenter the library as soon as possible. We offered the barest greetings to Gavin before Mourn sent the empty dishes and three kinds of cups up to the kitchen while I sat gingerly on the chaise.

The buas aren't going to be the only ones who are sore in the morning.

If Gavin smelled anything of what I'd been doing, he didn't seem to care. He set his writing aside, entwining his fingers and observing us for the first little while.

Finally, he asked, "Were you able to find paper and thread?"

Mourn and I had identical expressions.

Fuck.

"Um, no," he began.

"We forgot," I added.

"You forgot," Gavin repeated dryly, turning a page in his open grimoire. "I estimate I have about four left."

"As soon as the shops open tomorrow," Mourn promised.

The Deathwalker narrowed his eerie eyes, looking between us as Mourn greeted Graul coming out of his nest.

"Did Witch Hunters arrive again?" Gavin asked me.

He startled me partway out of my fog. "Huh?"

"Or some other threat?" The death mage's mouth turned down. "You appear concerningly ragged."

"Why?" I looked down. "Is my baby alright?"

"Still bright, though your personal aura is full of strange tremors."

"Ah. I was practicing."

"Practicing what?"

"Fighting."

When Gavin looked at me like that, I doubted how much focus I even had left.

"She is strengthening her mind and body together with some Yungian fighting techniques," Mourn explained, cradling his drake for some much-needed attention. "She overtired herself and needs food and sleep."

"Yes," I agreed. "That."

Gavin grunted, accepting this as he returned to his notes.

Food and tea arrived quickly with a warm bucket of water and stack of absorbent cloths. I sank into the task of feeding, drinking, and scrubbing down, determined to finish each with my limited energy such that even the air-puffing drake didn't seek to distract me.

Gavin, Mourn, and Graul were still awake when I collapsed into sleep on the chaise. I couldn't recall a time before where that would have been a good idea, but I believed I would be left in peace.

This may have been a first in my entire life.

CHAPTER 11

My bladder awakened me, and I'd made it to the waste closet before a clear thought came to me: I had not come from another dream in the Desert. My Reverie had been as still and quiet as an undiscovered cave.

Stepping barefoot onto the thick carpet, wearing only my black shirt and leathers, I crossed the library lit softer than before. Thinking of food, I spotted a platter covered with a wooden dome on the ledge of the delivery hatch.

Then I stopped in my tracks.

Gavin and Graul watched me from the same table. Neither had whites to their eyes nor were making a sound. Surreal enough that I reconsidered whether I was awake.

"Uhm, hello," I said.

Gavin was in the middle of carefully trimming the spine off a book broken into several sections.

Shit. What have you done?

"Good morning," said the death mage in a tone making me doubt he meant it. "Yes, that food is for you. It may be a little cool."

"Oh. That's fine."

I lifted the dome to peer at the familiar grain pods, broth, vegetables, and oiled noodles waiting to be mixed to my taste. They were still warm, the blended scent caressing my face as if in welcome.

"Mmm, mine," I murmured, taking the whole platter with me to sit on the chaise, balancing it on my lap.

That was when I noticed Graul stretching his neck so far out toward me, I thought he might tumble forward off the desk and onto the carpet. His hazy red eyes didn't blink, his chin hairs bristling as scaly nostrils expanded with constant sniffing. Even after I began to eat, neither his posture nor interest level changed.

Would he do anything besides pout if I simply ignored him and finished the meal? He could get his own food, couldn't he? Smart enough to follow simple instructions.

"I believe he has been waiting for you to awaken," Gavin said, using his scalpel to cut through the binding before reaching for another tool to scrape off some discoloration. "Mourn asked him not to disturb it or you while you slept."

I made a face. "Implying I would share when I woke."

Gavin shrugged with indifference and reached for blank pages from a stack to his left, laying them gently over the segmented book as if to measure them for a cut to match the size.

"Wait, where did you get the paper?" I asked, food stuffed in one cheek.

"Mourn went out when the shop opened again," he answered. "You were still sleeping."

I missed it.

"So, that's your grimoire separated into pieces?"

"It is."

I paused in chewing, and Graul perked up as if I might be finished. I hurried to finish and swallow.

"How long has it been?" I grumbled. "And why is Mourn gone again?"

"It's hard to keep time down here," Gavin stated, clearly not a complaint. "For certain you slept through the night. He also didn't volunteer where he was going, nor did I ask."

My belly hungered enough to keep eating, although I realized I could share with Graul and get something fresh if I needed more. Succumbing to the staring beast's silent begging, I spared a little of each in a bowl and got up to set it on the desk.

"No, not here," Gavin growled. "He may spill it."

"Mourn said not to pick him up," I said, lifting the bowl out of Graul's reach as he sidled next to me, churring. "And I'm not sure if he can jump down."

Gavin covered his trove of book supplies with his hands. Graul's tail began to lash back and forth while I held a bowl out of reach; this was clearly teasing the drake.

The death mage groused, "Yes, he can jump. I've seen him. I certainly didn't lift him to get up here in the first place, and neither did Mourn."

"Ah, okay."

Graul clicked his teeth and hissed to watch me walk away. I placed the bowl beneath the second, unused desk, a far distance from the book supplies. The shadow drake snorted with annoyance but stretched out his wings and expanded his throat pouch, preparing to leap off.

Seeing that brightly colored signal, I backed up quickly as he expelled it, creating enough of a gust to tuck his wings into, slowing him to a glide to touch the carpet without crash or injury. He then slithered beneath the desk and stuck his head in the bowl, snarfing the food.

I sat back down to finish my meal in relative peace, though now I was troubled by the length of time I'd slept. *An entire night.*

The last time I'd done that, I'd been so ill from the ordeals with Brom, the Ma'ab, the warp rot forest, and Soul Drinker that I couldn't hold myself upright long enough to piss without help.

I felt fine now; sore from the intense sparring, bruises which were making themselves known, but neither as bad as I might expect after lying inert and dreamless from then until well after sunup.

What is happening? Is it the exertion while pregnant, or another early sign of psionics?

The Davrin called our rest periods a "Reverie" mostly because we may dream lucidly at any point, most commonly of our life's memories. Reflecting in sleep became more frequent, even controlled, as one aged while children and newly mature caits and buas rested without dreams if they were tired enough.

Since reaching the Surface, I had been debilitatingly tired and dreamless more than once, but now I worried that my sleep would continue to change and become unpredictable to me. Even worse, I neither knew why it was changing nor how different my Reverie might appear over the next few years.

I may not be able to do much about it.

I breathed in slowly then exhaled, trying to recapture the elation after I'd completed the enormous task of testing a score of Human buas in their own trials, one after the other. I might even have one of them to play with as a result.

Some enticing intrigue was happening, both with stories intended to spread and in Mourn's minor yet well-timed interference last evening. I was certain the Dragonblood knew the student with the rose and skull tattoo wasn't a beginner or just modestly practiced like the Shi brothers.

An untrained death mage who can still gain an erection.

Gavin was so intent on rebuilding his book with new pages that I watched for longer than I meant to. I got up to request a second serving of hot food and enjoyed it, though was not quite able to finish. Graul flicked his tongue at me until I gave him the rest to distract him and make me stop smiling.

Finally, I said the most interesting thing so far.

"I found another death mage in Yong-wen."

Gavin grunted, lowering his head to squint and measure something before puncturing a layer with his needle and coarse thread.

"He's younger than you, I think," I said. "For certain, untrained."

"And how did you determine this?" he asked without looking up.

"Well, Mourn said it. He seems to know something about the boy outside the *dorji-ka*."

"What is that?" Gavin muttered. "For that matter, where have you been?"

"It's a school where Yungians learn to fight without weapons."

"Ah, that explains your interest."

"Yes, I wanted to learn something new to practice, and Mourn said if we presented ourselves right, I can be the 'life warrior' balance next to your 'death spirit' journey, which would give us some options if you must interact with more Yungians."

Gavin grunted, pressing his hand tightly on the folded pages as he did something out of my sight. "Such as this hand-fighting death mage?"

"Maybe. Though I noticed this boy doesn't have any scars like you have. He does have a tattoo that suggests death."

"My scars are the result of Manalari and Ma'ab pressures," he said. "Yungian death mages may have different methods and foci than self-harm. What was the tattoo?"

Despite that intense scowl and coarse tone, he *was* interested in talking about this.

"A white flower Mourn called a winter rose, and a human skull. They were bonded together with artistic beauty."

"Hm. No other scars on his hands or arms?"

"Nor his back or chest, nor his abdomen, flanks, or feet."

Gavin finally looked up. "What?"

My grin turned smug. "The *dorji-ka* practices wearing only pants." I paused. "Kind of like Mourn, now I think about it. The older ones mimicked his hair, too."

My scholar sighed, looked back down. "I suppose this explains the red sash wrapped around your ribcage after you returned."

Reminded, I looked around for that sash. It was folded, neat and clean, on a bookshelf with spare space. "A gift," I said. "They were pleased to see me fight. Although, for how long I might be active, they also offered something to cover my breasts."

"Unsurprising."

"Well, they do ache. I was glad for it."

Gavin grunted in answer, securing the book bind for one section of new folded pages to his old ones, then started measuring another handful. I wondered how thick his grimoire would be by the time he finished, and if he intended to use all the paper Mourn had brought him.

If he does, the book will be almost twice as thick, and he won't be able to wrap the leather around completely like before.

I sat frowning for a moment. "Would you have any interest in meeting the Yungian death mage? He speaks Trade."

"I would not," he replied. "I have no use for a distraction unrelated to my task."

That refusal was far firmer and more specific than death mages merely not tending to seek each other out.

I sighed, "What is the most interesting thing you have learned down here?"

The Deathwalker took his time thinking this over, his hands careful and his gaze intent on a possession equally as valuable to him, I bet, as Jacob's soul shard.

"I found a Manalari court record of a witch execution," he said, "which makes no mention of the Bishops and was conducted by a 'Lord.' It was dated roughly four centuries ago. I am looking for other references to better determine when the Bishops seized power over the sacred pool."

Graul lifted his head from his bowl and craned his neck stiffly. I raised my eyebrow at him, wondering what caught his attention. Gavin hadn't changed his tone.

"Mourn probably knows if more are here," I suggested.

Gavin nodded disinterestedly. "Only one of many lines of thought I pursue, Sirana."

"Don't the Bishops tell their people a history of when they 'claimed their rightful place?'"

"If you listen to that, the Consecration could have happened up to a thousand years ago," Gavin muttered. "It is intentionally kept vague, even as it was clear to me, as soon as I left, that the people outside Manalar's influence see the Bishops as a newer power. Dwarves, especially."

"Hm. So, less than four hundred years."

"That is the most recent evidence, yes."

"Indeed, not very old," I said. "The Ma'ab are older."

"And even they are a new intrusion per the tales of some."

"Both these younger powers want control of the sacred pool. That is why the Ma'ab are bypassing Taiding and Augran and going for Manalar."

Gavin paused to look at me. "Oh?"

Belatedly, I recalled my ally hadn't been there for that discussion. "This is what Mourn's Dwarven handler said."

"Dwarven handler?"

"Yes. I met him briefly. Talov Baradum from Taiding. He was the one who got the contract for Mourn to go after Kurn and Castis and retrieve the ruby. Mourn doesn't speak directly to those who hire him. They speak through Talov of the Guild."

"Aha."

Gavin stopped building his book for a moment as he straightened. I heard a deep crack in his spine. "Was this a young Dwarf or an old one? Or middling, like Rithal?"

"Old," I answered. "Very old. Grey beard, wrinkles, hazy eyes."

"Really." Gavin looked at the shadow drake, who had been curled up on the carpet but now blinked at the Deathwalker. "So, this is someone who has likely been aware of this Dragonchild for as long as Krithannia?"

"Oh, yes. He said as much." I smiled. "Talov even teased Mourn about being near a female of his race for once. They seemed familiar with each other."

Gavin nodded. "If you were suggesting before that I 'meet' anyone before we leave for Manalar, I would like to speak with this Dwarf."

I was surprised by that but shouldn't have been. "Well, uh, that's not something I can decide, but we could ask Mourn."

My scholar nodded and returned to his book binding, apparently satisfied with that answer. I caught his nonverbal cues soon enough that he was finished talking for now.

Graul continued watching us for a while longer. His odd, swiveling ears tuned up and toward us now and then before twitching back to their lower, resting position. When we were quiet, the drake lowered his head back down on the carpet. He seemed to prefer remaining outside his den and in our sight if he didn't need to count his hoard.

I decided to take the opportunity to figure out how to request hot water and washing supplies as Mourn had last night. While I'd had plenty of time to check over my dwindling supplies and repair or strengthen what I could on the boat, here was a better time for a deeper clean than I'd had since leaving Rausery at the cave.

I could use another body scrub and a hair wash after yesterday.

Mourn didn't return during the lengthy time this took to get set up. I opted for the bath and hair wash first and, as by the river, worked in the nude as I laid everything I owned over the chaise. This assured that I missed nothing as I worked smallest to largest, and I didn't think Gavin and Graul would care too much about how I worked.

Or so I assumed.

"Hai," I hissed, pointing at the drake as he sneaked into view. "I see you. Do not snatch or blow on anything to annoy me. I will burn the snacks in front of you."

Graul seemed to understand as his rear end and belly settled where he was. He stretched with an innocent whine and claws out front.

Then I thought to ask. "You haven't given the pouch away, have you, Gavin?"

"I have not," he replied, his pale face turned down to the table. I knew exactly what I meant. "I also haven't inspected the shelves near his den yet."

Graul looked between us. His red eyes seemed a bit wider than before.

"You mean," I clarified, "not even one?"

"Correct."

Oh, goddess, maybe the drake hadn't known?

Graul stared at me the entire time I deep cleaned my gear, and I worked faster, diligently pretending to ignore him while I waited for any rustle of air that might mean he'd shadow jumped to steal something for his hoard. At least I'd used good sense to keep Soul Drinker apart from everything else and set my spiders on the same bookshelf to guard it.

"You've already had food," I whispered.

"Hm?" Gavin asked.

"Nothing."

The drake churred, the tip of his tail flicking. He still watched me.

I gathered up the items to return to their assigned pouches, cinched things closed, knotting them where necessary. Finally, I started putting a very clean belt back together.

Next, I spot cleaned my bracers and armor, leaving my boots for last. Mourn had done me the favor last night of using his magic to refresh my shirt, stockings, and leathers along with the red sash.

Graul had crept forward when he thought I wouldn't notice.

I glared at him. "I see you."

He stopped, blinked again, flicked his tongue out and fluttered his throat pouch. Apparently, he was bored and sought entertainment. Or attention. *Or snacks.*

I sighed and put off buffing my boots. What exactly would I do if Graul pushed too close? Pick him up if he touched anything? Then what? Force a shadow jumper to go to his den and not come out while I bandaged lacerated arms?

Pfeh. Laughable. I wish you could talk and tell me what you want.

"Snacks?" I asked him.

Graul lifted his head quickly, chirped a new sound, and nodded.

Smart little beast.

"Gavin, do you know where they are?"

My scholar sighed deeply, slow and suffering as he reached inside his robe for the pouch Mourn had given him. "Just one. I may need some for later."

I placed my belt high and outside of shadows on a shelf then stepped over to take the pouch from him. Looking inside first, I tugged one out.

Long, tough strips of dried meat?

Graul simply *appeared* from beneath the desk, slapping my bare ankle with his tail.

"Hai!" I cried, stepping back, and peering underneath. I held up the treat. "You want this?"

He purred, nodding his muzzle again.

"No crawling or jumping toward me or my things. Stay quiet, stop staring, and you can have it. Yes?"

Another nod.

Then he lunged, his jaws snapping closed on the strip with a growl.

"Hai!"

I wasn't ready to let go, regardless of if he initially surprised me with the strength of his pull. Digging in my heels and bracing myself, I managed to keep the meat out of the desk's shadow and stay on my feet.

After testing back and forth, it was clear I could drag the beast out if I wanted to but didn't see the point. Graul seemed entertained rather than agitated, assuming his deflated throat pouch was a good indication. Gavin grumbled when the reptilian tail slapped him next beneath the desk, and the drake turned his head to gnaw the tough strip across his jaws.

"Sirana," he complained, "just let the creature have it."

"He's playing," I said, starting to smirk as I stared at Graul's narrowing eyes.

"Don't you have work to do?"

"It can wait."

The Deathwalker rested his face in his hand, waited through more growling beneath the desk and some returned giggling from me before the mage looked up, hearing the same suck of magic I did.

A chill darted up my spine as I felt eyes on me.

"Ah, good, you're back," Gavin said.

I let go of the treat and turned around just as Graul vanished beneath Gavin's chair to somewhere. I didn't look for the drake because Mourn was watching me and hadn't said anything yet. I was still naked.

"Oh, uh," I said. "You're back."

Brilliant.

Mourn exhaled, glancing at the obvious cleaning supplies now abandoned by the chaise, then said, *"Clax tivol,* Graul?"

I heard a sound from the drake's den, an odd sequence of chirps and purrs that seemed to mean something.

"He denies taking anything from you," said the half-blood, stepping closer, "but I suggest checking just to be sure. Sometimes he cannot resist shiny things, though he does not usually lie outright to me."

"So he mimics crows," Gavin muttered, evaluating his bookbinding progress after the disruption.

"He gets it from me."

I checked over my belongings as suggested and got dressed as well. My face warmed up a lot with the lingering realization of Mourn's first view after jumping in here.

Me bent over, everything from my netherhole to my fluff on display as I play tugging war with his drake under a desk for a treat.

Well, whatever he thought about it, he kept a good stone face. One might think he would have chuckled.

"I have something good to tell you, Sirana," Mourn began once I'd put myself together.

I smiled. "You do?"

"Mm-hm." Mourn bowed his head the smallest bit but clearly reminiscent of all the sparring bows I'd done the previous day. "Shi Mu Kuo, the patriarch for the Shi family with land on the western hills, has invited us for a midnight meal tonight."

"Oh?"

"I have accepted on our behalf."

"Oh."

"Midnight meal?" Gavin asked before I could.

"For privacy," he replied. "While an honored guest would usually be invited for the afternoon and evening, that will be too busy and potentially dangerous for them as well as us." Mourn looked back at me. "They want to keep it secret until after it's happened, so we will arrive in the middle of the night after their first sleep."

I squinted. "Wait, first sleep?"

Mourn nodded. "A lot of humans sleep twice in a night, awakening to perform any number of activities before returning to bed."

"I've…" I glanced at Gavin and back. "I've never heard of that."

"It is indeed common," the Deathwalker said, pausing to look up. "Just not for me. I often couldn't sleep at all or slept during the day. Rarely in regular shifts like the other monks." He shrugged and went back to work. "Another reason I was 'cursed' by my Ma'ab blood."

"Is that why Kurn and Castis slept through the night?" I asked.

"Possibly," Gavin said, "though it's a bit late to ask, and I've never been to Ennikar to observe their habits."

"Not just the Ma'ab but Mathias and Rithal were often awake in shifts, keeping watch," Mourn reminded me.

"And Troshin Bend?"

"Did you not hear some nighttime activity?"

"I did, but…"

"And the Witch Hunters and the extensive fire would have disrupted normal patterns."

That was a night that could've ended sooner.

I shook my head. "So, I should just accept this. There is a first sleep, a midnight waking, and a second sleep?"

Mourn nodded. "Correct. Though in this case, a formal family meal is very unusual, so servants will probably be short of sleep thanks to us."

"Aha. Is there a reason for the invitation besides further honoring spirits?"

"Indeed, there is." Mourn chuckled. "Shi Mu Kuo, father of Renshu and Hulin, wishes his sons to apologize to the spirits for what happened in the *dorji-ka*, and both Master Shi and his brother are desperate to correct this 'youthful disrespect.' Feeding us their best meal is the first step."

I read something in his calm face. "Only the first…"

He smiled without showing teeth, metallic eyes sliding to Gavin and back.

Aha.

I smiled back.

I could wait to hear more.

MOURN PLANNED TO GET SOME FOOD FOR HIMSELF AND ENJOY time with Graul but we would not stay here until midnight. Gavin had no qualms but also asked about meeting Mourn's handler.

"Hm. Might be possible. Why?"

"I understand he is a well-informed, outside perspective on both the Ma'ab and the Manalari, older than both of them."

"True." Mourn glanced at me. "I will pass the message."

The mercenary had also brought a vial and an ointment that would soothe my still-aching muscles; they were just what I needed. While Shyntre's pellets might have helped, I didn't have an abundance of them, and it seemed a pity to waste them on pains not caused by an open wound.

Mourn asked again that I leave my weapons belt and armor behind. "Would you consider wearing the red sash beneath your shirt?"

I smiled. "Sure, but I need help putting it on."

He nodded, and we got started in preparing to leave. "I recommend your blindfold before stepping out. It is midafternoon, clear and sunny."

Speaking of pains. I sighed, enjoying the caress of hands as he finished wrapping the sash around me.

"What about you?" I asked as I dressed myself the rest of the way, slipping the last bit of muscle relief ointment inside my bracer just in case.

"I close my eyes at first and open them gradually." He paused. "I suppose you could do the same."

"Nah," I said, tying it in place. "I haven't been up here as long. Even eyes closed, it's distracting, but if I slip or look too soon, the light leaves me with a headache well into evening."

"Ah. Then you *should* take the precaution, so tonight may have your full attention."

There was a hint of amusement in his voice. Something he still hadn't said in front of Gavin.

Hmph.

We bid farewell once again and stepped out into the alley. The air was shockingly warm and moist, streaming through the narrow, shadowed passage, and all scents of the city assailed me at once, good or bad.

"What are we doing until midnight?" I asked, showing my relief that I wouldn't be sitting cooped up until then.

"We thought you could use more practice with living horses."

"We?"

"Could be a practical skill in aiding your sister."

"Wait, horses hate you," I said.

"They do."

"And you said 'we.'"

That was her cue. "Hello, Sirana."

Uh-oh.

She'd been standing downwind.

"Krithannia," I replied, reaching to take my blindfold off as Mourn made room for her.

"Go slowly," she said, approaching. "You are in no danger. Anyone who looks down the alley will see it empty for now."

Rather than ripping the blind off, I untied it with care, keeping the darkness close a little longer as my ears sharpened to the noise around me. To my right, Mourn grunted softly in discomfort, and I heard an unsettling pop or two like he was cracking stiff joints.

A rare occurrence.

Then I smelled something odd the same moment I got goose-flesh, as if magic had been used next to me. I'd run across the scent before but couldn't remember where. *Like an injured animal…*

I couldn't open my eyes without pain yet but tucked the blind away sooner since we stood in the shade.

"Hold still," Krithannia said. "I am casting an illusion on you."

"What will I look like?" I asked, a hint of stress slipping out.

"The same Manalari woman you were on the ship, blue eyes, brown hair, not as pale as me. Please keep your hood up and gloves on so we may draw less attention overall."

"No walking around as spirits?"

"Not this time."

When I could open my eyes a slit without pain, it was enough to see Krithannia as the short, elder Yungian woman I'd first met giving instructions to Mai and Ting in the inn. She appeared to wear the same layers of floral robes as before.

"Ai-Ling," I said.

She was pleased. "Ah, very good."

Looking to Mourn next, I wasn't truly surprised to see Roewn, the tall, pale-skinned Noiri who had sailed with us on the ship. But I *was* confused.

"And we'll be horse riding?" I asked, my accent matching my appearance for once.

Ai-Ling smiled, her eyes crinkling at the corners. Her accent shifted as well. "We are. You and me."

"But Mourn's not."

"No. He frightens them. He has never ridden one."

I smirked to imagine the big half-blood sitting astride some poor swayback, so heavy that the legs wobbled. Then I turned a dry, mildly accusing expression on him without saying a word.

"I have tasks to do but will find you well before the meal," he said. "Krithannia has means to call me if she needs help. As long as you stay with her, you should be as safe with her expertise and guidance as you are with mine."

Right. You want her to convey something specific.

The Dragon son was not my bodyguard yet, so any protest about that would be petty. *Damn it.*

I sighed, grasping for something appeasing. "I don't suppose these tasks you go to have anything to do with finding my sister?"

"Maybe. Too soon to tell."

"Right."

Roewn's face smiled a little, he bowed his head to Krithannia, then me, and he excused himself. "Enjoy the practice. I will return toward dusk."

Ai-Ling brokered a ride for us from something she called a *duk-duk*: a small, two-seated cart with a sunshade, drawn by a stout Dwarvish pony whose slight, Yungian guide rode on his back.

"Come, up," the elder invited me after giving the male rider a coin, climbing into one of the seats.

With my hood over my paler face, I followed her in.

I had seen a few of these rides from afar but Mourn had given significant effort to choose streets and narrows very light on animals. We'd never stumbled into a rider or cart close enough for the beast of burden to catch the Dragonblood's scent and panic.

Not to say that horses don't have their own pungent scents.

As I knew from riding behind the Ma'ab, Mathias, and Rithal out of the mountains and across the plains. I looked ahead and between the ears of the cart's brown pony, to the hills outside of Yong-wen. I tried to imagine the vast distance I'd covered since the Ley Tower.

How much had changed for me to be riding in a tiny, specialized cart over clean, well-tended streets, and shoulder-to-shoulder with a Naulor Elf in disguise.

"Where are we going?" I whispered in Trade.

Ai-Ling placed a finger to her lips and smiled with her eyes, full of patience as she watched the people and their works pass by. I sat back, swallowing my grumble, and divided my attention between the high activity surrounding us and the gradual strengthening of the other Elf's warmth and scent.

Numerous questions came to mind to pass the time, but I must assume our driver understood Trade if Krithannia was willing to sit in silence watching the scenery. I'd thought Mourn wished her to discuss something with me, or perhaps the elder female had her own opinions on what he and I had done in the field yesterday. I failed to see her opening if we were carried from the city center to wherever I'd be practicing with living horses.

Why not just walk? Plenty of time to talk then.

The pony drew the cart out into the open fields and dirt roads becoming familiar to me. I could grant that we might arrive much more quickly than on foot, but we hadn't said a word this whole time. Did I feel bored or dismayed at the wasted time? Perhaps I'd become accustomed to Mourn's generous teachings, giving me plenty to ponder about where I stood in this foreign land.

"Do you speak Davrin, elder?" I asked lowly in my native tongue.

The older woman's brows lifted high as she peered at me then glanced at our driver and back. *"Some,"* she replied. *"Plain talk. Not web speak."*

Web speak.

I'd never heard that phrase before but understood what she meant. I also knew she could fake a broken accent so retained the possibility that she could be underselling her comprehension, deliberately setting limits rather than admitting ignorance.

Plain talk. Very well.

"You agreed to this simple outing Mourn could not do," I said, *"though you are a leader in a complex city, seeking knowledge on war and prisoners. This seems a distraction from your goals."*

She nodded that she understood, perhaps even agreed.

"There is more than teaching me to ride," I said. *"Something you want to know, or something you want to say. What is it?"*

Krithannia listened, smiled a little, and nodded. *"Wait to see. No danger to body, baby, or pride."*

An impatient growl rumbled through my head as I settled back again, scowling at the green fields. The copse of trees where Mourn had shown me his prick was coming up ahead; beyond that, the road came to an end, and we would turn either right or left. North or South.

He and I had turned right, walking in silence back to the city center. I wagered to myself that the *duk-duk* would turn left and South, although I had no prize to award myself when it happened.

Wait to see. Arrgh…

Eventually, we turned up one of those long, thin pathways bending off the main road. The trees and line-bushes grew thicker which, aside from splashes of color from patches of flowers, obscured the view of the fields beyond. Nonetheless, I smelled the undeniable mix of scents from a dwelling and straightened up in my chair.

Fire, smoke, dung, garden, food, horses… I sniffed deeper. *Leather and metal.*

And, of course, a lot of Humans.

The cart came to a halt next to a stable and series of fenced pastures, still some distance from what appeared to be the main dwelling for the Yungians tending this place. I was taken aback by the final details of our destination.

Twelve Humans gathered outside with half as many horses saddled and bridled. All were female wearing colorful, layered robes like a clutch of mages, their hair piled high on their heads and decorated with jewelry or flowers.

Only one older woman wore tan, loose bottoms like the men of the *dorji-ka*, though her shortened robe, covering her from shoulders to below her waist, appeared much like the other women. I didn't see how any except her could ride in those clothes without baring a lot of leg to be lashed by branches or bitten by bugs.

What the fuck?

I snapped my eyes back on Krithannia in her Yungian guise and spoke in Trade. "I'll be practicing with horses and docile, ill-prepared women?"

The Naulor smiled peacefully. "This will be useful to you."

I narrowed my eyes. "I am the only one wearing black. And pants."

That I appeared as a Manalari outsider wasn't worth pointing out.

I looked again. *At least they wear reasonable shoes.*

Krithannia motioned for me to get out of the *duk-duk*, and with another grumble, I complied. She followed behind me to hand our guide two coins this time, conveying her thanks and anything else with Yungian speech and their female mannerisms. After accepting and bowing his thanks, the driver nudged his pony with his heels, turning the passenger cart around to leave.

"Are we walking back?" I asked, considering whether Mourn would have to find us at dusk walking along the roads.

Krithannia shook her head. "He will meet us near here."

"So, I'm stuck here until dusk?"

The Guild Mistress chuckled. "Indeed, you are. Is that so bad?"

The Yungian girls near the barn broke into titters like a flock of birds, and I made a face, looking to the departing *duk-duk* and seriously considering a sprint after it. They pointed at us, whispering between themselves.

"I don't know, Ai-Ling, is it?" I said with sarcasm she could see in my sneer if not hear in my tone. "Will they all faint when I stomp on their demure little customs?"

"You judge them too harshly," she remarked.

"You were the one who placed Mai into a circumstance she wasn't ready for," I retorted, "just to see what *I* would do. The same that any cleric or mother back home would do to a child to test a competitor."

The Naulor cocked a brow. "Ouch."

"Truth," I bit back. "You could have told me long before we reached here, but you wanted to see my response now. You said no web speak, yet you play games Mourn did not the last two days."

Her mouth curved with amusement. "This was his idea, *Janshi.* I am not certain I agree with him if you choose hostility toward women weaker than you simply because they *are* weaker."

I glared at her. That possibility was as likely as my accusation, and I couldn't tell whether Krithannia was lying.

Meanwhile, the Yungian girls had gone quiet, watching us.

"It was his idea to say nothing until I saw it for myself?"

"Yes."

The elder woman waited for my response, her face impassive.

I stood there, deeply rankled to imagine that she *knew* what I needed from Mourn yet might lie so well that she could alter my behavior with the mere mention of needing to satisfy him.

On the other hand, the Dragonblood had plenty of time to arrange this while I'd been sleeping in the library, and he left just as much unspoken as the Guild Mistress. I could not discount that he *was* of Davrin origin and not indifferent to my presence.

Could I truly think this trip was *all* Krithannia's doing as if Mourn had no say in it? Those were the Matrons at home talking at the back of my mind. Apparently, this outing held some importance, enough to drag Krithannia out from whatever she'd been doing to find Jael. The Naulor didn't seem eager but wasn't here with me under protest.

This will be useful to you, she said.

I exhaled my annoyance, reminding myself to enjoy the open air I'd been looking forward to.

"Ai-Ling," I murmured, rubbing my eyes which had begun to ache, "the only time I spent with 'weaker' groups acting like these girls was at a castle when I tried to coax them into my bed."

I could swear Krithannia smothered a laugh. "Ah. I see. Well, there are other ways to interact with the timid. Coaxing them into the loft is not an option here."

No jesting.

"What about my being Manalari?" I asked. "Will they recoil from or ignore me?"

"No, this is permitted if I introduce you." Ai-Ling opened her arm gracefully out toward the girls. "Are you ready to join them in the paddock?"

I swallowed a groan and nodded.

Finally, we approached the group of girls and six saddled beasts swishing their tails by the tall fence. Two of the Yungians showed their relief as they came to meet us. One was the elder wearing pants, and the other appeared much younger but with far finer dress.

"Ah, Ai-Ling, wel-com back!"

"Tanzi! A gift to see you again!"

Krithannia met the pants-rider, Tanzi, with a genuine delight which surprised me as the two older women embraced.

Tanzi had some crooked teeth and deeper wrinkles in deeply brown skin on her face, possibly from day exposure. To keep her hair off her neck, she wore simple, metal rods crossed through her bun. She wore a colorful top but no flowers or jewelry.

The paler, smooth-skinned girl next to her, by comparison, could be a fine decoration not meant to be taken outside. She and I met eyes, and the girl smiled, keeping her gaze and chin up while dipping her body down, crossing her ankles and bending her knees in some mysterious move beneath her robe.

I'd never seen this before.

Unsure how to respond, I bowed, startled when she laughed abruptly. She said something to Tanzi, who sighed gently to look at me. I couldn't read her expression.

Now what?

"Respect is good, child," she said to me in Trade, "but you greet Shi-lu Dandan like two men greet each other. You are not men."

If I'd succumbed to the impulse to roll my eyes, I might have permanently strained my vision.

"Still good form," Krithannia said with admiring amusement. "She shows practice."

"Curious of her company to practice," Tanzi remarked with a smirk. "Perhaps a curtsy in return?"

I puffed air through my nose. *Not if it's whatever that teetering balance act was.*

"Ah, Janni is recovered from Witch Hunters, three year past," Ai-Ling explained, gesturing in front of her heart and belly which seemed to mean something to the two women. "She has learned to fight with men in Niss and shows talent but is fearful of horses after her trials in the south. Your teaching is kindest, Tanzi, your beasts the gentlest. Always, we come to you."

Always?

I saw a recognition in Tanzi's eyes which was not present in the fine girl's, which instantly had me suspecting whether the older woman was linked to the Guild. Perhaps she worked not only with Krithannia but Mourn, too, without knowing.

The exchange back on the boat sang in my memory.

"You have a lot of female contacts."

"They are easily overlooked, and I know how to find the best among them."

"Ai-ai, let us begin again?" Tanzi chuckled.

"Indeed, show her," Krithannia said.

Pressing her palms and fingers together, with tips just touching her lips, Tanzi bowed to me with eyes down. "I am Juo Tanzi, tutor for ladies who sit a saddle."

"The only one in Yong-wen," Ai-Ling added as if to be sure that detail was not left out.

I watched Krithannia bow to Tanzi with her palms together, fingers touching her lips, her eyes gently closed. The horse trainer nodded happily and bowed the same to me.

"Like this, Janni. Is proper for rough women like you and me."

Sigh.

I copied them, satisfied with an alternative, although the fine-dress girl simply repeated her curtsy when we were formally introduced.

"Shi-lu Dandan," she said.

I repeated the modified bow.

"Shi-lu means 'Lady Shi,'" Krithannia murmured helpfully. "Dandan is the only daughter of Shi Mu Kuo."

I froze before I could fully straighten up.

The Shi brothers' only sister?

Whom I would be dining with at midnight.

Fuck.

Alright, Naulor, you win.

Mourn had planned this for certain. I only had to discover why before he arrived.

CHAPTER 12

TANZI PROVIDED ME WITH A LIVING HORSE AS UNLIKELY TO REAR up as Nightmare had been before Troshin Bend, then she evaluated my comfort and skill in directing the animal alone. Not all the signals I'd learned from Gavin were understood by this animal, and the confusion and hesitation showed in us both.

"Ah-ah! Two bad habits!" the elder commented, remarking on my hold on the reins and how I held my heels. "Let us begin again with good form. Very basic."

Basic, good form.

I perked up. After learning and practicing three "forms" yesterday at my request, the idea of learning a new form for horse riding translated in an instant.

"Yes, Tanzi, I am ready."

Krithannia's elder Yungian persona relaxed with genuine enjoyment as the instructor gave me the beginning lessons. The twelve girls still on the ground were clearly bored as they sighed and waited.

Shi-lu Dandan was the only one to whom I was introduced; these other eleven daughters seemed either to answer to her or were looking to her for signs of how to act around me. Mostly, if I caught them looking, they smiled and nodded their head before turning to busy themselves.

So much like servant buas.

All of them listened when Tanzi occasionally said something in Yungian, seeming to request they pay attention to what I was doing. Within half an hour, the elder seemed satisfied, even pleased.

"Good!" she said, not unlike Master Shi. "You learn quick when you desire, Janni. Bad habits change." She indicated five of the other girls. "Faru, Caili, Lu, Zaiwen, Baibai. Mount up. We practice."

The girls' behaviors weren't so bad once I grew accustomed to the whispering. While old memories had put me on edge at first, I realized I conflated possible danger in their gossip with the expected behavior in buas. Gradually, I sloughed it off in favor of learning as I walked and trotted a coal-grey gelding around the pasture.

"Will horses outside Yong-wen respond to these signals?" I asked Krithannia at a point I drew close.

She nodded. "These are common horse training methods shared from Taiding to Augran, Manalar, and Ahj'Zayr."

"Ahz-where?" I interjected. "That sounds familiar."

Ai-Ling smiled. "Ahj'Zayr. Near the South Sea and neighboring the Red Desert. Due to the stronger sun, the Humans there have darker skin than by the Great Lake and farther North."

Neighbors of the Red Desert.

Somehow that brought back Mourn's multiple corrections in what I'd called them. The Humans there were not Cris-ri-phon's Zauyrians anymore, but Sal-zayr.

Yungian, Paxian, Noiri, Ma'ab, Kurgan, and Sal-zayr.

So many breeds, and the Pale Elf seemed to be implying at least one of these looked more like me. She was also saying that, in theory, I could use Tanzi's lessons to ride the horses farther to the South.

Useful, indeed.

I spent almost two hours riding, eventually moving out of the dirt paddock and into a long, grassy pasture. I was aware how my hands held the reins and what they signaled to the docile gelding beneath me. Although hand sign was a natural observation for me, thanks to the sunblind and hostility of the men, these were gestures that I hadn't ever caught and interpreted correctly by watching Gavin, Rithal, or Mathias.

This new knowledge combined with the deliberate way I could use my heels to urge more speed from the animal caused excitement to swell in my chest. How responsive the mount could be! Wholly different from both the plodding riding lizards and Nightmare's unique method of control, with the advantage of being transferrable if I must ride another equine beast elsewhere on the Surface.

"Very good, very good, Janni," said Tanzi after I'd come back from another gallop. "You learn quick! Dismount, please, and allow another girl her practice for today."

Damn.

I didn't want to but relinquished my training companion. Tanzi pulled a reddish-orange root from a bucket and held it out to me. I took it, showing my bewilderment.

"Break in pieces and feed Ku-lu with open hand," she instructed, indicating the gelding.

Oh, it's for him.

"Scratch behind ears," Tanzi continued, "tell him you honor his effort for you."

I cocked a brow. *Alright...*

After watching me break off a piece and prove that I knew how to feed a horse without having my fingers bitten off, she turned around to tend to another girl. I broke off another piece and slipped the bite of root into my own mouth to chew.

Mm. Yum.

The gelding consumed the rest almost as fast as I could offer them. We crunched and ground our roots together as I scratched his ears and muttered in Davrin after I'd swallowed.

"Thanks for your effort and, um, for being calm. Ku-lu."

Finally, I stepped back, surprised to see the next girl to practice was Dandan, herself. She adjusted the stirrups on her own but in the most baffling way, making one longer and the other as short as it could be, before taking her turn with the coal grey mount.

I'd glimpsed this oddness earlier with the other girls but had been too focused and, in some cases, too distant to see how they sat in the saddle. Now standing beside Krithannia, my hood up and the lowering sun behind me, I held my first remark until the Lady rode out of earshot.

The Naulor handed me a hefty pouch of dried travel rations, and I took it without hesitation. Pouring seeds, fruit, and meat into my palm and tossing it into my mouth, I observed Lady Dandan go through the first, familiar exercises while I chewed.

"Is this like the eating sticks?" I asked.

"What?"

"The eating sticks." I motioned to the girl riding with both her legs hanging off one side of the animal. "I'll grant I wondered how the girls would keep their legs protected, but I didn't expect them to make it even *more* difficult to stay on a horse's back to achieve this."

The Naulor chuckled. "The unmarried ladies are not supposed to part their legs so wide lest it damage their purity before their future husband's wedding night."

What?

My jaw sagged, and I fed it another handful, chewing on one side, speaking out the other. "Oh, no. Is this about the moon blood, too?"

"Ah, you know about that." Krithannia tucked a finger beneath her chin in thought. "It could be. It could also be a bit like the Manalari, some men discomforted by other men's attraction if their female family performs lewdly. Easier to control the female than to control other men's thoughts."

My teeth sheared through some meat as I rolled my eyes.

She sounded saddened. "Add to this an ever-mindful need to predict the world and spirits, which is by its nature beyond their comprehension, and practical reason for their rituals becomes obscured even to them. Lost in a morass of claiming to know that which cannot be known for the sake of those in their care or whom they hold in their power."

The Naulor spoke all that with a straight face, as if the idea was familiar enough to have been spoken many times before.

But then, she has been up here a long time.

Finishing my pouch all too soon, I observed the lessons of each Yungian daughter riding side-saddle with more curiosity now.

"The same heels signals don't work," I pointed out. "They need to use the crop to strike the horse."

"Correct," Krithannia said with a firm nod. "It is not an accident that there is an advantage on how horses might respond to a male or female rider, one with more pain signals than the other."

I felt anger in the pit of my stomach. "But there is no difference. Tanzi is teaching me the 'men's signals.' She uses them herself."

"Indeed. I am impressed how quickly you put that together."

I sneered, "And the women just accept these fake limitations and disadvantage by design?"

Krithannia looked at me, her face impassive. "The alternative is to compete with their fathers and brothers in ways which earned them respect from other competing men while, at the same time, fighting against the wishes of their mothers and threatening their positions as well. Perhaps they would be sabotaged by their sisters and cousins. I know you've seen in the Witch Hunters how violent some can become toward one unwilling to obey."

She paused. "And I understand your 'buas' face similar pressures?"

I bit my cheek hard and didn't comment on that last remark. "This is like the prostitutes not being allowed as independent merchants like letter writers or food preparers?"

Ai-Ling smiled widely. "My, my, you have had some fun conversations these last two days." She cleared her throat. "Indeed, like that. Whether a lady or a washer, their bodies are not sovereign. They can be well cared for just as easily as not should their actions or words threaten the power of others, especially the pride of the man seen as responsible for her and what she learns."

Also like our buas. I sighed.

"Yong-wen is healthy and peaceful because most do what is expected to maintain the order," Krithannia continued. "Although other places and breeds of Humans may be more or less strict as they must always test their limits."

"They must?" I asked.

"Indeed, they are extremely adaptable if their resources or territory changes quickly, more so than the Dwarves, and would probably make my people's heads spin to keep up. I have seen women become like you under the right circumstances."

"Truly? Where?"

How interested I sounded even to my own ears. Ai-Ling smiled to hear it.

"Currently, among the Noiri along the ice coast up North. Also in Taiding, working among the Dwarves. I have heard interesting stories for the Kurgan women on the Steppes as well, frequently fighting the Ma'ab to deter them from invading their land."

It wasn't difficult to see the pattern.

"Where order and safety are less certain," I said, "the women can shed these restrictions which are enforced in Yong-wen."

Krithannia nodded with patience.

"You have traveled far," I said.

"I have."

"Have you been to the Desert?"

She disappointed me by shaking her head. "I have not. I've had no reason thus far to travel that far. Even the Sal-Zayr rarely go deep into the dunes."

"Why not?"

"It is harsh and dangerous, and there is little reward for the risk of dying from thirst. The Humans say nothing is there but lost ghosts."

Hmm.

We stood watching the Yungian daughters practice their difficult skill in silence. I estimated dusk was another two hours away and wondered if I could get another chance to mount up. Perhaps on a different horse who was livelier, to test my budding skills.

The Naulor scattered this coalescing question with her next topic.

"Dandan has been well tutored in her role and has never rebelled against it." Krithannia spoke in a tone I could hear only the Guild Mistress using. "But she is not without promise. She is intelligent with many aptitudes."

I squinted at her, waiting for the point to be made.

"I have seen reports recently suggesting Dandan may have mage potential," the Pale Elf said at last, "though this means she would not only be untrained for her life, but her role would require her to suppress it until after she married, to protect her father's name. Any safety in exploring it would depend on her husband."

My squint became a frown. "Are Yungian female mages considered 'witches,' too?"

"Yes, though accepted more in the elderly, the 'crones.' As a way she may contribute if she outlives her husband and must rely on her son to care for her. Young witches are too threatening to the men until she's had children."

Of course.

The silence stretched for a while, then I finally gave in.

"Why are you telling me this, Guild Mistress?"

Krithannia's "crone" face smiled with apparent satisfaction; she checked to make sure none were close enough to overhear before speaking.

"We know the Shi patriarch is willing to provide you with his youngest son's company after the gathering."

I straightened. "Bohai?"

Krithannia nodded. "But there is absolutely no way Shi Mu Kuo would provide a companion for a sky warrior in this way without also providing one of equal or greater value to the Dragon Spirit of Yong-wen."

My eyes widened despite the low-key ache, and I looked at the girl riding the grey gelding.

"Precisely," the Guild Mistress murmured. "But to further consider the importance of this, *Janshi*, Dandan has never been with a lover, yet she would be ordered by her father to satisfy the Dragon Spirit for the honor of the family. This is probably one of the only circumstances where a young woman could give her purity before marriage and *not* be punished or disowned by her father."

"I would think not," I growled, "as it's his idea and command!"

"That it is." Krithannia chuckled softly. "You are open to this? You enjoy your chosen *bua*, and Mourn takes the patriarch's only daughter to her bed?"

I hadn't yet thought that far ahead. I swallowed as my stomach did an odd and uncomfortable flip.

"I can see why he'd want *you* to present this to me," I grumbled, folding my arms.

"True, he did not want you to be caught by surprise, but the circumstances are very unusual." The Guild Mistress smiled gently. "I know him well enough. I would say he is nervous."

Nervous. Ha!

That was an amusing mental picture.

"Has he experience rutting a 'pure' girl?" I asked bluntly. "I mean, he *is* large. I remember how even a normal size burned my sex at first."

Krithannia seemed intrigued. "Are you concerned for her pain?"

"I know he doesn't enjoy harming women lacking choice or defense," I replied. "And this situation is exactly that. In theory, he only considered this on my account. To have one, there must be the other. Otherwise, it is neither. Too late for that, as he has already accepted the honor."

"Ah, I am glad you see all this." The Naulor contemplated.

"He likely also desires it," I continued, my arms tightening around myself, "as I understand it has been a while. He claims to have few sources for such release that don't cause some lasting pinch of regret."

"Indeed, he has more than a few."

"I hope I'm not standing next to one."

I eyeballed Krithannia blatantly after saying that, and she laughed loudly enough that Tanzi and a few others looked our way.

"This goes better than I imagined," the Naulor remarked, her shoulders relaxing. "As you are so curious, once, and long ago, he and I were lovers. We are not anymore, but that is without regret. The drift was gradual and relatively painless."

I was confused. "What? Drift?"

"His growth is independent of mine, and we know our purpose apart from each other even as our paths have been parallel for some time." The Naulor shrugged. "We did not feel the physical attraction at the start, then circumstances changed, and there was a period where we did. We embraced it. But we no longer feel the urge now."

I don't believe you.

Krithannia looked at my face and shook her head sagely. "Make no mistake, Baenar, I still care deeply for him and his well-being, and I will come to his aid should he ask me."

"Like now," I interjected.

"Like now. But you must understand, because this is important."

I looked at her. Her silvery-grey eyes were a bit bluer now, and she stared back at me unblinking.

"I do not control or manipulate his body, and he does not control or manipulate mine," she said. "We have learned, as long-lived races among the young ones, we are better off accepting these natural changes. It is best that our concepts and understanding of love need not cage each other, like they do where we come from."

Where we come from?

"We are no longer trapped in a dead past while the younger world flows on without us," Krithannia continued. "We are part of it again because we could relearn this evolving joy. To experience this is a stronger pleasure than any simple rutting we could do today. It has allowed our spirits' growth in ways such as I've never known before."

My chest was in significant discomfort to hear her summarize a few centuries of a unique connection with the Dragonblood. I grew nauseated as the idea struck me like a flood, and I couldn't help but see my Valsharess caging Shyntre, Wilsira caging Kerse, the Priestesses caging the Consorts, and the Matrons trapping their sons.

Jilrina caged me.

We were all trapped in their past until they died.

Krithannia's gentle but firm voice filtered through the haze.

"You would be wise to contemplate this as well, Sirana, while you are up here. You are not too young to do so, and thankfully, not too old."

Wasn't I?

I'd already seen and understood where I had come from. Releasing a bua to find his own way once the attraction changed was... well, if one was responsible for him, it was unheard of. He could be given to someone else, but he could *not* choose his way or his companions. No one of whom his mother and sisters didn't approve. He sooner died.

Because someone would kill him for defying her.

"Are you alright?"

Ai-Ling sounded concerned.

"No," I muttered, "but it'll pass."

Exhaling slowly, I refocused on Dandan as she rode. She smiled with a simple joy, guiding the gelding within the fenced area she was allowed to explore without being surrounded by other girls.

I asked, "Does Shi-lu know she is intended for the Dragon Spirit?"

"Not yet. I pray you will not deliberately scare her."

"*Pfft.*" I snickered, welcoming any laugh to neutralize the venom of my memories. "No. If Mai was any example, I do not seek my entertainment in such ways. It is also not useful, more trouble than reward."

"I believe you." Krithannia sounded curious. "How would you claim entertainment in this circumstance?"

I thought about that and smiled easily to think of Jael yet again, this time as the new recruit in the Cloister. A flash of hot desire passed through my gut as I relived the first eve we'd shared together.

She had been exhausted and already abused by others; I'd let her sleep in my room until we woke up naturally. My new younger Sister was reluctant and afraid, yet I had gradually coaxed her to cum against my mouth.

My smile remained as I answered the Naulor's question. "I would share my experience with her. It's not unusual for more than one female to share space with their chosen buas, though the mood depends on if they have any attraction for each other."

The Naulor lifted her brows with clear surprise. "Ah. So this is the same in both underground cities."

I grimaced at this reminder. "If you say. I never knew the other was there until I came up here."

"Indeed, I heard."

"What about you?" I posed the question. "Your garden-tending sister seems more Yungian than Davrin."

"Hm, true enough," Krithannia granted, clasping her hands behind her back. "We value privacy as much as our pair bonds. We do not share rooms with other couples."

"Pity." I grinned with satisfaction in my collection of boasts far beyond one-and-one coupling.

Although, this *did* suggest another reason for Tamuril's reluctance to show me her skin. More to do with her fathers' and brothers' expectations before my Lead discovered her trespassing.

That would also explain why the Druid thought Auslan was more important to my baby than I was.

Some daylight remained when the Yungian girls had all finished their lessons. They returned as a group to the house for tea, leaving me behind with Ai-Ling, so I asked Tanzi to try another mount. She granted it easily.

"One more, Janni, one more," she laughed, choosing a deep sorrel mare with a black mane and tail and more spring in her step.

With the older women observing, we ran through the basics once more, and soon I was trotting off toward the far end of the pasture. I nudged her into a canter and then a gallop.

I regained that sense of the free wind that, as we approached the back fence of the pasture forcing us to turn around, a temptation whispered plainly in my ears.

Jump.

My unobtrusive spiders tightened up with anticipation.

Under necessity, we could always jump over the boundaries together. For now, however, I chose to turn around, chose to obey that stated limit of my hosts and my tutors to maintain the peace for now.

They couldn't keep me here, after all. I would be riding into war soon enough.

"Come," said Tanzi, taking the reins from me after we'd "cooled" the mare down, tilting her head toward the open stable. "You help brush down."

I narrowed my eyes with suspicion after the instructor turned around, glancing toward the gaggle of Yungian girls in a covered, open-air space doing no work at all. From here, though the shadows were long and growing deeper as the Sun went down, I could hear them clearly, laughing and squealing between one another.

"Would you rather be up there?" Krithannia asked me.

She sounded serious.

"Fuck, no," I muttered. "I only wonder if looking Manalari makes me a lesser worker in Yong-wen?"

"To some, yes. Though, Tanzi is normally the lesser here. She tends all the horses alone when the group is like this one, all from wealthier families." Ai-Ling looked toward the stable. "We could help her. It might be good for you to know."

"What about Mourn finding us here?"

"He won't walk in. He'll wait for us." She touched my shoulder. "Come. Only two horses each. Very quick."

With an inward sigh, I joined the two older women in the stalls, helping to remove their tackle then dry and brush them down. I had observed Gavin enough already to have an idea.

Tanzi was pleased, assisting me only with the side-saddle storage I wasn't familiar with while thanking us for the help. She even had a nicely scented soap to wash my hands to get the horse sweat, hair, and dirt off our skin at the end.

I'd noticed an exchange or two between Ai-Ling and Tanzi that I couldn't interpret, but as the "rough" woman began the next steps of preparing feed for the horses, the Naulor in disguise moved close to me.

"He's outside," she whispered. "I will stay here. You go."

Instead of asking how she knew—that concept was obvious to any Red Sister with a message pellet—I said, "Are you returning to the city center?"

Her mouth curled on one end. "Not to worry. I will tend to myself. Go outside."

I glanced at Tanzi, who had her back turned to fuss with measures of grains as if she wasn't listening. I didn't want to get caught in the guesswork of farewell rituals, however, so I nodded and turned to the partially open door, pausing long enough to skim the grounds outside before slipping out alone.

When the half-blood didn't reveal himself immediately, and I felt too close to burring horses and twittering girls anyway, I began a fast pace walking down the nearest pasture toward the road.

I kept going for almost a quarter hour, finding the firmest and least obstructed grounds which were still off the main roads and staying aware of the wind's direction. I knew when my scent would be safe from the noses of Tanzi's animals, thus, Mourn's would be as well.

If you're meant to find me at dusk, mercenary, the time has come.

The sky had grown dark enough that any Human would have tripped over dirt clods and rodent holes without a lantern or torch to guide them. Yet, for me, the lingering ache behind my eyes eased and vanished in that time. I slowed down, simply having no destination in mind, kept my gait steady and my footing sure in the grass and brush.

My skin prickled, and I looked to my left, spotting something like liquid shadow coming out of the trees. The metallic sheen of his eyes had me realize I'd been tracing his tail.

"Hah," I breathed, pointing at him as if I hadn't failed to see him in enough time to escape if I was prey.

His low chuckle rolled from his chest as he stepped up to walk beside me in the grass.

"Not bad," Mourn said in our native tongue. "Where are you headed?"

I shrugged. "How far is the Shi plantation from here?"

He looked North. "Off the main road, about two hours on foot, though we could make it faster."

"If we did, what do we do until midnight?" I asked. "How and where do we present ourselves? You know, I smell like sweat and horse."

He showed his white teeth, flicking out his tongue as if to confirm. "That is easily mended when the time comes. We'll approach their manor from the rear and present ourselves to two guards at the garden gate who shall be prepared. They will lead us in."

"And until then?" I asked again.

"Aside from the travel? We haven't seemed to run out of topics of conversation."

I smirked. "You want to talk."

"Don't you?"

"Can we start with Dandan being a 'pure' gift to you?"

His tail flicked once. "That was what I expected."

I chuckled. "First. Does this have *anything* to do with Mai?"

He looked surprised. "Well, in the sense of 'proving' you are a life protector, yes. But I'm sure you grasp the custom of perceived balance."

"With one as important and revered as you? Oh, yes!" I huffed. "But you could have hinted in the *dorji-ka* that choosing one for me also meant choosing one for you."

"I didn't know what Shi Mu Kuo would say until this morning."

"Yes, but I might have chosen a less *entangled* male if you had suggested the possibility."

The Dragonchild smirked at me. "Would you have? Do you not enjoy better the challenge of earning your true choice, not making do with less? Haven't you engaged with me in maneuvering and intrigue over the last day, even a little?"

Yes, I have. Tongue dipper.

"Learned habits," I countered. "Yet I was under the impression you cut all ties with the viciousness of the web in the Deepearth, choosing to learn more generous, balanced lessons up here."

"Viciousness is one thing. Measuring the impulses and intelligence of one who cannot harm me but could harm others is quite another. Surely, you've seen already there is a web up here as well, one even more complex for its sheer size and span."

He'd staked my foot on that one.

"I have begun to see it," I replied, "and it's a game in which you hid your enjoyment well at first. I trust you anticipate your earned 'pure gift' as much as I anticipate mine?"

"With appropriate caution. Many more steps to reach that point."

I thought of his pointed glans and chuckled. "Another question."

"Yes?"

"Bohai admitted being a flirt. Have you any insight as to his own 'purity' like his sister?"

"Unfortunately, no," Mourn answered, sounding genuine. "Young men like him aren't watched as carefully as his sister is. He could be flirting with his clothes on and share her lack of experience, or he could have found some good hiding spots to practice."

I was grinning despite myself. "I wager I will read him quickly enough. Whichever way doesn't matter. I have ideas for him which don't involve squatting on his pole as first thing."

"Oh?"

"Oh, yes."

I let the silence fill a bit then asked, "So, what happens to Dandan after she is permitted to use her first time with you instead of a bartered husband?"

Mourn considered his answer with care.

"A few possibilities," he said. "It depends how tonight goes."

"Oh? Does one include seeing her life devalued or destroyed after bedding the Dragon Spirit?"

He sighed. "That is always a possibility, but not the most likely one here. It is possible I can *raise* her value to her father by doing this."

"How benevolent of you."

"Less that, and more this is her father's view on it."

"Which matters most."

"His influence over his family, male and female, does mirror a Matron."

"*Hmph.* With one big exception."

The Dragonchild smirked. "Which one?"

"I'm quite sure Matrons prefer consorts to have a good amount of experience in sex before they're made into long-term companions. 'Purity' is undesirable. It means he hasn't practiced any read or rhythm with females and is perhaps too quick to spurt."

Mourn shook his head and looked at a few stars. "If you say."

He didn't like that reality but declined to say more. I looked out at the eastern fields, spotting the first of two moons rising, before trying to fill the void myself.

"Speaking of the purity of sons, what about Bohai? Will my dalliance have any impact on his status with his father and others?"

"Yes," he answered, still willing to talk, "but assuming he satisfies you, Bohai has many more choices than Dandan in using it to his advantage. Imagine this parallel to him being you as a Noble coaxing a son from a higher House into your bed."

I laughed out loud. "Oh, no need to imagine, Mourn. I did that."

A lot.

"Ah, good. Then you know how he has similar benefits and obstacles. Some might be envious enough they will not work with him later for spite, but some most certainly will, depending on how he plays it."

"Can his older brothers use it against him?"

"Yes, and probably will. But given that Bohai will not inherit the manor or land and is considering his choices, backbiting is more likely to enhance his reputation instead of diminishing it. His brothers would harm him more by *not* talking about it, but I doubt they are capable of such restraint."

I chortled. "I see. So, I need not worry. Wearing myself out will enhance options for him."

"Agreed, though this should be enjoyable for both of you."

I smiled at his tone. "Oh? Do you want to stay in the room with us, bodyguard, to make certain I don't harm him or take my pleasure at his expense?"

The Dragonchild's expression turned dry. "I *do* have my own focus to minimize harm and enhance the pleasure of an initiate."

"Agreed, and much more challenging than mine!" I felt my hips sway in stepping down a soft hill as I beckoned to him. "So bring her with you. If you wish, you could wait until Bohai and I are tired out. While you guard, perhaps Dandan might grow accustomed to you holding her."

He was painting that in his mind, I could tell.

"She may even accept she is safe with you, and learn what is expected of her from watching me," I coaxed. "When it is your turn, her body may be further awakened and warm to you. In addition, Dandan will have an additional witness in her family to confirm that she has pleased and was blessed by the Dragon Spirit. It may even aid Bohai against his detractors if he is bold enough."

Mourn didn't reply at first; he was just looking ahead.

Then he turned a stern gaze on me.

"What?" I challenged him. "I understand this is known in Vuthra'tern as well as Sivaraus."

"What is?" he rumbled.

"Being present during a group rut, even choosing your time to engage in it, while making certain an agreement is kept and one Davrin is not abused by several." I shrugged. "This *does* happen in

Sivaraus. While this circumstance may be unusual for Yong-wen, it feels like home to me. Unsurprising, now that you have called it a web."

Once I'd completed my offer and argument in favor, I pressed him no more, as I'd detected in him that same mood as after he'd ejaculated on the ground between my ankles. At least this time, I'd stirred up deep memories with a purpose, bringing to the fore that he and I had a shared custom between us, even being born in two different cities.

As before, it was a long wait before he spoke.

"Let me think about this," he said.

I smiled. That was good enough for me.

We walked the rest of the way to the Shi manor in a more companionable silence. Only three notable things happened before we would eventually approach two guards at the rear garden. First, the two sister moons would rise together, each not quite full but spilling tremendous silver light across Yong-wen and its surrounding hills.

"A good night for this," Mourn remarked. "More moonlight is a time for benevolent spirits."

"And nights with no moonlight are for dangerous ones?" I guessed.

"Exactly."

"I imagine that has to do with how well they can see a shape coming toward them in the dark."

The Dragonblood laughed, and a small, furry animal nearby darted away. "Probably, though the stories which the dark inspires are impressively complicated. Humans dislike complete darkness more than any sentient I've met."

The second event happened as we watched the main road in the distance. A carriage drawn by two horses, plus another rider on horseback, caught up and passed by us at a strenuous trot.

"Ah, Dandan is late," Mourn commented.

"Oh, is she now?" I chuckled.

"The other girls would stay the night and return in the morning, but it looks like her sire Shi sent a runner to get her."

"So, she's not likely to get that 'first sleep' as she bathes and prepares for you?"

Mourn was amusingly hesitant to address that directly. "I dare say all of them will miss that sleep. This is a lifetime event for the house of Shi."

I nudged his elbow with mine. "While you and I just want volunteers for a pleasant, last rut before Manalar."

His tail snaked behind him. "Hm. Indeed."

The last thing to happen, before *Wen-yung* and *Janshi-lantiu* greeted the quaking guards in the garden, was Mourn's magical cleansing. We sloughed off the sweat and dirt from my horse riding and our journey here, to present ourselves as fresh as the wealthy family with access to baths.

At the same time, Mourn opted not to keep me guessing.

"I would prefer to guard as you enjoy Bohai," he murmured. "If you do not protest."

Unbridled heat filled my middle as a spread of tingles rushed between my legs. I looked up at him in astonishment. "I do not. Why would I?"

"Is that an agreement?"

I huffed a laugh. "Is Dandan coming, too?" I grinned wider. "Both ways?"

He smiled, though just a bit. "That is a firm goal for tonight."

I hummed in anticipation. "Then yes. That is an agreement, To'vah-krav."

CHAPTER 13

THE PATRIARCH SHI MU KUO AND HIS BROTHER MASTER SHI greeted us personally just after I'd removed my boots and Mourn had scrubbed his scaly feet at the rear entrance.

They waited with poise, their backs straight, while the guards opened a large, double-paneled cabinet into which we placed our cloaks and my boots. The guards then closed it up, using a red ribbon to tie the two handles together with care and deliberate design. Meanwhile, I felt my spiders hide deeper within my braided hair.

"Father Shi," Mourn greeted in Trade, bowing to each man. "Master Shi."

"*Wen-yung!*"

"You have returned!"

The greetings held an incredible joy barely contained. Just looking at Father Shi's charming eyes made the feeling a tangible part of the room.

"With pleasure, I have," the Dragon Spirit answered. "I escort our most honored guest, *Janshi-lantiu*."

I was relieved that I might be allowed to understand more of our night's rituals as the Father and Master bowed in the same manner to me, just a bit less deeply. It was easy for me to match it and keep my expression pleasant.

The elder man's facial hair was mixed black and silver, finely trimmed, and braided into three deliberate twists leading off his chin. He was a well-fed man, plumper and less defined than the *dorji-ka* instructor next to him.

Both men wore fine clothing meeting my expectations for the loose-fitting, layered, and highly colored styles of Yong-wen. Their robes reached to the upper thighs, overlaying baggy dark trousers, and I found not a smudge or frayed end on them. They wore well-crafted sandals which did not appear to have ever been worn outside. Shi Mu Kuo's toenails were very clean, his brother's, somewhat less so.

"Your wild beauty astounds a mortal man, *Janshi-lantiu*," said Father Shi, beckoning us forward. "Come within my home, come! It is too tight here!"

I peered around the open room with woven mats and no less than ten places to sit, lie down, or even swing close to the ground. Plants hung in pots beside what must be large windows covered by tightly bound reed shades.

If this is tight, what is the interior like?

The elder man led us forward while the two guards remained in the garden room. We passed without pause a wing I knew to be the servants' quarters by scent alone, then another which would be the kitchen. Both were full of heat, scents, and quite lively in their blend of sounds.

My stomach awoke instantly, measuring how long it had been since I'd poured Krithannia's bag of trail rations into my mouth.

Oh, goddess, what magnificent Yungian dishes are in store for us this time? What does Father Shi consider his 'best?'

Before I would find out, I must meet the Shi brothers again and confirm whether Dandan had made it back in time to be ready for our arrival. If her preparation was anything like our Nobles back home, the chances were even.

Meanwhile, I was treated to a reverse look at these sloped-roofed manors. Our way from the servants' sections narrowed a bit further before opening wide toward the front. I saw enough rooms on the main floor to operate the entire family business, yet the ceiling seemed low enough to anticipate another floor and the multiple narrow stairways leading up to them.

The Shi private suites.

The care taken with the designs utilizing storage space beneath stairs and between rooms was impressive. When we reached the front entrance, I understood why Father Shi called the rear space "tight."

Fucking goddess.

"*Chinzui, chinzui!*" announced their patriarch, firm but jovial, as he lifted his hands and spoke rapidly in Yungian.

By his hand motions alone and the ripple of murmurs, I knew he introduced us to all those awake at this late hour, so many present which didn't include those working in the kitchen.

A sweep of the front room counted more than thirty Yungians: a minimum of two guards and two servants for each Shi family member who stood together in the middle. Of those dressed in finery, I recognized Renshu, Hulin, and Bohai first, as they stood in the front of two more males I didn't recognize, with four older women behind them and…

Ah, yes, there she is.

Dandan stood delicately without an age-mate, to one side of her mothers and grandmothers. She was even more decorated than she had been beside the corral, wearing three or four layers of colors which all reached the floor to cover her feet. She appeared petrified to do anything which might mar her complicated hairstyle and exaggerated face paint.

Before Mourn has the chance, anyway.

Did this mean that she'd been told what had been decided for her, or was she simply intimidated with the rest?

I wasn't sure I liked the painted mask on her. Even if colored enhancements of our best features existed back home at Court, even if I understood their purpose, there had been no time or place for that in the Cloister.

Even Elder D'Shea only showed Sivaraus her natural beauty.

With all present in this grand, well-lit entrance, plenty of clean floor space remained. The all-wood expanse beneath my feet was a lighter color than I had been seeing in town, somehow polished to a high gloss. Long, narrow carpets arranged to guide stockinged or sandaled feet suggested pathways to various exits while adding huge swaths of vivid details to the room.

The carpets led in four directions: forward to the front double-wide doors, to the right-side set of wide stairs leading up to the next level, and to the left to yet another garden seen through an open window. This courtyard had flowers and elegant bushes but no herbs, soil roots, or fruiting trees.

Lastly, the enormous space expanded behind us, wrapping around to the left to double back toward the rear of the house. I spied the indoor room parallel to the flower garden, widening into what seemed a space for dining or other gatherings.

The Shi manor held enough similarity to a Davrin manor, I pondered Mourn having had influence in this as well while, at the same time, wanting to deny it. The basic design was functional for any family of wealth, while the crafts and artistry were not at all like home.

I don't know what a Matron House looks like in Vuthra'tern, anyway.

My attention snapped back when Mourn took a step forward.

Subtly, he signed, ★Don't laugh.★

Don't laugh at what?

Renshu and Hulin stepped forward, mirroring us before lowering themselves in front and facing us with their legs folded underneath, their backs straight and eyes down. They bowed so low that their foreheads touched the carpet. Their arms stretched forward toward us, their palms up, implying beseechment.

"We beg forgiveness for insult, Janshi," Hulin murmured against the carpet, nonetheless intelligible. "For embarrassing our fathers and grandfathers with our mischief."

Renshu repeated the statement less audibly.

"Renshu!" Shi Mu Kuo barked.

"We beg forgiveness for insult, *Janshi-lantiu!*" he repeated loudly. "For embarrassing our fathers and grandfathers with our mischief!"

Oh, goddess!

Now I understood Mourn's warning; I had to bite my cheek hard to prevent the untimely snigger.

"Accept, and do not be vicious," Mourn whispered in Davrin. *"There is no need."*

"Understood."

Before I accepted, however, I found and made eye contact with Bohai first, winking when I did. He threw his gaze back to the floor as his cheeks darkened, and a few of his family dared to hum in their throats.

He looked almost exactly like a bua at Court who knew I'd soon corner him in my bedroom, and he wasn't seeking an escape.

Oh, this is going to be fun.

I could wait a little longer for our meal.

I stepped forward and bent down to tickle one open palm of each older brother at once. They jumped, pulled their arms back in reflex, and began to lift their heads when I spoke.

"For the honor of the city-wide generosity of Shi and their superior schools in Yong-wen," I said, reaching into my bracer to pull out the small vial I'd tucked inside, "the brothers' mischief is forgiven once by the sky warriors. Stand, please."

They had probably been waiting for their patriarch to instruct them but obeyed me all the same. I grinned as Hulin unfolded and raised his body more slowly, wincing with soreness.

I reached for his arm. "Here, hold it straight, pull back your sleeve to the shoulder."

I demonstrated doing the same as I uncorked the vial, the oil's medicinal scent wafting out. Equal parts shocked and afraid, the second born son pulled back his fine and vibrant sleeve, eventually showing his upper arm like I did. Hulin was indeed bruised from the number of times I'd struck him; his face darkened with embarrassment.

I poured a bit of oil onto my fingertips and rubbed it into my forearm to prove it wasn't poison before dabbing out more and reaching for his arm to massage the ointment into the darkest bruise.

"Ow," he complained but didn't withdraw from me.

"This helps with the pain," I said, replacing the cork and pressing the vial into Hulin's palm before folding his hand around it. I squeezed it with both of mine. "A gift for your mending."

The young man blinked at me twice then held the vial in both his hands as he bowed to me and then Mourn with a mild tremor. "Ah...thank you, such... *much* gratitude, *Janshi! Wen-yung!*"

I bowed my chin to him, keeping my back straight, and easily spotted Father and Master Shi's approval while sensing the intensity of relief in all present. I also enjoyed how minimal we needed to acknowledge the more stubborn firstborn son. Renshu only used the second born brother as camouflage for his own actions; there was simply nothing much of him *to* acknowledge.

The empty space in my middle gurgled loudly: *Enough delay.*

"Ah!" I chuckled, patting my middle, and looking to the patriarch. "I must say, your meal smells delicious, much desired by this new body of flesh."

"Yes! Oh, indeed! Let us sit!"

Father Shi motioned grandly to the left and back, toward that open space set on the rear, long side of the garden. The large crowd began to shift, seeming to know in what order they were supposed to be walking. I could only follow Mourn's lead as he walked right behind the patriarch and in front of the master of the *dorji-ka.*

Likewise, I assumed a known rank to the seating as well but couldn't begin to guess. The largest table was round, and none of the chairs looked like a throne.

Mourn signed, ★Wait to be invited.★

★Confirmed,★ I motioned back.

Shi Mu Kuo took grand enjoyment in seating everyone himself, a task I could not imagine any Matron doing. First, the Father Shi pulled out and stood before a comfortable chair and motioned Mourn to be seated on his right and myself on his left. The family filled out the rest of the circle seemingly according to age. Master Shi sat on the other side of Mourn, with the rest of the males curving around, becoming younger as they got farther away, with Bohai almost across from his sire.

The seating orders for females mirrored this on the patriarch's left, although with an exception. The age-peer to Father Shi, his "wife" probably, was seated next to me, then the rest from eldest grandmother to youngest, with Dandan next to Bohai.

Orderly and predictable. *So far, so good.*

The table had been set with glossy bowls, cups, and plates far more fragile than the wooden ones I'd been using thus far. A set of pale and polished eating sticks had been placed neatly on a small, marble rest, the sticks themselves made of something rarer than wood.

★No fingers, please,★ Mourn signed.

Glad I practiced with the sticks a little before this.

He'd said there would be many more steps this night before I could coax him and the siblings to share the same room. I'd already seen plenty of formalities, yet I was about to see how much ritual a wealthy Yungian might shove into every aspect of life.

So be it.

In the end, Jael still awaited our bargain, and I would not fail her.

The hot, fragrant food arrived on large serving platters, each placed in the center of the table upon a low, finely carved wooden platform. I blinked to watch them spin it in place as they added each one, grasping in an instant that everyone would be eating from the same source.

Any worry about tampered food evaporated as the scents collectively enveloped my face. My chest expanded to its limit without volition, and I felt dizzy as my mouth flooded with saliva. I swallowed as Father Shi chuckled and bowed his chin to show his pride and pleasure.

Oh yeah, baby and I are ready for this.

With that spinning platform, I'd also be able to reach anything that suited me without having to ask for it like a child.

★No,★ Mourn gestured as my hand started to rise. ★Wait for the sire to serve you.★

I bit back a growl with my hands clasped in my lap. Father Shi stood alone as he picked up Mourn's plate and then mine, serving us first with small portions of each dish on the platform.

Too small, I thought. Hopefully I could request seconds.

Even worse, I was forced to sit and stare at it when the Dragonblood didn't touch his. He was clearly waiting for everyone else to be served.

Sigh.

The family passed their plates to him one at a time; Master Shi reached low and around Mourn's plate and his wife did the same around mine. I'd begun to lose hope that I would enjoy the meal while it was still hot, even though Shi Mu Kuo worked with graceful diligence to serve all the plates the same starting out.

Meanwhile, Dandan stood up and moved with great care to pour tea and wine for everyone as if she was a servant. I didn't understand that but could say nothing to Mourn as all eyes watched her approach us, even his.

I studied her face carefully when Mourn thanked her for his drink. She curtsied with grace, but I saw her bottom lip quiver, her eyes filled with trepidation as they swept over his bare chest and patches of glossy scales.

Oh, yes. She knows.

The girl barely seemed to hear me when I followed Mourn's lead, though my accent was no doubt muddled. As she passed me, I caught her scent even through the powder on her face and neck.

The girl was sweating fear under all those layers.

I'd thought to note how much appetite Bohai had and added both Mourn and Dandan to the list as I waited for the signal to begin eating.

First, the patriarch offered a formal welcome and prayer of thanks to the Dragon Spirit and the Sky Warrior in Yungian, repeating a shorter version in Trade. If I could have blended everything I had heard in Yong-wen up to this point into one short speech, I thought Shi Mu Kuo had done an impressive job.

"Please! Cherished family and blessed spirits. Enjoy your meal."

He sat down.

Finally.

But I still waited for Mourn to take the first bite before diving in.

Picking up my bowl of a thin and flavorful vegetable soup, I sipped from it as I'd seen them do in the rest of Yong-wen. This was the correct behavior as about half at the table chose to start with the same dish.

In a Matron's House or at Court, soup was to be eaten in silence with a spoon, so it was amusing to hear rounds of audible slurps. At least I didn't have to burn my lips to be quiet.

Meanwhile, others demonstrated how to eat the rest, their motions neat and deliberate most of the time. They sucked in whole noodles through their lips, licking the different sauces before chewing, closed mouthed.

Many dishes highlighted the meats from the waters: fish cut raw and wrapped in a green waterweed, filets seared with fire, or broken chunks steamed with water. We had crawlers boiled whole or shelled and mixed with minced vegetable, and I recognized a soft-bodied squid from Mourn's description, though I'd thought they were bigger.

It certainly mimics a tiny, boneless Ornilleth's head.

I firmly pushed that mental view aside to tuck the seasoned morsel between my lips using the sticks. Neither stringy nor chewy, very mild yet my mouth knew this was a good thing to eat for lasting energy.

Sort of like eating a soft-cooked egg. Tasty.

In addition to the lake and river creatures, my plate presented darker cuts from land-walkers, while light-colored meats from feathered birds had been hidden in a crunchy crust, discovered only after I bit into one.

"Ah-ah!" said Father Shi, grabbing my attention. "Plop!"

Plop?

Holding back his sleeve with one hand, the patriarch demonstrated dipping his crunchy fowl into a dollop of thick, orange jelly I hadn't tasted yet. He consumed it with relish.

"Favorite," he assured me after swallowing.

I dipped the other bite of my bird into the congealed sauce and tried them together, taken aback by the strong sensation of heat and sweetness on my tongue, and a powerful scent of a sour fruit overtaking my nose. It lasted for several instants before gradually mellowing and…changing.

The flavor turned floral and very sweet by the time I swallowed, nearly the heat gone.

Oh, that was *much* more interesting!

"I understand why, father," I said with a lopsided smile as I reached to snag another piece. "Delicious!"

How the fuck did they make this?

Father Shi laughed with clear pride and joy. This brought smiles to the faces of his entire family, even Dandan.

Once I'd emptied my plate of each carefully crafted dish, I realized Mourn and I had pulled a bit ahead of the Humans. The patriarch responded by pausing his own meal to serve us again, something truly shocking to me if I might've equated him with a Matron. He even asked which ones we liked best and seemed to enjoy plying us with more of our favorites.

"Plenty to have, plenty!" he assured everyone.

Indeed, and they must have begun this plan in earnest once Mourn had agreed to come tonight.

No 'first sleep' for anyone.

Other family members served second helpings for themselves, yet when I'd finished my plate the second time, the father laughed heartily and served me smaller portions of each dish again. Perhaps he got a perverse pleasure out of the fact I would eat anything that he placed on my plate.

Shameless, I enjoyed this third platter, only realizing as I grew thirsty that my full cup of yellow-green tea had grown cold. I used that to quench my thirst, ignoring the sour wine after the opening toast. The room quieted around me as the family finished their meals, and Mourn made sure to catch my eye, signing to remind me.

★The meal will not stop until you leave food on your plate.★

Pity.

I was still annoyed by the idea of deliberately leaving food to be wasted to say I was finished, but perhaps the servants would consume what was left over from the nobles, like at the safehouse.

Unfortunately, our servants at House Thalluen didn't dare eat from Noble plates because my sisters had thought it was amusing to spoil their leftovers on the chance that someone in the kitchen got "greedy." I'd heard this reasoning a time or two at Court as well, so any uneaten food may simply not be safe to eat.

I'd fallen into the habit of clearing my plate so I could set myself apart from those cunts. The amount I'd been served had rarely been enough to satisfy, anyway.

Here in Yong-wen, however, even my pregnant stomach could be satisfied to the fullest it had ever been on the Surface. That in itself was an impressive feat, considering the abundance I'd found anywhere I'd been since spring, excepting the warp rot.

The final nudge to end the meal came from a glance across the circular table. Bohai had finished a while ago and seemed to be waiting patiently, though he had not looked directly at me through the meal.

I watched as he reached to touch Dandan's sleeve, seeming to ask after her wellbeing without words. She glanced at him and offered a nervous smile but dropped her eyes to her half-empty plate, which may have been her first helping provided by her father.

Hm.

His sister hadn't had time to grow at ease to the "honor" of helping two randy spirits find release, but the thirdborn son was ready to try.

Thirdborn like me.

I set down my eating sticks, leaving my last few morsels where they were. Taking up my cup, I sipped the tea with no intent to empty it while a few men took some final bites. I even heard a handful of satisfied belches, even from the women, which surprised me.

So, now what?

Father Shi stood up first, and everyone remained seated. He offered a closing speech like at the beginning of the meal, bowing to Mourn and me in turn, although this one was wholly in Yungian without a truncated Trade translation.

The moment the patriarch finished, we received a wave of bobbing heads and agreeable sounds not only at the family table, but from the numerous Yungians who had been watching us eat this entire time.

I even noticed a handful had come from elsewhere, probably the kitchen, while it had been going on. Father Shi called them forward specially to bow as he seemed to thank them as well. One of them even appeared to be female.

Mourn chose then to stand up with me following close behind.

"The Shi family meal preparers," Mourn said to me in Trade, "three generations, now. Highly valued, bringing their knowledge from Yong-ch'hai and adapting it to the new trade. Some of what we've enjoyed in the city center was inspired by their efforts."

My eyes widened. I interpreted this to mean I'd just consumed the results of a mere century of Humans experimenting with their abundance, while more than a thousand years had left the isolated Sivaraus with very little resource to change or enhance our food.

How could I return to the meals down there and taste *anything?*

"Magnificent," I said aloud, pressing my hands together to touch my lips and bowing to the cooks like Tanzi had taught me.

While I half-expected a laugh for choosing the wrong gesture, Mourn seemed impressed, and the five cooks responded in kind whilst trying to breathe a little slower.

★Good,★ he signed.

I had gotten it right. *Yes.*

"Now!" Shi Mu Kuo said, startling a few peering at Mourn and me a little too hard, and the family stood up as one. "It is a beautiful night, clear and lit by the two sisters! Let us gather for special entertainment."

Two guards opened yet another double-door to the fragrant front garden. Spotting benches and seats but not much else, I could only guess what the "special" entertainment was.

Mourn smiled without showing his teeth. If he felt any impatience whatsoever with the formalities before we might retire to a bedroom, I couldn't spot a single tic.

As for me, my belly was too full to ride Bohai this moment, so scratching up more patience wasn't much concern. Dandan's inexperience and lack of preparation still was, however. I genuinely didn't know how long it might take to settle a terrified, untouched slit into a state where Mourn squeezing his girth in would be "enjoyable for both."

To be accomplished before sunrise, preferably.

Yet for all I knew, Dandan would collapse into second sleep after having skipped her first one. *Or worse, she'll just faint like Mai.*

With a mental sigh, I joined the family gathering and continued celebration outside. Only two lanterns were lit, throwing long shadows softened by the high and bright sister moons above our heads.

Belatedly, I realized that the women had retrieved a few string-plucking and metal-tapping instruments from a closet in the front room. Rejoining us, they also placed seats spaced evenly within a beautiful, circular design created by many pieces of colored glass, shell, and fired clay.

Once Mourn had chosen his seat, taking up an entire stone bench by himself, the placement of the male audience was less strict now, if a bit competitive. Male family claimed other benches or set seats for themselves in no discernible order besides staying off the intensely decorated circle.

Hm. A separate performance area?

While they each sought their best view, they also seemed to have forgotten about me. I didn't mind this because Bohai hadn't chosen a seat yet. There seemed to be few left; he might have to drag one out from inside the house.

Before he could, I took my opportunity to slide next to him, behind the backs of his relatives, and lightly touched his shoulder with mine. I enjoyed the visible flutter pulse in his throat as he stoutly looked forward.

As the family completed their set-up for an all-women performance, which included Dandan, I leaned closer to the thirdborn son, drawing in the scent near his neck. Bohai was clean and warm, tense but not afraid the same way his sister was.

"Smells good," I whispered.

More color crept up his tan face.

"You know you were chosen to please me this night?"

Bohai swallowed, and I heard his heart thudding in his chest. He nodded slightly, reluctant even to whisper lest we draw attention.

Ah, good.

"Your first time?" I asked forthright in the same casual way we asked down below.

He thought this over for a suspiciously long time. Perhaps I wasn't clear.

"Have you touched a mortal woman for pleasure?"

Now, my meaning was clear, yet he hesitated. I'd seen this look before; he was trying to guess the answer I wanted to hear.

Heh. To be pure or impure?

"Sky warriors enjoy explorers unafraid to get wet," I whispered in his ear, flicking my tongue against his lobe.

Bohai gasped softly as his eyes met mine, as close as they'd been when I had him pinned.

"Don't lie," I said. "Yes or no?"

"Yes, touch," he whispered.

Excellent.

"But," he added. "Um."

But?

I waited.

"Never…"

His pulse throbbed as he struggled for the words.

Touch, yes. But never what?

I narrowed my gaze, glancing when I heard a pleasing strum as the women were about ready. Renshu and Hulin had noticed where their brother stood, and with whom.

"Stay," I said, reaching behind the bua and lightly cupping his ass. "Watch with me."

Bohai's fascinating eyes fixed on the women as they began to play a soft and relaxing song, quite the opposite of the tension I sensed in him.

"Yes, *Janshi*," he whispered, folding his hands in front of him to better hide an unwieldy phallus beneath his robes.

I grinned, squeezing his buttock through the smooth texture. I rested my hand there, allowing him to grow accustomed while never allowing him to ignore my presence. I imagined any servants looking out the garden window from the front room might see a sky warrior who was still hungry.

Every so often, I stroked his ass, tracing the hidden cleft, pressing as far as I could go between his legs with the clothes in the way. I watched him try not to shiver or jump, my smile stretching my lips.

The wealthy man's son never leaned away from me. At Court, this meant the bua was interested and willing to be seduced, but I didn't ignore that Bohai couldn't outright refuse any more than Dandan, not without horrifying their father and all their family.

In a way, I'd been in his place as the initiate in the Cloister. I could not escape someone new intending to use my body for her pleasure, but more patient Sisters had teased me about this first, as I teased this young man. The sex had always been better if I'd been given the chance to build some appetite and anticipation while being cornered.

It seemed to be working with Bohai. He smelled good, not sour, and I aimed my smile at the stage when he furtively pressed his buttock firmly into my hovering palm. *The flirt.*

I had two kinds of entertainment, now.

Mourn was probably aware of where I was and what I was doing, but he didn't give me away to the more distracted eyes and ears. He sat like an attentive honored guest, front and center, and quite still yet drawing as many eyes as the women. I saw his tail move only once.

It was when Dandan began to sing.

Bohai and I were drawn out of our private play when her voice lifted tentatively above us, her soft nervousness reminding me of his sister's fear and quivering lower lip as she poured the tea.

Her brother responded to my touch and mannerisms in familiar ways which enhanced my confidence we'd both enjoy my climbing atop him. Yet, I'd truly never known a female in this situation or one who acted like this.

Simultaneously, I wasn't sure how Mourn would go about his own seduction. He hadn't given away much of his plan for the bedroom part, assuming he had one before I suggested we share the same room.

He does want her, though.

Or he wouldn't have arranged all this for tonight, wouldn't be taking the risk that this could be a net gain for the girl. He wouldn't have agreed with me that enticing Dandan to climax was both a goal and a challenge.

I knew how difficult it could be to learn how to peak after knowing only pain and fear with anything between my legs, but how would that compare if this Human cait was simply afraid because she never had the opportunity to learn?

Dandan's singing voice finally strengthened in the wake of her father's encouragement. Krithannia's voice returned to me as well.

"How would you claim entertainment in this circumstance?"

My response: *I would share my experience with her.*

Mourn hadn't asked what the Naulor and I had spoken about while he'd been elsewhere. It was possible the Pale Elf had sent him a message, though. After all, she'd chosen her moment to tell me he had arrived and waited outside. She'd stayed behind.

"Not to worry. I will tend to myself."

Dandan had closed her eyes during the second song to concentrate on her singing, which carried a higher pitch. She projected a tremulous wobble which was intentional yet still pleasing to my ears, like some birds I'd heard. She kept her back straight, her feet close together, and prevented her hands from fidgeting by curving each set of fingers then hooking them together in front while lifting her elbows.

It was an interesting pose, and admittedly enhanced the impression of the girl being a pretty decoration, pleasing to look at while listening to her song. But this wouldn't help her when the Dragon Spirit was nudging his cock against her slit. No one maintained the illusion of beautiful perfection with a phallus that size spreading them open.

Hoo, bua…

My hand had tightened unconsciously on Bohai's ass, becoming aware of it when he pulled in a deeper breath. I smirked, squeezing my thighs together in anticipation. *How many more songs?*

One more, as it turned out, for a total of three. They were each fairly similar, calming and delicate, with the focus on peaceful beauty. I didn't know what her words said, but the men paid attention with a pleasant twinkle in their eyes. Mourn's tail moved a few more times, but rarely; I couldn't see any of the expressions he might have shown the women or Dandan, whenever she chose to open her eyes.

Eventually, clapping hands and murmurs of approval signaled the women to stand up and curtsy multiple times, first to Father Shi, then Mourn, then each elder man after them, including the sons. They also searched for me, spotted me in the back and curtsied in my general direction, which made me snicker.

Dandan should have been blushing deeply, yet I couldn't see her complexion through the powder on her face. I also didn't imagine it tasted very good, especially to a long, inquisitive tongue like Mourn's.

A bucket of water and a couple scrub cloths shall be my first request.

Considering those washcloths, I *was* curious whether Bohai had a pleasure spot behind his cock like all my Davrin buas. I wasn't sure whether we'd get to me tonguing his pucker before stretching it out to explore with a petrified virgin sister in the room.

Bohai would need to have a taste for humiliation already to submit to that, and I didn't know what "woman touch" he meant which he'd done before. It could have been just fondling her as she laid passive, since he was male.

Hm. Regardless how I do it, I should urge his first squirt quickly, so he'll last longer when I finally climb on top.

Lost in my arousing plans, I assumed the sudden rise of men talking would be like Matrons congratulating themselves on their sons' pleasing performances. I just had to wait through it, maybe try to catch Mourn's eye since he was involved. Meanwhile, the women put away their instruments and moved their chairs from the stage to the audience without crowding Bohai and me.

Once the noise had lessened and my lusty imaginings had just resumed, Mourn stood up, guided Dandan to take his seat, which she did demurely.

Then he stepped into the circular mosaic.

I blinked. *Hello, what's this?*

The Dragon Spirit summoned one of his sliders from his bracers, and the Yungians cried out in amazement, even Bohai. An open smile overtook my face. Not only was this powerful magic they may never have seen in their lives, but it was the sort on which Human mages may not even have a basic, collective grasp.

This audience couldn't know the magic came not from him but his bracers, the weapon-bound manacles from his dead Matron with which he'd had to make peace. If any but me had known of their origin, I doubt the Dragonchild would have displayed it with such flourish.

Mourn extended his arm as he unlocked the weapon, testing the blade's maximum reach in the garden well before he would gain any momentum. Six male servants dived in to move several heavy, potted plants farther away while Mourn said something appreciative.

Once he was alone in the circle, the Dragonblood locked the first weapon in its balanced position and called its twin to his other hand. The cries were even louder than before but he showed no distraction in beginning a slow exercise unfamiliar to me but reminiscent of the *dorji-ka*. His bare, callused feet settled in a familiar position while his tail became the third limb bringing balance to his weapons and adding complexity to his unique form.

The Human awe and adoration were obvious.

I understood Mourn was about to perform a weapons display. Just scanning the Yungian faces, I could see the men embraced their pride and honor in hosting such a rare performance while the women seemed like they had rarely seen even the mundane version.

It was a fantastic choice, because Dandan suddenly lit up like a sunrise, her bottom bouncing in her chair as she patted her hands together and chattered encouragement. She froze when Mourn looked directly at her with a small smile, which I believed was his *least* frightening one. She clasped and squeezed her hands in her lap, but she didn't look down in terror like I expected.

Ah, a good sign. She's eager to watch this.

So was I.

I hummed, leaned closer to Bohai, and grabbed his other buttock. He jumped slightly but still did not shy away. Boldly, he leaned closer, so I didn't have to strain. I grinned, keeping my eyes on the Dragonchild.

Mourn demonstrated a practiced, choreographed routine appropriate for his body and the double-swords now locked in position. Smooth and stylized, this was unlike the urgent, lethal use I'd witnessed after he'd cast the first spell to burn and cut down a horde of warp rotted corpses.

Not an attack. More like a dance.

His initial sets could have been a novice's first lesson on how to hold and balance the sliders. In his second and third movements, he unlocked them and showed us how quickly the weight shifted and responded to the tilt, the angle, and the downward pull of the world.

"*Ai!*"

"Oo!"

"Wen-yung jei!"

A couple chairs scooted back as Mourn "danced" through a basic turn and slashing cut, which looked much stranger when the weapons moved both on their own and by the strength of powerful arms. A few women couldn't contain their gasps and fluttering hands, and I spotted Dandan's backside bouncing again.

My thoughts darted to her doing the same naked with her sex wrapped around a large, dark pole. *Huh bua...*

Meanwhile, some of the audience seemed to have trouble following the blades, like these were the distraction as well as the focus. Mourn's feet remained on his invisible boundary chosen to protect his watchers. His golden eyes did not seem focused on anyone specific, nor was he staring hard at something unseen.

I heard the soft double-click as he locked the blades, anticipating before the rest how the weapons seized in mid-swing. They'd returned to position in the middle despite the movement, or maybe because of it. Only then did Mourn's swings pick up speed, fluidly rotating around him and above his head.

He breathed a word, and a soft hum arose, a tremor beyond the rush of the edges cutting the air. Gooseflesh spread along my upper back and caused my guardians to stir as the half-blood tightened his focus and his aura.

I felt the first true magic enter his performance.

What was he going to do with it?

The rest of the family seemed hypnotized, transfixed, no longer crying out or whispering to each other every other moment. As Mourn tilted the flared weapons this way and that, catching the moonlight and creating circles of light as they spun, the Yungians as a group grew excited when something else became clear to me.

They could finally hear the hum as well.

The tone was constant at first, trembling with only a little variation, until he unlocked the blades again and gave them their full span, increasing his speed even more. The tone changed, creating something deliberate.

A rhythm. A melody.

Like the women's instruments, he manipulated the sounds of his blades by the way he interacted with the space around him; like Dandan's singing, he spoke under his breath now to enhance the harmony. One pitch flowed to another within a sliding hush, and the tune responded to his steps and spins, to how he flexed his spine and tail, or where he moved his arms.

My heart beat harder as I accepted it as a song.

Blade song.

I remembered a distinct and unbroken hum as he'd fought against the warp rot, punctuated with a powerful voice in his sire's language, but I'd *never* heard anything like this before. Like the awestruck Dandan, I listened with my mouth agape to this new swelling and coasting of magic and light, together in motion, trans-formed into a caressing feast for my ears which flowed into and entered my core.

Painless. Welcome.

Missed.

I knew not how much time had passed when Mourn finished up his performance with a final sweep, locking his blades, his mo-mentum slowing to a halt. He lowered his body down into an ele-gant crouch, extending a few of his fingers out to touch the ground while his tail and both blades hovered just above it.

He waited for the music to dissipate into the night air.

I blinked and felt the dampness on my cheeks. *What the fuck?*

Glancing around, I wasn't the only one dabbing moisture from their eyes with a sleeve. I studied the half-blood in the silvery moonlight as he slowly stood up and sent his weapons back to their storage, seeking an anchor for the lingering roil of thoughts I could not yet name.

I might have convinced myself that I saw the half-blood's aura as a thin shimmer of gold and purple, lifted just above his skin that was also burning up. His body emitted enough heat that even an enhanced cloak of the Deepearth could not have concealed his outline in the full darkness.

No one moved in the garden until silence had fallen. Then, a few peeps of tiny frogs and the chirps of insects returned. The Dragonchild stood up straight and bowed at the waist to his audience.

Shi Mu Kuo broke into the first applause, nearly breathless. *"Weida du songyei! Ging-shi!"*

It took time for the entire Shi family to follow suit as Mourn received his admirers' social intricacies one at a time, including from Bohai. I could almost think, with their uncertainty of balance, that everyone here felt intoxicated on his performance.

Hmm.

I stood with arms loosely crossed over my middle, choosing this time to listen to my own body. I felt no haze of drunkenness in my head, although my womb, oddly, felt like a campfire coal at the base of my abdomen. Had this been some stress on my baby? I hoped not; I could do nothing for it.

A strange tremor still lingered within my ears, or perhaps within my aura? A feeling which *should* have driven me mad, yet I welcomed it. I was in no hurry to shake it off because my skin felt primed to receive and enjoy even the softest breeze passing through this garden.

I had stopped squeezing Bohai's ass at some point—I couldn't remember when—so I tested his receptiveness now with a caress, using the back of my hand to glide against his.

He reacted as if I'd just cradled his balls and pressed my fingers on the ridge between his legs.

"Janshi...!" he gasped.

Well, well.

The thirdborn wasn't the only one superbly sensitive. Father Shi and Master Shi stood first and, instead of following the solitary formalities of the evening, they reached out for the bare hands of their age-mates. The women accepted with eye-glittering delight, confirming for the first time that they were indeed bonded pairs.

Ohhh...

Had the blade-dance cast a spell which may allow *everyone* to relax a little more? Perhaps help persuade us all to bed a little faster?

Interesting.

I knew this tactic in Sivaraus, even if it usually took a mix of incense and oils rather than sharp blades and a huffing half-Dragon to help carry the magical effect to an entire crowd. Nonetheless, it had worked.

Father Shi made the formal announcement I'd been waiting for, clasping his wife's hand while raising the other one high above our heads. He spoke Yungian first but translated for me.

"A wonder of celebration with our Dragon Spirit and his companion this night! We shall be telling stories for generations! But now we must all rest."

He bowed to me specifically, having already spoken in his native tongue whatever made Dandan and Bohai flush just now.

"Please rest here with us, Sky Warrior. My obedient flower shall host the Dragon Spirit, and my charming and attentive third son will gladly host you, if you will have him."

I bowed, my heart sounding in my ears. "I accept, Father Shi." I smirked at Bohai. "With great pleasure."

"In wonder, in wonder! Our eternal gratitude!"

I tried not to show my deep amusement that a powerful noble was begging me to fuck their son.

That's a switch.

Mourn had done what I'd asked, and not only that. He'd found me someone safe to fuck while selecting all who were connected to him to add their stories in Yong-wen. I had enjoyed everything so far, and I would relish what came next.

Bohai might not get any sleep before Sun-up.

CHAPTER 14

MOURN APPROACHED DANDAN AND OFFERED HIS HAND TO guide her out of her seat. She accepted, seeming far less frightened as the servants filed out and the guards reassigned in their night watches. The girl's eyes focused on the half-blood's huge hand curling around hers when Mourn said something else to her father, and they came to some understanding.

While Mourn and I stood in place with the two siblings, the rest of the family headed toward the nearest door into the house and climbed the wide, carpeted stairway. Renshu and Hulin lingered the longest, watching us through the window for as long as they could, but Mourn was in no hurry to follow them up the steps.

He smiled closed-lipped at me before speaking in Davrin. *"How do you feel?"*

My long breath slipped into a leer. *"Like I might ride the bua so hard we'll break through the floor."*

He chuckled.

"Was that you? A lust spell, perhaps?"

"A nudge," he admitted. *"Only an enhancer, if one felt any lust at all."*

No problem there with me or Bohai. I glanced at Dandan, finally noticing that the tip of Mourn's tail had slipped beneath her robe. He was probably touching her ankle or calf out of view.

It explained the look on her face.

"So, she is…" I chose my words with care. *"Curious? Afraid of what is unknown but also anticipating?"*

"No doubt this overwhelmed her in a short time, but she is not weak." He met my eyes. *"That wasn't will-bending magic, Sirana. I have never forced or tricked someone to bed me, not in will or body."*

I looked back. *"I believe you."*

No will-bending, but he would manipulate an opportunity the same as me, if not as often. I maintained my smile but allowed this topic to drop away, perhaps to return when it wouldn't spoil the mood.

"I have a question, Bohai," I continued in Trade, slipping my hand into his, entwining our fingers.

The Human bua looked at me, at full attention with heart galloping.

"Wen-yung and I wish to stay in the same room. Is one of your beds larger than the other? Are they the same?"

The brother's mouth opened but no sound came out. I glanced at his sister, who had taken the surprise as an excuse to reach for Mourn's forearm with her free hand, turning toward him like he was her protector. I supposed that he was.

Bohai managed to speak. "Ah, I-I have never peeked, *Janshi,* since Father built her bride's room."

Bride's room?

The siblings showed similar discomfort, but Dandan explained after Bohai spoke to her. Unfortunately, her spiel was in Yungian as she gazed with large, dewy eyes at her intended mystical lover. If she understood any Trade at all, she couldn't speak it with the confidence of her brothers.

Once she'd finished, Mourn explained to me. "The short answer is her bed is larger. A bride's room is intended for her first ten days and nights following her marriage to whomever her father chooses as her husband." He paused. "Father Shi was considering three suitors when we arrived."

"I see."

Delightful. Would any of those men dare follow after *Wen-yung* into her bedchamber? Tonight would add a unique challenge for those suitors, and clearly Father Shi hadn't been deterred by this.

I bit my cheek on a snicker, making sure the urge was gone before speaking to Bohai. "So, her bed is large enough for two while yours is intended for one?"

The youngest brother nodded earnestly.

"Alright." I offered a small bow to the girl. "Then Shi-lu Dandan must lead the way."

If she doesn't faint on our way there.

The dainty daughter led us up the stairwell, pausing at the left main hallway once we reached the top. From the way both siblings glanced down it and the scent of the others lingering, I knew this was most familiar to them.

"Your bed is that way?" I whispered to Bohai.

He swallowed and nodded. "Next to Hulin."

Ah.

Perhaps it was doubly better that we headed to the bride's room. Everything so far suggested Dandan had been set apart from the rest of her family recently while she waited to learn about her new mate.

Some added space and quiet from the older brothers would be good. I need not taunt Renshu and Hulin *that* much with my moans.

The four of us walked straight ahead into a shorter pathway with more storage to another hall at the end which turned right. Four doors down, Dandan opened her room so we could step inside.

At once, I saw the bed was perfect. A solid wood platform built low to the ground with storage drawers sliding beneath, supporting a well-made mattress laid out on top. More surprising was its size, if this was meant for two Humans to sleep and play upon. I could line up three or four of the cot-like beds from Brom's Inn on top.

The four of us will fit just fine.

In addition to this masterwork of resting places, the suite contained a dark, standing wardrobe, a matching folding screen which could easily move around the room, and a vanity with a tidy seat to sit and apply one's face mask using a mirror. Lastly, a few thoughtful servants had left two fresh buckets of water and a stack of cleaning cloths.

Yes.

On the far end of the room stood a writing desk, visiting chairs, some fine storage chests and, in the corner, what was likely a waste closet like in Mourn's library.

Hmm. We're on the second floor. I wonder where the dung lands?

Bohai stared at the floor even though he probably couldn't see in the dark room, and Dandan was reluctant to leave Mourn's side to seek a light.

I signed to the hybrid, indicating the washing supplies and patting my cheeks. ★Take off the face?★

He agreed. ★I will help her with this. Start as you will with the bua.★

Mourn had some reasonable instincts as he led his Human companion over to her vanity and sat her down before lighting a candle. They exchanged whispered words in Yungian when Mourn dipped the first cloth and started to wipe the paint and powders from her skin.

Meanwhile, as soon as we had candlelight, Bohai stared about the room in such a way that I was convinced he had never seen the inside before. Abruptly, he turned around and faced the closed hallway door, as if he were about to open it and bolt.

I snapped hold of his wrist. He didn't run or pull from my grip.

"What is wrong?" I whispered.

He swallowed. "I should not be in here, *Janshi.* This is meant for her husband."

Ah, yes, the private pair bonds Krithannia mentioned.

"You are not here *as* her husband, who is not yet chosen," I said. "You are here to please me. You may also bear witness and be certain your sister is not harmed."

Bohai blinked at me incredulously. He grew bolder whether he realized it or not. *"Wen-yung* would not harm her!"

I grinned, stepping closer and pulling up his sleeve to run my fingers along his forearm. He was still feeling enough of Mourn's blade spell that he shivered, and I spotted the lump pushing against his robes.

"Mm. Very well, Bohai. I will tell you a secret."

"A secret?"

"Yes. *Wen-yung* is also here to be certain *I* do not harm *you.*"

The Yungian looked at me like a Davrin bua seeing a red uniform. "W-would you do that, warrior from above?"

I chuckled, leaning close enough that he would feel my breath on his skin as I spoke. "Nothing worse than in the *dorji-ka*, which you handled fine."

His scent grew stronger, his skin so warm that I dragged my open lips lightly along his jaw. *Mmm.*

"By my nature, Bohai, I am a violent creature, and *Wen-yung* guards Yong-wen against savagery from outsiders like me. I have done much to convince him I will follow these mortal rules to get you naked beneath me... yet he is still less sure of me than you are of him. He guards you and Dandan together. Thus, by his decision, you *should* be here."

The Yungian youth shuddered, but he still hadn't tried to pull away. I reached out and traced the swelling of his crotch. He swallowed a groaning whimper as he moved his hips back and then forward again, not entirely aware of it.

"You asked, *Janshi*," he blurted, "and I must say...I have not known a woman's secret."

Goddess, his face burned with embarrassment. His cheeks would feel wonderful between my thighs.

I challenged his confession. "But you *have* touched one for pleasure, you said."

"That is not a lie, spirit. I have."

"Touched her where? On her body, where?"

"Her lips, neck. Um, breasts. I-it was dark."

"Oo."

I pulled out my blindfold and held it up. He stared without recognition until I wrapped it expertly around his eyes.

"Was it dark like this?"

He jumped, whispered a curse of surprise, and quivered as I pulled it tight into a simple knot at the back of his head.

"A-almost."

I used the opportunity to call my spiders out of my hair before I forgot. Bohai shouldn't encounter them with his fingers.

That would be bad.

Once my little guardians were safe on the wall and crawling toward the ceiling, I closed with Bohai and took his feverish face between my hands to kiss his mouth. I inhaled his earthy Human scent again, tasted a musk not so pungent as Brom or Kurn.

I kissed the bua's neck next, biting it gently to suck some of that intriguing flavor off. I detected a hint of that marvelous dinner in his sweat. He groaned as I did this, and then again, louder, as I cupped his genitals through his clothes and bit him again.

I whispered, "Did you spurt after touching in the dark, too?"

"Ah, y-yes."

"Did she help?"

"N-no. After she left."

"How?"

He grimaced, glad for the blindfold now. "My hand."

"Heh. Yet, unlike her, *my* hand is eager to help."

I snaked my fingers into the opening of his robes and searched through two more layers before I found bare skin. He gasped as I slid my hand along his middle to find the waist of his pants. I stopped when he started to hunch over, already knowing this could be too much, too soon for an inexperienced male.

"I like your honesty, *bua*," I whispered, gradually dipping my hand inside now that he could anticipate it. "Keep telling me what you feel, and do not lie to me, Human. You are new for this body, but I can sense deceit. You are here to please me, not impress."

Thanks to the scalding heat of his turgid pole, I did not really need the belly fur that would lead me to the base. My fingers combed its coarse texture with delight anyway, and Bohai shuddered as soon as I wrapped my fingers around him like I'd seize the bottom of a fiberstalk shoot.

Mmm. A nice start.

"J-Janshi!"

He sounded extremely concerned. His hand covered mine as if imploring me to be still. I leaned close to nip his ear.

"Is it a knife's edge? You are about to spurt?"

"Y-yes!"

The sweet bua didn't lie. Truly, Mourn's "enhancement" trick seemed to have affected him the most, and this wasn't the best state for either of us to use my cunt.

I whispered so that only he would hear.

"Pull it out for me. I want to taste you, Shi son. Await my mouth then have your release when you feel my tongue. Understand?"

Shocked to stillness at first, he offered me the barest nod while obedient, trembling hands freed his cock and sack from that bulk of layers. At least he knew his way around in there.

His cock was longer than I had thought and had an interesting downward curve toward the floor. I took to one knee with firm grip on his hip before reclaiming the dark, furry base with my other, lifting his prick toward my lips while taking a closer look.

Hmm.

I already had my ideal position in mind once we got that far. And my slit would be the first of his young life wrapped snugly around his pole.

I don't think I've ever been any bua's first. Well, everyone's a novice at some point.

I slipped Bohai's erection between my lips. His unusual shape slid flush along my tongue and partway down my throat before I realized it. Compared to the Feldeu crammed down at an unnatural angle, requiring I turn in some strained position to go deep, this Yungian was quite comfortable to take nearly to the root.

"Ah!" he cried.

He was clean yet with a new, alluring scent flirting with my nose. I hummed, my mouth watering around him; I enjoyed several good sucks before he uttered a noise and his cock flexed. Hot liquid splashed across my tongue, and he hunched over, filling my ears and my mouth with that familiar male climax.

Ah, well.

Callitro lasted only a little longer the first time.

I pulled off him and swallowed his cream, thinking it a bit thinner before I saw his knees wobble.

"Careful," I warned, maintaining my hold on him.

The youth let himself drop quietly to the floor rather than fall with a thump as he caught his breath. He straightened his clothes from habit, hiding his bua bits underneath those damnable layers again.

Just wait till we get rid of those completely.

I tugged off the blindfold first, thinking if I could see those exotic eyes, I'd be better able to tell when he was ready for more. When I thought to look at Mourn with Dandan by the vanity, I felt a bit shaken that I'd been so deep in my play that I hadn't gauged the hybrid's mood at all.

Why hadn't I? I wasn't *that* foolish, was I?

Fortunately, the Dragonblood's humor seemed to be good as his tail curved and coiled languidly beside the chair.

He had moved the Shi daughter to sit on his thighs; her back rested against his bare chest, and his arms wrapped loosely around her. Dandan was still fully clothed, though only now could I see that she hadn't been wearing indoor sandals like the men but had her feet wrapped up with bindings, like I sometimes did for extra warmth inside my boots.

I smirked, signing to him, ★The cait must be exquisitely warm.★

He smiled and signed back. ★The bua might need help onto the bed.★

That was my next step, yes.

Had Mourn enjoyed watching and wanted me to continue? How much had he heard of my teasing exchange with Bohai? That might depend on when the Dragonblood had finished his cleaning task and reassurances with his Human companion.

Dandan's face now free from paint and powders made me realize she had been wearing some even while riding the horses. She was still paler than many Yungians but not so falsely flawless; worth the change for how many expressions she had that I could read.

First, she wasn't disgusted or horrified by what I'd done to her brother, but perhaps that was Mourn's influence. She was surely confused for not seeing much with Bohai's back to her and me kneeling in his shadow.

She would have heard plenty of interesting sounds, though, and I read she was curious, waiting to observe more or whisper questions to Mourn. No longer a doll on a shelf, perhaps she was ready to be touched more.

And to show us some real responses.

I stood slowly, offering Bohai help up as I had in the *dorji-ka*. "Come, let us move someplace softer."

The bua's beautiful eyes widened, telling me this would have been unthinkable just yesterday. Nonetheless, he accepted my hand to get up and finally turn to face the luxurious room; with a nudge, he let me guide him next to the bride's bed. I looked forward to putting it to good use.

Crossing my arms at the hem of my shirt, I pulled it up over my head and tossed it aside. Bohai followed the dark article to an even darker spot on the floor, as if he couldn't believe I would be so slovenly.

Mourn whispered something, catching our attention, then four candles flared to life: two set upon the stands at each side of the bed. With this grand but windowless corner illuminated, the bright red sash drew my bua's gaze and pulled an admiring gasp from his sister. Dandan murmured an exchange with Mourn, but I was more interested in circling my chosen bua. I narrowed my eyes critically at his clothes.

"Wh-what is wrong, *Janshi?*" Bohai managed to ask.

"Remove your sandals," I instructed, still pacing as he bent over to obey.

Mm. Tasty.

I held my temptation to pinch his backside until he straightened up. Completing my turn, I paused in front, peering up at him from beneath my brow and licking my lips.

Excitement and fear clashed in his expression, and I chuckled, tugging the leather ties of my pants and letting them hang while I loosened the waist of my bottoms. With one, slow rotation of my hips, the black leather slipped down a little to show new skin from which Bohai couldn't look away.

I stood there long enough to let him forget his question before answering it.

"I tell you what is wrong, Shi son," I said, my voice strong and blinking him awake. "Your robes. They are in my way. But I grant you a choice."

He swallowed. "A choice, *Janshi?*"

I motioned to one of the storage chests. "You may remove your clothing and set them neatly aside, but it must be all of it. Every stitch. Or…" I grinned. "I will remove them as I remember to do it, but we will be on the bed. I will try not to tear them, for they are fine work."

The thirdborn son's gaze on the chest and the way he dropped hands to his sash told me which option his sire would choose for him: neat and orderly. What interested me was that his next thought seemed to conflict with it as he took his hands away.

He would rather I forcibly strip him?

Delicious. We can do that.

Dandan said something, and her brother looked from me to her. This annoyed me until I realized she had done me a favor. Whatever she'd said, I saw the resistance in Bohai's face and he made no move to undress himself.

Spoken or not, he'd made his choice.

I hooked my thumbs into my pants and skimmed them swiftly down my legs, bending over so both Mourn and his playmate had a nice view of my ass and my cunt while I slipped each bare foot through. I enjoyed feeling the air caress my slickened sex; I also heard Mourn's tongue leave his mouth.

Grinning, I tossed the garment into a rumpled heap atop my shirt. Bohai's eyes followed its path to the floor.

He never saw me coming.

"Hai!" the Human bua cried as I seized his robes by his pits and hurled him onto the bed.

Bohai landed on his stomach but rolled onto his back, propped on his elbows. Nervous until he fixed on my hand sliding over my bare belly to ruffle my white fur, his tension transformed to lust when I dipped one finger between my pouting netherlips and showed him pink as I massaged my clit. His mouth opened with admiring awe, his lids half-closed, as I proved how wet I was between my legs.

By the time I crawled onto the bed to straddle him, I ached and wanted so badly to keep climbing him, to settle my knees on either side of his head and mash his face into my crotch.

How long had it been since I'd felt like this light and welcome? There'd been Shyntre but also too many webs sticking to us. Before him? I still couldn't remember much of how I'd caught with Auslan.

Callitro, then.

Whose well-crafted ring was still on my finger.

Exaggerating my impatience, I loosened Bohai's belt and growled while I sought every inside knot keeping his robes straight, snug, and above all, closed. Looming over him like a bird of prey preparing to feed, I flung wide the first two layers of Bohai's clothes before kneeling on them, mashing them into the mattress to enhance his feeling of restraint and to wrinkle them for the sin of obstructing me.

This excited the Shi son further, adding the spice of the forbidden as I showed him how much this sky spirit wanted him.

She cares less for the look of your clothing, sweetmeat, and more about what lay underneath.

His last layer was the least decorative as a plain dark cloth, beautifully framing his light brown skin when I tossed it open to reveal his torso. Taking his wrists, I pressed them down beside his head, arching my back as I dipped down to test the sensitivity of his nipples with a swirl of my tongue.

"Ah!" he cried, arching his back, lifting his pelvis against me.

Quite sensitive.

I breathed in his scent at neck and collarbones, dragged my lips and tongue across his chest while grinding my dripping sex against his abdomen, crossing over from his belly fur to the waistline of his pants and marking both with my slit smears. Thanks to his natural bend, I missed caressing his new erection often.

When I next lifted my head to kiss him, I could tell he was highly aware of the stains I'd left on his clothing and of the mirrored ache down below. I laughed softly, tightening my grip on his wrists, spreading them out a little more as I studied him up close.

"What about your face?" I whispered, pressing my crotch to his belly again and leaving a streak upward. "Would you be proud of similar markings on your face? I would *relish* the feel of your tongue this moment."

Words left him at first, but he nodded and forced out, "I am here to please, *Janshi.*"

Oh, yesss...

I took reasonable care getting into position, aware of his breath on my thighs as I kneeled upright. I caressed his short hair with both hands before reaching for his and guiding them to a good hold on my thighs while I got settled.

"Kiss me," I instructed, hearing a quiver of anticipation in my own voice. "Like a girl's mouth. Use your tongue to stroke me as I did for you. And suck on my lips sometimes."

I pressed his forehead against the mattress when he would have begun immediately, waiting until his eyes lifted to meet mine.

"When your tongue finds firm flesh," I said, "press harder but not rough. Listen well. I will guide you, perhaps without words, so do not forget me."

He blinked, adjusting his hold on my thighs. "Never, *Janshi.* Guide me, please."

"Good." I released his forehead and spread my legs, squatting to get my crotch closer to his face. "Kiss. Use your tongue."

His tentative start was the exquisite tease I knew it'd be. My eyes stared at a blank spot on the mattress while his slid closed to concentrate on gradual, deliberate exploration. I experienced his mouth learning a female's shape for the first time, perhaps before his hands ever had.

Ohhh, good…

Though my crotch was awash with sensation, my ears picked up the sound of scales sliding across the floor. I turned my head toward the foot of the bed and slightly beyond, where Mourn still sat with Dandan beside the vanity, although not as they'd been last time I looked.

The Dragonblood had made progress with his meek companion. At some point, Mourn had unwrapped her feet, for they were bare, pale, and perfectly clean. In addition, the three brightest and most decorative layers worn by the daughter had been drawn open with more care and neatness than I'd shown those of the son.

In contrast to Bohai's black underlayer, Dandan's was like the palest cream, offering a stark contrast with Mourn's large hands as he massaged her breasts through this final layer. His pace was quite slow and circular. I witnessed how gradually his fingers clamped down on her nipples, catching them between his second knuckles until she squeaked, the deep, rosy nubs showing turgid through the sleek material.

Meanwhile, Dandan's brown eyes had fixed wide on my thighs caging her brother's head, captivated by the way he seemed to savor pressing his nose into my snowy thatch and sucking on my folds with his lips. Her eyes contained a curious glitter, and I wondered if the effects of the blade song remained with her.

The magic could very well still be with me, because I whimpered as a sudden wave surged through me from where the Yungian's eager mouth attached and held on.

"Awyiss," I squeaked, my hips pressing slow but firm against him. "Good. Good sucking…"

Bohai drew much needed air in through his nostrils, squeezing my legs with his fingers at my praise, but kept his eyes closed. His focus was on his feast, and perhaps he had lost track of time, but my glance over my shoulder confirmed his prick had been hard for a while. A damp spot grew larger where his glans would be.

His tongue flickered side-to-side across my clit, making me gasp and reclaiming my attention. The bua returned to sucking and stroking and did not repeat that thrilling test; he believed my gasp to be one of pain.

"Again," I demanded, bracing one fist against the mattress, shifting my hips forward so I could slip a finger under his jaw and partway into my slit. "Flick your tongue like that, but harder."

He did.

"Yes!" I cried. "Continue!"

He obeyed, and I reached farther inside myself to press on my inner bump as well. *Oh, goddess, yeah!*

Pleasure rising, roiling toward me. Sensations filled me to the brim.

"Oh!" I tensed up. "Don't stop!"

Oh, fuck, please don't stop…

Bohai kept that tongue moving, his fingers digging deep into my tense thighs as he pushed hard with the muscle in his mouth. My toes curled up.

I was coming.

Fucking shit… Yes! Almost there!

A groan filled my ears as pleasure broke over me, and I began shaking before I could stop myself. My hips pushed, eager and greedy, against the bua's face, wringing all I could out of this moment.

Oh, yeah! Drink that last drop…

As the last wave passed, I fell to my elbows, knowing to draw my ass up into the air before it became too much. I needed to let him breathe. He gasped and shook as much as I did.

My inner thighs were drenched, but his face and brow were far worse.

"Oh…" I breathed in Davrin. *"Wow."*

Mourn spoke while I was still dizzy. "Has Shi-bin Bohai pleased you, *Janshi-lantiu?*"

I huffed a laugh at the formalities. *Give me a moment, half-blood.*

Licking my lips, I looked down between my legs and confirmed, "Very much. I am… immensely pleased."

Bohai's face was such a mess, too. He blinked up at me, adorable and a bit stunned, and I chuckled for a bit longer.

"Would *Janshi* still be interested in anything below his waist?"

Of course I was.

What are you hinting at, Mourn?

Craning my neck, I saw that Mourn had unwrapped the Shi daughter's hair as well as that final layer at some point. Dandan's blush extended from her face down to just above her breasts, which were now bare.

The half-blood's dark hands cupped them gently as if to display them for me, showing off her nipples of dark rose-red, standing up so tall it seemed they might never go down again. They even glistened as if a certain lavender tongue had been lashing them like a whip.

I was almost sorry I'd missed it to see the way she quivered in his lap now, but I wouldn't have traded it for Bohai's firm attention on my cunt.

As I carefully pushed myself up and shifted to one side of the dazed young man, I considered Mourn's question of being interested below the waist. *Of being interested in cock.*

Dandan had crossed and locked her ankles, and a tiny wrap of soft, pale cloth still covered her entire pelvis from view. Even as she writhed with apparent enjoyment in the Dragon Spirit's attention, she was reluctant to open her legs or remove that last garment.

For certain, she would not reveal herself while her brother still had his trousers on.

Mourn had demonstrated incredible patience so far, but even he must be starting to ache by now. Even then, he wouldn't rip her small clothes off and bring his other lively weapon out from beneath her cushy ass only to force her reluctant legs open.

Alas, that imagining woke me up a little.

She needs further persuasion? Very well.

I leaned down to taste myself on Bohai's lips, snaring his attention from wherever his thoughts had wandered while he fondled
his cock through his clothes.

"Ready?" I asked, pinning him with a thirsty grin getting
thirstier.

He was with me enough to ask. "For what, *Janshi?*"

Wise to ask anyone.

I answered him by leaping off the bed and reached for his
waistband. In one smooth motion, I dragged the dark cloth off his
hips, sliding my hands beneath his ass to pull it free. His pants were
around his thighs and his prick exposed to the air before he reacted.

"*Woh!*" he cried, trying to cover his genitals with his hands.

This was one of the funniest attempts I'd ever seen. I was still
trying to catch my breath as I freed his ankles, baring him from the
neck down but for his arms and their three layers of sleeves.

So lively and rumpled.

I crawled back onto the bed again to straddle my bua, pushing
his hands up and out of my way as I settled my soggy sex against
his pole; it hadn't shrunk much in his embarrassment. Summoning
more patience, I rubbed my cleft along his ridge instead of impaling myself first thing.

I reached for his hands and placed them on my hips. "Touch
my skin."

My red sash still bound my breasts and concealed my saphgar
necklace, and I'd decided to keep it on. The protection and support
had saved me many distractions already, and the Bohai wasn't completely stripped, either. From the sensations beneath me and the
naked look on his face, I'd awakened us both enough, and we
wanted more.

"Ready?" I asked again.

This time, he just nodded.

I pushed myself up and into a crouch, turning around quickly
to face his feet before straddling him again. Shifting forward a bit, I

let him stare at my ruffled cleft as I grasped the base, angled his cock, and wedged his tip in place. Groaning deep in my throat, I sank down steadily, pulled up again once, then sat on him.

All the way.

Bohai sucked in air, his toes flexing in the air. I chuckled, looking over my shoulder and reaching back. "Hands."

He gave them to me; I placed them on my ass.

"Bend your knees. Feet flat."

He obeyed, and I leaned forward to fold my arms atop his knees, sampling some regular strokes with his full length in my cunt.

"Ohh, yeah," I breathed. This *was* the ideal position for him.

Hits the spot perfectly...

Bohai's hands massaged my backside as I fucked him, squeezing and exploring my ass while attempting to stay in rhythm. Again, he grew bolder, nudging his thumbs tauntingly close to my crinkled pucker before drawing them down the softest part of my thighs. Then he did it again and witnessed me shiver.

Giving me tingles, bua.

I reached for my mound to massage my nub. "Do it again."

He took the command and ran with it, petting and caressing between my cheeks and thighs, anywhere he could see in candlelight, even around where his cock was swallowed by my body.

My netherhole winked at him once or twice as he teased me so pleasurably, but it wasn't intentional. Nonetheless, to my delight, he risked the interpretation of an invitation to lightly stroke my asshole from top to bottom.

"*Ohhhh, fffuck,*" I hissed in Davrin, needing to swallow some spit before speaking again. "Circle. Trace in circle."

The Yungian's fingers were already wet from my juices when he drew the pad of his thumb around the edge of my pucker, and my happy squeal encouraged him to keep going. He even reversed his direction without being prompted.

My cunt leaked and felt squishy and swollen around him; taking any length at all made my jaw sag open in seconds. My back hole relaxed as it was trained to do, and I arched my ass up, spreading my cheeks apart and pushing backward. The Human read my mute request to gently nudge my anus open.

"Ah!" I cried, massaging my clit above my stuffed slit. "D-deeper, Bo…! I'm… I'm gonna—!"

His thumb penetrated my ass; I didn't know how far, and I didn't *care.*

"Yes!" I called out, the contractions clutching and rippling along the new curvature of his cock were beyond my conscious control. "Yes!"

I climaxed with a glorious wail of pent-up lust, vividly aware when the thirdborn began thrusting with desperate urgency, clutching my hips to hold me against him as he threw his head back with an equally loud groan.

The Shi son's cock erupted deep inside me.

In time, I returned to the ground, shaking too much from fatigue to stay up like this. Stretching out both arms toward the foot of the bed, I leaned over and lifted one leg to pull my cunt off the softening prick, dismounting to one side of the drifting bua. I heard a couple thick globs of male cream land on his splayed robes, and I chuckled with immense satisfaction as I flopped on my side to catch my breath.

Once the languid weakness passed, a new scent and movements prompted me to check on Mourn and Dandan again. I rolled to my belly and rested my chin on my arms to watch them.

The Shi daughter had shed all but the final, pale robe. There remained a layer between her ass and his hard prick, which I could see much better outlined by the cloth, but he had managed to strip off her smallclothes and open her legs wide enough to touch her.

At last, I could see her dark curls and damp, rosy netherlips.

Mourn's right hand supported her right leg behind the knee, while his tail was wrapped around her left calf, subtly tugging that in the opposite direction. The clever Dragon's son still had one hand free to explore her nakedness, and she was unlikely to snap her thighs shut in a momentary panic.

Like Bohai, I could see everything but her arms; the thin, light fabric had even slid off her shoulders, exposing a grand expanse of near-flawless skin along which to run his scaly lips or his dexterous tongue. Dandan's breath was quick while he did so, her eyes wide and looking over herself as if disbelieving that her body was in this predicament.

I chuckled to myself. *You're not as bad off as he is, spring bud.*

The dampness which had leaked from his prick and onto her silken robe wasn't just a wet spot.

That's a waterfall.

I noted to snatch that piece and burn it rather than leave a trophy like that behind. *They'd probably display it for centuries while it turned yellow.*

Meanwhile, Mourn just wanted to come without hurting the girl; that much was clear. I almost felt sorry for him but lay still, thinking it took them too long to notice me watching them. Recognizing the deepening quiet, I glanced behind me and saw that Bohai had dozed off.

I grinned. *Ah. Good bua.*

When I looked back, they'd lost a bit of momentum.

Damn it, girl. Just work with him, will you? Why act so helpless and make him do everything for you?

Softly, I cleared my throat, asked him in Davrin, *"Anything else I can do to help?"*

Mourn's smirk was the first one hinting self-deprecation that I'd seen since we met. *"I don't know. Your partner's fallen asleep."*

"So?"

He kept any response unreadable, though perhaps he'd had one.

I sighed. *"My opinion, Mourn. I'd say she's had too much time to think about what's staining her gown. The rest of this is clearly enjoyable for her, but..."* I waved my hand vaguely.

He laughed dryly. *"Indeed, she has. And perhaps I have, too."*

I heard his tone and blinked slowly. *"Do you want to stop?"*

He exhaled. *"It's too late for that without making matters worse."*

After the big night's celebrations thus far, I had no trouble following his path of thought. Yet he *would* stop if all this had only been an attempt to seduce a companion who wasn't ready.

Many more expectations were attached to this, unfortunately.

"I can help," I said directly. *"I've used my mouth on more females than the greatest legendary flirt in Yong-wen. Let me try and give her something else to think about."*

"You'll just scare her."

"And you're not already? Come on, there's always fear at first with anything new. I'd be three fingers deep in this if it was the Cloister, but I'm asking you. May I join in? I'll even obey your 'tone' without question," I grinned suggestively at him, *"the moment you find a need to use it."*

The Dragonchild had plenty of reason to look at me with suspicion like he did, but it didn't last. While I'd grown accustomed to him taking a great deal of time to think over certain topics or agreements, Dandan was perfectly aware of us speaking in a language she couldn't understand.

She was also aware of the change of mood.

The young lady's eyes teared up, and a sob slipped out before she covered her mouth, as if realizing that she had made some mistake to cause the Dragon Spirit not to want her anymore.

Mourn didn't have much time to consider my offer.

"Please join us, Sirana," he rumbled.

CHAPTER 15

I PUSHED MYSELF UP AND STRETCHED A LEG OVER THE SIDE UNTIL my bare foot touched the floor, silently quitting the bed as Dandan's horrified panic reached its peak. She peered up at the Dragon Spirit, unable to read his closed, foreign face.

Once the girl had the mental resources to spare, she saw me in the corner of her eye. I didn't grant her time to expect the worst before placing my palms delicately on her naked thighs. Dandan's eyes snapped to my dark hands, absorbing this first contact as I leaned above her head, pressuring her to look up.

She watched as I touched my lips to the corner of Mourn's mouth with reverence, taking Shyntre's kiss in my dream as the inspiration. Mourn was just as surprised as I'd been but returned the light touch, granting a clear sign to bid me welcome. I smiled at them both.

"Tell her I will help prepare her to honor you with pleasure," I murmured in Trade. "Confirm that you still want her."

Mourn grasped these two points to refocus, and the Yungian listened with rapt attention as he spoke in her native tongue. Most importantly, I saw the despair leave and hope rekindle in her eyes, resurging in the flush of her cheeks. Even not knowing her language, I could tell she apologized to him, imploring his understanding, and he reassured her.

Before all this, the Dragonblood's tail had unwound from her left calf and rested on the floor. Now, his left arm slid gently around her waist, holding her closer while they spoke. Dandan's legs had closed at little as she relaxed; a good sign, and there was still enough room for me.

We can start again.

I waited for the first sign of renewed interest before I reclaimed their attention by caressing my way up Dandan's body, from her ankles to her soft hips. My hands drifted over Mourn's left arm and teased around her breasts, avoiding the nipples, before sliding up her neck to cup her jaw.

She stared at me in bewilderment. Clearly, she did not expect me to kiss her as I had Bohai. But I did.

Oh, wow… She was so soft.

My nose detected hints of her cosmetics, but the texture of her newly cleansed skin drew me into a luxuriously long exploration of her with my mouth. From her unbelievably tender lips to her flushed, smooth cheeks, I learned the first real hint of her scent near her ear from the sweat beneath her hair.

It reminded me of fresh fields and warm rain.

I heard her gasp as I kissed and tasted my way down her neck to the hollow of her throat. Mourn whispered encouragement to her, and she shivered and tilted her head back against him, seeming to present her breasts for me to kiss next.

Soon, little cait. Soon.

I didn't want to grope her tits without thinking; when my hands left her neck and ceased caressing her shoulders, they held the cloth of her robe before dropping to the half-blood's thick forearm. My right hand held firmly to the rising flex of muscle near his elbow, but my left landed on the hard metal bracer. I sensed that neither of us much liked this so shifted that hand farther to caress the back of his.

He took hold of it and squeezed, returning caressing the back of my hand with his thumb.

Unexpected.

I paused my kisses, shifting my balance to maintain this contact for a while. The first part of me to touch Dandan's breasts was my lips, brushing lightly down to the side and beneath. She peeped softly with renewed pleasure, squealing louder when my tongue swiped across and around each nipple which hadn't much chance to relax over the last hour.

Then my lips and tongue began to tingle.

Whoa. What?

I stopped. The sensation was disturbingly familiar. *Like contact poison.* From a Human girl's nipples? How was that possible?

"*J-Janshi,*" Dandan gasped like a protest that I'd stopped.

Mourn finally noticed my concern. Without speaking, he extended his tongue, dropping it down from between sharp teeth to snake around Dandan's left breast. He slathered the delicate skin with a slick and gooey saliva which set her off writhing, gaining some pleasurable grinds from her ass on his lap as he focused on me.

"*It's you,*" I said, licking the tickle on my lips with a prickling tongue. It was the oddest feeling.

He nodded once, lust and wariness in metallic eyes. "*Stronger when it's fresh.*"

"*How strong? Enough to intoxicate?*"

The Dragon's son shook his head, leaning to brush his lips along Dandan's bare shoulder. Gooseflesh erupted along her skin as he released my hand to cup her right breast. She moaned, appreciating his attention during our sudden exchange.

"*It enhances sensation but does not cloud or overtake the mind,*" he said, reading something in my face. "*You have my word. The effects are not like drunkenness or incense.*"

Ah, so he knew about the incense, too.

"*It works best on contact where blood is close to the surface,*" he finished, "*not under scales or calluses.*"

I narrowed my eyes, reaching to draw two fingers through the fresh goo on Dandan's breast in experimental circles. She sighed and offered me a wavering smile. My fingers tingled as well, but not as much as my lips despite being wet.

The girl was fully aware of who was touching her; she was not in a stupor. *Not yet.*

I smirked at him. *"Have you slathered any onto her slit yet?"*

Mourn chuckled and showed me how far that Draconic tongue could stretch. It couldn't quite cross his arm laid across her middle, but was still many times longer than any Davrin tongue.

"I haven't been in position to reach that area yet."

My smirk grew into a smile. *"No dripping or spitting on her?"*

"Not yet. It's very thick."

"I noticed."

"Indeed. Spitting without spraying my chin or neck is harder than you think."

My smile had become a full grin as I lifted four of my fingers closer to his mouth. *"Well, then. Let me paint her up pretty for you."*

The Dragonchild wouldn't stick his tongue out before gauging my intent again but didn't take long. The lavender probe slithered out, around, and between my loose fingers, coating every side thoroughly with this strangely viscous saliva he seemed to produce when he was aroused.

His gold eyes watched me the whole time.

I recognized a tease when I saw one.

I held that insolent gaze while sinking down to my knees between his thighs. His tail quickly coiled into its previous hold above Dandan's left ankle, pulling her open wide for me. Dandan flushed, gasping at her renewed exposure as I kissed her sex the same way I had the rest of her, licking reddened netherlips and taking in her true scent from the black curls adorning her mound.

"Oh!" She cried out loudly at first but, with Mourn's help, quieted down as she grew accustomed to my mouth this far down. *"Oh. Oh…"*

Soon enough the Shi daughter settled into this new view and the sensations, ready for the next step whether she realized it or not. I shifted my tongue up to rest the flat on her clit while I traced her plump folds with two sticky fingers, lightly painting a layer of thrumming Dragon spit.

I was grateful Mourn was paying attention because she tried to snap her thighs closed on my head. He caught her and kept her legs splayed.

"Aeii!" she cried. *"Ah-nah!"*

"Usha, Dandan, usha," he whispered, adjusting his hold on her, his big hands massaging her body as I focused on where his cock would need to go before the end of the night.

I ran one finger around the opening needing to be coaxed much wider, mixing her natural slickness with his livening lubricant. She still needed time to adapt and catch her breath before I dabbed the titillating slime to her clitoris.

Oh, but when I did…

"Ai! Oh, ah-nah, oh, oh! Ai-oh!!" she cried, getting louder in the Dragonblood's lap as I ramped up my touch, petting and massaging her sex with all four gooey fingers.

In truth, I hadn't realized she *could* get this loud, but it was helping. Mourn grew visibly more aroused listening to her, eagerly tonguing her, breathing in an enhanced scent through his teeth. His eyes shone, and his cock lifted the bottom of her white robe, announcing its presence rather than hinting.

We're almost there.

I slid my pointer finger smoothly into her hot slit, testing the ease and depth it would go. Dandan cried out with such astonishment to feel only one slender finger that I almost believed she had never done this herself.

If that's true, this'll be interesting.

At least Dandan's cunt felt familiar and female; no clumsy surprises between us, her body was pliant, hot, and slick around my finger. She stretched readily enough when I pushed in two fingers covered in Mourn's spit but also sucked in air to cry out.

"Ai, Janshi!"

I winced at the pitch, but Mourn growled with unmistakable interest, licking her breasts again and caressing her thighs, his fingers sliding close to her cheeks and parting them gently so that his member settled directly within her cleft. His cock bobbed once beneath the white robe, brushing my knuckles, and his tail adjusted its hold on her calf.

Then I heard a noise on the bed and glanced to confirm.

Yep. They woke Bohai.

The bua had removed his robes fully and now watched with his mouth agape, though I didn't know for how long.

I winked at him and mouthed, "Stay."

Bohai nodded, his hand creeping toward his awakened member. I chuckled and returned my focus to fulfilling the Shi family's promise. Their thirdborn had been intended to watch from the start, and he could indulge as much as he wanted.

We're just getting to the good part.

Adjusting my knees to squat a bit lower, I leaned to cover Dandan's firm, feminine bead with my mouth, sucking gently and feeling my lips tingle in earnest as I gradually worked three fingers into the inexperienced hole. I had to use incrementally deeper thrusts, pulling out before pushing in a bit more, like a practice pole.

Eyes closed, the Yungian girl moaned and traded active kisses and touches with her Dragon Spirit, reaching to caress wherever she could reach, even his pointed ears, his horns, and the coiled hair at his nape. She had *finally* let go of the assumption that she must lie passive while we used her body, and I saw at once how Mourn's own doubts and hesitation had vanished as well.

In time, her sex loosened up nicely, as receptive as any I'd known. With so much attention on most of her body, Dandan didn't seem to notice when her slit stretched around four of my fingers. On the third, careful thrust, she even gave my fingers a solid squeeze.

Stronger than I expected.

Good sign. She's ready.

The To'vah-krav could fuck the Shi's daughter without hurting her, and her sheath could accommodate him just fine.

Let us do it, then.

Slowly, I withdrew my fingers from her swollen hole and lifted her robe with my dry hand. I treated myself to another look at the hybrid's unique shape before cradling the pronounced underside with the hand which had just been inside Dandan. My soaked and tingling fingers caressed him, spreading the lubricant around.

Mourn had been watching me so wasn't taken off guard but the attention on his neglected member was a powerful hit. He sucked air through his teeth as his tail tightened enough around the girl's leg to get her attention.

Hmm. Maybe he needs a little prep before burying this inside her.

Grinning, I leaned to fit the spear tip of his phallus into my mouth, smelling his wild musk and my first salty taste of his tacky precum. He quivered, and I licked him clean before adding fresh spit to slicken him up.

"*Sirana—!*" he groaned, his voice tight.

Oops.

I stopped in place before opening my mouth carefully to back up, only lightly dragging my tongue on the underside as I straightened up. Out of habit, my fingers had begun squeezing the thick, scalding shaft just beneath the glans, a trick that sometimes worked to help a bua delay that edge a bit longer, though I wasn't sure I had the right hold on a Dragon's cock.

Either way, Mourn brought himself under control.

"She's ready when you are," I murmured, waiting for him to open his eyes.

The half-blood nodded his chin, finally looking at me. "Been ready."

He looked like he didn't want to think too hard anymore.

Dandan made eye contact with me, smiling shyly as I encouraged her hips to line up their sexes. With thighs quivering and breath shaking, she held on tightly to the strong, dark arms around her as I wedged the glans in and pressed firmly on the shaft to encourage the right angle.

The head of his black cock popped in beneath her black fur, nestling quickly between her bright red netherlips. She gasped, he rumbled, and they both paused to gather themselves. It was a good thing she stretched easily for four fingers, because that's about where she began with the Dragonblood.

Don't think too much. No need to see to feel it.

I leaned forward, wanting to taste where they joined, and drew my still-tingling tongue and lips across their straining sexes before sliding up to gently suck on her nub. Dandan's voice roughened as she groaned this time; she flexed her muscles somewhere deep inside and Mourn slid in a little farther without a thrust from him.

"Yes," he gasped.

Dandan arched her back a little, her head settling on Mourn's right shoulder as she stared with open eyes at the ceiling. She whispered to him in between two catches of breath, lifting her hips until he nearly popped out. I prevented this by pressing on the underridge again, holding it in place as she slowly pushed back down, impaling herself on him of her own accord.

She drew back with a small whimper and said something else that made the tip of Mourn's tail flick back and forth.

"What did she say?" I asked. "I could use the guidance."

"She says… she feels a 'pleasure spot' inside," he huffed, his legendary patience sounding frayed. "But she needs the 'outside spot, as well.'"

I pursed mildly buzzing lips, satisfied by now that the spit wasn't going to my head. *"She wants my mouth?"*

"Yes." His chest expanded, nudging at Dandan's back. *"I think she could peak with both, but she doesn't know how to ask."*

"Got it."

She might not know how to ask, but I knew how to make it happen.

I reattached my lips to hers. I could have been back in the Red Sister Cloister again for how sharp my focus held to my task. I knew how to overwhelm and even punish, but I also knew how to listen, to smell, to feel the small adjustments needed for a Sister's climax without ever releasing her cunt.

At the same time, Mourn took some control as well and pushed his cock in, only as deep as he'd been before. As his moist heat passed beneath my chin, Dandan sounded exhilarated. Carefully, he withdrew and stuffed himself back in while I sucked her, and I *felt* how Dandan responded to us both. I knew before I heard her encouragement that we had the rhythm right.

"Inyi, inyi!" Dandan cried. It was almost a shriek. *"Nui!"*

"More," Mourn translated, his voice strained. "Keep going."

Fuck, yeah.

The half-blood's thrusts grew confident as he heeded unspoken responses. I held on for the ride, my eyes closed, all senses wide open as Dandan approached her climax. I concentrated, and waited, and felt a drip down my inner thigh.

Goddess, what I might give for a Sister to drop behind me with her Feldeu right now.

"Nui...!" Dandan panted, her body shaking from an untamed tension about to break. *"Ai, inyi! Ai...! Oh!!"*

"Yes!" Mourn breathed, reaching for me.

He caressed my hair. Then my ear.

Almost as much of a shock to me as the orgasm crashing over Dandan.

The girl's pelvis jerked, and I strived to hold on, to keep my mouth in place as she howled with rising bursts of sound. Mourn helped me, lifting and keeping her back to his chest as he fucked her, and I sucked, letting her hit that peak uninterrupted.

"Ah! Ah! Ayeiiii!"

We listened as that blend of ecstasy and panic overtaking her present, the moment soon softening to herald that enviably deep sense of release.

"Ai... ai... ayei..."

I lifted my lips from her scorching sex before she grew too sensitive, leaning back to catch my breath. The air cooled everything below my nose and onto my throat. I looked up at Mourn, dizzy from forgetting to breathe, and pulled my glistening hand from my own crotch.

I signed, ★What next?★

His eyes were ablaze as he answered. ★On the bed.★

He hadn't come yet.

Withdrawing his sodden, unsatiated pole, Mourn swept Dandan up with him as he stood from the well-tested chair. He put her over his shoulder, her stained, white robe hanging down, and supported her ass with the crook of one arm while extending a hand to me as well. I accepted the help to my feet; I'd grown stiff enough on the floor to need it.

Bohai scooted back from the foot of the bed, offering plenty of room for us to join. I approached the bua from the side as Mourn climbed on and carefully laid his sister onto her back. Taking hold of her waist with both hands, Mourn shifted them both until they were near the center.

We watched the Dragonblood finally strip off the bride's pale robe to leave her fully nude. He grasped her hips, tugging her closer so that her legs draped over his open thighs. Even Dandan knew it was his turn; she cooperated, trying to assist as he wasted no time mounting up again.

She grunted as he penetrated, her wide eyes refusing to blink or look away as her Dragon Spirit shifted to find his depth from before. He cycled slowly at first, his hands lifting her ass while he stayed on his knees, letting them grow reaccustomed.

"*Wen-yung,*" she breathed, reaching to touch his hand.

"*Shi-lu,*" he replied.

Soon Mourn was thrusting much quicker than before, his pace urgent though not forceful. He kept this pace for only one reason: to attain that long-delayed release for himself and pump his jism into her wet and willing slit.

It's about time.

The distinct sound of another male stroking his staff reached my ears, and I peered at Bohai with a bit of incredulity. He was headed toward his climax as well but sensed my gaze, dragging his eyes from the Dragon Spirit to me. He flushed with embarrassment.

"*Ah,*" he gulped.

Chuckling, I climbed onto all fours and aimed my ass at him. "Put your cock here, Shi son. I am aching."

I had little grace or time left for him to overcome his shock, so I reached between my legs and spread my netherlips, dropping to my elbows and wiggling my hips impatiently.

I commanded him with more force, "Fuck me, Bohai. Now."

The nude Yungian scrambled to drop behind me, getting in one misaimed prod before I reached between my legs to snare his prick and gave him the guidance he needed. Once aimed properly, his hips lunged forward, and his cock landed deep before pulling back on his first stroke.

Oh, Goddess, yes.

His delightful, downward curve dragged his meat exquisitely along some extremely sensitive places. I exhaled in relief, braced on one elbow as I rubbed myself as well. "Now, fast and hard as you can!"

The youth fucked me with all the relish and attention I could ask for as I kept my attention on Mourn riding Dandan. I wanted to see the half-blood swept up in his intense peak again. We weren't as close together as we'd been by the tree, but we were comfortable, each of us with caresses *much* better than our own hands!

I looked for the modest knot at the base of Mourn's cock, unlikely to gain entry unless the Dragonblood simply lost control and crammed it in. While that remained to be seen, I also doubted that would happen.

He wouldn't hurt her.

The moment of truth arrived abruptly, though I didn't realize it at first, my attention distracted by the white spines rising on his back.

Fanning out along his spine.

Whoa.

That didn't happen last time.

Mourn drew his lips back in a snarl as he tensed, a familiar, guttural growl storming through his chest to pass through sharp teeth. Beneath him, Dandan shrieked in fear; she didn't recognize any of these signs as those of intense pleasure.

But I did.

"*Sssargt, rarrgh!*" he roared, shuddering, showing immense restraint to not slam his full length into her.

His tail lashed out as it had by the tree, whipping around as if desperate for something to grasp. This time, it found my wrist and in my present position, I couldn't avoid it.

My eyes snapped onto the scaled limb as it wrapped three times around my forearm and squeezed. *Hard.*

~What the…?!~

A powerful, new sensation coursed up my arm and into my chest before spreading from there to encompass all of me. An intensity so keen at first, I wasn't certain of pleasure or pain, yet it swept through me like a flooding river on dry sand as I drank it in.

I fell deep into the throes of orgasm, light exploding behind my eyes, and cried out with my hands clutching and tearing at the mattress. Someone behind me was coming, too, clutching my hips, far over the edge and squirting hot seed deep inside me with a hoarse groan.

This only made it better.

Suddenly, the male slumped onto my back, almost knocking me flat, his cock dragging a fistful of fluid across my thighs as it slipped out. His body toppled over with a thump; he just missed landing on someone's head.

The air filled with an intangibly high pitch teasing my ears, yet I was convinced I couldn't actually *hear* it.

It lived at the back of my mind.

Like walking on a Ley Line.

Then, just as quickly, it vanished, and the room was silent.

I blinked the haze away, pulling details to me like a blanket while tiny bumps spread over my back. The candles had blown out at some point; the room had gone dark except for the light of the setting moons flowing into the far windows.

What happened?

Enough light remained that I could see the Dragonblood mercenary without using Dark Sight. Mourn was upright but perhaps not for long. I watched him gingerly pull his cock free, supporting his weight on both fists pressed on either side of his playmate. The degree to which his weight sank into the mattress suggested he'd just caught himself from collapsing on her.

Her.

I studied her face.

Dandan.

She appeared asleep, arms out and hands relaxed, her head lolling to one side.

I glanced behind me to my left.

Bohai had fallen and rolled onto his back. He was also asleep.

Again.

Mourn rumbled in the quiet, dark room, and I was surprised he was visibly sweating. He looked feverish.

I cleared my throat. *"Need water?"*

He blinked as if surprised to see me. *"You're awake?"*

"Foreboding, Dragon son."

My grin slipped lopsided as I stretched out my back and legs. I asked again. *"Thirsty? I am. I'll be right back."*

I crawled partway off the bed to get my wobbly legs under me before ambling to the washstand, where there was a pitcher of water and two glazed ceramic cups. I poured them both to the rim and had drained mine dry before taking two steps toward the bed.

Ah, fuck it.

I drank the second one, too, before grabbing the pitcher and both empty cups to bring them back to the half-blood. By now he had managed to sit on his backside on the end of the bed, his feet on the ground.

I handed him a cup and poured it full of water, watched him drain it as fast as I had mine, and poured again. He emptied that one, and I poured a third time. Before *that* one was gone, I poured a final cup for me and *then* refilled his.

"Do you just want the pitcher?" I asked as he finished.

Mourn considered and nodded, reaching to take it as I held it out. I watched him drain what was left while slurping on my third cup. His heart pounded but his skin no longer seemed blistering when he set both items on the floor.

I didn't have the endurance to keep standing like this, so I sat next to him at the foot of the bed, wiggling briefly to wipe the excess fluid from my crotch.

"So, what just happened?" I asked, glancing pointedly over my shoulder at the two unconscious siblings.

Their chests rose and fell normally; their faces showed no excess sweat or strain, and their color overall was lush. Combined with Mourn's distinct lack of panic, I presumed they'd recover with some sleep.

Mourn sat with his elbows on his knees, the magic bracers all he wore. He'd slipped his pants off when I wasn't looking; I spotted them now over by the vanity.

"I'm not sure," he answered at last. *"It's normal that my aura surges when I find release."*

I nodded, recalling something like that by the tree. It hadn't been this powerful, though.

"You were surprised I was still conscious," I pointed out.

The Dragonchild grimaced like he regretted saying that but didn't deny it. He was looking out the window. *"Yet another reason I have sought less sex with Humans lately."*

"How long is 'lately?'"

Mourn shrugged. *"This has been happening over the last hundred years."*

"What's been happening?" I suppressed my smirk. *"They pass out when you come?"*

"Not every time, but this is becoming more frequent. And it's never happened to anyone nearby I wasn't fucking at the time."

True, Bohai had been fucking me on the far end of the bed. The brother's contact with Mourn's aura had been indirect, when that strong tail had snared my arm.

Despite his wording, the hybrid didn't look at all proud or amused by this new outcome. More frustrated.

I nodded. *"And this didn't used to happen at all?"*

He shook his head. *"No. There have been times I've enjoyed after-glow with a companion who was still capable of speech."*

I bit down on the laugh that nearly escaped, though he looked at me sidelong, cocking a brow ridge.

"Go on and laugh, Baenar," he grumbled.

His tail flicked once near the floor, striking my ankle, and a tight smile began to crack his dour visage.

I lost my struggle then, falling onto my back and cackling at the ceiling. I was sorry and yet not, because this felt *so* good somehow.

Mourn waited until my mirth had reduced to quiet chortling then reached to touch my red sash. I quieted and looked down, anticipating when he found the hard lump of Shyntre's pendant beneath. Neither of us would have seen if it had glowed, it was too well hidden. I thought it probably had, as the stone was still a bit warm.

"I am curious now," he said. *"Would you tell me of your last dream?"*

I shook my head as if to clear water from my ears. *"Huh?"*

"Do you remember it? You were eager to describe it before. Something about a very different sky than the cloudy morning here, and your queen being absent."

I propped myself on my elbows and frowned at him. *"Let me guess. 'Choosing your time' to hear about these dreams could be times you must regain control after seeing it slide?"*

Mourn shrugged, glancing either at my crotch or my belly, I couldn't tell which. *"You could see it that way. We have about two hours to sunrise, and I wouldn't leave before then."*

I made a face. *"Because we must reassure our host that we enjoyed our pleasures with his son and daughter now that they're no longer 'pure.'"*

He smiled dryly. *"Correct."* His expression softened. *"I offer many compliments to you, Red Sister, for all you taught them. An initiation like this will add a spiritual and worldly understanding to their lives with a balance unlike most around them."* He paused. *"I must thank you, and I truly do, for your insight and generosity toward them. It has been a long time since I've seen that."*

The tips of my ears burned as I tilted my head. *"A long time? But you have seen it before?"*

He nodded sagely.

"Krithannia?" I guessed.

Mourn smiled and shook his head. *"No. Another Baenar. In Vuthra'tern."* He hesitated briefly but decided to answer the unspoken questions as well. *"My commander. From my old squad. She was observant and generous with caits and buas in a similar way."*

I nearly asked if that had included him, but his eyes slid away from me and toward the moonlight again. His thoughts seemed far enough away that I decided it wasn't important; I felt mollified and willing to complete our lingering exchange.

"Alright. My dream."

Mourn brought his attention back as I sat up.

"Let's see. I was in the Red Desert again. Clear sky with stars and moons rising. No wind. Very quiet. The quietest it's ever been." I paused, squinting at the half-blood. *"I wonder now if this had to do with the 'protections' you mentioned. About magical interference?"*

"Possibly," he said. *"Go on."*

"Well. I was naked but didn't feel exposed. That's never happened before, either." I shrugged. *"For once, I was myself. Not someone else."*

The Dragonchild tilted his head, his eyes fixed steadily on me. *"Have you always been someone else in these dreams?"*

"No. I mean, I always feel like I am me, Sirana. But figures who talk to me in these dreams speak like I am someone else they know. They call me different names, and when I look down, I even wear their clothing and their body."

"Interesting." Mourn nodded once. *"And the point for this shift was when you came to the Surface?"*

I managed to nod.

"Tell me about this recent dream. The quiet one where you are your naked self."

I smirked and looked down at my white puff and bare hips and legs. My lower belly felt warmer than the rest of me.

"Hm. Well, I dreamt of my baby's sire again. But he was in trouble. Trapped in a sinking sand pit and couldn't lift himself out. He didn't want me to come down and help him lest I get stuck, too, but... I couldn't walk

away and just leave him. But there was no help anywhere. The sands were vast and empty."

Mourn's tail shushed over the floor. *"Is this the Davrin with gold eyes like mine?"*

I frowned. *"Not this time. He looked as he always did down below. His eyes are scarlet. They've only turned gold in a couple of dreams, but I have never determined a reason for it except that I once saw that painting in the Priestess Sanctuary. Maybe I'm just mixing them together."*

Mourn seemed momentarily confused at that description but then he grunted. *"I see. What happened next?"*

"I climbed down to try to help him out, but he was right. I couldn't do it alone. The more I might try, the more sand I kicked down onto him."

The bride's room fell quiet as I gazed at the moons setting through the far window.

"When I climbed up, I saw a... tower on the horizon. I described it to him, and he said he'd seen it in his dreams before. He said it was a 'spire,' not a tower, though I don't know the difference."

I glanced at Mourn then, and I was sure that he did.

"Have you seen a spire in the Desert?" I asked.

"I haven't been to the Desert," he reminded me.

"That's not a negative, To'vah-krav."

Mourn decided not to lie outright. *"I have seen one once in a lucid dream, but I never approached it."*

"A lucid dream. Like this one."

"Like this one." The Dragonchild glanced at my middle. *"I am somehow getting the sense that your child's sire dreams in a similar way that I do. Perhaps frequently enough to make contact with other dreamers."*

I swallowed as a deep chill entered my body, followed by a rush of heat. *"Isn't he rather far away to be doing that where I am?"*

Mourn shrugged. *"Not necessarily. But I don't know anything about him."*

"His… brother says he has visions," I volunteered, *"like the Priestesses or the Valsharess. He might be… as powerful? Maybe. But he's been trying to hide it."*

Mourn seemed like he hadn't wanted to hear that. *"He's hiding because he's not a Priestess, and that's a threat. The Abyss would use it to torment him, and change him to their likeness, if they can."*

My stomach froze. He understood perfectly.

"Is that where the dream ended?"

"Huh? Oh, no, it continued."

"I'm listening."

"Speaking of my chosen sire's brother," I said, *"they switched places in my dream."*

Mourn pulled out of his scowl. His golden eyes blinked. *"What?"*

"They switched places," I repeated. *"When I climbed from the pit and saw the spire and described it, it also looked like a sandstorm was coming. When I told him, I…well, I also noticed three others were watching us from far away. But, unlike the storm, they never got any closer."*

"Did you recognize any of them?"

"Two of them, no. Only one shaped like a Drider."

His Elven ears turned back in a way mine couldn't, somehow accentuating the rising aggression I read in his tail. *"Of course, her servant would be there. But tell me about the sandstorm and the buas switching places."*

I nodded. *"When I realized that the storm would blow enough sand to bury my baby's sire and suffocate him, I panicked and got back down there with him to… protect him, I guess. Except it wasn't him anymore, it was the wizard who made this."*

I tugged out the silver and blue pendant from my red wrapping, and Mourn's gaze dropped to study it again.

"Um. His name is Shyntre, and… well, he does have flecks of gold in his eyes. Metallic, like yours. He has for as long as I've known him, and I've seen the same trait in his sire's eyes."

The half-blood appeared baffled as he imagined this. Instead of asking more, however, he turned us again to our bargain. *"What happened in the dream, Sirana? How did it end when you woke up?"*

I took a deep breath. *"Well, Shyntre said he didn't know how he got there but understood the danger. My wizard summoned a shield for us, as his brother is unable to do, and we started digging him out, piling up the sand behind it as the wind got stronger. And louder."*

The imagery was still vivid behind my eyes.

"Shyntre scrambled out, and he was also naked. Um, we were still at the bottom, and it was almost too late. And..." I hesitated. *"I don't know exactly what happened."*

Mourn waited then prodded gently. *"Does it go dark? As if the sand covered you?"*

"No. We made it out. We found shelter from the storm."

"You did."

I heard some subtle relief.

"How did you get out?" he asked.

I pulled my lips between my teeth as I tried to choose the words.

"Shyntre couldn't hold the spell under the weight of the sand by the time the storm caught up to us. When the shield failed, I, um, remember screaming, I think. And punching the wall of sand. Or wanting to. It was all I could think of."

Mourn showed modest amusement. *"Punching the sand?"*

"Well, not with my fist." My face warmed to hear me say it as I dared to smile. *"Just... it worked. I thought about pushing it away as hard as I could, and it exploded upward where it was caught by the wind and didn't fill the hole. We kept climbing until we made it out and hid behind a boulder until it was quiet again."*

The Dragonblood watched me for a moment before nodding slowly. *"That is impressive, Sirana."*

"Um, thanks."

"Is this where you woke?"

"*Almost. Shyntre noticed the Drider was still there, but he couldn't see the other two. And the spire was gone once the sandstorm passed.*"

I paused, my hand covering my womb for the first time all evening. I had done better to train myself not to give away this unconscious tell of my condition, as I had in front of Gavin. Mourn observed without comment.

"*Shyntre wanted to touch my stomach. I think he could see the life aura somehow, like Gavin can. But he didn't because he said…*" I looked at Mourn. "*Almost exactly what you just did. That the queen would only use it to torment him. And that he needed to leave.*"

Mourn looked quite interested in that. "*Did he seem aware that he needed to awaken from this dream?*"

I nodded. "*Yeah. Then I woke up in your library, and you were sitting in the corner concentrating on Kurn's sword.*"

He grunted. "*I remember.*"

I waited for a response while he thought all this over, but I was also aware of how tacky my crotch had become. Having rested and recovered energy to spare, I stood up to retrieve a bucket of water and some washcloths from near the vanity, bringing them back to the bed.

Handing one to Mourn, I dunked and lightly wrung mine, lifting one foot onto the mattress to begin a thorough wipe down of my folds and creases. The half-blood watched me rather intently for a while before forcing a blink and standing up to do the same. I grinned to watch him in return, a pleasure to observe how he handled his own tackle.

When we'd finished, I nodded toward Dandan. "*I presume we should let her clean herself after she wakes?*"

Mourn turned to look, and his tail curved in a sensual wave at the sight of her open legs and flushed slit so recently enjoyed by us both. His offering had oozed out to leave a visible gloss along her creases.

"*Mm, correct,*" he murmured. "*Dandan must have no doubt the rut happened, and she may choose the clean-up ritual she wants.*"

"But we should take the robe."

He wasn't confused which one I meant. *"Agreed."*

I admired the sleeping siblings again. *"I'd say Bohai doesn't need that reassurance but regardless is capable of cleaning himself."*

Mourn chuckled, finishing up, and we took turns rinsing and wringing out our cloths. *"Climaxing three times and dropping asleep after two of them. He's a lucky bua, and there shall be some lasting and raunchy stories about you."*

I laughed with satisfaction. *"Aw. I forgot to reciprocate his thumb playing on my pucker. But I am curious if Human males have that pleasure gland one can reach through their netherhole?"*

Mourn gave me an odd look, narrowed-eyed and smirking as though trying to determine my jest, if any.

"What?" I asked, putting hands on my hips. *"I am asking."*

He shrugged. *"Purely by listening to others, it appears that they do."*

"Ha!" I laughed. *"I take it that you've never discovered for yourself?"*

The Dragon son showed a sardonic smirk as he held up his hand to show me sharp claws, saying nothing.

"I mean as the Human, Roewn," I clarified, *"or some other shape you take as a true form without those talons."*

"Then you are correct," he granted. *"I have never felt an urge to 'discover for myself,' though I have listened to many who do."*

"And those who have, do they enjoy it?"

"Of those who openly discuss it, I would say yes. Without doubt."

"Oo!"

"But," he continued, pausing to hold my eyes after that strong qualifier. He made sure I was paying attention. *"Those men who openly discuss it are **not** most men you will meet, Sirana. It's a forbidden subject in many Human settlements and can draw hostility from those who perceive such penetration as a threat. Like Kurn, for example."*

I rolled my eyes. *"Ah, yes, Mathias Briar mentioned that."*

"Oh, did he?"

I nodded, deciding not to describe the skin hunter with the Witch Hunter in the shed in any detail. *"He preferred men to women."*

"Some do. It's to be expected."

I frowned. *"Yeah? Why?"*

Mourn paused and folded his arms across his chest, beginning to smile close-lipped. *"Do you mean you can come from Nobility with long-term consorts, be recruited into a Sisterhood such as you've described, currently carry a baby caught from a tryst with very close brothers who have 'switched places' in your dreams, and you wouldn't have noticed a certain fluidity in preferences among Baenar?"*

I blinked at him in surprise. *"Well, I meant Humans, not Davrin. And while we're talking, what about Dwarves?"*

Mourn unfolded his arms, motioning an invitation to sit down on the bed again now that our skin was dry. *"As far as I've observed, yes. This flexibility is a quality of sensual bonding among all the sentient races I've had contact with. It seems to help protect them from overspecialization. A people can't adapt to a free-flowing world if all individuals must limit their bonds or their roles too much."*

He paused. *"I believe we all need multiple bonds to survive, whether or not they have anything to do with mating. These bonds have stretched and persisted even through extreme persecution and culling in mass, yet the races still thrive to bear children capable of these bonds. I do not see how they could not be part of the soul of the world."*

I nodded slowly in agreement, working this over to imagine Humans and Dwarves with preferences like mine. *Hm.*

Then his remark came back.

"Wait, um," I began, massaging my forehead. *"You included my catching from a 'tryst' with 'very close' brothers?"*

Mourn looked confused. *"You told me they shared no blood-bond but grew up together and call themselves brothers. They protect each other even now. Is that not true?"*

I nodded. *"That's true."*

"And you seem sure which one is the sire, but the other one, the wizard created those wellness pellets to help keep you and your child well on the Surface."

My face flushed unexpectedly. *"Oh. Well. Hm. I thought maybe he did that for... um. Me."*

"Aha," Mourn breathed. *"Did, um... have you never seen them together?"*

My mouth tightened. *"Just twice. The first time, they were arguing about something, and Shyntre pushed him. And the second time..."*

I grimaced. Auslan had been locked in solitary, reaching to me through the bars of a cell.

"Well," I finished. *"They have been kept separate for decades by the Priestesses and Matrons. So, no, I suppose I haven't seen them interact much."*

Mourn fell still for a beat. *"I apologize. Perhaps I presume too much."*

"Well, I mean, wait, no," I babbled, opening my hands to throw them at nothing. *"I wouldn't be **angry** if you were right, and of course they would have to hide such a bond! I mean, I know what would happen if they spoke openly about it. It's a forbidden subject, exactly like you said, and..."*

The half-blood's tail curled back and forth at the tip, giving me something to look at while this new realization took firm hold in my mind.

I heard Auslan and Shyntre from my dream again.

I am honored you still carry. I did not expect it to last even this long.

I shouldn't. She'll only use it against me later.

"How did you come to know them both?" Mourn asked, his voice interested and calming.

"Separately," I whispered, clearing my throat before speaking with more strength. *"I pursued them each, not realizing there was a connection until later. And even once I knew, I still sought after them. The one cycle we stood in one place wasn't safe to share much."*

"Hm." The curling and uncurling of Mourn's tail slowed a little. *"Would it be accurate to say they came to know you on their own paths? They weren't talking to each other between encounters with you?"*

Shyntre's voice erupted from my memory. *And he's known you this whole time. ... That fucking trophy. He never said a thing.*

I swallowed and nodded to the Dragonchild. *"Um. As far as I know, yes."*

"And you are attracted to each male on his own merit?"

My middle relaxed when I heard the amiable encouragement.

He wanted to know.

I tilted my head and smiled dryly. *"They're two **very** different buas. Sharing their merits isn't possible, they are like incomparable spices. But they might blend together nicely."*

Mourn chuckled, looking up at the window and around the darkened room again as if to be sure we were secure. His tail end had sped up again as he pondered what I'd told him, and I was about to ask why he wanted to know more about them when he lifted his right hand and carefully placed it on my left thigh.

Incredibly warm.

I stilled, staring at it as his finger pads caressed my inner thigh gently. It felt good. Consciously, I relaxed, left his hand in place, and turned my head to look at him. I quirked my eyebrows in silent question.

What do you want, To'vah-krav?

As if the partial swelling of the limb between his legs wasn't a hint.

"I remember something," Mourn said, *"from the Deepearth. I'd buried it with everything else until this conversation."*

I lifted my eyebrows the rest of the way, keeping my eyes on him while the rest of my body centered on his hand upon my leg.

"There were not many," he said, stroking my skin, *"but I remember a few caits and matas who had both sister bonds and sire bonds yet also weren't threatened by their brothers in arms having the same."* The half-

blood met my eyes. *"I mentioned my squads were mixed, because we were fewer in number than Sivaraus, and this is probably why more of these bonds arose to be seen. Out of necessity."*

I nodded, beginning to feel a sensation of being swallowed up by his gaze. His vertical pupils seemed to be tracing my face, studying it.

"The females who stood on their own, acknowledging and protecting the bonds of others while maintaining some of their own were, to me, courageous and strong. The opposite of those possessive and controlling in their violence." He paused. *"Those females were the few Davrin I admired when I left."*

"Admired?" I repeated with a cocked grin.

A nod.

"Why? Other than seeming strong." I waved my hand. *"Everyone wants a strong matron guiding their house."*

Mourn understood. *"I admired them because they'd found a way to be free within the forbidden set by the controllers, when most around them were afraid to reach out to anyone."*

His warm palm slid closer to my crotch. His teeth showed in a small grin when my eyes popped.

"What was more," he continued. *"Being close to these females spread freedom to others rather than cutting their bonds or cauterizing their ability to form new ones. Those close to her belonged not to her but to themselves, the same as she belonged to herself."* Briefly, golden eyes dropped below my face and back up. *"The only females I didn't fear and would protect without coercion."*

I swallowed as the knuckles on his last two fingers ran lightly over my mound fur. Although I blanked on a coherent response to all that, I didn't think I could be mistaking his signals.

I leaned back onto my hands and opened my legs wider. The Dragonblood accepted the silent invitation to caress my smooth netherlips.

"Ooh," I cooed, easing into watching him explore.

"You're warming up quickly," he said when I was taken by an involuntary shiver.

"Heh. Why wouldn't I?"

"Three climaxes in a night are a lot for some. Especially when each seemed so satisfying."

"And you cannot help but count them?" I chuckled. *"I think I only spotted one climax for you. Was it satisfying?"*

He nodded, moving his palm up in a firm sweep across my abdomen and other thigh. *"Very much."*

"But it's difficult to count beyond one when they keep passing out."

Mourn broke into a reluctant grin at my humorous tone, shaking his head. *"It's not funny, Sirana."*

"It is when I'm here to suggest a solution to this problem."

He gripped my hip with a soft intake of air; I felt only the barest tips of his claws on my flesh. *"What solution would you put forward?"*

I prayed to any goddess out there listening that he hadn't been teasing me this whole time.

I lifted my eyes. *"I think you must rub out another peak but this time with a Red Sister. Take as much as pleasure you like with my slit of greater experience, and I wager I'll still be awake afterward."*

His reptilian pupils broadened with interest. *"Wager what?"*

My eyes lifted skyward. *"My fourth orgasm for the night with that river log,"* I pointed at his fast-swelling prick, *"damming up my cunt."*

The Dragonblood emitted a sound between a growl and a laugh.

"Deal."

Excellent.

Mourn moved his hand up to caress one breast as tenderly as he had Dandan's. *"I wonder if the pendant helped protect you."*

"I became a Red Sister without it." My face felt hot as I pulled myself backward onto the bed and out of his reach, beckoning him

to follow. *"But perhaps there's insight to be had in more than a pin to the mat."*

He rumbled agreement, finally turning to crawl onto the bed. Tucking my blue pendant away, I watched him gather up Dandan with care and move her to the far side of her brother. This would give us about half of the mattress to rut on.

Once he'd cleared the space, I moved forward to meet him, determined not to fall into a state of hesitancy like Dandan's. He and I would just have to sort out the unseen limits as we went.

I knew one limit, at least. *No finger in his ass.*

Mourn and I met on our knees, and he reached to pull me against him as my hands slid around broad shoulders. He dipped his face low, deeply inhaling my scent between my neck and shoulder, then lightly licking it.

I remembered when I felt the tingle.

"Hey, just checking," I murmured.

"Hm?"

His hand slid down my back to squeeze my ass.

"I don't recall your tip lube tingling my fingers. Does it feel like your spit in any way when you spray inside someone?"

Mourn huffed a laugh and held me tighter, pressing a hard erection into my belly. *"I've long been grateful that answer is no."*

He brushed dry lips along my shoulder and upper arm. *"I doubt any female would have let me mount her a second time if she only felt burning after the first."*

"Oh, good."

We exchanged a few experimental kisses as I'd seen him practice with Dandan, though I thought this might be habit or expectation. He could pucker his lips and press them to mine, but I caught hints that the tiny scales reduced the sensitivity that a Human or Davrin would know, and he never opened his mouth. I could grasp why.

His teeth were sharp and his tongue mostly incompatible; the powerfully long muscle would overwhelm any sensual duel with a lover's tongue with any attempt. I didn't mind his quick, prickling licks along the edge of my mouth, though.

They were unique as the rest of him.

Time gave me opportunity to caress his ears and test that sensitivity as well. He inhaled with pleasure, his tail slowly looping once around my thigh, constricting and massaging up toward my crotch. Soon we stopped kissing in favor of exploring, licking, or nibbling a trait we had in common.

The room felt almost too warm to be wrapped up against the big hybrid, shifting slowly on our knees with a flared and turgid erection trapped between us, its tip leaving smears on our skin. He quivered as I did while we traced the textures and shapes of each other, up to down and slowly back up.

I learned Mourn was extremely aware of his claws and never dug his fingers into crevices he couldn't see, especially as I moved and reached, too. The half-blood was more likely to use his tail or his tongue in lieu of his digits for that exploration, and I discovered that to be a near-continuous series of thrills.

The first time his hands gently lifted and spread my buttocks while he nuzzled my throat, he also used his tail to test my slit's readiness.

"*Shhhiiit,*" I groaned as it glided lengthwise between my netherlips from behind, wriggling a little in the wetness. "*Oh, fuck!*"

He chuckled. "*I don't think you need my tongue to prepare you.*"

"*Might not need, but I want!*" I laughed, leaning back to look up at him. "*I'd enjoy knowing what Dandan knew.*"

He purred. "*Very well.*"

When he guided me to rest on my back, I cooperated at first. It was clear he wished me to be comfortable when he opened my legs to run his tongue between them.

It wasn't until he leaned low and over me to nuzzle the scents around the red sash that he became a dark shadow looming.

Void dark.

A presence that made me gasp with fear.

He stopped to look at my face. *"What is it, Sirana?"*

His eyes flickered between gold and sickly yellow.

"N-not on my back," I stuttered, pushing weakly against his chest.

"Of course."

Mourn didn't question but pulled me upright and drew me close, massaging and exploring me as we'd been doing.

"I should tell you something," he began.

I frowned but inhaled his scent to clear my head. *"Tell me what?"*

"You've seen the spines rise up on my back?"

I nodded, drifting less as I held tight around his waist. *"I have. Just tonight."*

"They make it uncomfortable to be on my back," he admitted, *"and I never cared for the position myself. I wanted to ask you what position you would prefer?"*

"Oh! On my knees," I answered, no hesitation. *"From behind."*

He sounded amused. *"Are you sure?"*

I blinked and looked up to see eyes sharply, beautifully metallic.

I grinned. *"With that low dip you've got on the underside of your cock? Fuck, yes, Mourn. You might make me cum twice before you're done. Especially if you play with my netherhole at the same time."*

He was convinced.

"Would you enjoy it if I licked you in that position, too?"

"Yes, please!"

Slipping my arms from him, I turned and dropped on all fours, opening my knees comfortably as I settled on my elbows. I heard him groan a little, and I chuckled, weaving my ass to entice him further.

I also detected the change outside the window, darker for the sister moons having set yet with a hint of diffused light drifting into view from the far horizon. It wasn't night's end already, was it?

Where did the time go?

I gasped in surprise as Mourn dragged a strong, slick tongue along my sex, tagging my white mound before coating my clit. He set me on end in an instant, slowly releasing the swarm of sensation across my ready folds.

My forehead dropped onto the mattress. *"Ohhhh!"*

He palmed my ass, holding me in place as he spread my cheeks wider and dipped down to start over again. The texture and rising intensity of his spit had me writhing like the Yungian virgin.

My eyes and mouth opened together when he finished his second taste by circling around my netherhole like Bohai had with his thumb. It flared awake as if it had never been touched before.

Oh my goddess!!

The tip of his tongue pressed into the twitching center of my asshole, and I clutched the mattress as if I were the one with claws! He penetrated just enough and swept around the rim, launching a spontaneous cry from my mouth.

"Mourn!"

"Mm-hm."

He knew it wasn't a complaint.

Tugging out his tongue, he slathered more saliva around my crinkled flesh before penetrating again. My well-trained orifice had already relaxed enough that he sank deeper without trying.

"Shit, shit!" I hissed, gulping before I drooled on the bed.

Large hands massaged my ass further before parting them again. His tongue slapped at my purple star like Jaunda did with her Feldeu before rimming me further and, in my delirium, I nearly asked him to put his cock there instead.

I bit my tongue. For that, he was *definitely* too big.

Fuck.

I could let him do this for *hours*, but that wasn't our bargain.

"Mourn, I…"

"Hm?"

"It's almost sunrise. Please…"

Mourn left my netherhole bereft of his tongue as he checked the sky.

"Oh, fuck," he muttered.

I laughed, *"Exactly!"*

Mourn took hold of my hips and pulled me backward and up, his thighs brushing up to the backs of mine. We needed some quick adjustments to line up our sexes, my knees lifting and the balls of my feet bearing the weight before I finally felt him squeeze the head in.

Yes!

The motion was achingly familiar, yet my flesh coated with Mourn's tongue glaze responded in ways entirely new. Now I understood how Dandan couldn't stay still as she received him. This wasn't only *her* inexperience; Mourn had to use more force to hold me still to go deeper.

"Ah, goddess…!" I screeched.

My breath felt hot as I pressed back against him.

"Not too fast," he hushed, pulling back to negate the distance I might have gained.

I growled rather than speak the first thought which leaped to mind.

Between my legs, the Dragonchild's spit intensified the sensations of being stretched and filled. He wasn't deep yet, but he was already as wide as I'd ever taken in the Cloister. We hadn't reached that low dip yet, which I anticipated soon to be savagely scraping along that delicious spot behind my bladder with each stroke.

Rarely had I enjoyed this position more than as he pulled nearly out to start over again, spreading, filling me up, and I groaned in ecstasy. Instead of pushing back to rush him, I composed myself and took a deep breath. Mourn followed my subtler encouragement forward as I stretched to accommodate him.

Finally, he sank that low, thick ridge inside, just past the entrance of my channel.

Thank fuck!

Mourn stopped and whispered, "Ohh, you feel good…"

I didn't doubt that but couldn't answer. My voice had been snared by the thrumming pressure on just one spot inside me, escalating like the time Shyntre had three fingers inside me casting sparks.

I thrust a hand down my belly to grip my mound, where my clit followed my cunt, harmonizing with that delicious buzz. I yelped when it suddenly spiked.

"Yes! Yes!"

"Sirana—!"

Mourn choked as I came as hard as I had in my life, my mouth open and drooling pure joy.

"Ohh-ooo-ohh!"

"Arrgh, Sirana…!"

He tugged backward on his cock, attempted a thrust, but my greedy body kept him in its grip until the strongest contractions of cascading pleasures had passed. A moment after the rush peaked, Mourn slipped his cock back and gave us another full thrust.

"Yes! Good!"

I had no other words!

Mourn held my hips firm as he pulled back and squeezed in a third time, my spreading sex finally pliable and relaxed enough for him to start fucking me with more speed. Braced on my feet and elbows while he huffed and pumped his hips, I wetly welcomed him with every lunge.

A drop of his spit landed on the small of my back, and my skin prickled as it slid up my spine. He gripped and massaged my ass with more force as he plunged into my depths, raking the lovely, murmuring ridge inside until I was ready.

I reached for my mound again, mashed my well-used folds against my clit, and although it wasn't as high as the first time, I came again.

"F-fuck, y-yeah…"

"Shit, Sirana!" Mourn growled, as incredulous as he was enraptured by our coupling.

"Keep going, don't stop!"

My shoulders down and face turned to the mattress, my cheek pressed to the drool spot from before, I sampled my tiring clit with my fingers, gauging if I could jump on just one more peak while I had such a unique prick plowing me.

But the half-blood gripped my sash in between my shoulder blades and lifted me up one-handed. My shoulders, elbows, and tits all left the soft bed and hung in the air.

"Whoa! Wha—?"

Then, like in the *dorji-ka* but mostly upright, the Dragonchild enfolded himself completely around me.

His tail snaked around both our waists and secured us together him on his knees with me impaled and my thighs splayed to the sides. His arms hooked beneath my pits and crossed my chest to grip my opposite wrists, holding me close. His chin hooked near my neck, his face close to mine, and everything seemed to tighten around me, assuring there was no way I could close my legs or draw away before he was finished coming as well.

Immobile and fully aware of his next several, decadent thrusts, I began to sweat from the rush of heat rising within his body. I heard that maddening pitch at the back of my mind again, wondered if it was his aura as the room seemed to shrink with all the sensations which filled it.

"Sirana—!" he gasped, on the verge of release as he pushed in one last time, as deep as he could go.

Deeper than he'd dared with Dandan.

My mouth dropped open as I felt it begin, his cock changing shape inside me! Just behind the low ridge I'd enjoyed so much, where that smaller knot would have been, his cock expanded to an astonishing size.

The fast-rising pressure edged me close to panic not knowing where it would stop. When it did, the seal around our sexes might've been tighter than any Sathoet.

Mourn ducked his head to press his brow to my upper spine and roared in release like a bear had gotten loose in the bedroom.

Oh, fuck!!

If my cunt had refused to let him pull out during my first orgasm, neither of us had that choice as his prick locked us together during his. The half-blood grunted and clung to me while he spurted deep with a lasting pleasure coming in waves. A couple of times I felt dizzy, my vision washing with colors and blurring as if I might pass out.

~No. Not now. Stay… awake.~

The hybrid was right about his cream not burning or tingling like his spit, but I could still feel several pumps of semen which were hotter than my own body's core. I also felt as if my body hummed to him, and more than his throat rumbled in return.

Low in my gut, as had happened before, my womb transformed into a slow-burning coal. Never more aware of my tiny passenger, I relished the affirming song in my head, my body lacking panic or pain or fear. Within this aura we were well, both quite alive.

And we knew it.

By the time his climax ended, Mourn was burning up again, gasped harder for breath than after he'd finished with Dandan. He leaned forward as if he might fall and crush me.

"Mourn, stop!"

He caught himself, wordlessly drawing us down onto our sides, facing away from the still-sleeping Humans and toward the window. We managed to settle with minimal discomfort, though his arms and tail still wrapped around me.

Deep within me, his prick seemed the same size; if it had shrunk at all, it wasn't much. When I tried to shift to ease that incredible pressure between my legs, Mourn hissed in pain and reached to lift my thigh, resting on top of his. He kept his hand there as well to assure I wouldn't squish his genitals between my thighs again.

Oops.

"Sorry about this," he breathed on the back of my neck, sounding barely conscious. *"It's… going to take a while. Try to lie still. It tends to…firm up again if we move too much."*

Well, that was… different.

I gauged our time by the faint light outside and listened past our breath and the low rush of blood to determine if we'd caused a rise in the household.

Everything was quiet.

I didn't doubt that at least some servants might be awake to have heard that last bestial roar, but it seemed no one intended to disturb us. We still had time.

"Don't fall asleep," I said.

"I won't."

He sounded physically tired and disinclined to carry a conversation, but I could believe he wasn't about to nod off like Bohai. I decided to trust him on it while I tried to absorb the quiet of the Shi manor to settle my own scattered focus. More than once, I tried to relax my spinning thoughts.

It wasn't working. The same worry kept coming back.

"Um, this might be poor timing, but I need to ask."

"Hm?"

"Will we confirm a bargain for my protection and for Jael?" I spoke through a grimace. *"Or did I just unbalance it, somehow?"*

Mourn chuckled softly, caressing my bare belly above where my baby rested. My womb wasn't as hot anymore.

"On the contrary," he said. *"This helped me to decide. You and I may begin settling the terms when we return to the library."*

His cock's bulge was finally starting to shrink inside my straining slit, but the early morning rustlings also grew louder. I agreed that we could talk later as I grew alert to rising activity around us, but I wasn't at all sure what he meant about settling the terms.

What had the mercenary decided? What did he want for payment?

And what had I just jumped into?

With both naked feet.

CHAPTER 16

ONCE I ACCEPTED LYING STILL AND QUIET, MOURN'S GENITALS relaxed quicker than I'd worried. He withdrew as soon as he was able and without my having to ask if it was time, although the uncoupling prompted simultaneous grunts in us both. My crotch was soaked.

"Whoo," I breathed, slowly closing my legs, and shifting to sit up. *"Gonna be sore all day."*

"I'm sorry," he said, dunking and wringing our cloths in cool water. *"I didn't intend to go full in like that, but—"*

"But," I echoed proudly, accepting the damp washrag from him. *"I remember telling you to keep going. I am glad you didn't hold back. I wanted to know what happens when you aren't protecting the cait you're fucking from yourself."*

He glanced at me. *"Hm. But I could have harmed your child."*

He sounded to already know he hadn't.

"You didn't," I confirmed, declining to borrow his worry. *"However your aura was acting, it felt better, not worse. Be at ease."*

Mourn eyed me as we cleaned up. I dabbed gingerly between my legs, parting my netherlips with my fingers to check just how reddened the well-stretched hole was.

"Whew," I said again.

He huffed. *"Nothing else on getting stuck? You're either unflappable or a shape like mine isn't unknown to you."*

"Well, you gave me an early look," I replied with a cocky smirk. *"I wondered about the function of that bulge, if and how you used it. Now I know."*

Mourn studied me as I gently patted myself dry and relinquished the topic in favor of getting clean and dressed. I was amused to watch him tie Dandan's soiled robe snugly around one thigh before drawing his loose pants to his waist, slipping his tail through the tailored hole in the back.

"No show of claiming a trophy, hm?"

Mourn shook his head, taking time to scrub the damp spot from when Dandan had first passed out. *"No. I am drained and should save what magic I can do. The robe will disappear. The rest is diluted or less convenient as sensual trophies."*

I suppressed the surge of unease and tried to sound casual. *"Hm. How likely is that?"*

Mourn smirked, finishing up. *"Father Shi indulges sometimes as part of his culture, but many Yungar create 'spirit relics' to trade without me spending the night. If there is one after tonight, the Guild will be curious who steps forward and if we know them."*

Shit. That sounded worse, somehow.

Farther reaching than I had ever considered when I walked in here.

Suddenly, I searched around for other rags not "diluted" enough and dunked them again, scrubbing at my own damp marks left behind. I began to fret about how many mages knew blood-binding magic besides Brom.

With so many unknowns, no wonder the Dragonchild didn't have sex very often if he must plan for *this*, too!

I knew this wasn't the time or place to dig deeper. I tried to neaten up and let things be rather than ask the half-blood what he knew or how many I should be worried about. Clearly, he knew the minimum of what I'd learned the hard way and was taking precautions.

The mercenary sensed the change in mood though. Why wouldn't he? He had observed me from the beginning, once expressing snide condolences for my claim of having experience with Priestesses of Braqth. He'd been there when I'd insisted Gavin burn the cloth he'd held to my bleeding nose after facing the demon of Soul Drinker.

The Dragonblood watched me intently now. He could probably smell I was afraid.

"Sirana?"

"Hm?"

"I am being cautious because that is my practice, but I am mostly taking the robe to prevent pointless or wasteful conflict between Humans, inspired by greed or ignorance. I am not taking it because of any personal danger or practical value it has to any mage."

No personal danger?

I frowned. *"What do you mean?"*

He thought on how to begin. *"Do I presume correctly that you've seen the Spider Queen's Priestesses use blood and semen in their rituals?"*

I swallowed and nodded. *"With bad outcomes for the one they drew it from."*

For certain a life-altering outcome for me.

Mourn nodded. *"I will explain to ease your worry. Such components must be fresh, but even that doesn't work alone. The mage must have direct contact and enough time with their target to break them in some way: their will, their aura, or their body. These influences and alterations on the victims cannot be accomplished from afar because they left a bloody cloth or a sex rag behind for the mage to find or for another to sell to them."*

This took time to sink in but, once it did, I felt how tightly tethered that worry had been at the back of my mind. I knew it only because of the pressure easing up now.

Is that true?

I exhaled, hearing my breath waver. Wilsira and Kerse had had that time and contact to break me and do what they did. The Conceiver had forced the arrangements with my Elder and the Prime, and I'd been with them for spans put together. I never truly escaped them.

"What about Brom seeing me cover my blood with dirt?" I asked. *"He knew what I was doing. He said he was the only one there who knew how to use 'blood magic,' and this wouldn't be a threat to me."*

Mourn nodded. *"I believe that he knows how and that blood spoiled with dirt is useless for that purpose. But even he would require the same time and contact as a Priestess to make use even of clean blood."*

The Sorcerer-General had tried to force that lasting contact with me as well. *He nearly succeeded.*

Mourn approached me slowly; at first, I didn't realize he meant to embrace me, but I accepted. We were as clothed as when we'd entered this room, him shirtless and missing his cloak downstairs, me lacking my cloak and boots.

"Use a bandage or a cloth as you need it," the half-blood assured me with earnest confidence. *"You need not worry about burning everything or taking it with you. If you bleed on something, do not let that distract you. Let it be. Only when one is a captive is the threat of this kind of magic real. Please believe me, Sirana, I have been there. The rules are the same on the Surface as they are below."*

A tightness in my middle broke completely. I *couldn't* doubt him. What Matron-Priestess with a Dragon's son in chains could resist drawing her nephew's blood to test the extent of power she could exert over him? This probably explained some scars on his back, where he lacked the natural armor of his sire's heritage.

"I-I believe you." I breathed out slowly. *"Thank you for explaining. I have never known enough about the limits of magic."*

He rubbed my back. *"You're welcome."*

We stepped back and Mourn took time to look around, finding another pale robe in Dandan's bridal closet before collecting her other decorative robes from the vanity. The half-blood instructed me to gather Bohai's robes while he brought the last bucket of water and fresh cloths.

"Will we clean and dress them?" I guessed.

Warmth and something tender touched Mourn's smile. *"If they accept, to thank them, before we leave the room together."*

Mourn proved he could awaken someone as well as put them to sleep. With a gentle touch and a word, our young companions opened their eyes and yawned next to each other. Their bodies shifted and stretched in luxury before comprehension swept their faces.

Bohai and Dandan gained their feet in a hurry, flustered to be naked and so sticky while the spirits stood clothed and clean. Mourn sounded amused but appreciative as he drew attention to their means of attaining the same state. He spoke their language when he offered the choice of bathing themselves or having us do it as a final thanks. The siblings were truly undecided at first, but then the brother bowed to me.

"I accept your grace with honor, *Janshi-lantiu.*"

I smiled in a way to see him blush. *Still, growing bolder.*

Modestly, Dandan echoed the same to *Wen-yung*, and the half-blood and I got to work. Taking the chance to caress them one more time was more fun than I expected; they both showed us in-numerable responses to our touch for every moment.

Some larger than others.

I winked at my bua while drying him off.

I also gained valuable experience in donning and securing Yungian robes in the correct order while Mourn combed Dandan's hair, leaving it flowing down her back. He instructed a well-dressed Bohai to do the same for me, which was unexpected but good and relaxing.

The siblings glowed with bliss by the time we were ready to leave the bride's room. All I had to do was be the last to step out into the hall to call my guardian spiders, letting them disappear into my free-flowing hair before I closed the door. I received the sense that they had fed well, too.

~After everything that happened in that room, my nameless ones,~ I thought with a dry inner laugh, *~it's good to know your only concern was finding a snack.~*

I wondered if it was possible for them to ever see Mourn as a threat. Or whether I still could as well.

Meanwhile, one glance at Dandan and Bohai from any servant, guard, or family, granted no doubt the night with the spirits had gone well. There wasn't a better ending to this new story about *Wen-yung's* gracious visit with his sky-eyed companion, sure to be popular in the retellings.

As the day grew brighter, the effort spent all night caught up to me. I was ready to leave Shi Manor, no disruptions or comments while the Dragon Spirit guided our rituals for departure. I just followed his lead.

MOURN HAD SAVED ENOUGH MAGICAL STRENGTH TO GRANT US some privacy from gawkers or possible taggers-on on the way back to the safehouse.

After vanishing through the gardens at the back of the estate and into the treeline, we took the long way around to the roads. The Dragonchild whispered into being a shadow-bending camouflage to augment our normal stealth required to lose the many eyes aware of the direction we'd gone.

Soon enough, we needed to leave the forest and regain the main roads toward the city center. Before stepping out, Mourn cast a simple illusion over us both to appear like common folk of Yongwen.

"Try not to let anyone bump you too hard," he said in Trade, still sounding tired. "It'll disrupt this spell."

I signed affirmative, but this also reminded me. "Hey, I wanted to ask something since we landed in Yong-wen."

"Hm?"

"The two times you changed from your 'Roewn' Noiri face and back, inside Yong-wen's borders, you smelled different and seemed feverish for a moment. I also heard some odd sounds as you changed."

Mourn looked at me with interest. "Hm. And?"

"And anyone could touch you and it wouldn't disrupt your appearance."

"Krithannia's different faces work the same." He smiled. "Or you wouldn't have had as much leisure with Tanzi and her horses."

"But you can maintain it for strings of days and nights together. Now that I think on it, you might even sleep wearing this form. You never changed from the moment we reached Port Fortnight to when we landed here. Not even the 'magic squall' in the Great Lake affected your appearance, while Gavin and I had to hide below."

"All good observations." The mercenary's smile widened into a grin. "What is your conclusion based on this evidence, *Vloszia Dalna?*"

I narrowed my eyes at him within my hood, tugging it down as we walked toward the morning Sun. "I say you're still using magic but not casting spells. You are changing your shape, your *actual* body."

"Very good. You are correct."

This confirmation answered the many related questions about how the rest of Augran still talked about demons and shadows. Mourn simply wore a mask which didn't slip outside of Yong-wen. If someone saw a demon or was tormented by shadows, then he had purpose.

"It seems stressful," I said. "Changing like that."

"It takes significant effort and is painful in ways, yes. There are other tricks and spells to hide and change my appearance for shorter durations, so I use it only when necessary."

"May I ask why it was necessary to change into a tall, pale man who stands out in Yong-wen when Krithannia and I left to ride the horses?"

Mourn nodded. "I needed to leave Yong-wen briefly and check up on something with Talov in Alran. Easier and faster using a face the right people recognized."

Well, now I was *more* curious.

"Anything to do with my sister?" I asked, unsure if I wanted an affirmative or not.

"Not directly," he answered readily. "But it has to do with Manalar, as most things will in the coming days and weeks. It's fair to assume any reports or leads we follow could uncover something about her, but the trail is not warm yet. When this changes, I will let you know."

When.

My patience settled more quickly than I'd been accustomed before when hearing him speak this way. Less evasive, no exclusion, and he spoke less vaguely than before, even still protecting his contacts.

I took a deep breath of fresh and fragrant air, struck by how quickly the day grew warm, hours before midday. "Are we in summer season yet?"

"We've passed the cusp."

"What do you mean?"

"The longest day and the shortest night of the year passed while we sailed on the Great Lake. Last night was the first of two full sister moons entering the sky together, following the Day of Hia-Yo."

"Hia-Yo," I repeated, trying to remember why that sounded so familiar.

"The Sun Brother," he prompted. "Also known as Musanlo."

Oh, yes. I made a face for having forgotten already.

"I mentioned last night was a time for benevolent spirits and a preferred time for celebrations of fertility of the waters, fields, and family." Mourn shrugged. "I admit the Yungians were open to the nature of your request due to the time of the year. A different season or timing of the moons, and even Father Shi might have been wary of sharing his daughter and son with us."

"Wow. So it took more than pinning Bohai to the mat to get this far, and repeat events are unlikely to be as 'lucky' for all involved?"

The Dragonchild bowed his head. "You could assume that."

"Lucky, indeed. Huh!" I pondered. "What about the Bishops of Manalar? How do they celebrate summer and Musanlo's 'longest' day?"

The half-blood caught the innuendo but only smirked. I waited for longer than I expected for an answer.

"In their own region," he said finally, "the Manalari are both more populous than Yong-wen and more fractured, so it is hard to say how this time is celebrated. Depending on wealth and status, if any, and on how close one lives to the Temple or the influence of the *Dyos Guerrimos*. If it has anything to do with fertility, as it does in Yong-wen, it might be justified in some convoluted way or a slight detour from the fixed patterns of codified worship demanded by the Bishops and their enforcers."

"Hm, so not nearly as fun."

"Not at all."

"Ugh. I am sorry I asked."

Mourn let the subject drop with an ironic smile. Still, my thoughts wandered deeper into the significance of summer, about the drumbeats of the Ma'ab marching on Manalar. Thoughts which could not be uncoupled from Jael's geas and Rausery's suggestion that our youngest novice must be there before these events coincided.

"You, um," I began, "you said we would settle our bargain once we return to the library?"

He nodded without hesitation or apparent regret. "We will make it binding with witnesses."

"Witnesses?" I frowned. "You've had no trouble parsing limits and possessions between us, mercenary, and it's not as if I've made one motion to walk away from this."

"Indeed, I understand that you can't."

"Nor have I any leverage over you, or treasure we haven't already set aside in prior negotiations."

Mourn glanced at me with a curious interest. "Are you still certain you want to be Soul Drinker's wielder?"

My eyes widened as genuine shock welled up, and I held his gaze despite the morning light.

"Yes, I *am*," I answered sternly. "It is a Queen's relic that is significant in the Red Desert history, and Innathi will talk to me. Bodyguard or not, I should have *one* weapon going into this war which works against anything with Vis or Vitas, whether alive, warped, mage, mundane, or the dead corpses arisen. Despite the cost, had I anything *less* to use amid the warp rot, I'd have been as lost as Gaelan."

Mourn looked away to scan the roads and fields. "I see. But have you any concern that it may draw the Deathless to you? Or others able to sense such a powerful weapon?"

"That's why I'm hiring you!" I huffed a bitter laugh, shaking my head as the cruelty and abuse heaped on me by that Abyssal curse swept my mind. "The gatekeeper is trapped in crystal on its throne, and I *beat* it to free Gavin and prove to you I could control it."

"Crystal?"

His expression reminded me that Mourn hadn't been present when Gavin had recorded my experience. I looked away and pulled my hood farther for more shade, grumbling, "It's all in the Deathwalker's grimoire."

"It is? Why?"

"He vouched for my strength of will, remember? He asked to know what happened since he'd been carrying the blade while I recovered, listening to its shrieks. So, I told him. Right after it happened."

"Was the crystal clear, or did it have colors?"

Oddly fixated on that detail.

My irritation escaped as I answered, "The crystal was clear. But I remind you again, Gavin vouched for me, and you and Krithannia have *already* agreed what I proved was enough. I didn't suffer that sickening touch again just so you could doubt me now, when you said just this morning that you *decided* to settle our bargain!"

Mourn slowed, lifting empty hands. "I apologize, you are correct. I am even convinced anew that the rune dagger must remain in your guardianship."

"What? Why?"

"Because the 'crystal trap' you described is likely to fall apart if it passes from your hands."

I felt his gaze and couldn't keep my eyes on the dirt road in front of us. "What do you mean?"

He smiled when our eyes met. "You and I already have a situational agreement, yes? That we work together to keep your psionic talent from affecting others whenever you sleep outside a protected den."

I nodded grudgingly. "Yes, and in return, I describe the dreams if I'm able."

"Then I must tell you, in my To'vah dreams, clear crystal is a powerful symbol of active psionics. If that's how you quieted the demon, Sirana, then you *must* keep the dagger. The prison won't hold in the hands of a new wielder, the creature would be free to start its tricks all over again. At least now I know it's unlikely to deliberately call out to the Deathless for his attention. You addressed my main concern, and I still intend to protect you from him."

Although this helped steady my breath after an intense exchange, it didn't address what I truly wanted and *still* needed from him.

"You've spent three days 'getting to know who I am' without the dagger's influence," I said, attempting to sound calm. "Have you not seen enough to know who you're bargaining with?"

"I have seen more than enough, Sirana."

"Me, too."

He smirked, and I nudged away an ill-timed impulse to glance at his crotch. *Focus!*

"What have you decided you want for this task, mercenary? We didn't need witnesses to renegotiate about Soul Drinker just now. Why do we need them before you'll even tell me your price?"

The half-blood gave this some thought. "I suppose because I've always had them when a contract is not negotiated by proxy."

"Not always," I countered. "Not now."

"Well, they await at the library."

I stopped in the middle of the road, and he paused to turn after another step.

"Let me guess," I said, "Gavin and Krithannia are your witnesses?"

"And one more."

"Have I met that one?"

"You have."

I pointed a finger at him. "Your handler, the greybeard."

Mourn smiled. "Talov Baradum, yes."

I shook my head. "You *must* tell me your price before we arrive there to settle."

He hesitated.

"Is it so complicated?"

Two men with a pony and cart were headed toward us, and Mourn answered with distraction as he gauged its pace. "Not really, no."

"You're teasing me to madness," I griped. "Unless you mean *not* to ask a price at all?"

"I have a price," he countered, looking at me.

"Oh? Are Shyntre's pellets for your apothecary sufficient after all?"

One eye squinted as he grimaced, glancing toward the cart. "Hm, no, it's more than that."

I growled at his split attention. "I haven't the faintest idea what you want, then! The only offer I *could* make you is one you've never accepted as payment!"

His eyes snapped like a bowstring back to me; the next instant I read his embarrassment.

Oh.

"Let us wait for the cart to pass," he murmured, motioning as he stepped forward. "Keep your eyes down."

I cooperated long enough to watch him bid a greeting to the farmers clopping and rattling loudly past us. The illusion as they saw it seemed intact, though Mourn still looked like a Dragonblood to me.

I spoke once out of earshot. "You've decided you'll trade sex for this mission?"

He exhaled. "For the first time in my life, yes. It may still be a mistake to bend on this."

His tail conveyed enough nerves for me to believe him.

I frowned with confusion. "So, you wanted your handler to negotiate the particulars for you?"

"No," he replied immediately, looking unsettled. "I would speak for myself. Talov would be there to help you and assure I don't take advantage."

"What?" I laughed, tilted an ear. "You take advantage of me? How fragile do you think I am?"

"Fragile isn't the word I would use," he said. "But you are in a vulnerable position and not entirely because of me. I thought it would be to each of our benefit to have knowledgeable witnesses. I've never considered this seriously before."

"Then why would you do so now?" I asked, more curious than flirting. "You've mounted me once, and I enjoyed it. You could persuade me to go again without a binding contract. And, knowing this now, I'd have *not* thanked you for surprising me in front of the Naulor and the Dwarf if I hadn't guessed it. Neither of them could advise me on my limits in this regard."

"Are you that certain?"

"Yes. I am of the Sisterhood, and whatever a Naulor or a grandfather Dwarf might consider unfair use of my body, I wager that none of you have ever met one like the Conceiver of Sivaraus."

Mourn probably didn't want to ask but did anyway. "The Conceiver? I take it she's a Priestess of Braqth?"

"The worst one. She was responsible for breeding and training the 'pleasure slaves,' and one of those collared buas is my chosen sire. *Barely* chosen, by the way. If the Conceiver had had her way, I would have caught by her Sathoet son, instead, and I don't know what would have happened to me after that."

"What…?"

His alarm and disgust naked on his face satisfied me to make my point.

"You and the Conceiver do not stand on the same *plane* regarding your appetites, and I am already pregnant. Exchanging the defense of my body with sharing pleasure in it is the fairest and balanced bargain I can think of. The fact that no others, only you and I, have any say how we do this is also a first in my life, Dragonchild. It's *quite* significant. I do not need a broker to reassure me whether it's fair. I don't care. I'll pay it."

Mourn didn't respond at once, brooding long enough for my stomach to complain loud enough for him to hear.

I shrugged. "We skipped breakfast."

The To'vah-krav sighed. "You are sure you wish to forego my handler's advice during negotiation?"

He sounded so formal and serious, even after I thought I'd made myself clear, that I could only chuckle. "Yes, please."

"Hm. We shall still need to go to the library so Talov can formalize it as a Guild contract."

"So be it," I replied. "I hope making it formal doesn't suck out all the fun to be had in this."

Mourn huffed a brief laugh though his teeth and bowed his head to me. "Let's get something to eat and talk elsewhere. Just you and me."

I exhaled. "Sounds good."

Ironically, a silent uncertainty nibbled at me after I'd swept aside part of his process. In my memory, the demon of the dagger shouted the only unfeigned warning it had ever given me, when Mourn had stepped out from warp-rotting trees.

Do not bargain with him. His words are binding!

We maneuvered through the midmorning streets of Yong-wen, first to pick up two skins of water from the seller who waited for workers coming in from the fields each day, then to find a food source which was not too crowded.

The hand pies weren't an option as we arrived to see a throng of city workers and servants waiting to trade their coin for what smelled to be just finished. *Damn.* But I supposed we'd had them twice already.

Maybe we can get out earlier tomorrow.

"Is an uncrowded place considered poorer food?" I asked, speaking Trade.

"Possibly, or simple fare served in between shifts," Mourn said. "If a cook doesn't draw the river or field workers, they do not serve long. The timing could also be luck, and the food is fine."

Fortunately, the half-blood found a quiet place for us, selling baskets of steamed dough balls I'd seen before, although these did not appear filled with anything. Needing to stand by Mourn to maintain the illusion, I got close enough to see into the back of the stand.

Three women of varied ages helped the merchant to tend fires beneath two large pots: one of steaming water with reedy baskets set on top, and the other filled with a thick bean mixture scooped with a large spoon.

"Shi'sheh," Mourn said, his voice not as deep as his natural one, trading coins and bows with the man.

At the same time, one of the women passed me two roughly woven baskets filled with buns and beans. No sticks with this meal, it seemed, but I hummed with anticipation sniffing the aroma. Even for Yong-wen's "simple fare," I could hardly wait.

Idly, I wondered where the mercenary had been keeping those straight-edged copper and silver coins on his person. Could the weapons bracers store other items as well?

Seems the only possibility, given he had nothing else last night.

"Where to next?" I asked once we'd stepped away.

"Not far. A garden I've visited before. High stone walls and a corner shaded by trees and low bushes."

A good choice to talk outside during the day.

His preferred spot wasn't far from Xijuan's grandmother either, though I couldn't spot her garden by the time Mourn jumped and pulled himself atop the warm, yellowish wall. He reached for the bun basket first, set that up top, then offered a hand to pull me up with the beans. He was strong enough to give me all the draw as I found toeholds and held the basket with one arm. I swung a leg over to straddle the wall like a horse.

★Stay low,★ he signed before dropping to the thick, green grass. After securing his basket by a flowering bush, he turned to reach for mine.

I gave it to him, chose my place to land, and swung my leg over. I caught him intending to reach up a third time, as if to take me down like one of the baskets, but I had gained the shaded ground already.

★Hungry,★ I signed, eyes pleading.

He nodded, and we chose our places to sit amid the quiet buzzing of insects and small, flapping wings from birds taking off on the other side of the shrubs. The air had grown warmer still, and the scents of several flowers in bloom surrounded us.

Our method of eating was simple enough this time; Mourn split a bun open with his thumbs and used it like a clam shell to dig some of the bean mix in the middle. He handed it to me; I eagerly accepted and bit into it.

The bun tasted good, if plain compared to the feast we'd had last night and would be filling. The two ingredients together could be thick to swallow, so I took some large swigs of my water with my first three buns to help wash them down. Mourn did the same and only got ahead of me by two because he could eat them in one bite.

He looked at my face as I leaned over the bun basket. "Are we splitting them evenly again?"

I shrugged. "I could eat three more easily. How many are there?"

"Fifteen."

"Then I want four more."

"Ah! I get the extra?"

"I'm feeling generous."

A hint of fangs peeked from between his lips as he counted them out, which he clearly enjoyed, and we consumed our late breakfast without much talk. Afterward, we sipped water as I sat against a tree and Mourn kneeled upright with his back to the wall watching the garden beyond.

With a burp and a sigh, my thoughts returned to the reason I'd wanted to delay reaching the library.

"So, first," I began.

His eyes levelled on me.

"Um, I must ask if I should practice saying your real name to make a long-term deal with you?"

He wasn't expecting that but hummed in thought, relaxing a bit. "I'd appreciate your effort, but it's not required. I've accepted many bargains under numerous names. The one I give at the time doesn't influence my actions to fulfill it."

That was interesting. *And reassuring.*

"And Morix still isn't acceptable?" I asked. "Something shorter to say under pressure, like a fight?"

He smirked at me. "Truthfully, I've grown accustomed to you calling out 'Mourn.' That's even shorter."

"*Heh.* Very well. So, you prefer either Mourn or… Morix-ksi—"

"*Morixxyleth.*"

"My tongue isn't shaped like yours."

"Indeed. I think you are more aware of that than ever."

My body heat rose looking at his face. Setting back my hood off my head, I squinted at him in the light. "Are we flirting now? I thought we were bargaining."

"We are." He was amused. "I confirm my To'vah name isn't required for a long-term bargain. The name we've agreed on is enough."

"Alright. I'll have to practice later." I repositioned my ass for comfort. "The trade itself seems simple to me. For as long as you are my bodyguard, you agree to utilize all your knowledge, skills, and resources of the Surface to protect me and my baby from harm and enslavement while we search for Jael. You also agree to recover me from capture should it happen."

He nodded in agreement.

"In return," I finished, "I agree to utilize all my knowledge, skills, and resources as a Red Sister to provide you any sort of body pleasures you want."

Mourn blinked, his tail reminding me of a wary serpent. "'Any sort?' You would leave that part *undefined* in a contract?"

Neither my smile nor my gaze wavered despite a niggling doubt.

"I'd rather be flexible on changing moods and tastes," I said. "The only limits I see are those that conflict with your role as my protector, anything physical or magical that would harm me or my unborn. I'm not concerned about your eagerness to test those limits anyway, so, yes. *Any* sort of sex that appeals to us, leaving it open for our desires to change. Perhaps some variety."

Mourn considered with great care. I could tell he would rather have heard specified boundaries, likened to counting the gems or coins he expected in advance and after the job was done. But what else than "do no harm" could I define when he might not realize everything enjoyable to be had? Especially if he'd found it difficult to choose partners on the Surface.

It's better this way. I doubt you can scare me the way you do Human women.

"How do you define 'variety?'" he asked directly. "This seems different from 'mood' and 'taste,' but I want to hear how you describe these words."

He had an idea but wouldn't continue without proper definitions.

"Fair question," I said, straightening up against the tree to ease a hard spot against my back. "A mood changes the fastest. As example, comparing when you first used that 'tone' with me by the trees with when you held Dandan in your lap. You were in a mood to direct me and tell me what I could do. Then you were in a mood to watch me with Bohai while I act as I saw fit, and in a mood to engage with us both while I kneeled in front of Dandan."

His tail shushed sensually over the grass as he reflected on these shared memories. "I understand. What about tastes?"

"Your tastes are more consistent choices for pleasure, what arouses you compared to what you avoid. You enjoy the scents of females and pursue them, but you also said you 'feel no urge' to seek male partners, even as you are aware of that possibility and do not resent it in others. Correct?"

"Correct."

"And your response to my asking about finding the nut gland through the male's pucker did not give me the impression that you want me to do that to you."

He blinked in mild surprise. "Correct, again. You should know that action has an extremely… unpleasant association."

I pursed my lips but dared to ask. "From Vuthra'tern?"

His eyes slid to one side. "Yes."

I nodded. "That's why I want to leave it open. I can't anticipate everything which is already familiar, which you may enjoy or possibly detest, and neither can you if memories were 'buried,' as you described. And there are actions which we might not realize *are* pleasurable, as one of us has not discovered it yet. Like your tail."

"My tail?"

He looked back, curious, and I smiled at him.

"Yes, your tail. That is new for me, yet you use it frequently in sex, as often as you do your hands and tongue. The constriction around my ribs during our spar in the *dorji-ka* was too much, yet other squeezes and caresses you've done are not. I think I could discover much more I would enjoy and am eager to try."

The half-blood nodded with more confidence; his eyes warmed with a small smile. "Fair. And wise, Sirana. I understand this definition of taste."

So far, so good.

"As for variety," I said, "I want to be clear in this bargain that I am not offering you a 'private pair bond,' such as came up with Krithannia when we visited Tanzi and her horses. Nor am I agreeing to be your personal pleasure slave."

"No, of course not," he replied with distaste.

"Thank you. But what's more, because this must be open but balanced, I agree as part of our bargain that I shall not do something impulsive or stupid for sex. I will not risk my freedom or yours, for I received a harsh lesson in Troshin Bend. I will not risk your health or mine, nor my baby's, nor the chance of seeing my Sister again."

He smiled modestly but didn't interrupt.

"The drive to obtain sex is not a strong enough temptation to threaten the goals of this bargain, especially if I may easily satisfy it with you. Do you believe me?"

Mourn bowed his head. "I do."

"Good. Then I want the bargain open enough that I am not 'cut off' from others, such as you described of your commander down below." I paused for a sip of water. "Now would be a good time to know if you felt contempt or resentment while watching me with Bohai."

Mourn shook his head with promising surety. "None. I believe we both understood intent and expectations."

I nodded earnestly. "And I *enjoyed* that dance with you, Mourn, very much. If we should be fortunate for an opportunity of including other playmates as we did Dandan and Bohai, I want to keep the discussion within this 'formal' bargain. Especially as I do not know how many weeks or months this might continue."

"Agreed. This benefits us both."

I showed my teeth in another smile. "I should tell you now, if we recover Jael, and she is well enough, I *will* be bedding her after we're safe. As she is not part of this agreement between us, I cannot say where you might stand at that time. I *can* say that I would be open to include you, but she may only be willing to let you watch, or perhaps you are not in the mood, and you will choose to be elsewhere. Or you have other options." I shrugged. "I cannot say, so I can neither speculate nor agree in advance to anything that involves her."

"I understand. Hm."

His tail shifted through the grass again, but this time it resembled a more relaxed serpent seeking a warm spot in the sun.

"I am grateful you can articulate this for me," Mourn said. "This is not as undefined as I thought you meant at first. You *do* have limits, Sirana, but they pertain more to sovereignty with our bodies. You are asking to navigate them with recurring discussions, like this one, which are understood to be part of the bargain."

It was my turn to follow his words carefully. *That feels right.*

"Yes. Exactly."

"I would agree to this bargain as you've described it, and trade sex with you for my personal payment, but only at appropriate times and places where we both agree."

"Yes," I echoed. "We must agree where and when to fuck."

He chuckled but soon continued. "There would still be the *other* payment which more broadly benefits the Guild and Augran as a whole."

"Shyntre's pellets?"

A nod. "Are you willing to trade two of them?"

I smirked and leaned forward. "If your apothecary figures it out quickly, could I have them replenished?"

"Those and at least two more, although I stress that without your wizard here to teach her directly, it is likely to take a lot of experimentation and waiting for the right components before Augran would have any supply proven effective enough to distribute."

"Oh." I sat back. "That makes sense."

"While we probably won't be able to replenish them at all during our bargain, you instead have access to the same healers and methods available to me, and that would be part of my knowledge used on your behalf as your bodyguard."

"Alright, then I can agree to that part of the bargain, too."

"Very good." Mourn glanced up through the trees, squinting as if to judge the time of day despite them. "We should return to the library as soon as we can. We are later than expected, and I don't want to worry them enough to send searchers out for us."

He leaned on one hand, preparing to stand up.

"Wait," I said, reaching out my hand to catch his eyes as well. "I still have a question."

He settled down and waited.

"In all I've witnessed, experienced, and heard from you, I could see this same negotiation and agreement between us *without* a formal contract with the Guild. I still don't understand why you need one and are so insistent. Is it because you've 'always had one?' Could you not simply say to your handler that you're taking a break from Guild clients?"

Mourn frowned in more than concentration. "I have always had one, yes, and you are considered a Guild client because of your association with Gavin."

I frowned back. "How? Has he made a contract already?"

"I believe Krithannia headed back to town last evening with that intent, after you left Tanzi's barn. We'll learn more once we arrive."

I held back a grimace. *Well, that's certainly a lot of time for the two to talk.*

Krithannia had called herself an archivist and a scholar before I learned she was also the Guild Mistress. Now I wondered how long one scholar might speak with another in the center of a book trove.

Probably longer than I'd managed so far.

"Well, alright," I acquiesced, "but I still want to understand something."

"Yes?"

"Do you owe Krithannia or Talov in ways of which I'm unaware that you need these contracts? Can you not make one like this, without a tangible treasure to add to your hoard? And if you must, could you explain how it might affect me? Do *I* owe them or the Guild anything besides the pellets?"

Mourn considered this, lifting his chin in the direction I thought the safehouse to be. He exhaled a slow breath through his nose then looked back at me. "These are good questions, and I would like you to understand more what I owe both Krithannia and Talov. It might be easier to explain with them present. You could corroborate any responses to your satisfaction."

I tamped down my rising frustration again. *Isn't this where we started on the road from the Shi manor?*

"Could you give me a hint what to expect from such a meeting?" I asked. "This seems as important as what you intended to ask for payment."

"Very well."

Mourn stood up first, collecting our empty food baskets and skins, and offered me a hand up. I didn't necessarily need it but accepted anyway, pulling my hood up against the Sun once on my feet.

"I will tell you before we arrive," he said, "that there *is* significant reward for me and my hoard in this bargain. Far beyond the physical pleasure, although I can't have one without the other."

He smiled with restrained amusement in watching me blink in honest surprise.

Then I narrowed my eyes at him. "What do you mean, Dragon son?"

"Your offer and this arrangement *is* unique in my lifetime," he explained, his metallic eyes shining, "but when I choose a lover for more than one night, the magic of my hoard changes and usually grows in potency. This lover gives me an *intangible* treasure but a treasure nonetheless and becomes part of my magic."

"Wait," I began incredulously, "you mean like Graul's pile has enough magic to ease his pains? Yours increases your magic when you fuck?"

"It's much more than that." His face set in earnest. "Every intense or influential interaction with another sentient counts. How I obtain gold or sex, and from whom? These choices influence my hoard, and thus my magic. It's usually incremental, but I notice changes as they happen, probably more than any other sentient race is capable to watch their own life evolving in the moment."

"Uhm…" I swallowed. "Another reason you obtain treasures through contracts with Humans? You have better… control? Or selection?"

One corner of his mouth turned up. "Bargains simplify some things, yes, but still have their challenges. Any ill-conceived, abandoned, or betrayed bargains affect me and my hoard the same as those bargains which are well-considered, balanced, and honored to completion."

My feet rooted in place as I grappled with that enormous mental tapestry. His insistence on obtaining the *Ridhian* ruby to complete his contract, even to the point of stealing it from me, made sense now. So did placing Kurn's sword apart for a while until he had a chance to study it.

The mercenary continued. "The Guild Mistress, my handler for contracts, and my only friend from the Deepearth—Krithannia, Talov, and Graul—are aware of this aspect of my To'vah magic. They understand why I was reluctant to name my price with you."

I peered up at him, glad we were still deep enough in the trees to stave off a distracting headache. I feared that I knew the answer already but asked anyway.

"Why were you reluctant? Because I am a 'Baenar,' and you didn't want any more to do with demon worshippers?"

He showed me that ironic smirk again. "True at the beginning, but this changed as I watched over you. Even more after we left the river."

"Did you watch me back then?" I asked because I had to know. "When I stopped Nightmare and went into the trees?"

"Watched you, smelled you. I told myself I guarded you." Mourn chuckled, looking down briefly. "My thoughts began to change, I admit, though what I told you on the ship was true as well, and I had no desire to bend this rule. Once you overcame the demon of Soul Drinker, and I had agreed to help you and Jael, I needed to talk with Krithannia after you left with Gavin about how best to do so."

He paused, and I prompted him, "Did you bring up sex as your price, or did she?"

"Our discussion was more complicated than that," he replied. "I was… frustrated that I could think of only one payment I wanted from you, and it was the trade I'd never accepted before. Krithannia had no suggestions that weren't a future payment we couldn't guarantee we'd receive from you, but we were both nervous about the consequences."

"What consequences?"

Mourn breathed out slowly, considering a moment before reaching up to touch my face and lightly sweating neck. I didn't know if this was thoughtful interest or a kind of affection. Whatever it was, my guardian spiders still made room for him.

"Past lovers who helped develop my magic and strengthen my hoard were not held to a bargain," he said. "This includes Krithannia. While she is not bound in any way and has no direct influence on my hoard, she still gifted us with part of her strength. It knew her as I did, and I'm reminded of these strengths each time I return to my den."

I stood mute, staring at him as I began to glimpse the extensive reach of what he was asking for payment. What he'd been thinking about for weeks.

The exchange wasn't as simple as I thought.

"Neither of us know what will happen negotiating with you this way," Mourn said, resting his hand beneath my jaw. His eyes seemed polished to a high shine. "I only know whatever comes of this bargain will be profound for me and my hoard."

I bit my lip. "But this could be a—"

Harmful? Regretful? Corrupting…?

"—a negative influence on your To'vah magic?"

He leaned closer, as if he wished for contact. Was he going to kiss me?

"Negative only if our Bargain is not kept," he said. "In any other outcome, as long as it's fulfilled, I will find Balance. I always have."

My eyes blinked involuntarily from the power of those two words as he spoke.

Bargain.

Balance.

Each felt like a thunderclap sounding too close to lie at rest.

I forced a smile; it wavered. "So, you're not afraid I'll ruin your treasure's magic by fucking you whenever you like?"

If Mourn were Human, he might have blushed.

"I am not at all afraid," he replied without blinking, stroking my skin with his thumb. "Not after you've provided me an answer to every question and doubt I had about your nature. Believe in my resolve to see our Bargain through, Sirana. This is something I want and *will* work for. I see a reward in the risk, and it is equal to a city's treasury."

Oh, Goddess.

I exhaled, my face hot and sweating within my hood. I took one step back, and he lowered his arm.

"That's quite a hint of what we'll be discussing in the library," I said, checking my waterskin to see if there was one swallow left. "Or perhaps that's all of it?"

"Most of it. You were right that we should discuss this in private first." He shrugged. "I apologize for trying to lead you to the contract table before you were ready. I am navigating something new to me."

Heh. Me, too. Fucking Goddess…

Finding no water, I fanned my face instead; the air's humidity wasn't helping. "Well! This surprise will take time to settle, but you spoke it well, and I think I understand. I see a reward in the risk that I want very much as well, and I am willing to work with you to get it."

"I see this, too." The Dragon's son smiled at me. "I think that's why we could make a Bargain at all. I just never thought it could happen with one from the Deepearth."

"Hm." I looked behind me in the direction of the safehouse. "Another reason to record it with the Guild, it's one of a kind?"

The Dragonblood chuckled. "Certainly the first and only I could expect for some time to come."

CHAPTER 17

WE APPROACHED THE SAFEHOUSE FROM THE FRONT WHERE I saw a painted wooden panel hanging on a metal rod above the door frame. The sign's script was still a mystery, but the design beneath caught my eye. It resembled two moons either rising or setting just above ripples of water. Both were in their crescent phase with the larger sister sloped underneath the smaller as if to catch her.

I pointed it out to Mourn, and he nodded.

"The inn, Luni Ti," he said. "Roughly means 'sisters of bounty.'"

"Are those the moons above the Great Lake?"

He nodded. "You could refer to it in Trade as Crescents' Inn, and most here would know where it is. Luni Ti was the first inn built when the Yong-ch'hai merchants began trading in Augran year-round. It's no longer the largest or wealthiest, now practically unknown outside of the enclave, but still in good shape."

The first, huh? I waited until we turned down the alley approaching the stable before arching my brow and whispering, "I imagine all that 'Dragon luck' included in their foundation helps soothe the sting of their decline?"

Mourn grinned. "The Fang prefer more subtle attention from the spirits than Shi and others."

"They get more attention than Shi?"

"Different, not more. But all they could want."

I squinted at this new piece teasing at that bigger picture but set it aside as we checked on Nightmare in the stable. She hadn't moved that I could tell, though her scent was less "alive."

She'll need another rat soon.

Incredulous that no one had messed with Gavin's horse. I would have expected some urchin, if not the stable boys, to be charging for peeks through a hole they'd dug by now.

★Everyone in Yong-wen *cannot* be so obedient at all times,★ I signed while we waited for the alley to clear. ★They're as curious and impulsive as anyone I've seen.★

★Agreed,★ Mourn signed. ★Krithannia placed stronger wards after the encounter with Mai outside. Even the stable hands do not think to check the last stall.★

★Why she is not being fed?★

★Correct, but we needed a ward regardless to be sure the inn still receives clients.★

I smirked. ★You mean word hasn't spread that the spirit of death is staying with the bountiful sisters?★

Mourn looked amused. ★No, because that would be bad for business.★

A good thing Dragons and merchants have so much in common.

When the alley had emptied for the moment, my bodyguard gave the signal. We slipped underground, an instant relief once out of Musanlo's light and heat.

THE LIBRARY WAS BETTER LIT THAN IT HAD BEEN THE LAST TWO times we'd arrived with only Gavin and Graul waiting on us.

The gaunt and ghostly Deathwalker sat at his preferred desk, but instead of a shadow drake curled on one corner, the Guild Mistress sat with him at one end to look over several scripts with him. Although Gavin still did not smile in any way, I thought the once miserable Human monk seemed engrossed, not at all annoyed by her relative proximity.

A good sign, I guess.

Meanwhile, someone else had taken the red chaise, his broad body filling it far more than mine had, and whose well-groomed grey beard I couldn't miss.

Talov Baradum wore a sturdy, well-made dark brown coat and blue pants. His boots were off to the side, his startlingly wide feet covered with thick, dark stockings reminding me of bear paws. Graul sprawled across his lap, and both were napping, their breath either wheezing slightly or rattling into a snort.

Krithannia turned and smiled in welcome while Gavin glanced up with a nod. Neither of them made noise that would wake up the two elderly creatures reclining in comfort.

★Take a seat,★ Mourn signed to me. ★I'll send for snacks and tea.★

Okay.

I might have preferred either Krithannia's seat by Gavin or where Talov breathed so deeply but gave no hint of that in removing my boots and cloak. I headed to the empty desk.

Graul's hazy red eyes opened as soon as I pulled out the chair along the carpet and sat down. The shadow drake lifted his head and sniffed the air while his tail woke up as well. His nose led to Mourn standing by the delivery chute, and his throat pouch vibrated with a calm and affectionate purr I hadn't heard before.

"Good morning to you as well," answered the half-blood out loud.

Graul's warm mattress inhaled suddenly and opened his eyes, and I was reminded of peridot stone for their color and semi-translucence.

"Ah, yer back!" The elder Dwarf grunted, pushing himself up to sit as the shadow drake climbed off his lap but stayed on the chaise.

"We are."

Talov swung his stockinged feet to the carpet and straightened his coat, twisting with a pop to his spine to find Mourn before turning in his seat to settle his gaze on me.

"So, how'd the night go?" His eyes crinkled at the corners as he asked, "Did the Davrin behave long enough at the Da's table tah get to after-dinner sweets?"

Enough flirting, informed delight livened his grizzled face that I wondered if I might blurt out more Tragar insults before this conversation was done. I began with a calm and satisfied smile.

"I did, elder Baradum. I savored a double helping, each distinct in their sweetness but equally delicious."

Mourn cleared his throat loudly as if it was to cover a laugh as Talov fully indulged in robust Dwarven mirth while Graul snickered along. At the same time, Krithannia covered her face with one blue-gloved hand.

Not in embarrassment, I noted, as her shoulders shook.

The Pale Elf's suppressed shuddering grew stronger when Gavin asked aloud, "Is there something noteworthy about after-dinner sweets?"

I looked at him. "Only in summertime, I'm told."

A soft sound slipped out of the Naulor as she leaned back in her chair, turning it out so she could see Talov and me. Crossing one leg over the other, the smiling Guild Mistress rested her hands in her lap and shook her head. "Will the entire report be in innuendo?"

I couldn't put away my smile yet. "I'll give it a try."

"Tempting!" the Dwarf replied, his cheeks red and round. *"Ach,* she's right, though. Guess I'm just eager tah know if it went well?"

"Extremely well, Talov," Mourn volunteered, turning around to lean against the wall as he waited by the chute. "Nothing outright damaging to the Shi reputation while we are likely to see more opportunities than we expected. There were far more witnesses than we estimated. This celebration will not soon be forgotten by the people of Yong-wen."

Me, either.

"Good! Good," Talov said with a demonstrative hammer of his fist in the air. "We'll let this brew some, then. Do we agree it's better if ya don't make further appearances fer a while?"

Mourn's handler had encompassed both of us in the question, but my new bodyguard answered for us.

"We're agreed. Further acts of favor would confuse the message or cause in-fighting too soon."

Krithannia asked, "Do you think Renshu will be humbled enough not to spoil his grandfather's work?"

"That's more likely now than it was three days ago," Mourn replied. "For one, Hulin may not enable him as blindly with how Sirana interacted with him, particularly the moment of encouragement when she gifted her muscle balm to him."

"Ya?" Talov perked up. "Ya didn't suggest that?"

"I did not. I didn't realize Sirana still had it. It wasn't necessary, our forgiveness had been granted, but she may have catalyzed a change in dynamic between those two brothers."

Mourn sounded proud as all three of his trusted contacts looked at me. Gavin finished up a note, now prepared to pay more attention to the conversation.

"Bohai will have more influence in the family as well, but it remains to see what he will do with it."

Krithannia nodded. "And Dandan?"

"I can confirm your report. She has mage potential for certain and is the only sibling who does."

"Could ya tell an affinity?" asked the Dwarf.

Mourn nodded. "Shamanistic, probably life magic as well."

Krithannia rubbed her lips lightly with one hand. "Hm. The talent skipped a generation."

Gavin seemed to know that word, but I didn't.

"What is shamanistic magic?"

Krithannia looked at me and smiled. "You've seen it. My sister, Tamuril, is powerful in this affinity."

"Ah. Influence over plants and animals?"

"That's the simplest understanding, yes."

I pondered. "I suppose Dandan was at ease with the horses despite the dirt and manure threatening her pretty shoes and robes."

The Naulor chuckled. "She and others are likely to assume a divine connection due to the nature of her awakening, but we can nudge them in the right direction as we did with her grandmother."

"Aye," Talov said. "A pity the woman ain't alive tah help her."

"Well, we'll see if any suitors step forward at all now and go from there."

"Aye, we can run the streams later." The Dwarf held his gaze on me for a beat before looking to Mourn. "More urgent is hammerin' out yer bargain with Sirana, ya?"

Mourn nodded as a single, reflexive wave ran the length of his tail. "We arrived later than expected because she and I worked out most of the details already."

Wiry, grey eyebrows shot up. "Oh?"

That tail couldn't be still while he explained.

"Yes, and I've confirmed she will pay my first choice of reward, so we have closed the bargain. As of now, I am her bodyguard while we confirm the other Red Sister's whereabouts, infiltrate Manalar, and retreat to safety."

Gavin's expression didn't change as he listened, but of the three, only Graul didn't look shocked. The shadow drake nodded his muzzle and fluttered his throat pouch in another purr, as if seconding a known fact. Krithannia and Talov each took note of this.

Graul already knew? How?

Krithannia's face eased into a placid mask while Talov seemed to remeasure his plans for this meeting. I was almost certain Mourn's handler *wasn't* angry at being cut out of the dealings, though he was perhaps a bit concerned.

"Well, awright," the Dwarf said. "Then I have a few questions."

"I expected you would. Go on."

A large tray arrived in the delivery chute before we could and Mourn served everyone a sipping bowl of the tea while it was hot, even Gavin and Graul. The latter partly filled his pouch with air to blow on the surface, red eyes peering down his snout at the ripples before his pink tongue dipped into the cooled liquid. Mourn and I passed on the snacks for now, although everyone gave me a look; even Gavin accepted a single grain pod to nibble upon.

"I've just eaten," I said.

"And there's plenty for later," Mourn added.

"Awright," Talov agreed, standing up slowly and carrying his tea and food to sit in the sturdy-backed chair across from me. Meanwhile, Graul shifted to lie in the warm spot just vacated, chewing on some bull.

Now we all sat in a loose semi-circle, able to turn our heads to see everyone. Krithannia passed Talov a sheet of parchment from Gavin's over-crowded tabletop, and the Dwarf surprised me by pulling out his own tiny bottle of ink and quill from inside his thick coat. We watched him prepare to take a few notes.

"So," the elder began, "assuming ya offered the Guild's resources to locate Sirana's sister and, if Jael is alive, a plan tah try an' retrieve her an' get 'em both out tah safety?"

415

"Correct," Mourn answered.

Talov scratched runes I now recognized as Dwarvish. "What can I note as payment fer services rendered?"

"Two of the anti-infection pellets for study by our apothecary of choice."

The Dwarf held up one thick finger for the Dragonblood to pause as he completed his notes then reached inside his coat for an empty pouch. Talov slid it toward me, smiling with slightly yellowed teeth. "If ya will pay those now, please?"

I straightened, looking to my belt hanging near the blank wall. "Ah, yes, one moment."

The room had their opportunity to exchange expressions or hand signs while my back was turned at the far end. I tried to glimpse anything out of the corner of my eye but found myself looking at the harsh red marks on the dark relic also on my belt as I drew close. For the first time in days, I touched it lightly with gloved fingers and listened.

Nothing.

Wrapped in crystal on its throne.

At least until it came into the possession of another carrier.

Detaching the pouch with Shyntre's pellets, I returned to the desk and removed two without ceremony, setting them on top of the empty pouch before pushing it back toward the greybeard.

Talov tugged it closer with a grunt of interest and carefully picked one up, giving it a sniff. "Smells like dirt."

I grinned. "Tastes like it, too."

"Heh. The kid said ya place it under yer tongue tah dissolve?"

"Correct. One or two a day will prevent fester and fever, or help break them if already set in."

"Fantastic." His quill strokes quickened briefly in his large-knuckled hand.

"I know only one component," I volunteered, "but it seems to be one of the most important."

"And that is?"

"A mushroom we call *genethsa*. Though Tamuril called it something else."

Krithannia nodded. *"Jeneth'te."*

I motioned to her. "That was it."

"Ach, that stuff," Talov grunted. "Yeah, we know what it looks like. Kinda hard tah find as it doesn't grow above ground or take well tah farming, but I'm not surprised." He chewed briefly on a tuft on his upper lip. "If we figure this out, we're gonna hafta change the appearance so shit-cons aren't passing out balls of mud they made in their yard."

Mourn and Krithannia nodded agreement with dry chuckles. The Dwarf finished up and gently transferred the pellets into his pouch, slipping them into an inside pocket.

"Okay, Sirana, the Guild is compensated fer the effort on yer behalf," Talov began in a tone of formality which turned warmer as he continued. "An' I know the kid can speak fer himself. So, he's convinced an' yer willing?"

A chortle welled up and out before I could stop it. "Quite. I like him, and this is *much* safer than what I've been doing to scratch that itch."

The crow's feet formed again. "Heh, that it is. Awright, an' ya already confirmed th' bargain fer him tah protect ya fer the time being, so we're good there. I just need a couple notes about contingencies or emergencies we should consider."

"Sounds good."

"Wait," Gavin interjected. "May I ask more clarity what Sirana is willing to pay? Am I correct that Mourn will continue on with Sirana and me to Manalar?"

Graul added a sibilant snicker as Mourn cleared his throat to answer. "Correct, Deathwalker, and the trade is simple enough. We both seek a safe sexual partner on the Surface. There is enough interest that we've agreed to indulge with each other for the length of this contract, at proper times and places only."

Gavin's black and blue eyes blinked slowly, his gaze holding on the Dragonchild. "I am glad to hear that last qualification."

The rest of us chuckled.

"So, all these activities between you thus far was to determine a certain…" Gavin waved his hand to choose a word. "Compatibility?"

"Correct."

"Hmm." The Deathwalker's eyes slid to his grimoire as if he had the impulse to open it, though I doubted it would be to record this detail. "I suppose it makes sense. You are the only two members of your race within hundreds of leagues."

"There is that," Mourn replied with a slight smile.

Gavin grunted again, tapping his fingers before nodding with an odd finality to it, like he decided something unyielding.

"I see an important benefit to my task in this bargain," he said, touching his fingertips together as hands rested on the table. "The journey from the Ley Tower was severely taxing from overbearing attention Sirana received due to her size and appearance, but we had little means to change it. Yet even with a disguise, the ship sailing here wasn't satisfied with my being her 'brother.' This would only grow worse as we approach Manalar or should we encounter Witch Hunters."

"When," Mourn countered with a smirk, his tail betraying a bit of aggression. "And I agree. She needs an escort with more means of dissuading them and others like them."

Gavin's eerie eyes shifted my way. "And you still intend to return to the Ley Tower to help me claim it?"

My middle jumped slightly, but I nodded jerkily to get past it. "Hopefully with my sister to help us."

The Deathwalker nodded firmly. "And your bargain with Mourn makes this more likely. Yes. This is unobjectionable."

I took the chance to laugh at his delivery even as I stared down that deeply challenging path. So many things had to go right to get there, and it remained my only path back home. Even now, it wasn't quite enough if Mourn simply completed his contract with me and left Manalar for Augran.

I clasped my hands to each other as the wave of tension passed through, finding hope in Krithannia's pale face.

The elder Naulor smiled with genuine interest at Gavin, no doubt pleased by this possibility of the Ley Tower being "open and neutral" once again. If the Guild Mistress had prior, successful dealings with a new death mage in residence at the Dwarven fortress, that was undeniably beneficial to the Guild. I could hope recovering Jael and escaping the siege wouldn't be the end of our dealings with the half-blood because of that.

Maybe I could draw Mourn to the Ley Tower next.

One step at a time.

"I'm glad you agree, scholar," I said. "Have you completed your own contract with the Guild Mistress for aiding your task?"

Gavin, Krithannia, and Talov nodded at once, but it was the Naulor who spoke with a captivating strength of presence.

"I've spoken with my contacts, and the Guild is highly invested in seeing Gavin's quest completed. This is the very catalyst we need, what we have been waiting for, and we shall contribute every resource needed to break the hold the Bishops have on the sacred pool *and* prevent the Ma'ab from taking it over."

I blinked, only now trying to visualize such an accomplishment. "How? Do you happen to have a third army I haven't seen?"

Each of them, even Mourn, smiled.

"Ova sort," Talov chuckled, though it had a dark touch to it. "Been building an' honing it fer three and a half centuries."

"Three hundred and seventy-two years," Mourn corrected.

"Most ov my life, kid."

"I am sorry about that.

"Bah. If not then, some other time. But since t'was then, I'd love tah see it put tah rest before dyin'."

"This is our best opportunity," Krithannia stated. "We shan't squander it, Talov."

Though I swiftly became confused, Gavin drew my attention when he turned suddenly, reaching for a pile of parchments to shuffle through them.

"Three hundred seventy…" he muttered to himself.

Mourn's tail coiled up as he straightened from the wall; he peered from Gavin to Krithannia. I wasn't sure what he intended by that look.

"Yes, the Deathwalker did find it," she told him, pointing subtly at Graul. "I believe in trade for the entire bag."

"*Rrrmm?*" The shadow drake lifted his head from the chaise and blinked hazy eyes.

"*Moxt fekiw,*" Mourn said to the drake who rasped back.

"*Loerchik ashne, Maekrix.*"

My mouth opened as Gavin looked up from his search and beat me to the question. "The drake can speak?"

"When he wants to," Mourn replied, his tail showing irritation with his small companion while Graul's tail responded in kind.

The Deathwalker frowned. "Does he speak only To'vah?"

Graul turned his head to Gavin. "Thanks for treats. Good fun."

He sounded exactly how I'd imagine a mischievous imp to talk.

"Two languages?" my scholar amended.

"*Three,*" Graul answered in Davrin, squinting at me next. "*Maybe six.*"

Surprised, I responded skeptically in my native tongue. "*Six? Which ones?*"

Graul showed his tiny teeth. "*Dwarf. The death-cold ones. The sun priest talk.*"

His accent sounded like Mourn's, and I supposed we didn't have a word for Ma'ab or Manalari yet. A good demonstration of speaking Davrin over just making the claim.

"But do you speak them well?" I remarked.

The beast snorted. *"Moments ago, I could not speak at all, Baenar."*

"True, that is an elevation of drakes I haven't heard of."

"Most nest-kin can't talk. Takes brains, magic, and time."

"Like most things we do below."

Graul hissed a laugh which led into a huge yawn with his dark mouth wide open.

"What changed that you decide to speak?" Gavin asked, returning to his page search.

"Maekrix decided about *Baenar,"* the drake replied. "Guild Mistress decided about you. Passed test. Will speak to you now."

"We're honored," I said dryly, earning another snicker.

Meanwhile, Talov and Krithannia had clearly known that the little beast had several tongues on him while not even hinting the possibility.

There were a lot of tests going on.

"Maekrix?" I asked Mourn then. "Yet another name you bargain with?"

One corner of his mouth drew up. "Not that one. It's a description, but the first To'vah word Graul learned. He uses it as a friend-name."

"Oh? What does it mean?"

"Leader."

I smiled instantly. "Given your solitary contracts, amusing to think of you as the leader of only one little drake."

His eyes glinted with equal amusement. "Not only, but let that come up again, given that I know where Graul led our Deathwalker."

I caught Krithannia's nod as Talov wrapped big hands around the small, Yungian teacup, but asked Gavin this time. "What did you find?"

The scowling mage had drawn out two separate documents placed within a leather folder, neither a scroll or book.

"I found what I desired to find," he said, his inverted gaze drifting across faded markings on brown parchment. "Another text written in an older dialect of Manalari which helped me pinpoint the start of the Bishops of Mount Sonai."

The way he touched his dry fingers to the dried page could have been affectionate if he was the sort. "Do you recall that earlier court record about the execution of the witch?"

"I remember. Four centuries ago, you said."

"Almost. Three hundred eighty-two years ago." Gavin touched another document. "According to this, that was ten years before Iarmod Tefornin seized power and proclaimed himself the first Archbishop."

Three hundred seventy-two years ago.

My eyes drifted from Gavin to Mourn. The half-blood smiled without showing his teeth; his eyes held not a hint of amusement.

Uh-oh.

A trickle of snowmelt filled my core just before I spoke. "I've heard of Tefornin. From the Witch Hunter Jacob."

Gavin looked curious. "Oh? What did he say?"

Mourn tilted his head skeptically, though that may have been in anticipation of the Witch Hunter's rant than any doubt of my truth. The greybeard and Naulor sat with somber patience, while Graul rested with his head up and front legs stretched out in front.

"Before Tefornin, Jacob spoke of sacrifices made to the Death Witch controlling the sacred pool, which gave birth to a fire-hair witch, supposedly the vessel of 'first witch' reborn. Of course, he accused me of being that same entity returned yet again."

Everyone in the room nodded at least a little.

I frowned in thought. "Jacob said a name, but... too much has happened since. I don't remember."

Gavin handled the parchment carefully, reminding me a bit of Shyntre in our archives. The Deathwalker reread a few sentences, his brow wrinkling a bit in concentration as he translated words in his head.

"Was it Halete Ebtryne?" he asked.

I blinked as the man's zealous intensity returned. "Yes, it was. He said Tefornin 'trapped and bound' her and revealed to the people that she maintained the pool's corruption by willingly coupling with the Hells' black hounds."

Mourn emitted a low growl, his tail slapping the wall as he kept his arms folded. "That particular legend has grown viler with the retelling."

My eyes fixed on him. "You mean Jacob was talking about *you?*"

"He was spouting his church's fearful delusions," the mercenary replied gruffly. "But it is fact that Iarmod Tefornin and his Lord Nikro Rophan arrested a red-haired woman named Halete Ebtryne. They tortured her to obtain a confession of witchcraft, heard some fantastical details about a black-skinned, yellow-eyed, horned devil with whom she loved, then brutally executed her publicly as a witch."

"Aye," Talov said softly, gesturing above his heart. "Lettie was a sweet girl that got in over 'er head. Tough life, an' she deserved better."

Oh, shit.

Gavin spoke while perusing his cherished parchments. "In the scriptures, I was taught that Lord Nikro Rophan was one of a long line of failed sinners whose family fell to worshipping these witches siphoning the pool's grace from Musanlo. The Sun God is said to have brought divine wrath upon the entire Rophan lineage, so that the faithful could finally hear the truth from his most devout servant, Iarmod Tefornin."

Mourn huffed. "Of course, you were. A self-proclaimed Arch-bishop needs to justify his coup to a people already frightened and ripe to believe him as their futures became uncertain."

Krithannia shook her head with apparent sadness, while Talov smirked and opted to comment, "Always was kinda morbidly amused how they explained it. Callin' ya 'divine wrath' like that."

Mourn sighed, looking away and toward the section of blank wall.

"Um, *entire* lineage," I said, looking at Gavin. "An exaggeration?"

My scholar had been staring at Mourn but forced his focus to me. "Apparently not. Both this document and the scriptures say that misfortunes, disease, and violence found all the Rophan heirs before the youngest could grow up, until there were none left. Manalar was then 'free' of all the corrupted governing lords, and Tefornin saved Manalar from its inevitable collapse."

"That part is mostly true," the Dragonblood admitted, his tail seemingly unable to stop coiling. "Krithannia and Talov tried to warn me not to leave a void like that and to focus on Tefornin and his closest officers. The man had gone into self-exile the very night Nikro was found dead, and we didn't hear from him for ten years."

He hesitated but then added, "The Guild didn't have the reach it does now, and I grew impatient for my revenge. I did not listen to them and made sure no Rophan of Nikro's governed Manalar for long."

I grimaced. "On behalf of one woman?"

The half-blood levelled his metallic gaze on me. "Halete was my first lover. She remained so up until she was caught, tortured, and executed by those men. It happened too quickly for me to re-cover her. I was young, and this had a... profound effect on me."

And on my hoard.

I could almost hear him say it.

Mourn curled one nostril with contempt, and I could not tell if it was for the killers or for himself. Regardless, Graul scurried to the rising head of the chaise and stretched out his neck with a rattling purr, waiting until Mourn broke his rigid stance.

The Dragonchild came forward to pick up the drake, cradling him like when we'd first been introduced. It seemed to help. Across from me, Talov and Krithannia displayed expressions affectionate and sympathetic.

In this moment of quiet, I wondered if the Naulor had been the next lover after Halete, or if there had been others in between? Either way, it seemed like the half-blood did not choose more than one female at a time.

Before our talk in the garden this morning, I'd have assumed it was another rejection of the Deepearth, a luxury of choice his Matron wouldn't have allowed him. Now I knew the importance of taking his hoard into account.

With Halete, his treasure had likely been smaller and less complex. What was it like now?

Rubbing his softly rumbling drake, Mourn finally continued.

"The man who would become the first Archbishop of Manalar sneaked back at just the right time. We hadn't the intelligence or opportunity to stop what he planned for the sacred pool. Killing him after that point would have been worse in too many ways."

Gavin nodded and touched a finger to another place on his parchment. "Around this time, the Ma'ab emerged from the Far North as a new threat. The largest group of raiders ever seen, stealing people and property. Taiding and Augran were busy forming defenses and new alliances. This included Manalar, whose own forces traveled quite far to help block the hostile campaign. Is this true?"

"Aye, it was somethin' tah see back then," Talov said with a cough. "Tefornin had been in the South around Ahj'Zayr. He an' his advisors brought back enough gold to have been feedin' the people of the Mount, rebuilding crumbling roads an' makin' connections fer seven years before the Ma'ab started their trail ov shit. Much as we hated 'im personally, the bastard had an' army we needed an' thousands ov workers backing 'im. The people loved 'im."

Krithannia nodded. "Manalar's forces *were* key to beating back the Ma'ab from the borders ov Bor and Alran that time. Despite our personal pain behind it, prosperity rose for the region under the new Bishops. We dared not destabilize it again so soon with the growing belligerence of the Ma'ab nearing the Great Lake."

"No, I couldn't do it again," Mourn agreed, studying a vague spot on the carpet. "I remember watching a steady three decades of decline *before* I sent events to the bottom with my plot to spread terror among them. I set off widespread impoverishment, starvation, disease, and suffering before Tefornin's people slowed it and turned it around."

"Aye," Talov admitted. "Human factions always gonna break apart an' reform intah somethin' else inna way my kin don't. Been hard tah advise on the 'Yungar' events sometimes, but Manalar probably didn't have tah get as bad as it did before it got better."

Ouch.

For a Dragonchild who claimed to prefer cities and held a tangible value in cultivating prosperity among Humans, I could see how this taught some harsh lessons about long-term consequences in the actions of a legend. Such a tumultuous era could have affected his hoard farther than he ever intended.

No wonder he tends Yong-wen like a precious garden.

"As much as I loathed their founder," Mourn said soberly, "the Bishops of Mount Sonai helped the ancient city to thrive again after I'd broken its back without mercy. As hard as it was at times to watch and do nothing, I had no option but to let Tefornin live his life while I rebuilt mine and allow what he'd created to exist for its natural cycle."

I wasn't the only one to look at Gavin, who merely wrinkled his nose in reply, as if he didn't want our attention or appreciation. *Only our aid.*

The Deathwalker focused his glare on his present arrangement of scriptures and scrolls. "You are correct about the natural cycle,

To'vah-krav. One way or another, the Bishops shall meet their end soon in the next transition of the pool on the mount. I've held nothing back in my intentions or my earnest suggestion that *we* should begin that transition before the Ma'ab do."

"Neither shall we hold back any guidance or assistance, messenger," Krithannia said with a regal dip of her chin. "The Guild is fully behind you in this, and we are much stronger than we were when all this began."

Talov nodded firmly. "Truth."

Graul squawked, "Aye!"

Mourn chuckled, massaging his hefty drake's shoulders and around his stiff wings until Graul groaned aloud, and I smiled despite myself.

The Guild Mistress focused on Gavin and me. "Trust us that a plan *is* forming to infiltrate the Temple City as we speak, but the timing is critical. I beg patience while we wait for further reports on the Ma'ab movement. When events come together, they will move fast, but there is some waiting yet to do."

Gavin nodded. "I would prefer to remain here until that time."

"That is fine with me, scholar." Krithannia looked to Mourn, who nodded agreement.

"I am glad you are content here, Deathwalker," he said.

The death mage drummed his fingers twice, managing a nod.

"Meanwhile," Talov said, "we could use some help pullin' together teams in Alran."

Unconsciously, Mourn's shoulders straightened. "Sirana and I will work on that."

I blinked. *My bodyguard taking me out of Yong-wen at last?*

Where we couldn't walk as ourselves, and he was still whispered to be a demon. Yet somehow, we'd be "pulling together" teams?

My smile returned. *That'll be interesting.*

The greybeard glanced at me, and his peridot eyes twinkled as he seemed to read my face before looking back to "the kid." "Good! Very good. Soon it's gonna be scary with all fuckery down South, but we've been watchin' fer this, huh?"

"Indeed, we have, old friend," Krithannia agreed.

"An' now it's here." Talov took a deep breath and stood up, running palms along his beard braids as he returned to the chaise to pull his boots out from beneath it.

"Gettin' late in th' day," he said, donning his footwear, "an' I need tah make it back tah Alran before dark. Keep in touch, an' we'll meet in there three days hence 'less ya hear somethin' sooner. Like always."

"Agreed," Mourn, Graul, and Krithannia said together.

Gavin and I exchanged similar looks, but I doubted he felt the same intense flutter in his middle that I did.

Without a similar explanation of where she'd be going, Krithannia prepared to leave the library as well. She approached Mourn to rub Graul behind his ears; the drake not only allowed it but hummed with satisfaction at the attention. The Naulor chuck-led but, at the same time, her storm-blue eyes seemed somehow older.

And troubled.

"I hope to have something tangible on your sister soon, Sirana," Krithannia said before bidding farewell. "No matter what we find out, however, please understand the Guild must put Gavin's mission first. If we discover the worst has happened to Jael, we can understand your pain but cannot allow you to sabotage this oppor-tunity. Do you understand?"

A nausea rose which had nothing to do with the geas. Still, I met her eyes. "I understand. All I need is for Mourn to go with us and protect me, so the worst doesn't *also* happen to me. I... I *need* to go back to the Ley Tower one day."

The Naulor bowed her head. "That, he can and will do. He has given you his Word."

Mourn didn't speak but bowed his head. Graul rubbed the mercenary's arm affectionately with his jaw.

"I ask only that you work with him, not against," Krithannia said. "No matter what else happens, we *are* your allies, Sirana, and Morixxyleth *is* your defender. There are no other guarantees in this war, and that is where we are headed next."

"I know, and I agree."

No demons but us. Always.

I started a cycle of breathe like in the *dorji-ka,* preventing the powerful sense of foreboding from overwhelming me.

I met the To'vah-krav's gold metal eyes and whispered, "Thank you."

CHAPTER 18

SHYNTRE CHANGED THE BEDDING ONCE A CYCLE IN THE FIRST three based on how frequently Auslan had broken into a fevered sweat, only to fret without cease about the "mess" when he next came aware.

"Stop that," the wizard murmured, quelling the simmering rage not aimed at the bedbound bua. "The Matron knows you're ill. Don't worry about Nobles for once and save the strength for yourself."

Over that time, the wizard had also coaxed his brother to eat and drink enough despite the lack of appetite. Shyntre breathed a sigh of relief as the Consort's face seemed less gaunt and his limbs no longer shook when he got out of bed.

Inevitably, this meant Shyntre had to rush to help Auslan out of bed when the healer panicked about soiling the bed with something other than sour sweat.

"Slow down!" he barked the first time the healer had fallen, kneeling beside him.

"I didn't want to bother you," Auslan whispered, tears of shame in his eyes. His hand covered his gut when it gurgled loudly; he grimaced from the cramps. "I am sorry…"

"Just tell me you need help," Shyntre groused, pulling an arm across his shoulder to help him off the floor. "I don't care what it is. That's why I'm here."

The healer's face tightened further with worry. "Is it?"

"Yeah. You're no good to anyone dead, right?"

"Right…" Auslan's eyes slid to the side. "But why you?"

"Because that's what D'Shea and the Valsharess worked out, alright? Now come on. On three, stand up."

This wasn't the first time Shyntre had tended a Royal Consort hand and foot, but none in the past had been as quiet and cooperative, nor had he ever cared this much. Instead of pampering and primping a temperamental ornament for a Worship Ball, the mage bent backwards to mend a once healthy body and aura from what appeared to be long and slow starvation. Shyntre was grateful for his stint in the army's infirmary before Elder General Rausery would take him to the Surface.

She said it might prove useful. She was right again.

When he wasn't feeding, tending, or cleaning, Shyntre shared the bed with Auslan but remained above the covers and kept his robes on. Frequently, his brother reached out to touch him while he tried to rest, whether fully awake or not.

Sometimes while the Consort slept, the wizard would trace the new streak of gold hair growing from his temple. *A permanent mark from the strain of cleansing Sirana of demonic taint.*

Now, after witnessing the outcome when the life mage used only half his gifts, Shyntre understood better why Sirana had caught during her healing. The wizard remembered how long Jaunda had been gone while he waited at the Cloister with Gaelan and Jael.

They weren't just being careless.

It wasn't hard for Shyntre to imagine a lengthy and desperate trance to mend the extent of the Red Sister's injuries in her body and aura. Eventually, Ta'suil needed something back if he would keep giving; he needed some strength or will to live. Some hope. If the Consort could have none of those, then he would take pleasure, even without true affection.

Sirana must have withheld nothing, giving back all that he needed and more. They'd known each other before that moment. Together, they had conceived a child which the Valsharess was *still* convinced Shyntre had quickened in the Wizard's Tower a span later.

Ta'suil had sired many children, yet none had captured the Queen's attention until now.

I'm afraid to understand why.

Thankfully, Sirana's Mother regularly disrupted his brooding. The Matron had returned to the room several times a cycle with clean bedding, food, and water, then took away all which had been dirtied including the bath water. She had done it all without contemptuous sneers or resentful remarks. At first, the young wizard had thought he was just missing them.

But no, he wasn't.

The Matron was clearly familiar with these necessities even before Shyntre's arrival, and she still kept a secret for D'Shea. No doubt Rohenvi had much to lose if word of this left her plantation, but resentment wasn't what compelled her to do the work.

Shyntre also remembered Natia, the garnet-eyed cait he'd met at the beginning. She obviously knew about them and had been blatantly concerned for Auslan, yet she hadn't entered the room again since Shyntre settled in. He recalled Rohenvi snatching the child back when she would have run fearlessly to the sick bed.

"Natia would sleep in here, sometimes," Auslan whispered when the mage finally asked. "She woke me if I grew noisy from bad Reverie. The Matron is worried I will harm her."

"Harm her? You?"

"She doesn't trust Consorts," his brother said. "I think... she fears us."

Shyntre stopped scowling. There could be just cause there, he knew. Perhaps Sirana's Mother had been one of the first to see the gradual corruption of the Consorts?

But I've never seen her at Court.

"How often do these bad Reveries happen?" Shyntre asked. "You've been quiet so far."

"It was frequent when I first arrived here," Auslan answered. "It's become less since then."

Shyntre knew already that "since then" was roughly the span after Sirana had left for the Surface. Auslan hadn't been alone and vulnerable to every Red Sister at the Cloister for as long as Shyntre had feared, even though it must have seemed like eternity while it was happening.

Soon after, the healer slid into a doze, and Shyntre was alone with his thoughts.

I know their torment, brother, and it took me longer than a span to see the Great Cavern again. At least you were strong enough to make it out as well. I wasn't sure if you would be.

Matron Thalluen had held Auslan in her care for almost half a turn afterward without the Valsharess knowing, an impressive feat before she eventually needed the Elder Sorceress's support.

She bartered with the Queen for me. I'm supposed to 'fix' him, to teach him to separate his healing magic from sex.

Then, because Shyntre had asked leniency for Sirana's Mother for keeping the secret, Shyntre also needed to somehow dream of Sirana on the Surface, maybe make contact, and inform *Her* about it.

That was a mistake.

"Difficult" did not describe the tasks ahead after Auslan regained his strength, yet Elder D'Shea had still taken these extra duties and claimed they could be done.

She better not have been bluffing.

When Rohenvi next arrived through her secret panel, Shyntre wasn't sure where they were in the cycle. She motioned for him not to get up, which was just as well. The healer was attached to his side, sharing heat, and Shyntre didn't want to disturb his rest by jostling or leaving him cold.

The wizard and Matron exchanged proper greetings in sign, keeping the room quiet. She added new portions of shelf-stable food to the tray on the table, confirmed plenty of water in the pitchers, and checked that the waste pot could wait. There wasn't much, and any smell had been neutralized by scoops of clay powder.

Shyntre watched as the Matron took a chair from the table and positioned it closer to the bed, facing them.

Uh-oh.

She sat down, her chin held high and her expression formal. ★Has he improved much?★

★Yes, Matron,★ Shyntre signed, ★but slowly.★

Rohenvi swallowed subtly. ★He did not want to serve as a consort after the Elder brought him here. I could tell he'd been recently abused, and I was glad to avoid the competition and distraction in my House. I did not know it could get so bad.★

Neither did he, I wager.

The corner of Shyntre's mouth tightened. ★How many has he healed?★

The Matron looked to one side. ★Only four times. Three Red Sister healings the Elder sent to us, and the last one, my guard, Drani... he saved her from a quick and brutal death. But that was when he grew ill.★

★What happened?★

Rohenvi's lips remained tight. ★An unknown threat had crept near; we've been unable to determine what. According to witnesses, most of the animals and Pytes were on edge for some time before an Uroan panicked and kicked Drani, shattering her ribs."

Shyntre frowned in thought. ★Has it happened again since?★

★Not yet. I've discarded pincerworms due to how many were affected all at once. We found no hallucino-sporing mushrooms nearby, no boot prints or sign of troublemakers from another House.★ The Matron shrugged, attempting calm with her next sign. ★I've considered a Sathoet, perhaps, or a…★

She hesitated.

★A Drider,★ Shyntre finished, where his mind had gone first.

Rohenvi exhaled, muscles in her throat tightening before she nodded.

Damn it.

★I could confirm either of those,★ he offered.

She frowned. ★Now?★

★Probably not, as it's been more than a cycle. But if I'm here and your property starts acting strange again, come get me. I could find them with a spell.★

Sirana's Mother narrowed her eyes. ★Are you not afraid if we find either?★

He smirked, letting her see the cynicism. ★Neither of those creatures will kill me, Matron, and I don't care if they hurt me.★

Rohenvi's eyes widened a little. After a quiet moment, she nodded. ★Thank you, Shyntre. I shall bear it in mind.★

He licked dry lips and tried signing. ★Could I ask for an exchange for information, Matron?★

She raised one eyebrow but replied, ★If I can.★

You and me, both.

★How many know that Auslan is here who are not part of your House? And can you give names?★

Matron Thalluen let out a breath. ★I am only aware of two in addition to you and the Valsharess. I presume their superiors must know as well.★

Mentally, Shyntre added another two or three Rohenvi knew about, and five she did not. Not ideal.

★Which two? My Mother,★ he prompted.

★And her Lead,★ Rohenvi added.

★Jaunda.★

Surprised but reading his face, she smiled a little. ★Yes. In fact, she was all three of Auslan's Red Sister healings. I do not know what she is doing, but she returns with injuries stemming from endurance travel each time.★

Shyntre nodded. ★Serving a mission for the Valsharess.★

★I'd expect nothing else.★

The Matron hesitated to ask, but a strong need lay in her eyes. Shyntre had no doubt she would ask.

★Do you know many Red Sisters by name?★

He looked at his hands when a rock seemed to land in his stomach, and an ironic smile stretched his mouth.

Would he truly be protecting Sirana's Mother by tightening his tongue now? The Matron was already in trouble thanks to D'Shea bringing Auslan here, from more than the wizard had guessed if either of those demonbloods had been skulking around recently.

★I know all of them by name,★ he answered honestly. ★I work with the Sisterhood more often than I'd care to.★

Rohenvi's eyes brightened a little, and immediately Shyntre realized what the next question would be. *Oh, damn.*

★Do you know one named Sirana?★

A laugh nearly escaped but he covered his mouth; it wouldn't have been a joyful sound. Rohenvi blinked at him multiple times and leaned forward in her chair, signing briskly.

★You know what happened to my daughter. D'Shea hinted that she'd been hurt while on a mission.★

His shoulders slumped. ★That I can't tell you, Matron.★

★Is she alive?★

★The last I saw her.★

★How long ago was that?★

Shyntre grimaced. ★Shortly after the Purge. Before the healer arrived here.★

Rohenvi sat back with detectable dismay. She contemplated something and added, ★What about a Red Sister named Gaelan?★

He stared at her. *What is the connection there?*

★I know her,★ he answered, ★but she was involved in the same mission as Sirana, also still alive last I saw her.★

★You can't talk about her, either.★

Shyntre shook his head. ★How do you know her?★

Rohenvi exhaled, resting her back against the chair. ★I bid to take in her child when she was recruited. I'd approved one of my past House Guards as her chosen sire.★

Shyntre's mouth opened. ★Gaelan's a mata?★

The Matron allowed a silent chuckle. ★So you know all their names but nothing about them?★

★Red Sisters tend to stop talking about where they came from, Matron,★ he replied, hiding his rash irritation. ★Their only consistent family is the Sisterhood. Talking about parents or siblings, children or sires outside of it is just a source of pain, something to be used against them.★

★I see.★ Her weak smile fell followed by her eyes. ★I believe that. If we may take a step back in our exchange?★

★Certainly, Matron.★

★Yes, Gaelan was a new mata when she was recruited. The cait you met is her daughter, Natia.★

That hadn't been immediately apparent, but the cait could have taken after her sire.

★I am somewhat heartened,★ Rohenvi continued, ★to imagine Sirana and Gaelan as shoulder-fighters together, to end up on the same mission.★

Shyntre swallowed and could only nod. For a moment, everything surrounding this subject seemed bleak. He sought another.

★Auslan told me Natia quieted his bad dreams,★ he signed. ★That she sometimes slept in here?★

Rohenvi's demeanor cooled significantly; she lifted her chin again as she leaned back from him. *That was before I learned he craves rutting just to stay in good health when using his gift. It's twisted, and even if it isn't his fault, I can't risk having him do something vile to her in his sleep.*

Shyntre straightened. *I don't think he would do that—*

I didn't ask what you think! Her nostrils wrinkled in disgust as her hands turned hostile. *I must keep him here, but I cannot risk tempting him! I know *too well* how the Abyss feeds, even on children!*

But he's not tainted by—!

Everything out of the Sanctuary is touched by the Void's hunger! Why would the Priestesses create any new creature in the first place if not to consume more of who we are and strengthen that power over us?*

Shyntre dropped his hands, taken aback how they dove straight into heterodoxy. Rohenvi realized to whom she'd blurted this and drew back as if seized by a sudden chill.

Forgive me, she signed smoothly. *I mean no disrespect to the Queen's Divinity or Her favored servants. I mean I am aware of the necessary sacrifices. My older children were tested too young. I want to protect my new little ones from the Sanctuary's appetites. I would prefer *any* Davrin child to grow strong before being tested in such ways.*

Rohenvi clasped her hands once she'd finished, as if to still their trembling as she waited for his response.

Meanwhile, Shyntre needed time to form a new idea of this Matron without knowing much about her except her thirdborn daughter. It seemed, like himself, and like Sirana, the Matron didn't accept the Abyss was entitled to such control over their lives.

That we're just being preyed on, restrained, and taunted for the entertainment of the powerful.

A *Matron* saw it and felt this way? To the degree that she would protect even the cait of a common guard and potion maker from possible abuse by a "Sanctuary creature."

She doesn't know Ta'suil.

But could he blame her caution?

★No insult or disrespect taken, Matron Thalluen,★ he signed, managing a genuine smile. ★We're of… like minds in this way. I wish any Matron would have thought of me or Auslan that way when we were Natia's age. We… do not think the Sanctuary is divine. Not at all. Only hungry, as you say.★

Rohenvi needed the moment to read him and decide if she believed him. He wasn't in a hurry and waited. Eventually, the Matron swallowed with discomfort at his words and nodded slowly, accepting the tiny hope she hadn't made a terrible miscalculation in their discussion.

★Well to know,★ she signed, hesitating before she continued. ★And what… are you saying about him not being 'tainted?' How do you know?★

Shyntre's smile remained much longer than he expected. ★Most of the youngest Consorts were tainted, Matron, you are not wrong about that. That's why the Purge happened. The Priestesses let what should have been enhanced breeding get out of control.★

Rohenvi narrowed her eyes. ★Was it ever *in* their control?★

Another heretical challenge. *Astonishing.*

★I don't know,★ he answered truthfully. ★But my Mother, Elder D'Shea, was also involved in the beginning.★

The Matron blinked. ★She was?★

★With reluctance, as I heard it.★ He stilled the quiver in his middle before continuing. ★The Royal Consorts were a blend of efforts that was supposed to strengthen our magic without turning us all into Sathoet, harnessing magic without letting it harness us. It was always meant to be only Davrin essence.★

★Yes, that was what they claimed,★ Rohenvi admitted. ★And I believed them. My two Consort-bred Daughters, however, left something to be desired."

Shyntre smirked, reflecting how he could expect such a statement from any Matron in Sivaraus about her children if they did not impress her. Yet, he also heard the personal rebuke against the Priestesses as well.

★Were they not mageborn as promised?★

★There seemed to be magical potential,★ Rohenvi confirmed, ★but my eldest wanted shortcuts. She started practicing on others here at the manor without the self-discipline to work with a tutor. She rejected all of them, claiming could join the Priesthood, that she was already chosen. She was... out of control from the start. Wholly unlike any child born in our House in the last four generations. She was responsible for my mind declining for a time, and for the death of my brother.★

Her lower lip quivered to share this. ★I was made to doubt the truth from multiple sources, but I am certain now. My First Daughter killed my brother because he would not bend to her will. I realized too late, he was protecting me from *her*.★

Shyntre swallowed. *Touched by the Abyss, without doubt.*

Rohenvi glanced at his expression and tried to shrug off her bitterness, both unconvincing and unsettlingly familiar.

★The Second was her first follower,★ the Matron continued. ★For my thirdborn, I'd sworn off the Consorts and chose another sire, but this only inflamed them. They targeted her next, but it took me far too long to see it. They...blinded me. By then, they'd turned Sirana against me as well.★

Shyntre frowned. ★Did she join them?★

That didn't seem like her.

The Matron shook her head, her expression guilty. ★No. They had... damaged her, to where she could not be my heir if I might choose her over them, and I was...planning on it. After the First died in her accident, Sirana was required to leave to attend Court. That was not all my decision.★

★It wasn't?★

Rohenvi shook her head. ★The Sisterhood watched my only sane cait there and seemed satisfied to claim her. Meanwhile, my Second tried to poison me as I carried my new baby.★

The Matron touched her head as if to smooth the memory behind closed eyes. ★the offspring of Sanctuary Consorts nearly destroyed me and all for whom I'm responsible. I regret *ever* pursuing the first one to bed.★

Shyntre was clutching his robe covering his thigh. He had to consciously release it to sign, ★I am sorry, Matron.★

With another silent laugh, she waved that there was nothing to be done, but the regret remained. ★I must try again with my Fourth Daughter, who is also not Consort-bred. I will give up the magic for some stability. Natia helps watch over her. I don't want to lose either of them to more Priestess ploys in their Consorts.★

Rohenvi's eyes flicked to Auslan as if to punctuate the end of her confession.

★I understand, now,★ he began with care. ★I would still hold that Auslan is different.★

How well he understood that look of skeptical disbelief.

★This Consort is one of the oldest ones,★ Shyntre continued, ★and nearly too old to be desirable.★

The Matron huffed a laugh, shaking her head, but the wizard bulled ahead, ★Yet his healing magic only grows stronger, and for that, Elder D'Shea saved him from the Purge to her own detriment. She is still trying to dig her way out of a pit with her superiors for making that choice. The Elder Sorceress has more ways than I do of sensing Priestess void-trickery. She would not have brought Auslan here if he were corrupted.★

Rohenvi seemed inclined to consider the truth but still signed, ★You say his magic grows stronger while he has been bent and conditioned by the Priestesses to need sex to heal others. Something about him is unnervingly attractive to any female who is near him long enough.★ She huffed. ★Even me! And I would not bed him if it meant evading the altar!★

Shyntre's hands rested in his lap when his thoughts fixed on Rohenvi's probable reaction to learn the details of Sirana's healing. Then he wondered how much of this could be true now, despite what Shyntre had known about him before.

This is exactly the concern that D'Shea had reported to the Valsharess.

Shyntre was mortified that Auslan had already confessed their past to Elder D'Shea, but despite her baffling acceptance, he still wouldn't condemn them both by flaunting touches of affection or worse, by getting caught with their cocks in their mouths.

Yet, Auslan *wasn't* recovering as fast as Shyntre had expected after he'd arrived, as if his proximity wasn't enough now when it had been before when they both lived in the Sanctuary.

The young mage had known him best when Priestess Juliran had been the healer's "mother." After she'd died, Wilsira had gotten hold of him, and the wizard hadn't wanted to learn about his brother's interactions with the Conceiver, nor did he care to hear details about the many Noble beds where the Consort had been pressed into service.

Perhaps I don't understand how he's been changed by it all. We have been kept apart for a long time.

Rohenvi audibly sighed, and Shyntre looked up.

★I apologize,★ she signed. ★Again, I did not let you finish.★

He shrugged. ★You have many good reasons to mistrust Consorts around your House caits, Matron.★

★But have you anything to add that I should know? You seem to know him and care for his well-being, and I trust Elder D'Shea's decision to bring you here. I also appreciate your offer of your mage skills, should we encounter anything suspicious. I know I should not make you bear the weight of my frustrations. You are not responsible. You are only here to provide the aid I need.★

The wizard blinked with slow surprise at Sirana's Mother. Had any Matron in his life ever *apologized* like this?

No, they haven't, even if they had an inkling whose son I am.

Matron Thalluen was acutely aware of the vulnerability of her House; otherwise, even she might have found a way to lessen the impact of admitting to a bua that she was wrong.

Had he anything to add? Shyntre considered. He couldn't tell her about the visions or Sirana's pregnancy or the Surface; he could not say anything of their shared dreams, or the time spent in the Sanctuary.

How else was Auslan different, other than being a healer willing to give pieces of himself to a fault?

★I am not sure I could convince you that Natia is safe with him, Matron,★ he admitted. ★I know Auslan admires her and misses her company. He's rarely been around children despite helping to conceive many, so Natia is one of the first he's become familiar with. He also knows you are wary, and why. He's accepted your decision, and I do as well.★

The Matron blinked slowly this time, settling down in her chair.

"Hmph," she said with a frown as she looked toward the door. She lifted her hands again as she stood up. ★Thank you for the exchange, Shyntre, and for your insights. You are an intelligent bua and a generous asset for the time I have you. Alas, it grows late for me, and I am tired.★

With care not to disturb Auslan, Shyntre slipped off the bed to stand facing her. He bowed with what courtly grace he could muster, as was her due; he felt very little resentment for doing so.

★Rest well, Matron Thalluen,★ he signed.

She dipped her chin, even as she still seemed uncertain about her thoughts. ★You will summon me, and only me, if you need something? Or if you have any concerns?★

★Of course. Thank you for the components to do so. I will use them if there is the need. I will only reach out to you.★

Sirana's Mother nodded again, took a deep breath, and saw herself out. The healer never woke during their meeting.

Shyntre busied himself checking over their supplies, reorganizing the taller shelf more to his liking. When the Matron didn't return immediately as if she'd forgotten something, he picked up a heating stone, whispered the command word, and slipped it into one bucket to begin warming the water.

He stared as the rock sank to the bottom, his sensitive eyes detecting the first Radiants rising from the heating stone.

Too often Shyntre was awake while Auslan slept. For all that time, he'd been wrestling with impotent anger, guilt, and fear at what had happened to his brother recently. Even the mercy of D'Shea pulling Auslan out of the Red Sisters' clutches and placing him here at House Thalluen had ultimately led to loss until he hadn't even wanted to eat.

It's wrong. All of it. No peace to be had.

Worst of all had been Shyntre's discovery when he first arrived, when he'd touched the clammy skin and felt for his pulse. He'd listened to the pitch of his brother's aura, recognizing in that frayed contact much more than his first lover.

He met a part of himself which he'd avoided for more than a century.

This connection had been numbed all that time, ignored somewhere cold and dark within him, so the spiders in the web couldn't follow the threads of passion and suck the life out of what they found.

Somehow, Shyntre had sloughed off the old dreams at the same time.

I never saw Sirana coming, but Ta'suil did.

Those dreams should have been his to experience if he wasn't so cowardly. Even when he was forced to drink Auranka's milk, Shyntre had thought he could just take another component to black out entirely. Whatever he dreamed, he wouldn't see it. He'd deny these sadistic rulers that extra source of knowledge with which to torment him.

I was wrong. But I didn't know until I touched him.

The dreams and most of the burden had gone over to his brother, and it only grew worse while Ta'suil had been left alone.

It's just wrong. There's no balance in anything here. It's spider shit!

"There's no way out," he whispered to his wavering reflection. "It'll get worse again, no matter what I do or don't do."

Shyntre drew in a deep breath, stepping back from the water to remove his sash. *I need to help him heal how he needs to be healed. He can't do it alone.*

The wizard undressed by the table, removing his robes and sandals to set them in a neat pile. The water had warmed enough for the mage to wet a fresh cloth and wipe down his skin in the nude. Once he'd removed most of the last cycle's sweat, he wrung out and set aside his cloth, leaving the stone to maintain the heat for later.

Returning to the bed, Shyntre pulled back the blankets and slipped beneath them, scooting close to the other bua, each lying on his side and facing the wall. He reached an arm forward to draw him close.

Auslan wore his long-sleeved shirt and loose bottoms required by the Matron, yet the moment his back touched Shyntre's chest, the Consort breathed a pleasant sigh in his sleep, and the wizard gained a startlingly swift erection despite the lack of skin contact.

Whoo… It has been a long time.

Shyntre settled closer, almost flush, and consciously slowed his breathing. Now that the healer's aura wasn't so raw to his senses, the wizard focused more on what *had* changed.

No, I don't know him as well anymore.

The wizard should be neither surprised nor jealous by the many caits and matas who'd bedded him; of course, the practice would have shifted his magic in a fundamental way. This was the reason he was born.

He could probably tell the same for me.

If the wizard allowed his brother close enough to tell that.

Shyntre sighed and tried again to relax, his eyes tracing where snow white hair met the dark nape of his neck. On impulse, he leaned forward to press a kiss there.

That felt and smelled the same.

"Mmm."

Auslan inhaled as if coming aware and would have rolled onto his back if Shyntre hadn't been there to catch him. The wizard's bare arm tightened while the rest of him focused on the warm, living pressure along his front. The healer's hand touched his fore-arm and paused, then slid upward, as if searching for a wizard's thick sleeve.

The Consort didn't find it.

Auslan turned his head and blinked toward the ceiling before scarlet eyes looked over his shoulder. Shyntre focused on his lips as they parted, as the bua breathed out, barely audible.

"Oh…"

The other bua was aware of the stiff pole nudging his back.

"You don't have to get naked," Shyntre whispered, keeping his hips from grinding. "I just… wanted to be. Sorry about that."

His brother was wide awake now. "Are you tired? Do you need Reverie?"

Mutely, he shook his head, and the other swallowed. For long moments, they studied each other's eyes.

Becoming familiar again.

"Do you want to kiss me?" Auslan asked, hesitant, as if he wasn't sure.

Shyntre huffed through his nose. He nodded. "A lot."

Eyes brightened, and their light lifted up the corners of his mouth, and the bred bua shifted in place to rest on his back, one hand clutching the blankets. He skimmed his eyes over what skin he could see on the wizard so far, each of them sensing the un-barred heat of more underneath.

"Please, kiss me," he said.

The rush was instant. Overwhelming.

A maelstrom erupted inside his chest, sweeping through his body as Shyntre climbed on top of his bedmate, making sure he couldn't roll away. Auslan gasped with shocked surprise but was eager and welcoming. Shyntre could see it when captured his soul brother's face between his hands and took that first kiss.

One of many he intended to seize.

Yearning for reunion at last equaled intense, tightly focused lust, each of which grappled with despairing loneliness and fear. Rage arose as well, strong enough to cave in the Great Cavern it-self. All of it broke free at once, no longer seeping through the cracks in his heart.

Oh, Goddess…

The Consort moaned in his throat. They could feel their twin erections lined up and pressed together between their bellies, sepa-rated by one layer of dull, dark clothing. Shyntre rocked gently as he could, pressed his pelvis harder against his first lover while kiss-ing and sucking on soft lips.

He heard and felt his brother's heart pounding within his chest as they dueled tongues, listened to the matured pitch of his aura at the back of his head while inhaling his intoxicating scent.

The keen hum was weakened but willing to grow.

Asking him for more. Longing to heal.

I'm sorry that I deafened us like this.

There hadn't been much choice what to listen to then; there was no choice except to listen now. The Queen would find out he heard eventually. She always did when Her Son wouldn't give up, when he refused to go limp in Her Web and cease to exist.

I don't care. Let Her wait for it.

Elegant hands reached to caress his naked back, sliding underneath the blanket, exploring down to his buttocks. Shyntre broke the kiss for an earnest thrust and encouraging gasp, shivering as soft fingers traced the curve of his muscle before gradually working their way back up.

His mouth dove back to Auslan's neck, breathing in deep, tasting and running his lips along his jaw and ear. They rocked together, their bodies shifting slow and firm. One or the other occasionally betrayed his urgent need before the other eased him back down.

Eventually, the Consort spoke.

"I am too hot," he said, reaching to tug up his shirt.

Shyntre seized for that first instant their stomachs touched, but he soon realized it wasn't a coy suggestion. The healer's hairline was damp; he *was* sweating again.

He's still weakened. Don't overpower him.

"Right. I got it."

The wizard braced and pushed himself up and off his companion, straddling his hips to settle upright. He kept their sexes together, their sacks nestled around each other while he helped Auslan pull his shirt over his head; he was struck admiring the trim figure from the waist up, the long hair spread over the pillow.

"Mmm," Shyntre groaned, tossing the damp shirt onto the floor.

Auslan looked after it, watching it land, and started to fret. "Um, it'll get wrinkled, shouldn't I—?"

The mage caressed naked shoulders, turning the healer's face back and quieting him with a kiss. He smirked a little. "You've been sleeping, it's already wrinkled. We'll wash it afterward and hang it to dry. Promise."

That was barely enough to nudge the worry farther out of sight while his hands and tongue refamiliarized the wizard with the intimacies of the healer's dark nipples, his pits, and his flanks. Shyntre wagered his companion had forgotten the shirt existed.

"Still hot," Auslan panted, grunting to kick off the blankets from his legs.

Or maybe not.

The Consort bucked beneath him, a delightfully mild attempt to push him off that made the wizard groan.

"Awright, hold on."

Shyntre twisted his spine to take the covers still clinging to Auslan's shin and fling them away. They landed part way off the foot of the bed.

"Oh, no! Are they on the floor?"

The wizard turned back around and took the healer's wrists as Auslan tried to sit up. Shyntre pushed him back down, tightening his thighs against the wriggling hips as he stretched out his lover's arms. He leaned to lick the exposed nipples again, blowing cool air over them to see them stiffen up, listening to the bua's sensual gasps again.

"Those are already dirty, too," he whispered. "We'll replace them afterward. Promise."

The Consort cocked one eyebrow at the wizard. "You're matronizing me, aren't you?"

Shyntre chuckled, shook his head. "No, I'm not. There's a time and place for some worries. I have a better question."

"Mm?"

"Do you want me to strip off your bottoms or just pull them down around your ankles?"

Auslan's dry smile melted into shocked passion as his lower lip trembled. The mage couldn't resist leaning to catch it gently between his teeth. He chuckled before kissing his mouth, holding tight to slender wrists until the healer answered.

"H-halfway," the Consort breathed. "My knees?"

Neither. Interesting.

Shyntre nodded and released him to shift from his knees to the balls of his feet. He curled fingers into the waistline of the loose-fitting pants, watching Auslan's eyes widen with anticipation, his chest rising up. Breath escaped as his wizard pulled out and down over the turgid staff; Auslan shuddered as fingers pressed into his flesh, slowly dragging the clothing out from beneath his ass and down his thighs to the top of his knees.

The Consort gripped the mattress with both hands and apologized, "I-I'm sorry, I haven't trimmed down there since before…"

"Shh," Shyntre shushed, gawking at the Consort's full arousal standing above his white pubic thatch. "You're beautiful. And I'm still less groomed than you."

"Oh, but that suits you," the other bua replied, his earnest delight blending with his embarrassment. "As does the short-cut hair!"

Shyntre smiled wryly.

"I also should have washed first—" Auslan began.

"Pfft, you're fine. My mouth is watering from scent alone."

"You're just saying—"

"I'm not lying, Ta'suil."

Shyntre straddled his brother's thighs, holding his own cock, and squeezed along the length. He was able to catch enough precum to smear the head to a shine which couldn't be missed.

"Look, I'm *dripping*." He paused long enough to enjoy the naked desire on the healer's face before adding, "And I won't lie. Not here like this. Trust me."

Slowly, Auslan nodded, consciously relaxing as the wizard gently pushed down bent legs. The healer couldn't stop quivering as Shyntre used both hands to gather up his brother's genitals, caressing and massaging his pole and sack together.

The sound which escaped sent tingles along the edges of his ears while the tip of the cock in his hands leaked with the first pull. He smeared the moisture around the glans and relished three firm strokes while his other hand massaged the smooth scrotum at the same time.

Another sound escaped which held a touch of desperation.

"That close already?" Shyntre teased as a grin tugged itself into place.

Auslan opened his eyes and blinked, forcing himself to let go of the mattress. He licked his lips and he took a deep breath as he quivered again. "I can wait as long as you need me to."

Shyntre knew he could. "Will you hold off until I tell you to cum?"

Though he'd expected a quick agreement, Auslan's scarlet eyes flicked to one side with new doubt.

"What?" he asked.

"Hm?" The Consort looked back, still nervous.

"You hesitated. Do you not want me to tease you this way?"

"It's fine! Of course you may, yes, I... you know that I enjoy this."

"But there was something else." Gradually, Shyntre resumed massaging and stroking him. "Tell me what you want, Ta'suil. I know we feel different from before. What were you thinking?"

"Um, well," the other bua gulped. "Could it be clean? When you command me to let go?"

"Clean?" Shyntre frowned. "What do you mean?"

Auslan looked troubled. "Don't make me spray all over myself. Please."

Ah.

"I won't do that. We'll keep it clean. Promise."

The healer relaxed again, smiling gingerly at him. "Thank you, and yes. I will hold off until you tell me to cum."

Shyntre relished listening to him say it, grunting at the rush of heat in his gut. *Hoo-bua...*

Easy to decide what he wanted to do next, and how best to give them the release they needed.

Shyntre shifted forward on his knees, deliberately dragging his scrotum along the other bua's now that it was fully exposed. Auslan whimpered softly as he pressed them gently together, lining up their hard and oozing cocks while the bua on top took them between his hands. Shyntre caressed and massaged their rods, squeezing them together and varying his grip to discover one which worked for them both, right now, in a simultaneous stroke.

"Goddess!" Auslan gasped, his heels scraping along the bed as his spine bowed a little. "Oh, yes...please, yes!"

Fuck, yes.

Shyntre pursed his mouth shut in concentration, easily pleasuring himself but distracted by the many ways his Sanctuary brother responded to his touch. Auslan cooed, his mouth lax and head propped on his pillow as he watched every stroke they experienced together with dazzling, wide eyes. Sensations grew before receding, rising steadily before slowing, as if he had them both under control from the bottom.

The tension climbed through him, through *them*, without force of any kind: between his legs, through his pole, causing his balls to draw up against the other's. Their aches strengthened, begged him for more, and he gave it without threat or humiliation, with guidance rather than dominance.

One of them seeped on Auslan's belly, and Shyntre wiped his palm across the flexing abdomen, stroking to create warm friction. Their heady, mingled scent encouraged the mage hunch over to better breathe it in, and Shyntre flexed his buttocks, thrust with his hips, harder along the other bua's length.

The wizard was probably closer to the edge than the healer, even with as much as the bottom bua writhed and trembled beneath him, reaching to touch his legs. The Consort would hold his climax for as long as necessary, his brows drawn down together like that, every so often biting his lip with concentration.

Perfect.

Shyntre admitted he would enjoy nothing better than to speed up, to stay just like this, and command his companion to climax with him. He would savor feeling them spurt between his busy hands, watching it erupt and spatter twice as much semen over his partner.

But…

Don't make me spray all over myself. Please.

Alright. Something else.

If not together in this position, then perhaps he'd turn around and kneel with the Consort's head between his legs? They could suck each other off without making a mess. But, even if it was cleaner, did he want the finish to be as lewd and muddled as the Red Sisters blindly cramming and sucking each other's Feldeus?

Maybe only if he asks.

Nothing wrong with enjoying their peaks one at a time.

Shyntre slowed his hands, easing his grip just as his heart started pounding in his ears. Auslan exhaled, releasing his new grip on the pillow as he breathed in through his nose.

"Shyntre?"

"We're good." He pulled his cock away and pushed himself backward to all fours, maintaining his hold on the healer's tacky pole. "I want to taste you."

"Oh, but—"

Shyntre's tongue glided along the underside before the Consort could say more, swirled around the top before closing on it to suck harder. Auslan cried out the loudest he'd been yet, covering his own mouth in surprise.

Shyntre chuckled, gladly filling his mouth again with cock, the sex musk striking him in the best way possible. It filled his mouth and nose at once, sending him into a single, glorious moment where he was wholly present with his actions.

I have a Royal Consort's aching pole in my mouth.

He would lavish pleasure on it, coax it to squirt down his throat so he could swallow it all.

Cleanest way possible.

And the biggest waste a Priestess could imagine.

"Oh, Goddess, Shyntre…!" Auslan squeaked, both hands clasping his pillow at once. His legs fought his pants around his knees for the first time.

Yes, hold on, I've got you.

Shyntre enjoyed the freedom to reach and stroke himself without obstruction, to relieve some of the ache as he took the Consort as deep as he could. He caressed this treasured length with his lips, worshipped it with his tongue, and eased it into his throat while squeezing his eggs.

"Oh my God—!" his partner cried again. "Y-you're…so good…ah!"

Depends who's asking, but I had the best instructors.

Further words were swallowed by a groan as Shyntre swallowed his little head, tempted to smirk around the hot prick before coming up for air. He was fully aware that the Red Sisters had made him one of the best cocksuckers among buas in Sivaraus. He saw a deeper irony that only one of those cocks in his lifetime would coat his throat with cream when the pleasure came.

No one else is worth the risk.

Shyntre drew his mouth off long enough to say, "Come for me, Ta'suil. Let go in my mouth."

He gobbled him back up; Auslan's hips jerked up and unintentionally pushed deeper.

"Shhhy—ah!" Ta'suil cried.

Shyntre sped up so he wouldn't have the choice to argue.

Or disobey.

"Ah! *Ahhh*, yeah!"

A hum rose in his ears at the same time hot seed splashed the back of his throat. Shyntre kept lips tight to catch every drop, cradling his tongue around the flexing pole until Auslan had finished. He tasted the salt and bitter tang only when enough had filled his mouth, then he pulled off and swallowed it all at once.

When Shyntre lifted his head, Auslan stared back at him. The healer seemed dazed, which made the wizard grin, though it didn't take long for the Consort to notice his yearning, bobbing member jutting out.

"May I?" Auslan whispered. "Do the same for you?"

Oh, fuck, yes, please.

"If you want to."

They traded places; the Consort having sweated enough all over to feel tacky, yet he didn't hesitate to take the same position. Auslan began with a long lick to the underside of Shyntre's prick before sampling his still-leaking head, proving he'd been paying attention.

"Ohhh, yeah…"

At first, the other bua's longer hair spilled down on both sides, caressing the wizard's hips but mostly covering the view. Shyntre reached to gather the silken tendrils into a tail so he could watch his cock passing between his brother's lips. Auslan's eyes were humored when he looked up, gradually and teasingly sucking the wizard's length, his tongue never still, dancing along the way.

Oh, Goddess…

It was Shyntre's turn to let noises slip. His brother was more careful with his mouth as he practiced, needing to grow reaccustomed to the act. He avoided pushing the erection down his throat, and Shyntre noticed, so he kept his ass tight to avoid thrusting up too far by accident. He remembered how sore his throat had been after even a couple horny Sisters.

He didn't need or want the same with Auslan. This still felt good; this was more than enough.

"It's coming," Shyntre warned, unsure if Auslan wanted to swallow.

He forgot to ask.

The Consort gave his answer as he nodded and moved his mouth and hand faster in tandem. He intended neither to stop nor remove his mouth to release the mess.

Not that I'd mind—

Further thoughts blanked out in the rush of release overtaking him.

The bua's heels dug into the mattress as his incredible break in tension flooded his body with mindless ecstasy, lifting him up, holding him weightless in suspension. His cock never left that warm and wet comfort as one joyful hand clutched his thigh as if to hold him down. Then, he was coasting, settling back onto the bed from where he'd been.

Feeling that last jolt of sensation as Auslan removed his lips.

"Mm," the healer hummed with a chuckle. "I remember your flavor."

Shyntre huffed a laugh, sweat cooling his brow as he opened his arm in invitation. Auslan pulled his bottoms to his waist and reached for the blankets still half off the edge, dragging them forward to cover them both. The healer settled on his side, pressing to the wizard whose arms wrapped around him. Several heartbeats passed before Auslan whispered it first.

"Thank you."

Shyntre turned to kiss his forehead, licked at the salt from his lips, and felt he was just now catching his breath. "Thank you for trusting me."

The Consort caressed the wizard's bare chest with delicate fingers. "I do not believe I ever stopped."

They sounded drowsy and on the verge of yawning. His limbs grew heavy, and he didn't want to move. Against Shyntre's better judgement, they slipped into Reverie together, lying as they were, before either could say any more.

SOMETIME LATER, SHYNTRE BOLTED UPRIGHT, MOMENTARILY confused where he was. His words had been caught tight in his throat, but he forced them out.

"Stop it! S-stop watching me every *fucking* moment…!"

"Shh, shh," Auslan hush, sitting up to hug him, kissing the side of his face. "You're safe. You're with me. Peace."

Shyntre shifted on his hip and clutched the other bua. His chest ached until his heart began to slow; he breathed in the scent of their sweat, listened to the Consort's soothing hum. He attempted to clear the oppressive darkness from his mind.

Eventually, the night sky came back. So did the dunes.

The sand pit, and the storm.

Sirana.

"W-was that real?" he whispered.

Auslan rubbed his naked back, patting it with comfort as they maintained as much skin contact as possible. "Was what real?"

"The… open sky. The stars. And that…"

"The trap?"

"Yeah. The sand. Sinking. Too tight to get out."

The Consort hugged him tighter. "I'm sorry. I didn't want to be alone again."

They hadn't met eyes since waking up but, eventually, the shaking eased, and Shyntre didn't feel so ungrounded. The presence of the Great Cavern's ceiling far above returned, as did the tangled, unseen labyrinth surrounding him. He sensed the unimaginable press of stone and earth, and heard the deep, ever-present thrum of the Deepearth.

The wizard exhaled, filled with an odd relief to look at the four walls of this room at House Thalluen. At least he could believe he'd break his nose if he tried to step through them.

"What happened?" he asked, gathering courage to meet his brother's extraordinary eyes.

Auslan was still apologetic. "We shared a vision."

"We did?"

"Yes. Of Sirana."

Shyntre stared. Did this mean he dreamed exactly what the Queen asked of him?

So soon *and* without trying?

Fuck.

Shyntre winced. "Is *that* what it's been like for you?"

His bedmate shrugged. "It's usually more confusing and frightful. This was… oddly quiet."

"Pfft! Quiet?" The wizard rolled his eyes toward the ceiling. "Until the sandstorm showed up. I thought it'd scrape off my ears when the roaring wouldn't stop. It sounded like a monster!"

The Consort smiled ruefully. "I'm sorry. But I saw some good signs."

"What good signs?"

"Most important, you got out of the trap before the storm would have buried you."

Shyntre squinted at him with suspicion. "But Sirana helped me."

The other bua squeezed him in his arms again, his face flush with a renewed wellbeing. "Another good sign. She's still alive."

"Is she?" he asked. "Was that her or an illusion?"

"That was her," Auslan answered with confidence. "Answering a mystical call. She's *alive*, and the Valsharess's vision is still on our path."

"Wait, what?" Shyntre drew back. *"Her* vision? Not yours?"

"Yes, the one that predicted Sirana will come back."

"How do you know about that?"

"Sirana told me. Or tried to."

"I don't understand."

Auslan swallowed, tracing his face before meeting his eyes. "She climbed into the pit *twice*, to help each of us, and she climbed back out. She could have turned away and left one or both of us there, especially when the storm arrived. She didn't. It means she hasn't forgotten us, and she isn't captured. She *could* come back."

Indulging in this fragile hope which felt far too dangerous. Shyntre felt nauseated. "She was still carrying your child, too. What does *that* mean?"

The Consort's expression sobered, and he shook his head. "Other than that, she still carries, I don't know. I haven't seen anything about the child."

"Have you…tried?"

"No." His eyelids fluttering as his gaze wavered. "It does not work like that. And I'm not certain I *want* to know."

"Why not?"

The healer dragged his eyes away, looking toward the washing buckets. He noticed the gently steaming water.

"Oh! You already activated the stone!"

"Wait, Auslan—"

The Consort had a spring in his step as he dipped to pluck his discarded shirt off the floor then pulled down his bottoms to slip them off as well; he was clearly eager for his standing bath. Shyntre sighed as he watched the cleaning ritual begin. Now that the healer could do it himself, the wizard wouldn't be able to distract him from doing it right.

"Come on," the beautiful bua invited him. "Scrub clean with me."

That was a good idea regardless. Much better if the room reeked less of sex and the buas weren't dozing naked in bed together the next time Matron Thalluen stepped in.

Shyntre swung his feet over to touch the floor and stood up to join in the baths and laundry. Now that there were two sets of hands, the work would be done quicker.

THE SECRET PANEL OPENED AROUND THE TIME THE BUAS expected their next meal, and they had plenty of dirtied supplies waiting to be removed. What neither males expected was for a familiar cait to poke her head in first.

"Natia?" Auslan asked.

She grinned. "Auslan! You're feeling better, I can tell!"

"Um, does the Matron know you're here?" Shyntre asked.

The cait slipped into the room and turned around to accept an infant from Matron Thalluen as she stepped through as well.

"The Matron is aware, yes," Rohenvi said dryly.

Both buas stood and bowed.

"Matron Thalluen," Shyntre said.

"Can we help you?" Auslan asked.

"No, it will be faster if I just take care of things. Natia agreed to watch Vekika during that time."

The adults watched the cait approach the fresh, neat bed, her face frowning in concentration as she carried an alert, baby Davrin held close to her chest. With care, Natia placed Vekika on her back before climbing up herself, sitting with her legs hanging off the side. She smiled again, looking between the two buas.

"You've done great work, Shyntre, wow! He looks so much better!"

Shyntre bowed his head mutely to the child and looked to one corner, biting the inside of his cheek while Auslan laughed without guilt.

"Yes, the wizard is discerning and clever in his solutions," said the Consort. "Plus, he never shies away from working hard with his hands."

Oh, fucking Goddess, Ta'suil…

Shyntre couldn't tell if Rohenvi suspected anything as she inspected the drying clothing and blanket, and checked on other changes of clothes, washing supplies, and sustenance.

"I would appreciate it if you sat with Natia and visit for a while, Auslan," she said, preparing her first trip out. "She's been asking about you every cycle since you healed Drani."

"Of course, my Matron." He bowed, his voice filled to the brim with warmth and gratitude. "I shall take complete care with her."

All waited until Rohenvi nodded once before the healer headed to the bed to sit with the two young caits. A mere moment later, Natia had convinced Auslan to try picking up and cradling the heir of the House.

Shyntre caught himself holding his breath.

"Hold her like this," the child directed. "Watch her head."

For a split instant, Shyntre saw Ta'suil holding Sirana's daughter instead of her tiny sister. The Consort's smile had always been gorgeous, but a fresh, unfamiliar joy touched it as he learned how to properly cradle a baby.

Now he's perfect.

Shyntre swallowed, shaking his head mockingly at himself before looking to Rohenvi for a distraction. "May I ask a favor, Matron?"

She paused and faced him. "Yes?"

"Have you any, well, any books?"

"Books?"

He shrugged. "I could read to them to pass some time until my Mother returns. Or I could even teach Natia if you've got any lessons for her?"

Rohenvi paused and frowned, thinking this over. "Hm. Interesting proposal. I'll have to think about that last one, but I *do* have a few books, mostly about the known dangers while Deep Trading."

He smiled slightly. "Sounds exciting."

The Matron chuckled, shaking her head. "If you use further imaginings, perhaps. Written mostly as detailed description and observations, for the benefit of a traveler coming after an early explorer. It's much too detailed to keep a child enraptured."

Shyntre's smile became whole. "That sounds amazing, Matron. And I have many imaginings I could add. I'd be obliged to see it."

She bowed her head. "Very well. I'll retrieve them from my office. Do take care of them, as they are priceless to me."

"We're agreed, Matron. I often care for the archives in the Wizard's Tower."

"Oh, really? Is any book or scroll is priceless to you?"

"For the most part, but it does depend on what it is. For example, a detailed account of what lies outside the Great Cavern?"

Shyntre shared a look with Auslan.

"Such shared experiences have no equal."

CHAPTER 19

THE PEOPLE OF MANALAR GREW FEARFUL AS THE DAYS warmed.

Those who could were hoarding supplies as the markets of the entire region burred with disappointments punctuated by impotent shouting. Short tempers flared in the streets every day, whether cobbled or trampled dirt, occasionally erupting into violence to fight over what remained.

In the wealthy district, the Templari might enter a manor every other day, by intimidation or force, to seize the taxes and tithing due to the Temple who strengthened their defense. Some would not fully disclose what resources were available otherwise.

In the poor districts, preferably outside the walls, the God Warriors would do the same as they conscripted the young men who did not answer the first summons. The work they'd been doing must be left to the women, children, and elderly.

Some Manalari were trying to escape as refugees before the Ma'ab army could lay siege. The *Dyos Guerrimos* were sent to chase them down on horseback, to capture them and drag them back.

"If men are well enough to flee," the Archbishop Keros said to his High Inquisitor, "they are well enough to fight."

"I have heard some of them claim not to be worshippers of the Temple, your Holiness," said the High Inquisitor Vene Kegyek, his tone neutral as he touched the sunburst pendant resting on black and grey garments. "There are Dwarves among them, and travelers from Augran and Taiding who were denied safe passage to the river."

Their leader, dressed in unique vestments of striking blue, silver, and gold, appeared amused and contemptuous at once.

"They use our roads," he said, "trade in our markets, drink from our cisterns, and pay their taxes to shelter with us. They are all pilgrims of a sort, chosen to be here in the City of the Sun during our time of need. By the end of this, some will see the error of their neglect, and those shall be grateful to He who provided that protection and prosperity."

The two men stood far above the streets, high inside the Temple, comfortable and quiet within the opulent tower office with a north-facing window. From so far up the slopes of Mount Sonai, they could see almost as much of the city and surrounding landscape as those assigned at the Crest watchtower.

"I expect we'll see the blackness oozing through the hills before we smell their stench," Keros mused. "I am told we have less than a day at that point."

The High Inquisitor nodded. This was one difficulty when a fight came to a city occupying the entire side of a mountain. The only direction with an unobstructed view was to the west, where the streets and roads sloped downward toward the visible rivers, farmers' fields, and Dwarven hills spreading their bounty out before the City of the Sun.

Even now, Musanlo's morning light touched the Big Ker River, making it sparkle like diamonds. No enemies had ever come from that direction in enough numbers to be worrisome.

To the east and behind Manalar was the massive, vertical cliff of Mount Sonai, a face impossible for even a small group to scale. At the bottom lay the jagged ravines and canyons filled with obstructive boulders and more steep land flanking both sides. The evergreen trees spread out enough to provide little shade or cover.

From the Crest watchtower, they could see any approach on their blind side in plenty of time for the mages of Manalar to use their proven methods. It took only a tiny fraction of the city's population to trap and crush men foolish enough to be seen coming from the direction of sunrise.

From the north and south, however, lay the rest of the Raguruos Mountains to which Mount Sonai belonged. This chain of peaks offered cover to close the distance with Manalar, though the series of smaller cliffs on either side of the city led to their famously tall defensive walls. Even better hidden, the land did not welcome hostile approach.

To use the Raguruos to reach the city meant there must be a point where invaders had only one direction to go to avoid the traps and kill points near the impassable walls. To make themselves known, an army must spill out onto the fertile fields of the west side.

"In past sieges," the Archbishop mused, gazing north, "the enemy always cut off the main city from the Big Ker river and its fields, confident to a fault that these were our only sources of food and water."

Vene smiled, understanding the peace in his leader's tone. "They do not understand the full blessings of *Pisc'sagrad*."

"Well for us that outsiders know little about the sacred pool, else we may welcome a siege year after year, until the grasses and crops are stomped into oblivion."

"Of course, your Holiness."

Emil Keros turned from the yellow-tinted window, still the fit and perfect image of an Archbishop after twenty years standing on high. His warm brown skin showed the decades he'd lived but his hair still possessed plenty of natural auburn alongside the silver in his wavy hair and short-trimmed beard, neither of which showed signs of thinning.

That his slate-blue eyes seemed as penetrating as the blond Capitan Isboern had convinced Vene that the people sought this trait in their leaders, or at least were more likely to trust them— unlike his own dark, Northern eyes. The Inquisitor still regretted that his much redder hair had not remained another decade; he'd gone silver and white prematurely.

"But we are quite familiar with our own lands, are we not?" Keros remarked. "What we lack sufficient information on is this shield our spitting daeva is bleating about."

"Yes, your Holiness," Vene replied, dipping his chin. "Although, the Capitan somehow gleaned that it will be familiar to us in the marking of the sun and perhaps as bright a color."

"Indeed? How interesting." Keros frowned. "Was the black demon to steal it, if such a relic exists?"

"I must assume so, but Isboern and I are in agreement that we should find it first if it lies within these walls as the captive seems to believe."

"Fascinating."

"I've found nothing in the Temple archives but haven't asked the Clast Brothers for their insights."

"Do not," the Archbishop replied firmly. "Not yet. There is somewhere I'd like you to visit first."

Vene felt a chill of premonition between his shoulder blades. "Where do I search next, your Holiness?"

"The Temporal library in the Bestirs Quarter. Chaplain Vorbines may help narrow your focus with mention of a 'sun shield.' Have no worry. He knows when to keep his mouth shut."

Vene clasped the sunburst hanging from his neck and bowed his shoulders, thankful to hide his consternation behind closed eyes. His feeling had been correct, and perhaps he should have borne the courage to go there first and not waste a full day among the fretting and arrogant scholars in the Temple.

From the smirk on Emil's face as the Inquisitor left the office, Vene was certain he remembered what happened the last time they had visited the Temporal Library together.

More tests of loyalty. More trials of faith.

I shall pass them all.

"SUN'S BLESSING, CATECHIST OF TRUTH. WHAT BRINGS YOU here today?"

Vene motioned a blessing to the Chaplain as he stepped out of the daylight; behind him, Vorbines closed and locked the door with his key as expected. The Temporal Library was not open to the public, and the Inquisitor was one of the few who could open the iron gates and arrive unannounced.

"My eternal mission," Vene answered, letting his eyes adjust as his nose tickled, threatening a sneeze. "Seeking answers from those who know."

The short and lean elder betrayed his nervous thoughts. "Ah, of course. A silly question. Forgive me, High Inquisitor."

Vene smirked. "Forgiven. For today, I expect those who know about what I seek have been dead a long time."

"Indeed, and I am here to assist with all that you need."

"Good."

The library was dusty and dim from too many packed shelves and not enough windows. A casual glance provided clear signs that many tomes and scrolls had not been moved in years.

"I am cleaning, Truthseeker," Vorbines volunteered, "but started on the top level, as dust tends to settle low. I have not made it to the foyer yet."

Vene grunted. "Are you alone?"

"I am, yes. My last apprentice was excused to join the defense training three weeks ago."

"Excellent."

The Inquisitor led himself in walking about that first level, passing through three doorways deep into the library and toward the stairs at the far end. He listened for whispers or shuffling of the living *or* the dead.

Nothing yet.

"Does it ever seem like you are not alone, Chaplain?"

"Musanlo is with me, Catechist."

Sigh.

"What of the less savory spirits?" Vene asked directly, inspecting each room as the old man in drab robes followed him. "Do they ever try to enter? Or do you hear objects moving around at night?"

Vorbines fretted with his swollen fingers. "Not such that I have borne witness, Truthseeker. I maintain all the protections recommended by the Temple, and my vigil has never lapsed. I am unaware of a breach but confess the dust encroaches without an assistant."

Vene placed his black-gloved hand on the banister, gazing up the unlit stairs constructed using the dark, ancient timber hauled from the Raguruos slopes. He was astonished how long this library had lasted with only modest repairs.

All their oldest governing buildings were like this, still in fine shape at their foundation. They were said to have been designed and constructed by Dwarves for the ancient Lords then consecrated for the Church's use when Iarmod Tefornin cleansed the sacred pool almost four centuries ago.

Vene could believe it. Frequent maintenance and major reconstruction always seemed to be happening with the newer structures of Manalar. Some of those just three centuries old served better to be demolished and rebuilt from the ground up.

These pre-Consecration properties required far less effort and expense to maintain them. For this reason alone was this archive still here, locked up with a curtain of evergreens hiding it from street view. Only select members of the Temple ever came here.

Sometimes even we must look beyond the light and into the darkness which necessitated our creation.

The High Inquisitor climbed the stairs, slow and deliberate, peering into the shadowed corners of the second-floor hallway which offered three doors. By design, this archive wasn't quick to navigate; the stairs upon which he stood did not continue to the top floor he knew existed. The same as he must cross the whole first floor to get to the second level, he must turn back across the library to reach the stairs to the final level.

Which door was it?

Chaplain Vorbines waited without speaking, swallowing the question if the Catechist needed help. What did it matter? Vene was going to check them all, anyway. He indicated the nearest one.

"Open this door, Chaplain."

"Yes, Catechist."

The old man brought out his long, metal keys and knew which one to use first. The mechanism clunked within the frame, and Vorbines pushed on the stout handle to open it a crack. He did not enter first, fearing offense to his visitor more than anything kept inside.

Taking the first step in, Vene knew this was neither the room leading to the stairs nor one holding any hint of death. He wasted a little time walking around the shelves, confirming the shelves were a bit cleaner up here but exited soon enough.

"Open the next one."

The middle door was similar to the first; no alcove leading to stairs, no whispers in a dead tongue. It was also pitch black until Vorbines brought in his lantern, for the center room lacked windows.

Hmph. Of course, it would be the one farthest away.

"And the next, Chaplain."

Vorbines had anticipated this, pushing the door open the moment the other man spoke. He stepped aside and waited as the Inquisitor entered.

The chill was here.

Vene crossed the threshold and encountered the sensation he'd awaited from the moment the Archbishop gave his directive. The third room would have an outside wall where a window would make sense yet was as lightless as the center one. An odd choice in construction but appropriate for the room most likely to hold a ghost.

One cannot pass to the third level without encountering her terror in the dark.

"Light," Vene ordered, holding out his hand for the lantern which the Chaplain relinquished promptly.

After his "silly" greeting, the old librarian did not ask what the Catechist searched for, if anything. Vene was glad for the lack of distraction. He wouldn't speak about records of any ancient sun shield until he knew all who may be listening.

She was there in the corner, maintaining a semblance of femininity in her wraith's form. Her hair must have been blonde in life, and quite long, but appeared now like mist barely kept and acting as a death shroud. Blended with her hair was a memory of robes. She seemed civilized, not naked, wild, and hungry.

Her face, however, was the worst thing about her. Where her eyes should be was only darkness. Twin voids gazed out of a chalk-white, expressionless mask, ready to draw the unwary into the endless pit.

Vene had faced that peril only once when he'd tried to banish her from the library. He could not draw out her true name, however, and this had led to his failure half-witnessed by the Archbishop those years ago. The Inquisitor was convinced he'd been forgiven because Emil couldn't sense her at all. His Holiness doubted she was real.

Vene wished he could be as certain.

"Chaplain?"

"Yes, Catechist?"

"I fancy some hot tea while I search this room."

"At once!"

"Make some for yourself as well."

"Certainly. Ah, are you peckish?"

"No, I will pass."

Vene closed the door once Vorbines had gone from sight and his feet touched the bottom of the stairs. With care, the Inquisitor set down the lantern of glass and metal on the center table, as far from the shelves as possible.

The translucid ghost didn't so much as turn her head while he crossed the room to check the opposite door which would lead to the next floor. He found it locked, so returned to stand near the warm light in the middle of the small room.

Vene wasn't sure whether her eyes followed him; he couldn't tell if she was in a damned state of limbo or aware of the present simply waiting for him to speak. Perhaps she would vanish when he next turned his back, or lunge and attempt to possess him. Either way, he could not turn from her.

I shall not tempt her.

Clasping his sunburst pendant, Vene spoke his command. "Give me sign you hear me, shade. Now."

The apparition turned her head toward him. He looked away, aware that his voice grew harsh from dread.

"Do you still speak?"

Her mouth opened, swimming with grey and without teeth or tongue. The whispers which emanated from her was no language of the living, and Vene shuddered. She was not one of those chained and damned in the crypt beneath the Temple but somehow conveyed the same meaning.

"Is it time, seeker?"

Indeed, the time had come to face her again, a purpose to serve in so clearly hearing the wraith where she lurked. There must be a reason, or Emil wouldn't have sent him here alone.

The High Inquisitor always had purpose in where he went and why. For as long as the Archbishop did not witness *how* he obtained his confessions, his verifiable truth, His Holiness upon Mount Son-ai could forgive him for the greater good.

"I do seek something, yes. But why are you here?"

"I cannot leave the library."

"Did you die here?"

She paused. *"I do not know."*

Vene swallowed. "Do you know this library?"

She bowed her head. *"Yes."*

"What purpose did you have to it?"

"Archivist. Caretaker."

"Can you read what you care for?"

"Yes."

Impossible. Vene ground his teeth. "What do you choose to read?"

She turned her head toward the far door. *"Mostly what is left open for me to read."*

The Inquisitor observed the partly dusted shelves. "You cannot move the tomes? Or unroll the scrolls?"

She shook her head in the negative. *"They drop to the floor. It damages them."*

Vene huffed through his nose. "Do you remember what was here which you once cared for?"

"Yes. I care for them still."

Vene weighed his next question, tamping down his regret. *We are running out of time.*

"I must find any records in this archive which speak of a day-yellow shield with the markings of the sun, a relic of note in a past time. Could you show me where to search?"

"Yes."

She turned her head away and began to float parallel to the far shelves. Vene froze in terror, watching her mimic a walk without a glimpse of feet touching the stone floor. Too late, he called out as she vanished through the locked door.

"Wait!"

She was gone, the chill fading with her.

"Oh, damn."

Vene opened the door to the descending stairs and clasped the banister as he shouted downward.

"Chaplain! Come up here and unlock this door!"

"I'm sorry, sir?"

"Come here and unlock the door! I must see the third floor, now!"

"But your tea—"

"Finish it afterward. Bring the keys, for God Eye's sake!"

"Yes, Truthseeker!"

The old man hustled up the stairs, wincing and out of breath by the time he met Vene in the third room, fumbling with his keys. Vorbines opened the door quickly enough that the Inquisitor could hold his tongue.

Vene took the lantern and strode up to him. "I've changed my mind. Keep the tea downstairs. I will come for it when I'm ready."

"A-and if you need more keys, Catechist?"

Vene glanced at the confusing mass of unmarked metal in the old man's trembling hands. He grunted. "I will call you again. Go downstairs."

"Yes, sir."

The Inquisitor hurried to climb the stairs to the third floor, only to spot the single door awaiting him. He shouted downward, "Wait!"

"Yes, Catechist."

The Chaplain hadn't left as promptly as the ghost.

THE THIRD FLOOR HELD ONLY ONE LARGE ROOM WITH A VAULT-ED ceiling, windowless, spacious, and recently cleaned. The air was a bit stale but comfortable; Vene thought it should have been much warmer during this time of the year. The walls seemed soundproof as he could hear absolutely nothing of the city outside.

His spectral archivist stood next to a shelf of no memorable feature. Once he had closed the door and stepped her way, the ghost pointed at a top shelf well above her head. Vene wondered why she didn't just float up to indicate her pick but said nothing while sought the step ladder and placed it where he could climb to inspect the high place himself.

"What tome am I looking for, shade?"

"The epic poem of Yuresti on the Longlands."

The Inquisitor frowned at her and peered at the few scripts visible along the edges; most were either unmarked or had no place to mark them. He began pulling them out one at a time, frowning at the foreign markings on the front. Several had not even that.

Some archivist.

"Kurgeshtuk," she said.

Startled, he clutched the ladder and shelf. "What?"

She did not repeat the sound, but continued pointing a long, hazy finger at something. The Catechist of Truth touched one piece after another until she moved. A nod.

This one. Very well.

Vene tugged it loose and carefully descended the ladder to bring the large, thin portfolio to one of the tables where he laid it out. Carefully opening the crackling cover, he scowled at the brown, brittle parchment.

I can't read any of this.

Suddenly, the ghost was looming over his shoulder, and he jumped in fright when he turned his head.

"Nomuli sancji," he whispered, crossing his surging heart.

The archivist did not recoil at the prayer but granted a slight nod as she seemed to recognize the text without her eyes.

"Can you read this?"

"Yes."

"Read it to me."

She started at the beginning, and Vene moved his chair back from the table, pulling out the modest book he kept for his interrogations to make notes for himself. He wouldn't use it for some time as he listened to a bard's tale spoken in a hushed, ethereal whisper without much inflection. The sound made him shudder multiple times.

Slowly, a tapestry formed in his head. Every so often, she would stop reading and wait, and he would turn the page for her.

Once, there had been a people here before the Diabolic Lords of Rophan, but their city was still called Manalar. A few Dwarves were mentioned, but no Ma'ab. Instead, there were the "Orchesh Sons" from the Longlands threatening to soil the sacred pool in the name of their fathers.

The barbarians began by destroying farms and raiding caravans, but they were not an army; not until the clans convinced each other to ride together and encroach on the "stone house" which had been built over their holy site.

Vene Kegyek frowned as he listened to the ghost describe the powerful horses and giant dogs which made the strength of one Orchesh Son seem like three.

Could they mean the Kurgan of the Steppes? But they have never come this far south. They stay on their side of the Raguruos in the colder climes and harry the Ma'ab.

The Kurgan did not tend to bother with Noiri towns unless it was a particularly harsh winter on their steppes, and even then, they were brief raids for supplies. The riders of the Steppes were among the wildest and sturdiest of men.

*But they **are** men. Just mortal flesh and blood.*

A Noiri man with the family name of Kegyek would know better than most in the City of the Sun that the Kurgan were not these "Orchesh" things described in the tale.

Somehow causing raging insanity to spread like a virulent plague among their fighter groups.

The region had been descending into chaos, and people grew hungry even before the Orchesh made their first attack to seize the pool which the defenders barely fended off. Finally, the long-winded tale introduced the Godblood Yuresti who swore a life-oath to be Defender of the Mount.

Vene sneered to hear this. *Godblood? Again?*

To discover this idea was a tradition from long before the Bishops shouldn't surprise him. The people of Manalar always needed their "chosen one" touched by the Sun God in times of vulnerability and violence.

Once, that chosen man had been Iarmod Tefornin.

But this was no siege or armies meeting to do battle. The threat from Orchesh embraced stealth and strategy, tactics meant to inspire a sense of everlasting conflict, where one did not know when the violence would break out next. Yuresti sought a vulnerability of the Orchesh to force them to parley, and he could only do so by traveling to the Longlands to learn more about them.

"He traveled by the Sun's light itself, carrying a shield of pure gold, bearing the blessing of sun and moons—"

Vene's boot clomped onto the wooden floor as he sat up straight in his chair. "Stop! What? Repeat that last line."

He evaded her black gaze by turning his ear, listening intently to the line again and what came next.

"A gift from the ancients long buried amid the bleeding sands," she continued, *"the Shield of the Soaring Sun, Mitneh'thran, awakened to reflect the spirit of its bearer. With Yuresti, they calmed minds and erased fear, aiding in the search for peace."*

"And what happened to it?" Vene asked. "What became of this shield after the Orchesh retreated?"

The archivist tilted her head. *"That did not happen."*

"What? What did happen?"

She returned to reading aloud, and the Inquisitor rubbed his face as the language was further draped in ribbons and flowers until he could not tell how much time had passed, either in the tale or in this attic. Eventually, he pieced together that the shield had been stolen and taken north before it could be brought back to the city. It was lost for a time.

"Stolen?" the Inquisitor groaned. "So, there is no shield within the city walls. The demoness wastes our time."

I shall make that smirking bitch suffer one hour for every useless one I spent tracking a vapor trail...

"Within city walls," the archivist repeated. *"Yes."*

"Hm?"

The shade stepped beside the ladder and pointed. Sighing, Vene climbed again and found what she wanted him to find: another bardic tale, but this one not as long.

About Yuresti's great-grandson.

The man who recovered the golden shield from the "exiles in ice." This time, Furdrick found aid among the Kurgan who understood the threat of this foreign menace.

The Ma'ab.

The High Inquisitor gripped the arms of his chair tightly, too long since he had taken any notes.

"They buried Mitneh'thran with the Magicept Furdrick upon his death, for he lived long enough without using it that many had forgotten its face."

"Buried? Where was Furdrick buried?"

"The undercroft of the Temple of Manalar."

The crypts.

Could it be that no one had looted those tombs of everything useful by now? Had the tombs truly been ignored and forgotten before Vene arrived?

The Inquisitor had begun to sweat. *I shall have to go down there after all.*

Perhaps he should have when insistent ghosts first blocked his path.

Vene swallowed. "While we're here, archivist. Do you remember anything about a 'deathless one,' who may be returning? Whether in a tome or not, what do you know?"

She was still for some time, the lines of her form vaguer than when she'd first left him for the top floor. After what seemed a trance, she answered.

"I know not of a deathless one."

Remarkably, the Inquisitor believed he had met the first woman who didn't attempt lying to him first.

She doesn't because she can't.

"Very well."

Unnervingly weak, Vene pushed himself up from his chair. He was truly exhausted as he replaced the documents where he'd gotten them, parched and seized with a ravenous desire to fill his belly. He had drained his mage's strength, he knew. For a time, the High Inquisitor could not cast a single spell even to startle inconvenient zealots.

By the time Vene had made it safely off the ladder, the shade was gone.

Or perhaps she is still here. I am only unable to see across the veil.

Having gotten what he'd come for, Vene returned to the bottom floor to drink that tea before returning to the Temple. Vorbines asked no questions, not even if the Catechist had found what he sought. The old librarian had a little food ready to eat on short notice, but it was cold and dry. It also wasn't enough.

I must recover before I tell Keros where to search for this shield.

Soon after, Vene passed back out of the iron gate and decided to stop somewhere to eat, first, lest he be summoned the moment his foot touched the hallowed ground.

If I do not, he will see what I've done to find our answer.

CHAPTER 20

SOMETHING WAS ODD ABOUT THE FALCON BOY, THE "PAGE" who did most of the dirty work while the Godblood's men guarded Jael's cell.

So overwrought without his bird in view.

A discussion between the Godblood and the Templari had been required, but the knights tolerated the trained bird down here for as long as the page cleaned up after it and kept it quiet.

Mostly, it remained unobtrusive and alert, occasionally pouncing on vermin that crept too far out from the wall. If anyone made a sudden move toward the boy, as Jael had unfortunately discovered, the bird shrieked like it intended to tear down the walls with its beak and talons. Ironically, the city soldiers saw more benefit in the falcon after this.

It sounds an alarm no one can ignore.

Jael realized by now that this was the same bird which had given away her presence and helped get her captured, though she also knew that the Godblood and his Templari had been searching for her anyway. The falcon had functioned more like a dog with a scent to follow rather than as the deciding mind in the hunt.

None had known why she'd come, however. Willven Isboern had needed to touch her skin, to ask her mind-to-mind. Shocking how he'd pulled her Queen's secrets out so easily, slipping around the geas. Jael had been instantly terrified.

How else could the mindflayer puppet her or disrupt the memories and willpower she had left? Perhaps he'd even plant a geas of his own!

She had attacked him while she had willpower to try.

Hoping they'd kill me quickly.

A few crossbow bolts had found their mark but didn't end her life. The Godblood had prevented his men from finishing her off. She woke here without so much as a scab or a scar to show where she'd been hit.

Someone healed me with magic.

The Godblood visited her when he could, as had many other snarling and sneering man-dogs, and Jael had determined that the psion's interference *hadn't* broken her geas.

I still have tasks to do.

What was more, now that she knew what to expect from Isboern, she worked much harder to cover her thoughts when the thought-reader wanted to "talk" without words. The blond man hadn't learned much more from her than he had on her capture.

But maybe he isn't trying yet to rip it from me.

Jael shuddered.

So, where did the page boy fit into all this? The youth didn't try to talk to her. Not that Jael wanted him to, but noteworthy in that every man down here had tried at least once before growing bored or unsettled with her silent stares.

The drab-looking boy only worked, doing the distasteful jobs around the prison while trying to hide tears from the men keeping the Witch Hunters away. Even Isboern's trusted men didn't seem too familiar with the falcon boy. Other than having a sharp-eyed and well-trained animal to help keep watch, why was he chosen to observe the "demon" when so few were?

They act like they believe I can't cast spells or do more than they can do.

The longer Jael remained alive, the more that possibility troubled her in determining her fate. At least a few of the Templari were mages, if not all of them, and Isboern seemed capable of psionics *and* magic.

A combination which explains his title with the people.

Even that dour, black-robed old man who'd visited a few days ago was a mage, scaring off the barking enforcers when they refused to leave.

I only have so much defense against mages while having nothing to turn back around on them.

And the longer the Humans kept her, the more they would see her thinning resistance with no way to hit back unless she got lucky with her fist or foot. They would do whatever they wished with her.

I am so fucked.

The youngest Red Sister was almost certain that failing in her geas would kill her. While the pain had only been hinted at so far, and it was excruciating, perhaps this would be the quicker way out of this cage. At least it wouldn't be decades of being passed around between Human mages, be they Manalari or Ma'ab, as an enslaved peculiarity.

Sometimes, when her guards were quiet or asleep, Jael closed her eyes against tears leaking out. Circumstances and her eventual fate hadn't changed that much from the one meant for her when the Sathoet first arrived at her House. Back then, Rausery and Sirana had appeared to rescue her, to hide her from the Sanctuary within the Sisterhood, and to give her a fighting chance against grey, psionic Dwarves.

That won't happen this time.

Jael had been given her base clothing, if not her boots, bracers, or leather armor; they were even clean. She had covered her nudity voluntarily after losing the wager that she could enrage the Witch Hunters to kill her. Shivering with cold wouldn't help anything.

She had refused to eat or drink at first. To counter this, Isboern not only swore his "oath" that she wouldn't be poisoned or drugged, but the mute falcon boy had volunteered as the taste-tester for every delivery so far. Jael consumed everything to keep up her strength in case she got lucky enough to break out during the confusion of the coming battle.

First, I need these chains off.

The hinged manacles were barely small enough to hold both wrists, and the metal links were long enough for her to stand and perform mild exercises. From this, she could tell they expected to move her at some point and wanted to do it quickly.

The long-term torture hadn't begun yet.

Jael recognized when the Godblood entered the dungeon; either the falcon or the boy gave her tells that this was neither a changing of the guard, a new prisoner being brought into one of the farther cells, nor someone unwelcome who must be discouraged from this area.

Isboern was the only reason the falcon made a weird but soft cheeping or when the cleaning boy smiled.

"Capitan!" greeted the four guards as one, offering their salute.

Their lead officer must have returned it yet his stride neither slowed nor stopped until he reached her door. She heard it being unlocked before torchlight poured in through a crack before splitting open wide.

Jael squinted, blinked through tears, and climbed to her feet, reading nothing but purpose and urgency in the blond man's demeanor. Her heartbeat picked up and her ears pricked as she readied herself.

Something's going on.

She recognized the first shapes stepping in as Isboern and the falcon boy, the former slipping off his glove to clasp the latter's hand. Jael pressed back against the stone as an angry tension seized her to watch the Humans "talk" with psionics, private and much faster than any other method. Even the Templari didn't see the way their Capitan briefed this lowly page first and out of their sight.

Though she tried, Jael couldn't read the lightning-quick mash of emotions smeared across the page's face before he and the bird simply turned around and left the cell. The hovering soldiers let him by, and Jael heard the light footsteps hurrying up the stairs and out of the dungeon.

What the fuck?

"Good, you are dressed," said the Godblood, warmth carried through his voice, face, and hands; none of them contradicted the other. He even sounded relieved. "We are looking for your boots."

Jael sneered with skepticism. "Boots?"

The blond man nodded, lowering his voice; he spoke slowly and in Trade for her sake. "I spoke with the man in black. He found where to seek the shield. He would not tell me first. He meets with the Archbishop. They will be here soon."

The Davrin felt a trickle of fear to understand him. Willven Isboern had managed several visits since the man in black had checked on her. Vene Kegyek had spoken solely in Manalari, and she'd understood nothing until he said "shield."

They are looking for it. She'd suppressed an involuntary quiver. *Good.*

Afterward, Isboern managed to make her understand—without a mindlink—what the Inquisitor had threatened about the Archbishop "breaking girls" who flaunted nudity. This possible torture seemed to upset the Godblood and falcon boy much more when it was nothing less than Jael expected as a Red Sister. Nonetheless, she had put her clothes on and gave up that taunting tactic, knowing that it wouldn't make death quick with the Archbishop as it would the Witch Hunters.

That Isboern had come ahead to make sure the prisoner was dressed before the man's arrival echoed the warning like a shout in a massive cavern. The Godblood hadn't been concerned by her nakedness and attitude when the man in black was here.

But he sure as fuck is concerned now.

"This is important," said the Godblood. "Try *not* to insult the man wearing blue, silver, and gold. Especially not for amusement or rebellion. His pride is everything here. He wields great power and uses it often."

So this would be like meeting a Priestess, or maybe even the Valsharess. *I got it.* Jael scowled but nodded. "I no insult."

"Will you cooperate?"

She squinted. "Why for?"

"To find the shield."

Instantly, she nodded. "Must... m-must give you."

The Godblood looked uncertain. "The Archbishop will keep it."

Jael jerked like she'd been punched.

Pain!

"No!" she shouted. "You! Take!"

"Shh! Quiet, quiet."

Isboern glanced behind them as his men crowded the door, and he signaled to them to stand down. As they took positions on either side, their Capitan looked back at her. "Why me?"

A boiling roar rose inside, and her bottom lip quivered as her eyes flew wide and began tearing up. She couldn't speak.

"Jael," he whispered, offering his naked hand. "Let me help you."

No!

Tears flooded her cheeks as she fell against the stone wall and locked her knees to stay upright.

"Please," he implored her, offering his hand again. "The more I know why you are here, the more I can help you against the Archbishop. I've tried to wait, but we are almost out of time."

Cornered again, she heard herself growl, words escaping in her native tongue. *"Don't touch me, mind flayer!"*

Her four guards turned quickly with more footsteps coming down the stairs. All tromped into a salute.

"*Suisantifa, Lus it Viti!*" they called together.

The Godblood's expression just before he turned around to salute as well told Jael that they *were* out of time.

She peeked at the men over his metal-armored shoulder, recognizing the silver-haired Inquisitor. The man beside him had much darker brown skin and reddish-brown hair; that he was important to this temple was glaringly obvious as his stark blue robe and white sash shimmered on their own, further enhanced with gold stitch-designs and silver trim.

No one else in Manalar wore anything remotely that beautiful.

Archbishop Keros carried a small, knowing smile as he greeted Isboern. His understated suspicion and delight with intrigue became clear in his every movement and tone of his remarks.

He acts like the Conceiver.

The Godblood bowed, saluted again, carrying a confident exchange with both elder men. It seemed like the three of them had been interacting with each other a lot lately, as Jael sensed the two older men's grudging familiarity from the first moment without any gap in comprehending each other's stance or rank.

Jael also estimated that if the Temple were the size of the Valsharess's Palace, and if Isboern had come down here in such a hurry just as Kegyek had gone into a "meeting" with Keros, then they must have left for the dungeon almost immediately to catch them like this. The Templari hadn't even had time to find her boots, much less for her and Isboern to exchange much information.

Keros mistrusts Isboern even more than Kegyek. Huh bua.

Jael recalled the confidence with which the falcon boy had taken the Godblood's hand, how he and his bird had run with whatever he'd learned.

He knows his Capitan is psionic.

She was too late to wonder what she might have learned if she'd just grasped his hand without question. She'd never been the type to do such things, except maybe with Sirana.

Archbishop Keros stepped past Capitan Isboern, smiling down at her in a way which seemed to hold all the hog oil she'd smelled on her way here.

Do not taunt him.

Jael lowered her eyes, adopting a standing stance with an air of submission like she did with the Prime after she was done playing.

Out of necessity.

Keros seemed to understand. He spoke softly, cooing with pleasure in his throat before reaching to touch her left ear with his blue glove. A spark crackled along her skin, and she winced as sharp pain struck her inner ear like a needle.

Argh! Fuck.

Stubbornly, she kept her eyes down, neither frightened nor impressed. So, he pulled the same zap-tricks as the Tower wizards?

Fine.

Keros hummed, turning to quip something which urged Kegyek to chuckle, while Isboern's expression stayed placid as they continued to negotiate. Midsentence, the Archbishop reached to twist her nipple through her shirt. This action surprised Kegyek and the soldiers while finally drawing a bit of concern from Isboern.

The high priest peered at her with anticipation.

Jael didn't meet his eyes but couldn't prevent tightening one corner of her mouth and quirking one eyebrow. *Is that all, bua?*

"*Fasinate,*" he murmured.

The man had ideas.

Pfft. Figured the Witch Hunters learned it from somewhere.

The man was just another Priestess, delirious and drugged on his own sense of importance.

You'd piss your robe to meet our Queen, infant.

"We will search for the shield now," the Archbishop said in Trade. "You shall guide us, *daeva.*"

His accent was much different from Isboern's. Jael had to reattune her ear to make out the meaning. Once she did, she felt the geas take solid hold of her guts. Her head nodded that she understood his command.

Yes. Now, I hope.

They'd already wasted so much time.

Isboern motioned, and a Templar brought in her boots. Neither Archbishop nor Inquisitor liked this apparent concession, but they didn't stop her from donning them without stockings, her hands loudly jangling the chains. Then two soldiers approached to take hold of her arms while Isboern unlocked her manacles.

Wewf. Strong grip.

Jael cooperated, making no sudden moves after her wrists were free. Before Isboern told her the Inquisitor might know where to look, she might have tried to take advantage of this.

Now I can't.

She must help them.

Or the deathless one will find the shield when this city falls.

VENE PAUSED WITH THE ARCHBISHOP AS THEY BROUGHT THE demoness up the stairs and out of the prison. The long, twisting hallway was wide enough for two men abreast hauling a body between them. Somehow, this path had always seemed too narrow for that.

"Lead the way to the crypts, High Inquisitor," Keros said with a refined motion he'd practiced in front of thousands.

Vene hid his trepidation as he bowed and turned to carry the torch ahead of the group. Behind him were His Holiness, the Capitan of the Wall, and Isboern's four loyal Templari: two of them holding the demoness prisoner, the other two bringing tools at Vene's request.

The Inquisitor considered warning them in advance if there was an area into which they should not step but opted to mention it only should the ancient monk or any of its ilk encroach.

The deathly whispers grew louder when, this time, he did not choose the way toward the light. Vene was tempted to look behind him at the faces of the others, to see if they sensed anything at all, but resisted.

There was an old story in the Far North about not looking behind one's self for the ghost trailing him out of the land of the dead, that his attention fed the thread between them and gave it strength to hold on and walk where he walked. How did it work if he were walking *into* the spirits' realm, not out?

We are about to find out.

Neither mist nor fog coalesced into any shape as Vene walked past the point he'd encountered the moaning wraith before. While not quiet, it was dry, dusty, cool, and dark. The torches caught and burned numerous cobwebs draping from the ceiling while robes and boots disturbed the fine layers of silt and dirt, leaving a trail behind them.

They descended two levels of stairs; the midway point was marked with a reinforced landing rather than another floor. At the bottom and to the left, they encountered their first locked, iron gate and discovered they had no proper key that would fit.

Beyond the gate, the hallway leading out of the stairwell had been sealed with bricks not five paces beyond iron bars. To Vene, it was obvious that these bricks had been made and placed by Humans, while Dwarves likely built the rest of this subterranean space.

"Well, well," Keros remarked. "So the records were accurate. The crypt has been sealed up since the Consecration."

Vene tried not to raise an eyebrow at him. The remark was so vague and obvious that he guessed Emil said it to save face.

Perhaps he did not expect to meet a factual wall, but it is true regardless. No one has gone this way for a very long time.

No Bishop had had reason to break down such a stout barrier until now.

Capitan Isboern and two Templari worked with the tools to break the lock by force, making tremendous noise which drowned out the ghosts. Vene watched the work with Keros, aware when His Holiness glanced twice behind him at the demoness and the men holding her while Isboern worked out a plan with his tool-bearers to open the sealed entrance.

"It sounds as though we shall have to retreat up the stairs, Oh Capitan of the Wall," Keros said with amusement.

"And wait for our signal that it is safe, your Holiness, yes," answered the blond man, either not catching or acknowledging the joke.

"I'm sure you'll need all your men's strength," Keros continued. "The High Inquisitor and I shall watch the daeva."

Oh, for the love of Musanlo…

No doubt Keros wanted this moment to cajole Vene to "share" the interrogation afterward, as they'd not had time to plan next steps. The Inquisitor's face twitched in a wave of distaste. It had been years since they'd done so, for good reason, but he might not be able to refuse.

An invading army could arrive any day and we have places to be, but you would keep me there to watch you train her to lick your boots. Ugh.

Willven Isboern smiled at their leader, his charm alone seeming to make the torches brighter. "Gracious, your excellency, but five of us would be too much, we might collapse the ceiling. Three will suffice, and we will not fail our Templari oath shall keep our greatest holy officers safe from the prisoner. This is our reason to exist."

Keros chuckled. "Boy, I've practiced the sacred powers and communed with *Pisc'sagrad* itself. The Templari simply attend the defensive school of magic apart from the Temple. I can handle her."

"None doubt your worthiness and magnificence, Archbishop, and thank you for coming down here with us. Please allow us to stand by our oaths and keep you safe. We are all expendable in the coming conflict, but you are not."

"Hmph."

Vene did not convey his opinion while they wasted time tugging the placement of the female creature between them. *At least she isn't nude and parting her cheeks as distraction in an escape attempt.*

Unfortunately, such predictable tricks would work even with Keros. The middle-aged man had grown accustomed to vulnerable young girls unable to leave his topmost chambers of the Temple unless he wanted to make an example of her.

We're not in your quarters, your Holiness, but down among death and devils.

Finally, Vene broke his silence when it was clear Keros would continue debating. "We should operate with abundance of caution, your Holiness. Now is not the time to let a dispatched mischief maker from the underworld poison us from the inside. She could do it in any number of ways, and we have yet to witness what magic she wields."

Keros was annoyed with him but quickly smoothed his face. "Very well, Kegyek. Lead the way, if you must."

"The landing will be far enough," Isboern said. "You need not go to the top. Be prepared for some dust."

With a nod, Vene led the climb back up the steep stairs to the midway point. He turned around to watch Keros stand next to him and the Templari remain on the steps with their captive.

Not so much as a twitch of rebellion.

Vene and Keros knew what to expect next, and although it would have been interesting to watch Isboern especially, they could see nothing of the men at work and could barely hear anything from the bottom of the stairs.

Then the Capitan called out in Trade, "Sunburst in the hole!"

The demoness jumped, her quizzical expression moving to stark concern as she witnessed her guards cover one ear and turn their heads, while the holy men covered both ears.

"Shuiblith!" she hissed, clapping both hands to her head just before the burst exploded below.

The light flash blinded them before a cloud of dust rushed up the stairwell toward them. The demoness cried out as Vene felt fine tremors in the stone beneath their feet. When only fluttering torchlight remained and the roar of sound had passed, he heard a few lone clatters of brick dropping upon brick.

"Clear and open!" Isboern called out again. "There is a long passage behind the wall!"

He's communicating with the demoness as well.

Why was he protecting her?

"Come," Keros grunted with a cough, impatient and irritable. "Let us find this golden shield supposedly buried in the heretics' crypt."

"Yes, Archbishop."

Vene was first to step beyond the broken brick wall with his torch. He had expected the rustling and agitated whispers of the dead to intensify as they walked deeper into the mountain but frowned to admit this was not so.

The spirits were neither silent nor vanished, but...

Calm?

As the first of the living to breathe here in centuries, Vene felt stale air flow into his chest and coughed. They continued to leave marks in fine silt and to burn dusty cobwebs above their heads. Quite different were the walls which displayed complex carvings and reliefs spanning the long distance, seeming to contain a suggestion of natural elements in motion.

He wasn't the only one to notice.

"Hm," Keros began. "I thought the builders would line the way to a crypt with skulls and haunting death's heads."

"Indeed, sir," Isboern acknowledged, studying with the rest of them by torchlight. "Carvings seems to be mostly fire and water, though some could be air."

"Here is a head, Capitan," said one of the tool-bearing Templari.

"What kind of head?"

"I do not know. A river monster?"

When Vene turned around, he noticed the "head" that everyone was looking at. The demoness's gaze was curious but nothing else; she didn't know what it was. The Inquisitor paused as he considered whether *none* of the others could see it for what it was.

How could that be?

"It is a Dragon," he said.

Keros turned to him. "You recognize it, Inquisitor?"

"I do, your Holiness. From my youth. The Dwarves carved similar images up in the north country, and they last for centuries. We found it on many ruins."

The Archbishop seemed amused. "Do the squat burrowers worship imaginary beasts, then?"

"I can't say, sir. I've never known one to say so, though there are stories even among men about encounters upon the caravan roads with a Dragon in disguise."

"Heh. Surely to keep unruly children obedient," Keros replied. "An effective trick if one believes everyone who passes them could be a Dragon ready to eat them. The peasants do the same with devils."

Vene nodded but said no more, as it would only be contradictory. He reflected perhaps the stories he'd heard of red Dragons at Manalar had only come out when someone had died in his presence. He'd taken the "beasts" for granted as existing in all lands, though the color changed with the people.

The Manalari don't speak of them in public, but the Dwarves who built upon the Mount certainly recognized them the same as my kin in the North.

"I heard out west that Dragons could also be guardians," said Capitan Isboern, tapping his chin with thick-gloved fingers. "There was one said to be wandering the Lonely Ones. You could meet him in the forest mountains or on the beach, but not on the roads or in towns. They said he disliked pathways set in stone or well-known trails trampled to barrenness."

Vene squinted at Isboern. "Did the stories suggest a color of his scales?"

The Defender of the Wall seemed surprised. "Yes. Like emeralds."

Green. Red. Blue…

Keros laughed with derision as the red-eyed witch glanced between them, bewildered. They were not speaking Trade.

"Enough about this," said the Archbishop, waving his hand, once again irritable. "There are no Dragons in Paxia, no matter the monsters said to exist in the barbaric lands. This is an ignorant import from the Dwarves before the Day of Consecration. I'll send masons later to erase this false idol." Keros glared at the stone face of the Dragon. "It seems the First Bishop missed a few."

Some turns later, right and left with descending stairs in between them, Vene wasn't sure how deep below the city they were when they came upon another locked iron gate identical to the first. Fortunately, there was no sealed wall beyond it they could see, though it did bend around again to the right.

The Inquisitor heard a whisper which raised the hair on the back of his neck. *"Welcome, seekers."*

As always, no one else seemed aware of this presence.

The Templari repeated their efforts to check over and open this second gate while the rest of them waited. The screech of the hinges when they pulled it open was enough to bother the demoness but was still not as bad as Vene thought it should be after this much time.

Only now did he wonder what records the Dwarves might have of Manalar's Temple in their Halls at Taiding, considering the evidence here that they'd built this foundation. It was far too late to bring up to Keros, yet the vulnerability now seemed plausible if this passage ultimately led to the outside.

The High Inquisitor led them around the bend, at once relieved and further concerned that they encountered no second wall blocking them off. He passed through an archway and abruptly stood upon a balcony high above a cavernous room. He heard the demoness gasp as she saw something in the darkness they could not.

"*Haxa luzi,*" Isboern whispered, creating a stronger light as high and close to the ceiling as he could.

"*Nomilu sancji,*" murmured each man present, making the sign of protection and purity against evil.

The crypt was massive. Far below, no less than thirty sarcophagi lined the center of the level, orderly stone floor before disappearing into darkness. Straight paths lined the room at the narrow ends of the coffins with plenty of room to cross the space in between each. Numerous arched shelves built high from the floor vaguely resembled an insect hive.

Vene counted twenty vertically, though most of these holes in the wall were sealed with a lesser version of the wall they'd just broken down. Still, a few had crumbled part way open; even from this distance, Vene recognized white bones when he saw them.

Hundreds or possibly thousands are buried here beneath the holy Temple.

The people of Manalar today either burned their dead to rise to the Sun or left the bodies of the unworthy on the Raguruos cliffs to be eaten by the birds. This underground vault was reminiscent of the way the Noiri and the Dwarves entombed their best warriors and leaders.

"Ugh," Keros grunted, gazing around with distaste. "For certain the work of the Sunless Squats, using stone boxes to lock up the souls lest they are seared out of existence by the Glorious Eye's Judgement."

"Yet the stone coffins are sized for a man, your Holiness,"Vene said.

"Yes, I believe the failed Lords *are* buried here. We must burn this place as soon as we have the chance, lest they soil our very foundation."

The Templari said nothing, not even Isboern, though the Inquisitor did not see fear or agreement with Keros's statement, but awe and wonderment at this proof of their ancient history on this Mount.

They'll be curious for more.

"Capitan!" the Archbishop barked. "Have the daeva show us where this shield lies. We don't have time to check every coffin."

Isboern pursed his mouth. "Certainly, your excellency."

The Capitan motioned for his men to bring the creature down the long, wide steps still in good condition. They passed yet more reliefs of fire, water, and the hint of Dragons along the walls. As they descended, carvings of the dead arose as well, the skulls and standing mourners Keros had expected. There were also carvings of birds.

Crows? Possibly vultures…

Upon several of the sarcophagi, Vene gazed on the blank but beautiful face of a woman without eyes wearing tattered shrouds. He swallowed, counting six images before realizing they would continue down the line.

Like the apparition in the library.

There were differences. The archivist had not worn tatters, her hair had been visible, and there were no cracks near the vacant eyes the way this enshrouded woman bore them. In addition, birds surrounded this visage, and the more crafted imagery Vene saw, the more he was convinced they were crows.

Who is this?

Clearly, she had been worshipped here on the Mount.

The Spirit of Death? The one the slant-eyes insist on placating in their legends?

495

If so, why could he not look away?

"Inquisitor?" Keros rumbled.

He blinked. "Sir?"

"No need to study so closely. This is all getting destroyed and consecrated once we find this golden treasure. We must do it before the Ma'ab arrive."

"Uh—"

Keros looked away from Vene to the Godblood and Templari, who were dragging the demoness between the coffins. The Inquisitor jumped, his heart launching into a sprint when he noticed the bald monk from the hallway above now stood directly behind Keros with its mouth open.

Sibilant whispers escaped that unsettling maw as it lifted a hazy hand to touch the holy robes.

"No!" Vene said, hand reaching out as the Archbishop spun around.

"What did you say?!"

"Sir, uh! There is a curse near that coffin! I sense it!"

Keros turned around to look at the well-lit crypt, coming face-to-face with the gap-mouthed specter without realizing it. Vene saw a smile on the ghastly, hairless face which gave him chills.

"I sense nothing odd, Inquisitor," Keros said.

"Your... your Holiness, come, stand next to me. An ancient death goddess and her black birds are engraved on these stones. I do not understand the significance of their placement but sense some spots are simply better not to stand."

Emil rolled his eyes. "I am *one* with the sacred pool, Kegyek. I feel no weakness in my power coming here. Nothing on this Mount can harm me." He scoffed. "I dare say nothing coming from off it, either!"

Of all the pompous statements he'd heard in this service, that one Vene knew *not* to be true.

"Your excellencies!" Isboern called out from a score of coffins away. "We may have found it!"

JAEL COULDN'T SENSE SHIT DESPITE THE GUARDS POINTING HER at random places like a hunting dog. She was certain the Godblood was doing the real searching while passing his motions off to anyone who cared as if he received the insights from her.

Stop trying to help me and get the shield before the Bishop does.

She knew he'd be able to sense the enchantment, and there would be nothing else like it in this cavern built for their dead. She had only to wait though she couldn't relax as the Archbishop kept arguing with the man in black what to do next.

If this is their leadership, they are as fucked as I am.

"We may have found it!"

The grip on her arms tightened to become painful while Isboern and his two Templari chipped the aged plaster from the seam of the stone box, revealing there was a lid which could be pushed off. The Archbishop approached quickly, crowding too close behind her as he'd been doing since they'd met the first iron gate. She'd have expected to feel a caress on her ass by now if she hadn't been wearing her cloak.

She sneered where he couldn't see. *At least my compulsion is forced by a spell, you shriveled bag of knotted guts.*

Eventually, the working men braced together, counting down to push, and the scrape of heavy stone upon stone began. Instead of toppling it off the far side, they rotated it to rest askew, revealing one end first.

"Oops," one said.

"The feet," said Isboern with a chuckle. "Let us try again."

The three took the opposite positions and braced to swivel the stone cover in the other direction while she and those watching shifted to better viewing positions.

Her heart leaped in her chest when a glint of gold reflected from the Godblood's light near the ceiling. Gazing down at the skeletal corpse mostly covered by the span of metal, the Templari made hand signs they wanted to have formal meaning but was only gibberish to her.

The Archbishop growled a derisive rebuke, jerking his hand toward the body in the box with his nose wrinkled in disgust. The Templari muttered something to acknowledge him but didn't seem very apologetic while Isboern again debated with the high cleric on their approach.

Meanwhile, Jael clasped her hands together, trying not to vomit with how strong the impulse was to dive into that coffin and yank the shield free of its skeletal storage before shoving it into Isboern's hands.

It won't help. There's still a chance he'll claim it.

She tried not to think about what might happen if he didn't.

At last, the Godblood reached in with obvious respect to tug the dusty shield upward, discovering it was not held by any part of the body but had been laid on top, covering the corpse from chin to groin. It was bulkier than she'd expected; Isboern needed to do some angling and request another set of hands on the other side to aid him.

Jael shivered as the correct man held *Mitneh'thran*, testing the weight with one arm before brushing off the face of it to better see the engraving of the full Sun centered and flanked by the asymmetrical crescents of the Sister Moons. Although numerous unknown markings remained, the three celestial bodies which traveled the sky, providing the Surface with all its light, were unmistakable.

The Archbishop sneered, pointing toward those unknown markings, and the Capitan replied with solemnity, straightening his back, and lifting his chin. The man in black was silent but seemed he had something to say.

After a few more exchanges, they all looked at her.

Uh-oh.

"I must ask," Isboern began, "why you have said I must carry this."

Tears pricked her eyes as she tried with all her will to answer.

"Deathless one," she croaked.

The man in black jerked his head, his eyes wide. "What did you say?"

Jael gasped for breath, spit out excessive saliva as her stomach jerked. "Death…less…one. Comes!" She stopped on a groan.

"You seem chilled, Vene," said the Archbishop, at last deigning to speak in Trade. "Do you recognize this?"

"In…among records," he stuttered. "Only a warning."

"Warning of what?"

"Just as she says, a deathless one must be drawn to the shield."

"The Ma'ab liches?"

"I do not know, but it has been stolen before and taken North, where it was later recovered and buried here."

Another pithy gesture toward the Capitan. "Then why him? Our Defender of the Wall should not carry it. If he falls in our defense, it may be stolen again. Such treasure would be safer in the Temple vaults. Here, give it to me, Capitan."

No!

As Keros stepped into her periphery with hand outstretched, Jael doubled over and heaved, hanging between the two men. She gagged, trying to breathe.

The Godblood hesitated. "Let me talk to her first. There is more we must—"

"That is an *order*, Capitan!" growled the man in black. "I will interrogate her and find out what she hides. You defend our city. As we've *each* sworn to do."

Willven Isboern weighed his next response, glancing at her.

Jael shook her head. *Don't.*

Then the blond man bowed his head and lifted the shield up toward his superiors. "Yes, your excellencies."

No, you fucking don't!

The Davrin's leg shot out to the side, her heel landing a devastating blow into the knee of the complacent Archbishop. Keros screamed with pain and shock as he staggered and fell against the open sarcophagus. The man in black shouted in alarm as Isboern ordered all four of his Templari to restrain her further.

"Black witch!" roared the interrogator as he dragged the Bishop back from her by himself.

"We need her alive!" the blond man said.

She shouted back. "Godblood shield! Godblood shield! Manalar falls! You hear? *IT FALLS!*"

"Silence, cunt!"

Isboern's men blocked the interrogator's fist meant for her as Keros made demands from the floor, rocking and clutching his leg.

"Get the shield, Vene! *The shield!*"

"*You all die!*" Jael raged, manic as she pulled and struggled against their hold. "All *die!* Godblood carry, *he must!*"

"We will *never* allow it!" barked the man in black, turning his focus from her and lunging for *Mitneh'thran.* "The Capitan shall give it up! *Now!*"

"Do not!" she cried. "P-please!"

Isboern didn't even put up a fight. He released the shield.

He *gave* it to the wrong ones!

The pain overwhelmed her as lightning struck at the back of her head and burned through her spine. Head tilted back, she screamed, the shrill crying sustained as magic scorched her flesh through her blood, as all her organs seemed to swell and ache at once, and her limbs stiffened and contorted so tightly as if attempting to break her back.

She kept screaming, legs failing, chomping anything that tried to cover her mouth or muffle her. Her jaw locked on something leathery, and she couldn't let go as her mouth frothed, as she growled and barked as men shouted to each other around her.

Her wailing continued through it all, her skin fevered and drenched with sweat.

Cool, bare hands captured her face; she tried to throw him off.

He held on.

~Jael! Jael, can you hear me?! What's happening to you?~

She couldn't think.

Couldn't answer him.

Didn't *know*.

~Vene says you're dying! How? Show me, I can heal you again!~

Again?

She convulsed in his hold as her vision faded to black.

She couldn't see.

"Nomilu misderncorda di Musanlo," Isboern murmured, his tone imploring. Earnest. *"Diex lakar me dortua, mi Solue!"*

She felt a single thread of warmth which was *not* agony.

~Hear me! I grant you mercy, Jael. I take your pain unto myself.~

She couldn't breathe, but she grew aware of it.

She could see blue eyes watching her.

I... I-I can't breathe...!

~I shall breathe for you. You can get through this.~

No, you're wrong. There's no way out while She lives! No way... I am meant to die here!

~Only if this noxious thing maintains its grip. I am granted the strength to take it from you, to lift that unbearable weight, and banish it back where it came from. But you must want to live, Jael. You must try to escape this coercion leeching your life away!~

The man was in more pain than her.

She was in less pain than him.

Blue eyes.

~Trust me, Jael. I serve others. I serve you. I know you're not corrupted. I know you have no choice. You've tried, and I believe in your mission. I will get the shield back from Keros. You have my oath.~

Relief.

~You have the will to survive this. I know you do.~

She sucked in a breath through her clenching teeth. *Yes... I want to live.*

Everything still hurt.

~Good. Breathe again. And another. Now... when I open the cage, step out. Don't be afraid. This pain will pass.~

The psion had found the core of the spell masked within her mind. The side of him which was divine, the same soul, *did* something to it... something which the Abyss loathed him for.

The next shriek sounding through her mind wasn't hers, though it arose from the barbs of blackness trying to shred her from the inside. It was failing, coming loose, slipping off the nurturing shield the Godblood had formed around her mind and within her aura.

It no longer had a sure hold on her.

~Begone, darkness. Begone from her!~

Her curse fell back into the Void.

She was free.

Oh, Goddess...

Raw feeling flooded her, rushing in to take up every mote of space the pain had left inside herself. She'd never known it before. *So unfamiliar.*

She only realized how much she'd missed it once it began to sing.

~What is that, Jael? Something's changed.~

I don't know!

The song grew louder within the youngest Red Sister and she groaned, wrapped her arms around herself. She discovered her body lying on its side, weeping.

It's so loud!

She had never heard this before. She didn't want it to stop.

Then an enormous set of golden eyes opened within the expanse of the crypt, seeming to float in the air. Its pupils were sharp and vertical, expanding outward.

Focusing on her.

She was unsure anyone could see them but her.

★Well, well, that took some time,★ the strange voice thrummed, wrapping around her like an inquisitive blanket. *★This will become interesting, I see.★*

He chuckled. She was *almost* certain it was male.

~Jael?~

Isboern? C-can you see him?

~Who?~

Those golden eyes. They're huge.

Isboern paused, seeming to redirect his vigor while mindlinked with her. He glimpsed enough that she heard a gasp of surprise, and the reptilian eyes narrowed with amusement to see him, too.

★Hello, there, boy. Powerful mind you have.★

~Who…who are you?~ Willven asked.

★A long-time dreamer of this world.★

~Do you have ill intentions toward Jael? Or toward Manalar?~

★None at all, Godblood. I merely confirm a bargain fulfilled.★

Jael protested. *I made no bargain with you!*

The metallic eyes shifted. *★I never said you did, small one. But you are the unfortunate daughter who must jump from the nest first. There is no tucking this treasure back into the chest now.★*

Tucking back? What treasure?

The eyes shifted briefly around the crypt, landing on the Inquisitor with the golden shield slung on his back. The man in black was still helping the Archbishop to his feet. They moved bizarrely, as if the entire crypt was filled with something more viscous than water, enveloping all to slow their motion.

The creature's laugh rumbled out like an earth tremor. *Ohhh, surrounded by mages who must deal with two old promises on top of all the rest.* He looked at her. *I suggest having some fun with it, Baenar.*

Jael shook out her ears. *Have… fun?!*

Up to you. He sounded to shrug. *Regardless, I think it's time for me to Wake. It seems your Queen has been searching for me.*

The hovering gaze blinked and vanished from existence. Time within the crypt returned to normal, and men's voices filled the once-silent depths with cries, confusion, and so much cursing.

Tamuril had sent Pilla to fly around the city while she waited outside for Willven. She hid in the ill-tended garden at the back of the Temple, where none of the common people were allowed to go. Few of the Temple mages seemed to care much for the trees.

For hours she waited, breathing in the fresh, warm air and fragrance while sitting in the shade. Gradually, she fell into her bond-trance with her friend, seeing through her falcon's eyes, and thinking how little seemed to change in the city day to day.

She did recognize one of her sister's Humans, though.

The man was strong with brown hair but not particularly striking or memorable. He walked around, seemingly casual when speaking to others, but she recognized a tracker's behavior when she saw it.

He's looking for something.

Or someone?

Should I send a message about Jael through him, or does Krithannia already know?

The Druid sat in indecision, daring not to leave until she received some contact from Willven. At the same time, she considered her elder's reach, who was so much smarter to be so successful living in Human cities for centuries.

Krithannia must already know, mustn't she?

When Camden's beloved grandson reappeared, however, Tamuril felt his distress and concern before reading his face. She reached out for his hand, and Willven clasped hers, his hold gritty and damp with sweat.

~We found the shield in the crypt, and Jael is alive for now. But Keros and Kegyek took her and the shield elsewhere in the Temple, probably the upper floors. She's no longer in the dungeon, and I have no way to protect her now.~

Tamuril gasped in alarm as many more details passed through her, almost too many to grasp.

~If you have any way to tell your sister,~ he thought as urgently as she'd ever felt, *~do it now. Tell her, if there's help planned for the Davrin prisoner, they must hurry. Come from the south, there will be fewer eyes on the wall. I want you to stay there as well, Tamuril. Please.~*

Y-yes, Willven. I understand.

The Capitan attended his infinite duties while the page boy slipped out of the garden and into the city streets, following her falcon to that tracker. She pressed herself hard, determined to reach him quickly. Long distances passed beneath her feet.

There.

Sweating in the setting sun, she approached the Guildsman in disguise but showed him the hand sign Krithannia had taught her. Her clever sister had insisted she practice until she got it just right.

His eyebrows lifted with interest. He was paying attention now, but she waited until he returned the proper response before moving somewhere out of sight to talk.

Yes. Tell your Mistress to hurry.

For even having suffered at the Dark Sisters' hands in their underground territory, the Naulor still did not wish upon their youngest the worst at the hands of the Bishops of Manalar.

Sirana had been wrong; the younger sister *wasn't* sent to kill Willven. She had been sent to give him something to help him in the war. Failing in this had almost killed her. Her Queen's punishment was death.

Tamuril wept once she'd left the Guildsman behind.

I… I believe him.

The Red Sister had survived her ruler's sentence and could tell them more, if she could be rescued from a very bad place.

She needs help. There must be a better way. An escape from the coming fall.

A way out for all of us.

The Guild has found my missing sister, and she is in grave danger. I am part of a team again, intent on slipping into the heart of a war. I failed to find Gaelan before it was too late. I would not fail Jael.

Battle For Manalar: Sister Seekers Book 8 Coming in 2022!

Thank you for reading about Sirana
and her journey on Miurag!

Help others to find the dark epic fantasy they want and leave a review for Book 7 at smarturl.it/ss7gd

★★★

Follow Etaski and Subscribe to her newsletter at www.etaski.com

Are you interested in reading more about Sirana's world? Do you like maps, timelines, and extra details about the people, places, and objects in the story? Be sure to visit Etaski's series lore at World Anvil! www.miurag.etaski.com

Follow Etaski on Amazon for new release updates and don't miss *Battle For Manalar!*

Acknowledgements

So many years at this, and you all are still here reading the rough stuff and cheering me on! Thank you so much my friends and beta readers, Eris Adderly, Ile Depak, Axelotl, Leonard, Dark Pulse, NecrosisBob, & Pastor of Muppets.

This is the first book I have written as a full-time author. I want to acknowledge and send so many thanks to My Hubs for believing in me and making this possible for us.

My gratitude endures, Doc Kangey, for your gifts of time, skills, and tutoring for the cornerstones of my career online. Check out our hard work and lore yet to come at Etaski.com & Miurag.Etaski.com

Finally, to my top patrons who helped make it possible and support all my efforts to develop my goals in every way:

Sir Cumference, Baelus, Jesse C., Does, John K., Julie S., Paul B., Carla H., Briana R., Josanna, RainbowNight, Lesley PLAY, Kalculyszero, NotSoWeird, Zenor☃, Kelly D., Lady Dia Meter, Raymond T., Lexanii, Zeroharas, Johnathon Matlock, Chris R., and Roy Meyer, and in loving memory, Stacy Meyer.

ABOUT THE AUTHOR

Etaski has entertained herself with fantasy stories since the first day she sat on a school bus looking out the window. When hand-written letters were disappearing, she scribbled no less than five pages to be worth the postage. Her early stories were written by hand, and she had a writer's callus and three embarrassing novels before graduating high school.

She studied science, archaeology, history, and theater. Frank discussion of sexuality was rare growing up, so she wrote fantasies, theories, and observations within stories for deeper contemplation or just be entertained.

History speaks little on sexuality, yet biology demonstrates how it sways basic choices. Drama reveals our strongest bonds but may fade to black at its most intimate. In the Sister Seekers, the sex and the story are inseparable, and their discoveries will change the journey of Miurag without cutting away.

Please consider leaving a review of this book. It truly helps!

smarturl.it/ReadSisterSeekers

www.goodreads.com/etaski

www.bookbub.com/authors/a-s-etaski

Sign up to Etaski's newsletter for Sister Seekers releases at:

www.etaski.com

NEW!

Read more about the setting of Sister Seekers at World Anvil!

miurag.etaski.com